PENGUIN  CLASSICS

RABINDRANATH TAGORE:
SELECTED SHORT STORIES

RABINDRANATH TAGORE was born in 1861, into one of the foremost families of Bengal. He was the fourteenth child of Debendranath Tagore, who headed the Brahmo Samaj (a Hindu reform movement). The family house at Jorasanko in Calcutta was a hive of cultural and intellectual activity. Tagore was educated by private tutors, and first visited Europe in 1878. He started writing at an early age, and his talent was recognized by Bankimchandra Chatterjee, the leading writer of the day. In the 1890s Tagore lived mainly in rural East Bengal, managing family estates. In the early 1900s he was involved in the *svadeśī* campaign against the British, but withdrew when the movement turned violent. In 1912 he came to England with *Gitanjali*, an English translation of some of his religious lyrics. It was acclaimed by W. B. Yeats and later published by Macmillan, leading directly to his winning the Nobel Prize for Literature in 1913. In the 1920s and 1930s he made extensive lecture tours of America, Europe and the Far East. Proceeds from these tours, and from his Western publications, went to Visva-Bharati, the school and international university he created at Santiniketan, a hundred miles north-west of Calcutta.

Tagore was a controversial figure at home and abroad: at home because of his ceaseless innovations in poetry, prose, drama and music; abroad because of the stand he took against militarism and nationalism. In 1919 he protested against the Amritsar Massacre by returning the knighthood that the British had given him in 1915. He was close to Mahatma Gandhi, who called him the 'Great Sentinel' of modern India; but he generally held himself aloof from politics. His own translations (*Collected Poems and Plays of Rabindranath Tagore*, 1936) have not proved sufficient to sustain the worldwide reputation he enjoyed in his lifetime; but as a Bengali writer his eminence is unchallenged. His works run to thirty-two large volumes. They contain some sixty collections of verse; novels such as *Gora* and

The Home and the World; experimental plays such as *The Post Office* and *Red Oleanders*; and essays on a host of religious, social and literary topics. He also wrote over 2,000 songs, which have become the national music of Bengal, and include the national anthems of both India and Bangladesh. Late in life he took up painting, exhibiting in Moscow, Berlin, Paris, London and New York. He died in 1941.

WILLIAM RADICE was born in 1951 in London. He has pursued a double career as a poet and as a scholar and translator of Bengali, and has written or edited nearly thirty books. In addition to his translations of Tagore for Penguin, his publications include eight books of his own poems, *Teach Yourself Bengali* (1994), *Myths and Legends of India* (2001) and *A Hundred Letters from England* (2003). He has also translated from German (Martin Kämpchen's *The Honey-Seller and Other Stories*, 1995, and Sigfrid Gauch's autobiographical novel *Traces of My Father*, 2002) and Italian (Puccini's *Turandot* for English National Opera). He wrote the libretto for Param Vir's Tagore-based chamber opera *Snatched by the Gods* (1992). He has contributed regularly to BBC radio, has lectured widely in South Asia, North America and Europe, and has been given literary prizes in both India and Bangladesh.

William Radice is Senior Lecturer in Bengali at SOAS, University of London, and from 1999 to 2002 was Head of the Departments of South and South East Asia. He lives in London and Northumberland.

RABINDRANATH TAGORE

Selected Short Stories

Translated with an Introduction by
WILLIAM RADICE

PENGUIN BOOKS

Dedicated to the Rivers of Bengal
Revised edition dedicated to Arun Deb of Konnagar
on the Shore of one of the Rivers of Bengal

PENGUIN BOOKS

Published by the Penguin Group
Penguin Books Ltd, 80 Strand, London WC2R ORL, England
Penguin Group (USA) Inc., 375 Hudson Street, New York, New York 10014, USA
Penguin Books Australia Ltd, 250 Camberwell Road, Camberwell, Victoria 3124, Australia
Penguin Books Canada Ltd, 10 Alcorn Avenue, Toronto, Ontario, Canada M4V 3B2
Penguin Books India (P) Ltd, 11 Community Centre, Panchsheel Park, New Delhi – 110 017, India
Penguin Group (NZ), cnr Airborne and Rosedale Roads, Albany, Auckland 1310, New Zealand
Penguin Books (South Africa) (Pty) Ltd, 24 Sturdee Avenue, Rosebank 2196, South Africa

Penguin Books Ltd, Registered Offices: 80 Strand, London WC2R ORL, England

www.penguin.com

First published in Penguin Books 1991
Reprinted with corrections 1992
Revised edition 1994
Reprinted with a new Chronology, Further Reading and corrections in Penguin Classics 2005
006

Acknowledgement is given to Visva-Bharati Publishing
Department, on behalf of the Rabindranath Tagore estate, and
to Macmillan London Ltd for permission to reproduce the following stories:
'The Living and the Dead', 'The Postmaster', 'Housewife', 'Little Master's Return',
'Skeleton', 'A Single Night', 'Fool's Gold', 'Punishment', 'A Problem Solved',
'Exercise-book', 'In the Middle of the Night', 'Elder Sister'
and 'The Hungry Stones'

The moral right of the translator has been asserted

Filmset in Imprint
Typeset by Datix International Limited, Bungay, Suffolk
Printed in England by Clays Ltd, St Ives plc

www.greenpenguin.co.uk

Contents

Preface to the 1991 Edition

This book was conceived as a companion volume to my *Selected Poems* of Tagore, published by Penguin Books in 1985 and revised in 1987. I originally intended to do for the stories what I tried to do for the poems: select from the full range of Tagore's stories from 1884 to 1941, and write an Introduction that would survey a lifetime of story-writing. I soon realized that this was not practicable: a one-volume selection from over ninety stories would either be too unwieldy or too thin. I also wanted to reach a fair critical assessment of each story before choosing or rejecting it, and it was difficult to do this for so many. It is possible (fairly or unfairly) to skim through a poem to decide whether it might be possible to translate it; this is not so easy with stories, which need to be read carefully from beginning to end.

I also realized that there were other good reasons for limiting my selection to the 1890s, Tagore's most fertile decade as a short-story writer, and that the Introduction could, in explaining these reasons, go more deeply into a particular period of Tagore's life than was possible in my Introduction to *Selected Poems*. I believe that any book of English translations of Tagore has to 'introduce' him in the sense that it should not assume prior knowledge; but that is not to say that we should be reluctant to move beyond the general portrait to examination of particular phases or aspects of his life and work. The Tagore of this book is a man in his thirties, with a wife and young children, not the majestic sage of later fame.

Selected Poems was designed for the Western English reader. One of the surprises that it brought me was the interest it aroused in India and even in Bengal itself. It is unusual for a translation to provoke controversy and interest among those who have no need for it; but I have come to see that the very special importance that Tagore has for Bengalis, their excellent command of English, and their understandable desire that he should be appreciated and properly understood by outsiders, all combine to make

translations of Tagore newsworthy in Bengal in a way that no
translation of an English author has ever been – to my knowledge
– in Britain. This book, while mainly intended for non-Bengalis,
has therefore been done with a sideways glance at Bengali readers
and critics. I have given Bengali language sources in my Introduction, and related what I have said quite closely to what I have
been able to learn of Bengali criticism of Tagore's stories.

It seems appropriate, now that there are many Bengali speakers
living in Britain and other Western countries, to assume a greater
communality of interest between Bengali and non-Bengali readers: to refer in a footnote to a book written in Bengali does not
seem as academic as it might have done even ten years ago. This
is an aspect of the way our societies are changing: Bengal is closer
to Britain than ever before – so Tagore is less distant from us
than he was. At the same time, the extreme difficulty and challenge of translating and presenting him properly remains. Just
because the stranger has become a neighbour does not mean we
have to work any less hard to understand him well.

I have used the same system of transliterating Bengali words as
I used in *Selected Poems*. For names of people and places, however, I have gone for commonly accepted spellings with no
diacritical marks. It is never easy to indicate Bengali pronunci-
ation by any system of Romanization. When in doubt, consult a
native speaker!

As always I must acknowledge the support of friends. Sujata
Chaudhuri, Ranjana Ash and the late Subhendusekhar Mukhopadhyay answered my translation queries (the last named also gave
me special help with the notes in Appendix B), and Prasanta
Kumar Paul – Tagore's leading contemporary biographer – gave
me vital advice while I was working on the Introduction. I must
also thank Visva-Bharati University in West Bengal and the
School of Oriental and African Studies in London for making it
possible for me to go to Santiniketan for six weeks in March and
April 1989. The Introduction was largely written in Rabindra
Bhavana, the most beautiful and civilized library in the world.
Finally I should like to thank those at Rajshahi University in
Bangladesh, who in 1987 took me by university jeep, and by
ferries over the Padma and Gorai rivers, to the still magical place
where most of these stories were written, a century ago.

Note on the 2005 Edition

To bring this book in line with the 2005 edition of my *Selected Poems* of Tagore, a Chronology of Tagore's life and a list of Further Reading have been added. From the list, readers can see that this is not the only volume of Tagore short stories to have appeared in English to challenge the old translations published by Macmillan. Readers can now compare new translations of a number of short stories.

I have made only one change to the text of the 1994 revised edition of this book. The end of the story 'Punishment' is a notorious crux: when I have given lectures in Bengal, I have often been asked how I translated it. After years of reflection, I have decided to revert to the translation of '*maraṇ!*' (p. 133) I arrived at in the first edition of 1991. I shall no doubt spend the next ten years wondering if this was, after all, the right thing to do.

Northumberland, 2005

Further Reading

The standard edition of Tagore's Collected Bengali Works is the *rabīndra-racanābalī* of Visva-Bharati, Calcutta. Vols. 1–26 were first published between 1939 and 1949, with two supplementary volumes in 1940–41; Vol. 27 appeared in 1965, and Vols. 28–30 in 1995–8. Visva-Bharati is also the publisher of volumes of Tagore's letters, his collected songs, separate editions of individual works, and many books relating to Tagore. Now that Tagore is no longer in copyright, other editions of individual works are appearing in India, and collected editions on CD-ROM: *Chirantan Rabindra Rachanaabali* (Kolkata: Celcius Technologies) and *Gitabitan Live* (Tagore's songs, with recordings, Kolkata: ISS Infoway). For many years, the standard edition (though it lacked any information or notes) of Tagore's own English translations was *Collected Poems and Plays*, first published by Macmillan in London in 1936. This has been superseded by a massive and excellent annotated edition, published by the Sahitya Akademi in Delhi and edited by Sisir Kumar Das. Vol. 1 (*Poems*) appeared in 1994, and Vol. 2 (*Plays, Stories, Essays*) and Vol. 3 (*A Miscellany*) in 1996. The stories in Vol. 2 are only those that Tagore translated himself.

The main library and archive for Tagore, and the largest collection of his paintings, is at Rabindra Bhavana, Santiniketan, West Bengal. In London, the Tagore Centre UK has an interesting collection of Tagore books and documents.

The fullest bibliography of Tagore in English is still *Rabindranath Tagore: A Bibliography* by Katherine Henn (The American Theological Library Association, 1985); also useful is Dipali Ghosh, *Translations of Bengali Works into English: A Bibliography* (London and New York: Mansell Publishing Ltd, 1986).

For on-line material about Tagore, go especially to www.visva-bharati.ac.in (an impressive and informative website), and to the Internet journal *Parabaas* at www.parabaas.com.

Please note that Calcutta is now known as Kolkata and has been so cited for works published since 2000.

Works by Tagore

For a useful list that includes older translations, see *Encyclopedia of Literary Translation into English*, 2 vols., ed. Olive Classe (London and Chicago: Fitzroy Dearborn Publishers, 2000).

Glimpses of Bengal: Selected Letters, newly trans. after Surendranath Tagore's translation of 1921 by Krishna Dutta and Andrew Robinson and with an introduction by Andrew Robinson (London: Papermac, 1991).

Gora (novel), trans. Sujit Mukherjee, with an introduction by Meenakshi Mukherjee (New Delhi: Sahitya Akademi, 1997).

He (fantasy fiction), trans. Kalyan Kundu and Anthony Loynes (London: The Tagore Centre UK, 2003).

The Home and the World (novel), trans. Surendranath Tagore (London: Macmillan, 1919); with an introduction by Anita Desai (Harmondsworth: Penguin Books, 1985); new edn with a preface by William Radice (London: Penguin Books, 2005).

I Won't Let You Go: Selected Poems, trans. with an introduction by Ketaki Kushari Dyson (Newcastle upon Tyne: Bloodaxe Books, 1991).

My Reminiscences, Surendranath Tagore's translation of 1912, revised and introduced by Andrew Robinson (London: Papermac, 1991).

Particles, Jottings, Sparks: The Collected Brief Poems, trans. with an introduction by William Radice (New Delhi: HarperCollins, 2000; London: Angel Books, 2001).

The Post Office (play), trans. William Radice, set as a play-within-a-play by Jill Parvin (London: The Tagore Centre UK, 1995).

Quartet (novella), a translation by Kaiser Haq of *caturaṅga* (Oxford: Heinemann, 1993).

Rabindranath Tagore: An Anthology, ed. Krishna Dutta and Andrew Robinson (London: Picador, 1997).

Selected Poems, trans. with an introduction by William Radice (Harmondsworth: Penguin Books, 1985, revised 1987, 1993; new edns 1994, 2005; New Delhi: Penguin India, 1995).

Selected Short Stories (various translators), ed. Sukanta Chaudhuri (New Delhi: Oxford University Press, 2000).

Selected Stories, trans. Krishna Dutta and Mary Lago (London: Macmillan, 1991).

Three Plays [*raktakarabī, tapatī and arūp ratan*], trans. with an extensive introduction by Ananda Lal (Calcutta: Birla Foundation, 1987; New Delhi: Oxford University Press, 2001).

Three Companions (novellas), trans. Sujit Mukherjee (Hyderabad and London: Sangam Books, by arrangement with Orient Longman, 1992).

About Tagore

For fuller bibliographies, see the books by Krishna Dutta and Andrew Robinson.

Chatterjee, Bhabatosh, *Rabindranath Tagore and Modern Sensibility* (New Delhi: Oxford University Press, 1996).

Chaudhuri, Nirad C., *Thy Hand, Great Anarch! India 1921–1952* (London: The Hogarth Press, 1987), especially Book 2, Chapter 5, pp. 595–636: 'Tagore; the lost great man of India'.

Das Gupta, Uma (ed.), *A Difficult Friendship: Letters of Edward Thompson and Rabindranath Tagore 1913–1940* (New Delhi: Oxford University Press, 2003).

Dutta, Krishna and Andrew Robinson, *Rabindranath Tagore: The Myriad-Minded Man* (London: Bloomsbury, 1995; New York: St Martin's Press, 1996).

Dutta, Krishna and Andrew Robinson (eds.), *Selected Letters of Rabindranath Tagore*, with a foreword by Amartya Sen (Cambridge and New York: Cambridge University Press, 1997). A wide-ranging selection, combining English letters with letters translated from Bengali and with extensive notes and commentary; an essay on Tagore and Einstein by Dipankar Home and Andrew Robinson is included in an appendix.

Dyson, Ketaki Kushari, *In Your Blossoming Flower-Garden: Rabindranath Tagore and Victoria Ocampo* (New Delhi: Sahitya Akademi, 1988).

Fraser, Bashabi (ed.), *The Geddes-Tagore Correspondence* (Edinburgh: The Edinburgh Review 109, 2002; Kolkata: Visva-Bharati (*The Tagore-Geddes Correspondence*), 2004).

Hogan, Patrick Colm and Lalita Pandit (eds.), *Rabindranath*

Tagore: Universality and Tradition (Cranbury, NJ, London, UK and Mississauga, Ontario: Associated University Presses, 2003). Includes essays on Tagore and nationalism, education, science, Yeats, Satyajit Ray, *Gora* and Jane Austen, Janusz Korczak, etc.

Kripalani, Krishna, *Rabindranath Tagore: A Biography* (London: Oxford University Press, and New York: Grove Press, 1962; revised edn, Calcutta: Visva-Bharati, 1980).

Kundu, Kalyan, Sakti Bhattacharya and Kalyan Sircar (eds.), *Imagining Tagore: Rabindranath Tagore and the British Press (1912–1941)* (Kolkata: Sahitya Samsad in collaboration with The Tagore Centre UK, 2000).

Lago, Mary M. (ed.), *Imperfect Encounter: Letters of William Rothenstein and Rabindranath Tagore 1911–1941* (Cambridge, MA: Harvard University Press, 1972).

Lago, Mary and Ronald Warwick (eds.), *Rabindranath Tagore: Perspectives in Time* (London: Macmillan, 1989). Includes essays on Tagore's Western career, his short stories, his educational ideals, Tagore and Elmhirst, Tagore's paintings, Tagore and Western composers, etc.

O'Connell, Kathleen M., *Rabindranath Tagore: The Poet as Educator* (Kolkata: Visva-Bharati, 2002).

Radice, William, *Poetry and Community: Lectures and Essays 1991–2001* (New Delhi: DC Publishers, 2003). Includes essays on translating Tagore, and on Tagore and the Nobel Prize.

Radice, William, 'Rabindranath Tagore' in *Oxford Dictionary of National Biography*, Vol. 53 (Oxford: Oxford University Press, 2004).

Ray, Sibnarayan, *From the Broken Nest to Visva-Bharati: Six Exploratory Essays on Rabindranath* (Kolkata: Renaissance Publishers, 2001).

Robinson, Andrew, *The Art of Rabindranath Tagore*, with a foreword by Satyajit Ray (London: André Deutsch, 1989).

Sahitya Akademi (ed.), *Rabindranath Tagore 1861–1961: A Centenary Volume* (New Delhi: Sahitya Akademi, 1961, reprinted 1986). Introduction by Jawaharlal Nehru; memoirs by several of Tagore's associates; essays on all aspects of Tagore's life and work; essays on Tagore in other lands; bibliography of Tagore's Bengali and English works (with dates); very useful

chronicle of his life compiled by Prabhat Kumar Mukherjee
(Tagore's biographer in Bengali) and Kshitis Roy.

Thompson, Edward, *Rabindranath Tagore: Poet and Dramatist*
(London and New York: Oxford University Press, 1926; second
edn 1948; new edn with an introduction by Harish Trivedi,
New Delhi: Oxford University Press, 1989).

Chronology

1858 The British Crown takes over the Government of India, following the Mutiny of 1857.

1861 Tagore born in Calcutta, in the family house at Jorasanko.

1873 Goes with his father Debendranath Tagore on a tour of the Western Himalayas.

1875 His mother dies.

1877 Starts to publish regularly in his family's monthly journal, *bhāratī*.

1878 First visit to England.

1880 His book *sandhyā saṅgīt* (Evening Songs) acclaimed by Bankimchandra Chatterjee, the leading writer of the day.

1883 Controversy over Lord Ripon's Ilbert bill, to permit Indian judges to try Englishmen, intensifies antagonism between British and Indians.

Tagore marries.

1884 His sister-in-law Kadambari commits suicide.

1885 First Indian National Congress meets at Bombay.

1886 Tagore's daughter Madhurilata (Bela) born.

1888 His son Rathindranath born.

1890 His father puts him in charge of the family estates.

Second, brief visit to England.

Starts to write prolifically for a new family journal, *sādhanā*.

1898 Sedition Bill; arrest of Bal Gangadhar Tilak; Tagore reads his paper *kaṇṭha-rodh* (The Throttled) at a public meeting in Calcutta.

1901 Marriage of his elder daughters Bela and Renuka (Rani).

Inauguration of the Santiniketan School.

1902 His wife dies.

1903 Rani dies.

1904 Satischandra Ray, his assistant at Santiniketan, dies.

1905 *Svadeśī* agitation against Lord Curzon's proposal to partition Bengal, with Tagore playing a leading part.

His father dies.

1907 His younger son Samindra dies.

1908 Thirty-five revolutionary conspirators in Bombay and Bengal arrested.

1909 Indian Councils Act, increasing power of provincial councils, attempts to meet Indian political aspirations.

1910 Bengali *gītāñjali* published.

1912 Third visit to England; first visit to America; publication of the English *Gitanjali*.

1913 Tagore awarded the Nobel Prize for Literature.

1914 230,000 Indian troops join the first winter campaign of the Great War.

1915 Tagore's first meeting with Gandhi.

He receives a knighthood.

1916 Home Rule League formed by Annie Besant and B. G. Tilak.

Tagore goes to Japan and the USA; lectures on *Nationalism* and *Personality*.

1917 E. S. Montagu, Secretary of State, declares the development of self-government in India to be official policy.

Tagore reads his poem 'India's Prayer' at the Indian National Congress in Calcutta.

1918 Rowlatt Act against Sedition provokes Gandhi's first civil disobedience campaign.

Tagore's eldest daughter Bela dies.

German-Indian Conspiracy Trial in San Francisco implicates him: he sends a telegram to President Wilson asking for protection 'against such lying calumny'.

1919 Gen. Reginald Dyer's Amritsar Massacre; Tagore returns his knighthood.

1920 Death of Tilak leaves Gandhi undisputed leader of the nationalist movement. Tagore travels to London, France, Holland, America.

1921 Back to London, France, Switzerland, Germany, Sweden, Germany again, Austria, Czechoslovakia.

After meeting with Gandhi in Calcutta, Tagore detaches himself from the Swaraj (home rule) campaign.

Visva-Bharati, his university at Santiniketan, inaugurated.

1922 Gandhi sentenced to six years imprisonment.

Tagore tours West and South India.

1923 Congress party under Motilal Nehru and C. R. Das ends its boycott of elections to the legislatures established by the Government of India Act (1919).

1924 Tagore travels to China and Japan.

After only two months at home, sails for South America: stays with Victoria Ocampo in Buenos Aires.

1925 Returns via Italy.

Gandhi visits Santiniketan; Tagore again refuses to be actively involved in Swaraj, or in the charka (spinning) cult.

Bengal Criminal Law Amendment Act crushes new terrorist campaign in Bengal.

1926 Tagore travels to Italy, Switzerland (staying with Romain Rolland at Villeneuve), Austria, England, Norway, Sweden, Denmark, Germany (meets Einstein), Czechoslovakia, Bulgaria, Greece, Egypt.

1927 Extensive tour of South-east Asia.

1928 Starts painting.

1929 To Canada, Japan, Saigon.

1930 To England (via France) to deliver Hibbert Lectures at Manchester College, Oxford (*The Religion of Man*); to Germany, Switzerland, Russia, back to Germany, USA.

Exhibitions of his paintings in Birmingham, London and several European capitals.

Gandhi's 'salt-march' from Ahmedabad to the coast inaugurates new civil disobedience campaign.

1932 Tagore travels (by air) to Iran and Iraq.

His only grandson Nitindra dies.

Gandhi declares fast-unto-death in jail in Poona; later breaks his fast with Tagore at his bedside.

1934–6 Tours of Ceylon and India with a dance-troupe from Santiniketan.

1935 Government of India Act emerges from Round Table Conferences of 1930–32, with all-India Federation and provincial autonomy as its main aims.

1937 Tagore delivers Convocation Address to Calcutta University, in Bengali.

Starts Department of Chinese Studies at Visva-Bharati.

Congress Party ministries formed in most states.

Tagore falls seriously ill in September.

1939 Congress ministries resign on grounds that the British

Government has failed to make an acceptable declaration of its war aims.

1940 Tagore's last meeting with Gandhi, at Santiniketan.

Death of C. F. Andrews, Tagore's staunch friend and supporter at Santiniketan.

Oxford University holds special Convocation at Santiniketan to confer Doctorate on Tagore.

Muslim League under Jinnah demands separate state for Muslims.

1941 Tagore dies in Calcutta.

1942 Congress Party calls on Britain to 'quit India' immediately.

1946 Congress forms interim Government under Jawaharlal Nehru.

1947 Viscount Mountbatten announces partition: India and Pakistan become independent dominions.

1948 Assassination of Gandhi.

1950 India is declared a Republic.

... I may, if I am lucky, tap the deep pathos that pertains to all authentic art because of the breach between its eternal values and the sufferings of a muddled world ...

Vladimir Nabokov, *Lectures on Russian Literature*

Introduction

Rabindranath Tagore wrote over ninety short stories during his long and abundant literary career. It would be possible, though not very satisfactory, to make a one-volume selection from the full range of his stories; but a selection of those written during the 1890s is indicated not only by the need to limit numbers. Tagore was specially committed to the short story during this decade, and fifty-nine stories belong to it. From 1891 to 1895 he wrote forty-four – almost one a month. In 1896–7, and again in 1899, he stopped writing short stories as such, but his interest in story-telling was sustained in the narrative and dramatic poems that made up his books *kathā* ('Tales') and *kāhinī* ('Stories'), published in 1900.[1] If we count these in with the prose stories, we arrive at over eighty narratives in prose or verse, an astonishing flow that only waned when Tagore's interest shifted to the psychological novella. *cokher bāli* ('Speck in the Eye') and *naṣṭanīṛ* ('The Broken Nest') appeared simultaneously in serial form in 1901. With their greater length, narrower time-scale, and emphasis on detailed analysis of emotion rather than factual life-history, they mark a break with the short stories that preceded them. The stories that Tagore produced at intervals over the rest of his career are related to his novellas and novels, rather than to his earlier stories. For this, and for several other reasons, the stories from which I have made the present selection form a group.

Why did Tagore – always primarily a lyric poet – write so many short stories at this time? The simplest answer is that the periodicals with which he was associated, and the readership for those periodicals, demanded them. Most nineteenth-century Bengali literature reached its readers initially in the pages of periodicals. The leading literary figure of the 1870s and 1880s, Bankimchandra Chatterjee (1838–94), established new artistic, intellectual and typographical standards in his journal *baṅgadarśan*,

---

1. Later published as one volume, *kathā o kāhinī* (1908), with some narrative poems from earlier books added.

serializing many of his own novels in it; and Tagore recalled in
My Reminiscences (1917) the feverish excitement with which each
monthly issue was awaited. His own first attempts at prose
fiction, such as *bhikhārinī* ('The Beggar-girl', 1877) or the historical romance *rājarṣi* ('The Royal Sage', 1887), were published in
periodicals; and he was fortunate, as he strove to establish himself
as a writer, to live at a time in which Calcutta's literary-magazine
culture was reaching its zenith. The periodicals to which he
contributed so extensively were packed with ideas, debate, reviews
and counter-reviews, as well as the latest poetry and fiction.
Writers and editors were keenly alive to literary developments
abroad; and as the taste for short stories developed in America,
Britain and Europe, so it did in Bengal.

On 2 May 1891, an advertisement appeared in *The Bengalee* for
a new weekly magazine, *hitabādī*, listing a number of prominent
writers among its contributors. Tagore's name was among them,
as well as Nagendranath Gupta (already established as a short-
story writer) and the great Bankim himself ('religious subjects
only'). No copies have survived; but Tagore certainly contributed
at least one short story to each of the first six issues. It is said that
he stopped contributing because the editor, Krishnakamal Bhattacharya, complained that his stories were too sophisticated for the
general reader. Before long, however, he had a much better
showcase – the magazine *sādhanā* ('Endeavour'), whose signific-
ance in the development of modern Bengali literature is comparable to Bankim's *baṅgadarśan* or Pramatha Chaudhuri's
sabuj-patra ('Green Leaves', started with Tagore's encouragement
in 1914).

The first issue of *sādhanā* was advertised on the back of
another leading journal, the *tattvabodhinī patrikā*, in its Āśvin
(September–October) issue, 1891. It was clear from the list of
contributors that it was to be virtually a Tagore family magazine,
with eight of Rabindranath's brothers or cousins included. The
contents of the first issue included poetry, criticism, 'Modern
Science', music, reviews of books and other journals, and short
stories by Sudhindranath Tagore and Rabindranath himself. But
such was the size and prestige of the Tagore family that the
magazine instantly acquired a central position in Calcutta literary
life. Rabindranath's nephews Sudhindranath and Nitindranath

(sons of his eldest brother, Dwijendranath) were named as editor and manager, but it soon became obvious that Rabindranath was the magazine's prime mover, closely directing not only its contents but its printing and design. Like *hitabādī*, *sādhanā* was paid for by persuading wealthy Calcuttans to buy 'shares' – which were actually more like subscriptions, as no one received any return for his investment.

Tagore published his story *khokābābur pratyābartan* ('Little Master's Return') in the first issue of *sādhanā* (30 November 1891). He also wrote all the reviews of recent books and other magazines, and a selection of scientific reports. Although other members of the family shared the reviewing in later issues – covering English as well as Bengali publications – Tagore's dominance continued. To the sixth issue, for example, he contributed a short story, an article on 'Ignorance of Bengali Literature', an instalment from his *yurop-yātrīr ḍāyāri* (a diary of his second visit to England in September–October 1890), *bimbabatī* (a 'fairytale' poem, later included in *sonār tari*, 'The Golden Boat', 1894), translations of Heine's poems from the original German, two songs written for Brahmo worship,[1] reviews, and replies to readers' letters.

sādhanā continued until October 1895, with Tagore becoming its official editor in November 1894. In the end, financial difficulties, weariness with what had become an unshared editorial burden, and attacks from literary opponents, all got the better of him, and he closed the magazine down. In a letter to one of the contributors to the magazine he wrote: 'I have broken my ties with *sādhanā* completely. My enemies will sneer no doubt, but I can't go on exhausting myself merely in order to ward off the sneers of my enemies.'[2] From other letters we gather that he had been tiring of the magazine for the past year. Not the least of his difficulties was his distance from Calcutta: collection of material, editing, arranging the printing, proof-reading, all had to be done from remote Shelidah in East Bengal, as we shall see.

1. Tagore's father Debendranath was *ācārya* ('Minister') of the Brahmo Samaj, the Reformed Hindu Church founded by Rammohan Roy. Following a schism in 1866, Debendranath's branch of the Samaj was known as the Adi ('Original') Brahmo Samaj. Rabindranath was its Secretary from 1884 to 1912.

2. Letter of 22 October 1895 to Thakurdas Mukhopadhyay, quoted by Prasanta Kumar Paul, *rabijībanī*, Vol. IV (Calcutta, 1988), p. 77.

Thirty-six of Tagore's short stories were published in *sādhanā*. It is quite possible that he would not have written them at all if the magazine had not existed. His story-writing paused when it closed down, and revived again when he reluctantly became editor of another monthly journal, *bhāratī*, from May 1898 to April 1899. This magazine, however, was more of a forum for the writings on the political and social questions that were preoccupying him at the time. All in all, it is with *sādhanā* that his best short stories of the 1890s are most closely associated. It was *sādhanā* that was their *sine qua non*.

In various letters, interviews and comments on the stories (which the reader of Bengali can conveniently find in the Appendix to Volume IV of *galpaguccha*, Tagore's collected short stories[1]), Tagore repeatedly gave a rather different explanation. In 1909 he told a questioner:

To begin with I only wrote poetry – I didn't write stories. One day my father called me and said, 'I want you to take charge of the estates.' I was astonished: I was a poet, a scribbler – what did I know about such matters? But Father said, 'Never mind that – I want you to do it.' What could I do? Father had ordered me, so I had to go. Managing the *jamidāri* gave me the opportunity to mix with various kinds of people, and this was how my story-writing began.[2]

In an English interview given in 1935, when asked about 'the background of your short stories and how they originated', Tagore replied:

It was when I was quite young that I began to write short stories. Being a landlord I had to go to villages, and thus I came in touch with village people and their simple modes of life. I enjoyed the surrounding scenery and the beauty of rural Bengal. The river system of Bengal, the best part of this province, fascinated me and I used to be quite familiar with those rivers. I got glimpses into the life of the people, which appealed to me very much indeed. At first I was quite unfamiliar with the village life as I was born and brought up in Calcutta and so there was an element of mystery for me. My whole heart went out to the simple village people as I came in close contact with them. They seemed to belong to quite

1. These comments were collected by Pulinbihari Sen, bibliographer of Tagore. They can also be found in the Appendix to Pramathanath Bisi's study of Tagore's short stories, *rabīndranāther choṭa galpa* (Calcutta, 1954).
2. Conversation with Jitendralal Bandyopadhyay, May 1909.

another world, so very different from that of Calcutta. My earlier stories have this background, and they describe this contact of mine with the village people. They have the freshness of youth. Before I had written these short stories there was not anything of that type in Bengali literature. No doubt Bankimchandra had written some stories but they were of the romantic type; mine were full of the temperament of the rural people ... There is a note of universal appeal in them, for man is the same everywhere. My later stories haven't got that freshness, that tenderness of the earlier stories.[1]

This explanation of the origins of the stories is what Tagore believed and has been widely accepted by Bengali readers and critics. In many ways it is true, and the reader of the marvellous letters that Tagore wrote describing his life as manager of the family estates will find passages that relate quite exactly to characters, feelings and places in the short stories. The description of the boys playing at the beginning of *chuṭi* ('Holiday'), for example, is taken straight from observation, though the girl who sits on the fallen mast becomes a boy in the story:

There was a large mast lying on the mud by the river. A bunch of naked little boys had, after much debate, realized that if they heaved and puffed and shouted they would be able to roll it along, and that this would be an exciting new game. They set to work to carry out this plan: 'Heave ho! Watch her go! Heave ho!' Each time they managed to roll it over, they all cheered. But there were a couple of girls among the boys, and their feelings were different. They were forced, because they had no friends of their own, to join in with the boys, but were obviously not enjoying such a violent, physical game. One of the girls, solemnly and coolly and without speaking, firmly sat herself down on the mast . . .[2]

But some of the passages often quoted as sources for the short stories do not seem to be sources at all. Tagore *was* friendly with a local postmaster: early on, a post office was actually situated in a ground-floor room of the family house at Sajadpur. But the real postmaster does not seem to correspond with the postmaster in Tagore's famous story of that name: it is hard to imagine the dreamy, lonely postmaster of the story telling this amusing anecdote:

---

1. The interview was published in *Forward* magazine, 23 February 1935.
2. *chinnapatrābalī*, Letter No. 24, June 1891.

Yesterday he told me that the local people so revered the Ganges that if a relative died they would grind his bones into powder and keep it; then, if anyone came who had drunk the waters of the Ganges, they would mix the bone-powder with his drink and, by so doing, imagine that part of their dead relative had mingled with the Ganges. I laughed and said, 'You're making it up.' He thought soberly for a while and then confessed, 'Could be, sir, could be.'[1]

Moreover, many of the characters in the stories are not 'simple village people', but of the middle or gentry class. Some stories are more urban than rural; some are supernatural fantasies; and many of them contradict Tagore's statement in the same English interview quoted above that he had 'no social or political problems' in mind when he wrote them. The thirty stories translated for the present volume convey, in fact, a complex and varied picture of a society in transition, and are far from being simple scenes of timeless peasant life. So what was the exact nature of the relationship between Tagore's short stories and his experiences as a zamindar in East Bengal?

There is no doubt that the decade in which Tagore's main address was 'Kuthibari, Shelidah, Nadia District, East Bengal' was crucial to his emotional, intellectual and spiritual development. His pantheism, his involvement with rural economic improvement, his dislike of the city, his calls for Hindu–Muslim unity, his interest in folk-literature and the songs of the wandering Bauls,[2] were all rooted in these vital years away from the cultured yet oppressive atmosphere of Jorasanko, the Tagore house in Calcutta. The Tagore family owned three *paragana*s (estates) in the Padma river region, acquired by Tagore's grandfather Dwarkanath: Birahimpur, Kaligram and Sajadpur (all now in Bangladesh). The *kāchāri* (estate office) for Birahimpur was at Shelidah; for Kaligram it was at Potisar; Sajadpur was named after the village where the Tagores owned a large (but little-used) zamindar's house. In November 1889 Tagore's father, Debendranath, transferred the management of the estates from Jyotirin-

---

1. Ibid., Letter No. 17, February 1891.

2. He used Baul patterns and tunes in the patriotic songs he wrote for the *svadeśī* campaign against Curzon's partition of Bengal in 1905. Close study of the Baul songs did not, however, come till the *Gitanjali* period and after (1914 onwards). See Ghulam Murshid, *rabīndrabiśver pūrbabaṅga pūrbabaṅge rabīndracarcā* (Dhaka, 1981), pp. 78, 137–41.

dranath (Rabindranath's fifth eldest brother) to Rabindranath, with the clear understanding that he would be an active, resident landlord rather than the absentee that most Calcutta landowners had become. Debendranath had striven hard to pay off the debts incurred by the extravagant Dwarkanath, and had kept his share of the inheritance in his hands (the sons of his late brother Girindranath, on coming of age, received two-fifths). Because the estates had previously been in danger, and because Debendranath was a man of the highest moral principles, he believed that the tenants should have a resident landlord. Perhaps he also felt that practical experience would be good for his poetically inclined, formally unqualified youngest son.

Tagore had been to the Padma once as a child with his brother Jyotirindranath, and near the end of his life he recalled the trip in his book *chelebelā* ('My Boyhood Days', 1940). But he had no real acquaintance with the region. Immediately on taking charge of the estates, he took his wife, a maid, his daughter Bela, his son Rathindranath and his nephew Balendranath on an exploratory visit – vividly described in one of his first letters to his niece Indira Devi.[1] Then as now the journey from Calcutta was quite complicated. Kusthia could be reached by rail via Ranaghat: from there Shelidah could either be reached by boat, north-west along the small Gorai river and then east along the Padma; or else the Gorai could be crossed and Shelidah reached by land from the south.

He took his family back to Calcutta, but immediately returned to Shelidah. His isolated *jamidāri* life now began in earnest. Shelidah was his headquarters, but he also stayed at Sajadpur, and spent many nights on the magnificent family houseboat – which his father and grandfather had kept on the Hooghly in Calcutta but which Rabindranath brought to Shelidah, naming it the 'Padma'. It had two main bedrooms and a dining-room, and was handsomely fitted out in nineteenth-century aristocratic style; and in this boat Tagore could travel along the Ichamati and Baral rivers to Sajadpur, or the Atrai river to Kaligram.

Legend has it that the name 'Shelidah' derives from an English indigo-planter called Shelley, and the *daha* (whirlpool) formed by the confluence of the Padma and Gorai rivers.[2] An older *kuṭhibāṛi*

1. See Appendix B, Letter No. 1.
2. 'Shelidah' is an Anglicized form. In Bengali it is *śilāidaha*.

(indigo-factory house) had fallen into decay, and an attractive two-storey house was built by Jyotirindranath. It can still be visited today, and there are relics such as the *pālki* (palanquin) in which Tagore was carried round the villages. The Padma river has retreated a long way from the house, and in the dry season can barely be seen; but the peace and isolation of the place can still be appreciated.

Tagore felt lonely at first, missing his four-year-old daughter and two-year-old son; his early letters to his wife do not always describe the region in rhapsodic terms.[1] His estate-duties, which he always carried out most conscientiously, were sometimes irksome and interfered with his writing and thought. His letters give glimpses – not always complimentary – of some of the staff with whom he had to work, including 'Maulabi-saheb', an Urdu-speaking non-Bengali Muslim who seems to have exhausted Tagore with his endless talking:

Maulabi-saheb follows me around all the time. He drives me mad with his constant chatter. He's as hard to bear as the rheumatism in my shoulders that I suffered at Sajadpur ... This morning he isn't here, so I'm getting some relief.[2]

But irritations apart, Tagore quickly came to love the region profoundly. Its rivers, skies, fields, sandbanks and changing seasons pervade many of his stories, inspired numerous poems, and were above all celebrated in the magnificent letters that he wrote between 1888 and 1895 to his niece Indira Devi, daughter of Satyendranath Tagore. These letters are much more consciously literary than the letters he wrote to his wife or to friends such as the writer Pramatha Chaudhuri (who married Indira) or the scientist Jagadish Chandra Bose; and in March 1895 he asked her to copy them out. From the two *khātā* (exercise-books) that they filled, preserved in the Tagore archives at Santiniketan, he made an extensive selection of letters, calling them *chinnapatra* ('Torn Leaves', 1912).[3]

1. See Appendix B, Letter No. 2.

2. Letter to Pramatha Chaudhuri, *ciṭhipatra*, Vol. V, p. 154.

3. *Glimpses of Bengal*, an abridged English translation by Surendranath Tagore of some of the letters, was published by Macmillan in 1921. *chinnapatrābalī*, a fuller edition of Tagore's letters to Indira Devi, was published by Visva-Bharati in 1960.

His restlessly itinerant life (the family also owned estates in Orissa which he visited from time to time), long absences from his wife and children, and a growing conviction that life and education away from the city would be healthier for them, made him decide to bring them to Shelidah. Moreover in February 1895 he and his nephews Surendranath and Balendranath had started a business venture, 'Tagore & Co.', dealing in grain, jute, and sugar-cane-crushing machines, and the office was at nearby Kusthia.[1] So in August 1898 he brought his wife and five children to Kuthibari. His son Rathindranath in his memoir of his father recalls their life there affectionately: the houseboat trips in the winter, botanical expeditions with Jagadish Chandra Bose, the medieval ceremonials with which the village headmen would greet the arrival of Tagore the zamindar, and the unusual arrangements that were made for the children's education:

Our teacher of English was an Englishman of a rather interesting type. He was given a bungalow in the compound. There he lived with thousands of silkworms in which he had become interested through Akshoy Kumar Maitra, the historian. On Sundays, discarding all clothes, Mr Lawrence would wrap himself in old newspapers and lie amongst the caterpillars, which delighted in crawling all over him. He was very fond of them and used to say they were his children.[2]

Reading between the lines of Tagore's letters to his wife, however – before she came to live at Shelidah, and afterwards when she was visiting relatives in Calcutta – it is not hard to see that she never really shared his fondness for a remote and peaceful rural life far away from the city. This was but one of the many temperamental differences between them. Eleven years his junior (she was only eleven when he married her in 1883), she did not live long enough for him to understand fully that it is not fair for a poet to expect his wife to be a soul-mate. The attempt to live as a family at Shelidah lasted only two years. In the summer of 1901, arrangements for the marriage of his eldest daughter, Madhurilata (Bela), were put in train: Tagore's wife was no doubt

---

1. The venture was never very successful, and was eventually wound up in 1901, leaving Tagore with heavy debts.
2. Rathindranath Tagore, *On the Edges of Time* (Calcutta, 1958), p. 23.

relieved to make this an excuse to stay on in Calcutta. But there were other factors weakening his ties with Shelidah. Three grandsons of Debendranath's brother Girindranath were of age now and were entitled to a share of Dwarkanath's bequest. After a court-case in 1897, the Sajadpur estate and some other lands were transferred to them, and Debendranath's final will of 1899 laid down further divisions. Rabindranath kept the Birahimpur (Shelidah) estate until 1921, when it passed to Satyendranath's son Surendranath; but long before then Tagore's interests had shifted to Santiniketan, where his unique experiment in education and community living was inaugurated by the foundation of the Santiniketan ashram in 1901. His visits to the region he had loved so much became more and more infrequent. In a letter to his wife written towards the end of 1901, we sense the closing of a chapter:

I find it very poignant to be back here at Shelidah. It's human nature always to find what we are about to leave more beautiful. I associate Shelidah with both happy and sad memories – but more of them are happy than sad. This is not, though, the best time to be here. Everything is soaked in dew, there is mist until eight o'clock in the morning, and in the evening there is fog. The water is very low in the well and the pond – malaria is widespread. We were right to leave Shelidah: the children would have fallen ill if we had stayed. Bolpur is much purer and healthier. But what masses of roses are in bloom! Huge, beautiful roses. And there's a lovely smell of acacia-flowers all around. Your old friend Shelidah sends you a few acacia-flowers with this letter.[1]

Tagore is recalling here the realities of his life at Shelidah with and without his family, and he typically uses in his third sentence the Bengali words *sukh* ('pleasure', 'happiness') and *duḥkh* ('sadness', 'trouble'). These are frequent words in Tagore's writing, and the euphonious and rhythmic compound *sukhe-dukhe* ('in happiness and sadness') often trips off his tongue in poems and songs. It is sometimes tempting to translate this as 'in joy and sorrow', but the spiritual connotation that these English words have is probably not right for *sukh* and *duḥkh*, which always seem to refer to immediate, physical, material moods and feelings ('joy' would be *ānanda*).

In order to capture the exact nature of Tagore's experience of

1. Letter to Mrinalini Devi, *ciṭhipatra*, Vol. I, p. 96.

riverine Bengal, and its relationship with his stories, let us begin on land, as it were, with immediate day-to-day reality, using one of the headings that Tagore gave to a brief three-part selection of his letters to Indira Devi that he included in *bicitra prabandha* ('Miscellaneous Essays', 1907).

sthale (on land)

Because the beauties of the Padma region inspired Tagore to such rhapsodies and ecstasies – in his letters to Indira Devi and in many of his poems – it is tempting to see this as the dominant mood. But romantic though he was, he always kept his feet on the ground. If we take the totality of his life at Shelidah, including his practical work as a zamindar and businessman, his domestic life, and his editorial work, as well as the whole range of his poetry and stories, we find that realism is just as much present as lyricism, romanticism or pantheism. Perhaps the most moving of his poems of the 1890s are to be found in *citrā* and *caitāli* (1896); and it is worth looking at them in order to understand that even in his lyric poetry the note of realism is strong. The best modern critics of Tagore – especially Abu Sayeed Ayyub[1] in his celebrated book *ādhunikatā o rabīndranāth* ('Modernism and Rabindranath', 1968) – have rightly associated this realism with the strain of uncertainty, foreboding, despair or agnosticism that runs right through Tagore's work, in his youthful writing as well as in the stark poetry of his old age. Ayyub rightly quotes *sandhyā* ('Evening') from *citrā* as a touchstone for this realistic, doubting mood. The beautiful rural evening is exquisitely described, but at the end of the poem this is what the earth seems to draw to her breast as darkness falls:

> . . . such sadness, such torment,
> So many wars, so many deaths:
> No end! The darkness gradually thickens
> As it falls; silence deepens; the world's
> Consciousness sleeps. From the lonely
> Earth's huge heart arises a solemn
> Painful question, an agonized weary

1. His objectivity may derive from his non-Bengali origins (he was a North Indian Muslim), though his mastery of Bengali was complete.

> Melody flung at the empty sky:
> 'Where now? How much further?'

Most of the poems in *caitāli* are sonnet-like poems of fourteen lines rhymed in delicately precise couplets. They cover many moods. Some are pen-portraits of rural people – a girl looking after her little brother by the riverside, or a herd-boy coaxing a cow into the river for a bath; and sometimes what Tagore observes and feels is bleak. In *karuṇā* ('Tragedy') a child is run over by a cart and his mother rolls on the ground, her clothes coming adrift in grief. In *mauna* ('Silence') the poet himself succumbs to despair: 'Today, everything I have said seems pointless ... In the depth of the night, nothing but the cry of dumb, idiotic silence seems to speak out of the dark.' In *anābṛṣṭi* ('Drought'), we have a world deserted by the gods:

> I have heard that in a former time the gods
> Used to come from heaven to earth
> Out of love for womankind. That time has gone.
> By the dried-up, burnt-up river and fields
> Of this Baiśākh day, a peasant-girl
> Pitifully entreats, 'Come, send rain!'
> She keeps on looking at the sky
> With sad eyes, in pathetic expectation.
> But rain does not come; the deaf wind
> Impatiently drives away all clouds;
> The sun licks up all moisture from the sky
> With his fierce tongue. In the age of Kali,
> Alas, the gods have grown old. A girl's
> Plea can only be directed, now, at man.

Moving from this poem to the short stories in the present volume, can even the most cursory reader deny that the world and age they describe is the same *kali-yuga* (age of Kali[1]) in which the gods have grown old? Story after story is tragic, often unbearably so. What consolation is there for Raicharan in 'Little Master's Return'? Or for Ratan at the end of 'The Postmaster'? Or for Banamali in 'The Divide'? What salvation is there for Yajnanath in 'Wealth Surrendered'? Or for Kadambini in 'The Living and the Dead'? What future is there for the princess in

1. See Glossary.

'False Hope'? What reassurance for the dog at the end of 'Un-wanted'? No wonder Tagore was stung when critics accused him of writing unrealistic, poeticized stories! At the very end of his life, in May 1941, in a conversation with Buddhadeva Bose, one of the leading Bengali critics and poets of the 1930s, he stressed with some pain that his stories were true to life:

I have written innumerable short lyrics – maybe no other poet in the world has written so many – but I feel surprised when you say that my stories are over poetical. At one time I used to rove down Bengal's rivers, and I observed the wonderful way of life of Bengal's villages . . . I would say there is no lack of realism in my stories. I wrote from what I saw, what I felt in my heart – my direct experience . . . Those who say that my stories are fanciful are wrong. Maybe one could say that in stories such as 'Skeleton' or 'The Hungry Stones' imagination predominates, but not completely even in those.[1]

Defenders of Tagore have taken pains to point out the close observation that does indeed lie behind many of the characters, scenes and situations in his stories – the vivid picture of Bengal that is found in them. Buddhadeva Bose himself, for example, in a fine essay on Tagore's stories, wrote:

All of Bengal can be found here. Not only facts, but her living soul: we feel her pulse as we turn the pages of *galpaguccha*. Her changing seasons, the vital flow of her rivers, her plains, her bamboo-groves, her festival canopies and chariots; her cool, moist, richly fertile fragrance; her mis-chievous, noisy, lively boys and girls; her kind, skilled, intelligent women . . .[2]

His patriotic list goes on for several more lines, and other Bengali critics have repeated or extended it; or they have pointed to the accuracy of the stories as social documents. We find in Tagore's stories ample evidence of his reflections on child-marriage and the dowry-system ('Profit and Loss'); bigoted orthodoxy or casteism ('Son-sacrifice'); changing landlord–tenant relations ('A Problem Solved'); the political frustrations of a rising educated class ('A Single Night'); the growing gulf between town and country ('The Postmaster'); ruinous litigation ('The Divide'); dehumanizing poverty ('Punishment'); cruel and corrupt official-

1. *galpaguccha*, Vol. IV, *granthaparicay*, pp. 306–7.
2. Buddhadeva Bose, *prabandha saṃkalan* (Calcutta, 1966), p. 60.

dom ('Thoughtlessness'). But to find elements of *naturalism* in Tagore's stories does not seem to get to the heart of his realism, which was essentially the realism of *feeling*. This is what Tagore clearly felt he had achieved, and this was why he was not prepared to dismiss as unrealistic even the supernatural stories – 'Skeleton', 'In the Middle of the Night', 'The Hungry Stones', and several others not included in the present selection. Such stories are just as full of pathos, grief, anguish and terror as the more naturalistic tales. They are also full of humour and irony – and this is another aspect of Tagore's realism that is found in both 'supernatural' and 'natural' stories. In many the narrator of the story is a shallow, jaunty, self-regarding individual, who is changed and deepened by the events of the story, or by a story told to him by someone else. This 'Ancient Mariner' technique is particularly characteristic of the supernatural tales, as if Tagore was concerned to place the fantastic and other-worldly within an ordinary, realistic frame. But the same tone is found in the 'natural' stories like 'Kabuliwallah', 'The Editor' or 'Ṭhākurdā'; and Tagore's capacity for scepticism, mockery and hard-headed rationality contributes just as much to his realism as does his awareness of grief and suffering.

jal-pathe (by water)

This is another of the headings under which Tagore printed his brief and early selection of his letters to Indira Devi: evocative of his splendid houseboat, or the small 'jolly-boat' which can be seen today in the Kuthibari Museum. It has been said by some critics that his characteristic view of East Bengal was, as it were, 'through a window' of his houseboat: the life of the people passed before his eyes like the banks of the Padma. Distanced by his status as zamindar, his aristocratic lineage and demeanour, his refinement and education, Tagore could never really know the ordinary people, and his stories are unrealistic as a result. Again, this is a charge that he vigorously denied. In a speech at a felicitation ceremony in 1940 he said:

People have often ganged up against me to say: 'He's a rich man's son. He was born – as the English put it – "with a silver spoon in his mouth".

How can he know about villages?' But I can honestly say that those who say that know less than I do. How can they know anything? Conventional wisdom isn't true knowledge. In true knowledge there is love: the heartfelt love with which I have observed village life has opened the door for me. It might sound like boasting, but I would say that very few writers in Bengal have looked at their country with as much feeling as I have.[1]

Just as in understanding Tagore's realism we have to go beyond naturalism to something deeper, so we have to probe into the exact nature of the knowledge from which his realism derived. It *did*, no doubt, include a quite detailed knowledge of the customs, agriculture, dialect and religion of the villagers who were his tenants, and he started to take a special interest in folk-literature at this time.[2] But this was not exactly the knowledge that impelled his short stories or poems. We do not find in them the technical rural terms, or the ear for dialect that we find in more recent Bengali writers. Islam, the faith of most of his tenants, is almost completely absent.[3] In many ways Tagore's rural characters are generalized rather than specific, and the language they speak is standard Bengali: only rarely does he attempt to give his dialogue a truly peasant flavour. So in what way did his knowledge actually run deep?

In Tagore's art – even in his most realistic, prosaic, ironic or sceptical art – we are never far from the transcendental Spirit that Indians through the ages have attempted to know and articulate. The sages who wrote the *Upaniṣad*s in the seclusion of their forest hermitages realized there must be a supreme cosmic force behind the *saṃsāra* (world) of mortal existence, the *māyā* (illusion) of sense-perception, or the *svargaloka* (heaven) of the Vedic and Hindu gods; and Tagore's spiritual endeavours were in direct descent from theirs. He took it for granted that higher levels of human consciousness are made of this Spirit. The aim of spiritual

1. *galpaguccha*, Vol. IV, *granthaparicay*, p. 306.
2. The three essays which later made up his book *lok-sāhitya* ('Folk-literature') were published in *sādhanā* (1894 and 1895) and *bhāratī* (1899).
3. When Muslims do appear, however, they are treated with respect: Achimaddi and his mother in 'A Problem Solved', for example, or the 'old Muslim' who comes for medical treatment in 'The Gift of Sight'. In 'The Hungry Stones' and 'False Hope' we find romantic fascination with pre-British Islamic culture in India.

life was to unite human with cosmic consciousness. As a romantic artist, Tagore strove to do this through art rather than through meditation or mysticism: but in this he was extending the central Indian tradition, not diverging from it.

Tagore's love and knowledge of riverine Bengal sprang from a deeply religious response to its natural beauties and human simplicity. He needed to keep his distance, watch the rural scene through the windows of his boat, because his response *was* essentially idealistic, springing from his own religious needs rather than from practical or scientific observation. When he writes of his love for the Padma river itself, in letters or poems, he is writing not as a fisherman or scientist but as a poet. His letters to Indira Devi are a kind of continuous song of praise – *padmār mahākābya*, 'an epic of the Padma', as Pramathanath Bisi puts it in his important study of Tagore's short stories.[1] In its movement, peace and isolation, he found the freedom, solitude and solace that city life and literary fame could never give him:

I'm now in the boat. It's my own private home. Here I am my own master: here no one else has any claim on me or my time. This boat is like an old dressing-gown: whenever I enter it I feel relaxed and at leisure. I can think what I like, read what I like, write what I like, and if I want I can put my feet on the table and sink myself in the wide, bright, lazy light of day . . . Even after only one day, how different my mood is from what it is in Calcutta! Yesterday afternoon sitting out on the roof I felt one way, and today sitting in the boat at noon I feel quite another way. What might seem sentimental and poetical in Calcutta here seems totally real and true . . .[2]

Tagore is aware that there is an idealized aspect to his response to the Padma scene, which from the city point of view might seem sentimental or poetical; but for him the Ideal Spirit is just as real as the *sukh* and *duḥkh* of ordinary material existence. The river is a symbol of 'the spirit that impels / All thinking things, all objects of all thought, / And rolls through all things' – through human life just as much as through the natural, non-human world. Indeed, it is hard for an English reader not to be reminded of Wordsworth. Mooring the boat at the small town of Pabna on the way to Sajadpur, he watches the people on the *ghāṭ* as the sun

1. See p. 4, n. 1.
2. *chinnapatrābalī*, Letter No. 93, 2 May 1893.

sets: he feels all the works, desires, hopes and conflicts of mankind as notes of a single melody whose mood is unbearably still and sad as darkness descends. This is the timeless Spirit that lies behind the *sukh-duḥkh* of mortal life:

The essence of the matter is this: that men are small and their lives are fleeting, yet the stream of life, with its good and bad and its happiness and sadness, flows and will eternally flow with its ancient solemn murmur. On the edge of the town and in the darkness of the evening that constant murmuring sound can be heard.[1]

Furthermore, this *prabāha* (stream) is intimately bound up with Tagore's own creative life as well as with the laws of Nature and humanity. It was in the 1890s that he began to express his profound sense of a *jīban-debatā* (life-god) guiding, impelling and harmonizing all his creative and practical endeavours. His book *citrā* (1896) includes a poem called *jīban-debatā*, but the most thorough-going exposition of the concept is found in an essay on his poetic development that he published in 1904 in a collection of essays by various authors called *baṅgabhāṣār lekhak* ('Writers in the Bengali Language'). The essay – which quotes two of his letters to Indira Devi[2] – is an extreme statement of an inspirational, deterministic theory of artistic creativity: the poet impelled by a God who is himself a poet:

To this Poet, who fashions my life out of all my good and bad, strong and weak points, I have given the name of *jīban-debatā* in my poetry. I do not just think that he forms all the separate fragments of my being into a unity, so as to bring it into consonance with the universe; I also believe he has brought me to this present life from some previous existence, *via* a strange stage of forgetfulness; and that a strong memory (derived from his power) of my flowing journey through the universe continues to remain subtly within me. That is why I feel so ancient a harmony with the trees and animals and birds of this world; that is why I do not find the vastness and mystery of the world either alien or terrifying.[3]

1. Ibid., Letter No. 128, 6 July 1894.

2. This was almost the first time any of them had appeared in print. Their very first appearance was in Mohitchandra Sen's Introduction to the second edition of *kābya-grantha* ('Collected Poems', 1903) where two 'unpublished letters' are quoted.

3. *ātma-paricay* ('About Myself', Visva-Bharati, 1969), pp. 7–8, a collection of autobiographical pieces taken from various sources.

Such notions can be dangerous, giving the poet a 'divine right'
beyond criticism or self-criticism; perhaps it is a weakness in
Tagore's artistic philosophy that he could never quite abandon
them – though his relationship with his *jīban-debatā* grew steadily
more bewildered and humble. The essay was criticized for its
dambha o ahamikā ('arrogance and egotism') by the poet and
playwright Dvijendralal Ray (1863–1913), and Tagore felt obliged
to write a reply in the periodical *bangadarśan*.[1]

How does Tagore's spiritual sense relate to the short stories? In
what way is the guiding hand of his *jīban-debatā* present in
them? Stories as rational and ironic as 'Forbidden Entry' or 'A
Problem Solved' cannot obviously or superficially be attributed
to the motion of the Padma, or 'the milk of paradise'.

For Tagore the Spirit has two main facets. On the one hand it
is enormously rich and ever-changing; it is powerful, frightening
and awesome as well as beautiful; and it manifests itself in the
abundance and creativity of Nature and the endless variety and
complexity of human life. On the other hand the Spirit is something very still, quiet and simple. If we look at the poems of the
1890s we find both dimensions. We find the first in energetic and
elaborate poems such as *basundharā* ('Earth'); or *Ūrbaśī* – a
paean to the courtesan of the gods; or *mānasundarī* ('Lady of the
Mind'), in which the *jīban-debatā* is identified with the Spirit of
Poetry and is given the female form that Tagore always henceforth
preferred. The whole of his book *kṣanikā* ('The Flitting One',
1900) is devoted throughout to the evanescent, uncatchable nature
of the Spirit, expressed in a brilliant range of novel verse forms.
But the other, quieter side is conveyed in a poem such as *acal
smṛti* ('Unmoving Memory') in *sonār tari* (1894), in which he
speaks of a 'still silence' that never leaves him, 'a silent mountain
peak' ever present in his mind; or *dhyān* ('Meditation') in *caitāli*,
in which the same inner stillness is seen as a single lotus floating
on a calm sea. In other poems, and in *chinnapatra*, beauty and
happiness are seen as ultimately very simple. The famous poem
sukh in *citrā* describes a serene afternoon scene on the Padma and
concludes: *mane hala sukh ati sahaj saral* ('I feel that Happiness is

1. In 1901 Tagore was persuaded by the publisher Shrishchandra Majumdar to
edit a revived series of *bangadarśan*. Bankim's journal had come to an end in
1883. The revived series ran for thirteen years; Tagore was editor till 1906.

very simple and easy'). In a letter, the refreshing beauty of the weather after rain gives him the same feeling:

All my work and all my dealings with people feel very easy. Actually, everything is simple. There is one straight road – if you open your eyes you can go along it. I don't see the need to search for all sorts of clever short cuts. Happiness and sadness are both on the road – there is no road that avoids them – but peace is found only on this road, nowhere else.[1]

These two facets of the Spirit, the complex and the simple, are found in the short stories just as they are in the poems and letters. In terms of *content*, we find the former in rich descriptions of Nature – sometimes beautiful, as in 'The Postmaster' or 'Guest', or when the adolescent Nilkanta in 'Unwanted' awakens to the beauty of the river; sometimes awesome – like the storm in 'The Living and the Dead', the brooding valley in 'The Hungry Stones', the sandbanks at night at the end of 'In the Middle of the Night', or Giribala's sense of her own physical beauty in 'Fury Appeased'. There is especially significant symbolism at the end of 'A Single Night': in the same way that the narrator is able to rise above his humdrum existence in a moment of mystical communion with the woman he should have married, so also the divisions of the land are overwhelmed by the unity of the water, *sthal* by *jal*, world by Spirit. Morality is transcended: indeed the Spirit in its complex form lies beyond good and evil – it is a creative, evolutionary power, 'the force which through the green fuse drives the flower'. The Spirit in its simple form, however, shows itself in qualities of human goodness: kindness, sensitivity, simplicity, innocence, humility and love. The reader of the stories in the present volume will find many characters with this simple, spiritual quality of goodness, and this is how the Spirit enters the content of even the most realistic and ironic stories. The subtlety of Tagore's perceptions and the depth of his sympathy is shown in the way he discovers good qualities even in foolish or vain characters like Baidyanath in 'Fool's Gold', Taraprasanna in 'Taraprasanna's Fame', or Ṭhākurdā in the story of that name.

We need, however, to look further than the content of the stories, for they are linked to Tagore's perceptions of the Spirit at

1. *chinnapatrābalī*, Letter No. 57, 21 June 1892.

the deepest levels of style and expression. In Tagore's Bengali
prose we find both complexity and simplicity. On the one hand
we have, in passages of heightened description or feeling, long
and elaborate sentences unprecedented in Bengali prose; on the
other hand we have a startlingly direct, simple, sometimes almost
bald manner of narration. It is the latter quality that will probably
strike the reader of my translations most forcibly, as the music of
Tagore's long sentences, with their relatives and correlatives,
strings of participles, and parallelism of phrasing – at their best,
broad and grand as a Bengali river – requires its original orchestra-
tion, whereas in the translation of his simple mode probably less
is lost. But perhaps an *overall* vitality and energy will be sensed,
running through all the stories; and perhaps their countervailing
simplicity will be felt, even in translation, not only as an aspect of
their realism, but of their poetry.

We have here the essence of the way in which Tagore expressed
in his stories the deep spiritual bond that he felt with rural
Bengal. His realism operated at the level of feeling rather than
naturalism; his idealism at the level of style and expression as
well as content. When he writes with such eloquence of the river,
landscape and sky in his letters, we recall not merely comparable
descriptions in his stories but – in Bengali at least – a *general*
quality of rhythm, breadth and complexity in his prose style.
Similarly it is not so much the touching goodness of particular
characters as a *general* quality of honesty, directness and innocence
in the writing that is associated with accounts in his letters such
as this:

Sometimes one or two old, simple, devoted tenants come: their devotion
is so unaffected, they seem to love me so truly that tears come to my
eyes. Recently an old tenant came to me with his son: he took the dust of
my feet with, so it seemed, all the simple tenderness of his heart. In the
Bhagavata Krishna says, 'My devotees are greater than I am.' I can
understand that idea a little now. Truly in his beautiful simplicity and
heartfelt devotion this man is much larger than I am.[1]

Maybe, as Tagore himself admitted, from the city standpoint this
does seem sentimental, but it is something that those who know
Bengali villages can still find – a quality that Tagore felt in the

1. Ibid., Letter No. 96, 11 May 1893.

Padma region and tried to convey in stories that were, as he put it, 'full of the temperament of the rural people'. After all, many of his characters are neither rural nor innocent; yet simplicity and innocence in the *writing* is nearly always present.

ghāṭe (at the *ghāṭ*)

Why did the goodness of the old tenant described above bring tears to Tagore's eyes? And why are so many tears shed in the stories? Or why, even if the tears are not described, do we know that they are being shed – by Raicharan at the end of 'Little Master's Return'; by the narrator in 'The Editor'; by Nilkanta at the end of 'Unwanted'?

ghāṭe is the third of the headings that Tagore used for his selection of letters in *bicitra prabandha*. A *ghāṭ* can be the steps down to a tank or pond, not necessarily a river, but in the context of riverine Bengal the *ghāṭ* is more than just a place where people bathe, wash clothes and utensils and gossip; it is also a mooring-place, a place of arrival and departure, of welcome and farewell. In Tagore's letters, stories and poems, the *ghāṭ* usually has poignant associations. Many examples could be given. In one of Tagore's earliest short stories, *ghāṭer kathā* ('The *ghāṭ*'s Story'), published in the journal *bhāratī* in 1884 when he was twenty-three, the *ghāṭ* itself narrates the sad history of Kusum, a girl who often comes to the *ghāṭ* to gossip with friends. She goes away to get married, and returns as a young widow. An attractive *sannyāsī* (holy man) comes and stays in the village, gathering a circle of devotees: Kusum attends to him. She has a dream in which he is transformed into her lover. She tells him about the dream. Gently – and with a hint that the feelings between them are mutual – the *sannyāsī* tells her he must go, and she must forget him. After he has gone, Kusum descends the steps slowly saying, 'He has told me to forget him', and drowns herself. In *chinnapatra*, there is a letter describing a young bride standing at the *ghāṭ* and trying to bring herself to leave:

At last when it was time to leave I saw them trying to coax that girl, with her cropped hair and big round armlets and bright and innocent beauty, to get on to the boat; but she didn't want to go. Eventually they

managed, with great difficulty, to pull her aboard. I realized that the
poor girl was probably going from her father's house to her husband's.
When the boat set sail, the other women stood watching from the bank:
one or two of them were gently wiping tears away from their noses with
the ends of their saris . . .[1]

It was an incident that obviously made a special impression on
Tagore: in interviews on the stories he cited it as a source for
samāpti ('The Conclusion' – not included in the present
volume).[2] Of all the stories it is perhaps 'The Postmaster' that
makes the most haunting connection between the *ghāṭ* and poignant leave-taking; but here there is a difference between the grief
of Ratan and the melancholy reflections of the postmaster himself.
Hers is real, live, human loss and rejection – *duḥkh* – but his is
more metaphysical: the current as it carries him away makes him
udāsīn, detached; and it is this kind of mood – alienation rather
than grief – that many passages in the letters seem to link with
the *ghāṭ*, with its meeting yet separation of land and water, world
and Spirit. There is a letter, for example, that Tagore included
under the *ghāṭe* heading in *bicitra prabandha* and whose mood
was likened by his biographer Prabhat Kumar Mukherjee to his
most famous single poem of the 1890s, *sonār tarī* ('The Golden
Boat').[3] Tagore describes the scene at the Sajadpur *ghāṭ* in the
heat of midday in June, with a market on one side and crowds of
boats on the other; he notices the way the day's work and
movement is subdued by the heat but still goes on, and then
writes:

I was thinking, why is there such a deep note of mourning in the fields,
*ghāṭ*s, sky and sunshine of our country? I think perhaps the reason is
that Nature is constantly before our eyes: the wide, open sky, flat and
endless land, shimmering sunshine – and in the midst of this men come
and go, crossing to and fro like a ferry-boat. The little noises that they
make, the ups and downs of their happy or sad efforts in the market of
the world, seem in the context of this endlessly reaching, huge, aloof
Nature so small, so fleeting, so futile and full of suffering! We feel in
Nature's effortless, unambitious stillness and serenity such vast, beauti-

---

1. Ibid., Letter No. 26, 4 July 1891.
2. See *galpaguccha*, Vol. IV, *granthaparicay*, p. 321. C. F. Andrews' translation
of *samāpti* can be found in *The Runaway and Other Stories* (1958).
3. See *rabīndrajībanī*, Vol. I (Calcutta, rev. edn 1946), pp. 318–19.

ful, undistorted, generous Peace; and compared to that such an effortful, agonized, tormented, petty, perpetually unstable *lack* of peace inside ourselves, that when we look at the distant blue line of the shady woods on the river-bank we are strangely unsettled. Where Nature is swathed and cramped by mist and snow and dark clouds, man feels in command, feels that his work can leave a permanent mark: he looks towards 'posterity',[1] he builds monuments, writes biographies and erects huge stone memorials over dead bodies . . .[2]

The contrast between India and Europe is significant here, and crops up elsewhere in the letters. Woken up on his houseboat by the noise of the river, Tagore sits and stares out at the dimly moonlit night, and the day seems unreal; but when he gets up in the morning, the night seems remote and dreamlike:

If one sits up in the middle of the night and looks out at the scene, the world and one's own self seem to take on a new existence – the daytime world of contact with other people seems false. But when I got up this morning, my night-time world seemed distant and dreamlike and insubstantial. For man, both these worlds are real, but they are very different. To my mind, the daytime world is like European music – consonant and dissonant bits and pieces are combined to produce an overall harmony. And the night-time world is like our Indian music – a pure, poignant, solemn, unmixed *rāga*. We are stirred and moved by both, yet they are opposed to each other. What can be done? At the root of existence there is a conflict, an opposition; everything divided between the King and the Queen, day and night, variety and unity, time and eternity. We Indians live in the kingdom of the Night – we are attuned to eternity and unity. Our melodies are lonely and single; Europe's music is social and communal. By our songs the listener is taken beyond the limits of day-to-day happiness and sadness to a companionless, detached world at the root of the universe; and European music takes us on a marvellous dance through the endless fluctuations of human happiness and sadness.[3]

From letters like this, and from stories and poems contemporary with them, we can draw up a list of opposites which seem to lie at the back of much of Tagore's thinking at this time:

---

1. The English word is used.
2. *chinnapatrābalī*, Letter No. 23, 23 June 1891.
3. Ibid., Letter No. 142, 10 August 1894.

India	Europe
Night	Day
Country	Town
Padma	Calcutta
Single-line music	Harmonic music
Solitude	Crowd
Silence	Noise
Spirit	World
Female	Male
Child	Adult
Imagination	Pragmatism
Sensitivity	Cruelty
Poetry	Prose
Idealism	Realism
Peace	*sukh-duḥkh*
jal	*sthal*
Unity	Division
Eternity	Time

Pramathanath Bisi in his study of Tagore's short stories notices a tension between 'a longing to enter the human world of happiness and sadness, meeting and parting, and a longing to rove freely in a world of unfettered beauty'.[1] The former mainly finds expression in the stories, the latter in the poems: but Pramathanath stresses that they are not 'watertight compartments', and neither are the opposites listed above.

As we have seen, both are present in the stories – the realism of *sthal* and the idealism of *jal*. Tagore's ultimate artistic and spiritual goal was to reconcile realism with idealism: in *My Reminiscences* he defined this goal as 'the subject on which all my writings have dwelt – the joy of attaining the Infinite within the finite'.[2] There are many poems and songs where it is achieved, where the *sukh-duḥkh* of mortal life is perfectly in harmony with the Spirit that 'rolls through all things'. Is it achieved in the short stories?

Once again, one needs to distinguish between the *content* and the *art* of the stories. The essence of their content seems to be a

1. Op. cit., p. 17.
2. *My Reminiscences* (London, 1917), p. 238.

conflict, not a harmony, of Real and Ideal, *sthal* and *jal*. They belong to the *ghāṭ*, to the meeting-place of land and water, a place more often than not of sorrow and tears. His characters weep because of a conflict between goodness and cruelty, innocence and the world, sensitivity and insensitivity, depth and shallowness. Sensitive characters (Ratan in 'The Postmaster', Ṭhākurdā's granddaughter, Banamali in 'The Divide', Nirupama in 'Profit and Loss', Shashikala in 'Elder Sister', Nilkanta in 'Unwanted', and many more) weep because their feelings have been hurt; insensitive characters – those who have the potential for change and growth, like the narrators of 'Ṭhākurdā', 'Kabuli-wallah' or 'Thoughtlessness' – weep when they realize that their actions have been at odds with kindness and goodness. The sky weeps heavy monsoon tears in 'Housewife', 'Thoughtlessness', 'Holiday' or 'A Single Night': as if in sympathy with the tension that must always exist between division and unity, cruelty and goodness, world and Spirit.

At the more factual and historical level of content, too, we find that many stories hinge on a conflict between one or more of the pairs of opposites in the list above: between modern, Westernized values and traditional patterns of life – with Tagore sometimes sympathizing with the former (on child-marriage or female education, for example), sometimes with the latter (on, say, older patterns of landlord–tenant relationship in 'A Problem Solved'), sometimes holding himself ironically and quizzically aloof. Mary Lago, in her study of the stories, sees them essentially as a product of the clash between the new and the old ('town and country'), that characterized the evolution of nineteenth-century Bengal.[1] But what of the *art* of the stories? Do we find in them a balanced reconciliation of opposites, or an uneasy forced marriage?

Tagore's art is a vulnerable art. Nearly all his writings are vulnerable to criticism, philistinism or contempt, because of his willingness to wear his heart on his sleeve, to take on themes that other writers would find grandiose, sentimental or embarrassing, and his refusal to cloak his utterances in cleverness, urbanity or double-talk. The fact that his works are so difficult to translate

1. Mary Lago, *Rabindranath Tagore* (Boston, 1976), Ch. 3.

has made him doubly vulnerable to criticism by foreigners able to read him only in bad translations. By the same token, Bengalis have become fiercely protective towards him, and find it as difficult to face up to flaws and failings in him as parents do in a much-loved, vulnerable child. He himself lacked self-criticism, and was hypersensitive to the often harsh criticism he received from his compatriots.[1] His short stories are his most vulnerable productions of all, and some of them attracted scathing comments when they first appeared. Here is Sureshchandra Samajpati, editor of *sāhitya*, writing about *niśīthe* ('In the Middle of the Night'), after its publication in *sādhanā* in 1894:

'Niśīthe' is a short story. The story is utterly lacking in narrative skill; only in its beauty of language and wealth of description is it attractive. But sad to say, its language and rhetoric are not put to any meaningful purpose. The zamindar Dakshinacharan Babu knocks on the door of a doctor's house in the middle of the night shouting, 'Doctor! Doctor!' This is how the story begins. It's hard to find any reason why he should wake up the doctor at such an hour to tell him his life-story. It is also unlikely that Dakshina Babu would be able to speak with such linguistic and rhetorical skill at half past two in the morning. No one telling his life-story would give such minutely detailed pictures of scenes of so long ago, in the fine language of a poet: the pure white moonlight, the darkness, the night sounds, the fragrance, the sighs, etc. If Dakshinacharan were a sentimental poet, one might forgive him for it. But unfortunately he comes across as no more than a *yātrā*-actor with a good memory. He is merely reciting, at half past two in the morning, to meet the thirst of readers of *sādhanā* for short stories, lines which the author has given him. The story falls down because of the writer's lack of story-telling skill and inability to perceive what might be plausible, but it has to be praised for the way in which he handles language. Why waste such skill on something so worthless? It's hard to see clearly which part of the mystery of human existence he wishes to depict.[2]

It was this kind of thing, presumably, that drove Tagore to

---

1. For a characteristically extreme account of Tagore's journey from rejection by his countrymen to worship by them as 'a fetish . . . the holy mascot of Bengali provincial vanity', see Nirad C. Chaudhuri, *Thy Hand Great Anarch! India 1921–1952* (London, 1987), Bk. VII, Ch. 5.

2. *sāmayikpatre rabīndraprasaṅga: sāhitya*, ed. Nandarani Chaudhuri (Calcutta, 1970), p. 16. The review appeared in the Phālgun (Feburary–March) issue of *sāhitya* in 1894.

abandon the editorship of *sādhanā* and give up writing stories completely in 1896 and 1897.

Tagore's comments on his stories later in life show that he was aware of their weaknesses. He knew that not all of them would bear comparison with the best European stories – especially the French and Russian writers who were by then available to him in translation but were scarcely so in Calcutta in the 1890s. He defended himself by pointing out that he had to play the demanding role of a pioneer in the art of writing short stories in Bengali. In his interview with Buddhadeva Bose he said:

You speak about my language, and say that even in my prose I am a poet. But if my language sometimes goes beyond what is appropriate in a story, you can't blame me for that, for I had to create my Bengali prose myself. My language was not there, heaped-up and ready-made ... I had to create the prose of my stories as I went along. You often speak of Maupassant and other foreign writers: their language was already made for them. If they had had to create their language as they wrote, I wonder how they would have fared.[1]

It is not of course true that there was no Bengali prose to speak of before Tagore: Bankimchandra Chatterjee was a master stylist, even if his dry, compact style was not a model that the lyrically inclined Tagore could naturally adopt. It is also a fact that other Bengali writers started to write short stories at the same time as Tagore – particularly Nagendranath Gupta (1861–1940) – so Tagore was not totally alone.[2] But he was the first Bengali writer to think of the short story as a serious art-form, rather than merely as an entertaining way to fill up the pages of periodicals; the first to write about real, contemporary life rather than romanticized history or myth; and although some British and American models were available to him – and his brother Jyotirindranath perhaps gave him some acquaintance with French – the manner and provenance of Western short stories were really too remote from Bengal to be of much relevance. Some have argued that his 'supernatural' stories were influenced by Edgar Allan Poe and Théophile Gautier: one recent debunking critic has accused him of actually lifting material for 'In the Middle of the Night' and

---

1. *galpaguccha*, Vol. IV, *granthaparicay*, p. 307.

2. For the history of the Bengali short story, see Sisir Kumar Das, *bāṃlā choṭagalpa* (Calcutta, 1963).

'The Hungry Stones' from Poe's 'Ligeia' and Gautier's 'The Mummy's Foot'.[1] But a taste for the macabre and ghostly had long been fostered in Bengal by folk-tales, and Tagore's direct and straightforward manner of story-telling seems worlds apart from European *fin de siècle*.

Even if there had been a mature tradition of short-story-writing in Bengali, and even if the great French and Russian masters had been available to him as models, his stories would probably still have been vulnerable, would still have mixed the perceptive with the naïve, the realistic with the idealized, the rhetorical with the plain, the sophisticated with the jejune. His nature demanded it. He was never a writer who could learn from others: his own, unique literary demon, his *jīban-debatā*, had too relentless a grip on him. His stories – not only in their content but in their overall character and 'feel' – belong not wholly to the prosaic real, not wholly to the poetic ideal either, but to the *ghāṭ* where the two meet: sometimes happily (for the *ghāṭ* is a place of welcome and home-coming as well as parting), sometimes more uneasily. They leave us, I would say, with a sense of uncertainty: with the cry of the mad Meher Ali in 'The Hungry Stones' ('Keep away! All is false!') ringing in our ears as well as the song of love that Uma in 'Exercise-book' hears; with the rattle of the empty treasure-jar in 'Fool's Gold' as well as Tarapada's flute-music in 'Guest'. The reconciliation at the end of 'The Gift of Sight', between a wife whose blindness takes her deep into her Indian soul and a husband whose medical career takes him far away from his, is not, perhaps, total – but Tagore would be a much less valuable writer if it was. His blend of poetry and prose is all the more truthful for being incomplete.

1990

---

1. See Pratap Narayan Bisvas, *rabīndranāther rahasya galpa o anyānya prabandha* (Calcutta, 1984).

The Stories

The Living and the Dead

I

The widow living with the zamindar Sharadashankar's family, in
the big house at Ranihat, had no blood-relatives left. One by one
they had died. In her husband's family, too, there was no one she
could call her own, having no husband or son. But there was a
little boy – her brother-in-law's son – who was the apple of her
eye. His mother had been very ill for a long time after his birth,
so his Aunt Kadambini had brought him up. Anyone who brings
up someone else's son becomes specially devoted: there are no
rights, no social claims – nothing but ties of affection. Affection
cannot prove itself with a legal document; nor does it wish to. All
it can do is love with doubled intensity, because it owns so
uncertainly.

Kadambini poured her frustrated widow's love on to this boy,
till one night in Śrābaṇ she suddenly died. For some strange
reason her heartbeat stopped. Everywhere else, Time continued;
yet in this one, small, tender, loving heart its clock's tick ceased.
Keeping the matter quiet, in case the police took notice, four
Brahmin employees of the zamindar quickly carried off the body
to be burnt.

The cremation-ground at Ranihat was a long way from human
habitation. There was a hut on the edge of a tank there, and next
to it an immense banyan tree: nothing else at all on the wide open
plain. Formerly a river had flowed here – the tank had been made
by digging out part of the dried-up course of the river. The local
people now regarded this tank as a sacred spring. The four men
placed the corpse inside the hut and sat down to wait for the
wood for the pyre to arrive. The wait seemed so long that they
grew restless: Nitai and Gurucharan went off to see why the
firewood was so long coming, while Bidhu and Banamali sat
guarding the corpse.

It was a dark monsoon night. The clouds were swollen; not a

star could be seen in the sky. The two men sat silently in the dark hut. One of them had matches and a candle, wrapped up in his chadar. They could not get the matches to light in the damp air, and the lantern they had brought with them had gone out as well. After sitting in silence for a long time, one of them said, 'I could do with a puff of tobacco, *bhāi*. We forgot everything in the rush.'

'I'll run and get some,' said the other. 'I won't be a minute.'

'That's nice!' said Bidhu, perceiving his motive. 'I suppose I'm to stay here on my own?'

They fell silent again. Five minutes seemed like an hour. They began inwardly to curse the two who had gone to trace the firewood – no doubt they were sitting comfortably somewhere having a smoke and chatting. They were soon convinced that this must be so. There was no sound anywhere – just the steady murmur of crickets and frogs round the tank. Suddenly the bed seemed to stir a little, as if the dead body had turned on to its side. Bidhu and Banamali began to shudder and mutter prayers. Next moment a long sigh was heard: the two immediately fled outside and ran off towards the village.

A couple of miles along the path they met their two companions returning with lanterns in their hands. They had actually just been for a smoke, and had found out nothing about the firewood. They claimed it was being chopped up now and would not be long coming. Bidhu and Banamali then described what had happened in the hut. Nitai and Gurucharan dismissed this as nonsense, and rebuked the other two angrily for deserting their post.

The four of them swiftly returned to the hut at the cremation-ground. When they went in, they found that the corpse had gone: the bed was empty. They stared at one another. Could jackals have made off with it? But even the garment that covered it had gone. Searching about outside the hut they noticed in a patch of mud by the door some recent, small, woman's footprints.

The zamindar, Sharadashankar, was not a fool: to try to tell him a ghost-story would get them nowhere. After long discussion, the four decided they had best say simply that the cremation had taken place.

When, towards dawn, the wood arrived at last, those who brought it were told that in view of the delay the job had already been done, using firewood stored in the hut. They had no reason to doubt this. A dead body was not a valuable object: why should anyone wish to steal it?

II

It is well known that an apparently lifeless body can harbour dormant life which in time may bring the body back to life. Kadambini had not died: for some reason, her life-function had been suspended – that was all.

When she regained consciousness, she saw dense darkness all around her. She realized that the place where she was lying was not her usual bedroom. She called out 'Didi' once, but no one in the dark room replied. She sat up in alarm, recalling her death-bed – that sudden pain in her chest, the choking for breath. Her eldest sister-in-law had been squatting in a corner of the room warming her little son's milk on a stove – Kadambini had collapsed on to the bed, no longer able to stand. Gasping, she had called, 'Didi, bring the little boy to me – I think I'm dying.' Then everything had gone black, as if an inkpot had been poured over a page of writing. Kadambini's entire memory and consciousness, all the letters in her book of life, became at that moment indistinguishable. She had no recollection of whether her nephew had called out 'Kākimā' for the last time, in his sweet loving voice; whether she had been given that final viaticum of love, to sustain her as she travelled from the world she knew, along Death's strange and endless path.

Her first feeling was that the land of death must be one of total darkness and desolation. There was nothing to see there, nothing to hear, nothing to do except sit and wait, forever awake. Then she suddenly felt a chilly, rainy wind through an open door, and heard the croaking of monsoon frogs; and all her memories of the monsoon, from childhood right through her short life, rose in her mind. She felt the touch of the world again. There was a flash of lightning: for an instant the tank, the banyan tree, the vast plain and a distant row of trees showed themselves before her eyes. She remembered how she had sometimes bathed in the tank on sacred occasions; how seeing dead bodies in the cremation-ground there had made her aware of the awesomeness of death.

Her immediate idea was that she should return home. But then she thought, 'I'm not alive – they won't take me back. It would be a curse on them. I am exiled from the land of the living – I am my own ghost.' If that were not so, how had she come at dead of night from the safe inner quarters of Sharadashankar's house to this remote cremation-ground? But if her funeral rites had not yet been completed, then what had become of the people who should have burned her? She recalled her last moments before dying, in the well-lit Sharadashankar residence; then, finding herself alone in this distant, deserted, dark cremation-ground, she again said to herself, 'I no longer belong to the world of living people. I am fearsome, a bringer of evil; I am my own ghost.'

As this realization struck, all ties and conventions seemed to snap. It was as if she had weird power, boundless liberty – to go where she liked, do what she liked; and with the onset of this feeling she dashed out of the hut like a madwoman, like a gust of wind – ran out into the dark burning-ground with not the slightest shame, fear or worry in her mind.

But her legs were tired as she walked, and her body began to weaken. The plain stretched on endlessly, with paddy-fields here and there and knee-deep pools of water. As dawn broke slowly, village bamboo-groves could be seen, and one or two birds called. She now felt very afraid. She had no idea where she stood in the world, what her relation to living people would be. So long as she was in the wide open plain, in the burning-ground, in the darkness of the Śrāban night, she remained fearless, as if in her own realm. Daylight and human habitation were what terrified her. Men fear ghosts, but ghosts fear men: they are two separate races, living on opposite sides of the river of death.

III

Wandering around at night like a madwoman, with her mud-smeared clothes and weird demeanour, Kadambini would have terrified anyone, and boys would probably have run away and thrown pebbles at her from a distance. Fortunately the first passer-by to see her in this condition was a gentleman.

'Mā,' he said, approaching her, 'you look as though you come from a good family: where are you going to, alone on the road like this?'

At first Kadambini did not reply, and merely stared blankly at him. She felt totally at a loss. That she was out in the world, that she looked well-born, that a passer-by was asking her questions – all this was beyond her grasp.

The gentleman spoke again. 'Come along, *Mā*, I'll take you home. Tell me where you live.'

Kadambini began to think. She could not imagine returning to her in-laws' house, and she had no parental home; but then she remembered her childhood friend Yogmaya. Although she had not seen her since childhood, they had sometimes exchanged letters. At times there had been an affectionate rivalry between them, with Kadambini asserting that nothing was greater than her love for Yogmaya, while Yogmaya suggested that Kadambini was not responding sufficiently to her own affection. But neither doubted that if opportunity to meet arose again, neither would wish to lose sight of the other. 'I'm going to Shripaticharan's house at Nishindapur,' said Kadambini to the gentleman.

The man was going to Calcutta. Nishindapur was not near by, but it was not out of his way. He personally saw Kadambini to Shripaticharan Babu's house.

The two friends were a little slow to recognize each other, but soon their eyes lit up as each saw a childhood resemblance in the other. 'Well I never,' said Yogmaya. 'I never thought that I would see you again. But what brings you here? Did your in-laws kick you out?'

Kadambini was silent at first, then said, '*Bhāi*, don't ask me about my in-laws. Give me a corner in your house, as a servant. I'll work for you.'

'What an idea!' said Yogmaya. 'How can you be a servant? You're my friend, you're like –' and so on. Then Shripati came into the room. Kadambini gazed at him for a moment, then slowly walked out, without covering her head or showing any other sign of modesty or respect. Afraid that Shripati would take offence at her friend's behaviour, Yogmaya made apologies for her. But so little explanation was necessary – indeed, Shripati accepted her excuses so easily – that she felt uneasy.

Kadambini joined her friend's household, but she could not be intimate with her – Death stood between them. If one doubts or is conscious of oneself, one cannot unite with another. Kadambini looked at Yogmaya as if she and her house and husband were in a different, distant world. 'They are people of the world,' she felt, 'with their loves and feelings and duties, and I am an empty shadow. They are in the land of the living, whereas I belong to Eternity.'

Yogmaya was also puzzled, could not understand anything. Women cannot bear mystery, for this reason: that poetry, heroism or learning can thrive on uncertainty but household arts cannot. Therefore women thrust aside what they don't understand, maintaining no connection with it, or else they replace it with something they themselves have made – something more useful. If they cannot do either of these, they get angry. The more impenetrable Kadambini became, the more resentful Yogmaya became towards her, wondering why she had been burdened with such trouble.

There was a further problem. Kadambini was terrified of herself. Yet she could not run away from herself. Those who are frightened of ghosts look backwards in terror – they are frightened of what they cannot see. But Kadambini was terrified of her inner self – nothing outside frightened her. Thus, in the silence of midday, she would sit alone in her room and sometimes shout out loud; and in the evening, the sight of her shadow in the lamplight made her quiver all over. Everyone in the house was alarmed by her fear. The maids and servants and Yogmaya herself began to see ghosts all over the place. Eventually, in the middle of the night, Kadambini came out of her bedroom, wailing; she came right up to the door of Yogmaya's room and cried, 'Didi, Didi, I beg you! Do not leave me alone!'

Yogmaya was as angry as she was frightened. She would have driven Kadambini out of the house, there and then. The kindly Shripati, with great effort, managed to calm Kadambini down and settle her in an adjoining room.

The next day Shripati received an unexpected summons from the inner part of the house. Yogmaya burst into a torrent of accusation: 'So! A fine man you are. A woman leaves her own husband's home and takes up residence in your house – months have gone by but she shows no sign of leaving – and I've heard not the slightest objection from you. What are you thinking of? You men are a fine lot.'

In fact, of course, men are unthinkingly weak about women, and women can accuse them all the more because of this. Even if he had been willing to swear on his life that his concern for the pathetic yet beautiful Kadambini was no more than was proper, his behaviour suggested otherwise. He had said to himself, 'The people in her husband's house must have treated this childless widow with great injustice and cruelty, so that she was forced to flee and take refuge with me. She has no father or mother – so how can I desert her?' He had refrained from inquiring about her background, not wishing to upset her by questioning her on this unwelcome subject. But his wife was now objecting strongly to his passive, charitable attitude; and he realized he would have to inform Kadambini's in-laws of her whereabouts, if he was to keep the peace in his household. In the end he decided it would not be fruitful to write a letter; it would be better to go to Ranihat personally to find out what he could.

Shripati set off, and Yogmaya went to Kadambini and said, 'My dear, it doesn't seem advisable for you to stay here any more. What will people say?'

'I have no connection with people,' said Kadambini, looking solemnly at Yogmaya.

Yogmaya was nonplussed. '*You* may not have,' she said irritably, 'but *we* have. How can we go on putting up someone else's widow?'

'Where is my husband's house?' said Kadambini.

'Hell!' thought Yogmaya. 'What is the woman on about?'

'Who am I to you?' said Kadambini slowly. 'Am I of this world? All of you here smile, weep, love, possess things; I merely look on. You are human beings; I am a shadow. I do not understand why God has put me in your midst. You're worried that I'll damage your happiness – I in turn cannot understand what my relation is to you. But since the Almighty has kept no other place for the likes of me, I shall wander round you and haunt you even if you cut me off.'

Her stare and the tone of her words were such that Yogmaya understood their import, even if she did not understand them literally and was unable to reply. She could not manage any more questions. Gloomy and oppressed, she left the room.

IV

Shripati did not return from Ranihat until nearly ten at night. The whole world seemed awash with torrential rain. With its thudding sound, it gave the impression that it would never end, that the night would never end.

'What happened?' asked Yogmaya.

'It's a long story,' said Shripati. 'I'll tell you later.' He took off his wet clothes, had something to eat and after smoking for a bit went to bed. He seemed very preoccupied. Yogmaya suppressed her curiosity all this while, but when she got into bed she asked, 'What did you find out? Tell me.'

'You are certainly mistaken,' said Shripati.

Yogmaya was rather annoyed at this. Women do not make mistakes, or if they do men are wiser not to mention them; it is safest to let them pass without complaining. 'In what way?' asked Yogmaya heatedly.

'The woman you have accepted into your house,' said Shripati, 'is not your friend Kadambini.'

Such a remark – especially from one's husband – might reasonably cause offence. 'So I don't know my own friend?' said Yogmaya. 'I have to wait for you to identify her? What an absurd thing to say!'

Shripati replied that its absurdity or otherwise was not the point: proof was what counted. There was no doubt whatsoever that Kadambini had died.

'Listen,' said Yogmaya. 'You've got into a complete muddle. Whatever you heard in whatever place you went to can't be right. Who asked you to go anyway? If you had written a letter, everything would have been made clear.'

Distressed by his wife's lack of confidence in his efficiency, Shripati started to explain all the proofs in detail – but to no avail. They went on arguing into the small hours. Shripati believed their guest had been deceiving his wife all this time, and Yogmaya believed she had deserted her family; so both were agreed that Kadambini should be evicted from the house immediately. But neither was willing to admit defeat in the argument. Their voices rose higher and higher, and they forgot that Kadambini was lying in the next room.

'It's a terrible thing,' said one voice. 'I heard what happened with my own ears.'

'How can I accept that?' shouted the other. 'I can see her with my own eyes.'

Eventually Yogmaya said, 'All right, tell me when Kadambini died.' She hoped, by finding a discrepancy with the date of one of Kadambini's letters, to prove that Shripati was wrong. But they worked out that the date given to Shripati was exactly one day before Kadambini had come to their house. Yogmaya felt a racing in her heart at this, and Shripati too began to feel unnerved. Suddenly the door of their room blew open, and a damp wind put out their lamp. The darkness outside instantly filled their whole room from floor to ceiling. Kadambini came and stood right inside their room. It was half past two in the morning: the rain outside was relentless.

'Friend,' said Kadambini, 'I am your Kadambini, but I am no longer alive. I am dead.'

Yogmaya yelled out in terror; Shripati was speechless.

'But other than being dead, what harm have I done to you? If I have no place in this world, or in the next world, then where shall I go?' And again, in the rain and the night, as if to wake God from his sleep, she screamed, 'Oh, tell me, where shall I go?' Then, leaving the dumbfounded husband and wife in the dark house, Kadambini fled in search of her place in or beyond the world.

V

It is hard to say how Kadambini returned to Ranihat. She did not show herself to anyone at first: she spent the whole day, without food, in a ruined deserted temple. When evening came – early, as it does in the monsoon, and oppressively dark – and the villagers, fearing a storm, had retreated into their houses, Kadambini emerged on to the road again. As she approached her in-laws' house, her heart started to pound; but she pulled her heavy veil round her head like a servant, and the gate-keepers did not prevent her from entering. Meanwhile the rain had come on even harder, and the wind blew more fiercely.

The mistress of the house – Sharadashankar's wife – was

playing cards with her widowed sister-in-law. The maid was in the kitchen, and the little boy was lying in the bedroom, sleeping after a bout of fever. Kadambini entered the bedroom, without anyone noticing. It was impossible to say why she had returned to her in-laws' house – she herself did not know why – but she knew that she wanted to see the little boy again. She gave no thought to where she would go after that, or what would happen to her.

She saw, in the lamplight, the thin, frail little boy lying asleep with his fists clenched. Her racing heart thirsted when she saw him: how she longed to clasp him to her breast one last time, to protect him from all misfortune! But then she thought, 'Now that I am not here, who will look after him? His mother loves company, gossiping, playing cards; for a long time she was happy to leave him in my care; she never had to bother with his upbringing. Who will take care of him, as I did?' The little boy suddenly turned over and, half-asleep, said, '*Kākimā*, give me some water.' 'O my darling,' she inwardly replied, 'my treasure: you haven't yet forgotten your *Kākimā*.' At once she poured out some water from the pitcher and, raising him up against her breast, helped him to drink.

While he remained half-asleep, the little boy showed no surprise at taking water from his aunt as he had been used to doing. But when Kadambini – fulfilling her longstanding desire – kissed him, and then laid him down again, he came out of his sleep and hugged her, asking, '*Kākimā*, did you die?'

'Yes, my darling,' she said.

'Have you come back to me? You won't die again?'

Before she could reply an uproar broke out: a maid had come into the room with a bowl of sago in her hand, but had then screamed and fallen down in a faint. Hearing her scream, Sharadashankar's wife dropped her cards and came running: she stiffened like wood when she was in the room, unable either to flee or utter a word. Seeing all this, the boy himself took fright. '*Kākimā*, you must go,' he said, wailing.

Kadambini felt for the first time now that she had not died. The ancient house, everything in it, the little boy, his affection – they were all equally alive to her; there was no gulf intervening between her and them. When she had been in her friend's house she had felt dead, felt that the person whom her friend had known had died. But now that she was in her nephew's room, she realized that his *Kākimā* had never died at all.

'*Didi*,' she said pathetically, 'why are you frightened of me? See – I am just as I was.'

Her sister-in-law could not keep her balance any longer; she collapsed unconscious.

Informed by his sister, Sharadashankar Babu himself came into the inner quarters. Clasping his hands he begged, 'Sister-in-law, it is not right of you to do this. Shatish is the only son in the family: why are you casting your eye on him? Are we strangers to you? Ever since you went, he has wasted away day by day; he has been constantly ill, calling out "*Kākimā*, *Kākimā*" day and night. Now that you have bid farewell to the world, please stop attaching yourself to him, please go away – we'll perform your proper funerary rites.'

Kadambini could bear no more. She screamed out, 'I did not die, I did not die, I tell you! How can I make you understand – I did not die! Can't you see: I am *alive*.' She seized the bell-metal bowl that had been dropped on the ground and dashed it against her brow: blood gushed out from the impact. 'See here, I am alive!'

Sharadashankar stood like a statue; the little boy whimpered for his father; the two stricken women lay on the ground. Crying out, 'I did not die, I did not die, I did not die,' Kadambini fled from the room and down the stairs, and threw herself into the tank in the inner courtyard of the house. Sharadashankar heard, from the upper floor, a splashing sound.

It went on raining all night, and it was still raining the next morning; even in the afternoon there was no let-up. Kadambini had proved, by dying, that she had not died.

The Postmaster

For his first job, the postmaster came to the village of Ulapur. It was a very humble village. There was an indigo-factory near by, and the British manager had with much effort established a new post office.

The postmaster was a Calcutta boy – he was a fish out of water in a village like this. His office was in a dark thatched hut; there was a pond next to it, scummed over with weeds, and jungle all around. The indigo agents and employees had hardly any spare time, and were not suitable company for an educated man. Or rather, his Calcutta background made him a bad mixer – in an unfamiliar place he was either arrogant or ill-at-ease. So there was not much contact between him and the residents in the area.

But he had very little work to do. Sometimes he tried to write poems. The bliss of spending one's life watching the leaves trembling in the trees or the clouds in the sky – that was what the poems expressed. God knew, however, that if a genie out of an Arab tale had come and cut down all the leafy trees overnight, made a road, and blocked out the sky with rows of tall buildings, this half-dead, well-bred young man would have come alive again.

The postmaster's salary was meagre. He had to cook for himself, and an orphaned village-girl did housework for him in return for a little food. Her name was Ratan, and she was about twelve or thirteen. It seemed unlikely that she would get married. In the evenings, when smoke curled up from the village cowsheds, crickets grated in the bushes, a band of intoxicated Baul singers in a far village sang raucously to drums and cymbals, and even a poet if seated alone on a dark verandah might have shuddered a little at the trembling leaves, the postmaster would go inside, light a dim lamp in a corner of the room and call for Ratan. Ratan would be waiting at the door for this, but she did not come at the first call – she would call back, 'What is it, Dadababu, what do you want?'

'What are you doing?' the postmaster would say.

'I must go and light the kitchen fire –'

'You can do your kitchen work later. Get my hookah ready for me.'

Soon Ratan came in, puffing out her cheeks as she blew on the bowl of the hookah. Taking it from her, the postmaster would say abruptly, 'So, Ratan, do you remember your mother?' She had lots to tell him: some things she remembered, others she did not. Her father loved her more than her mother did – she remembered him a little. He used to come home in the evening after working hard all day, and one or two evenings were clearly etched in her memory. As she talked, Ratan edged nearer to the postmaster, and would end up sitting on the ground at his feet. She remembered her little brother: one distant day, during the rainy season, they had stood on the edge of a small pond and played at catching fish with sticks broken off trees – this memory was far more vividly fixed in her mind than many more important things. Sometimes these conversations went on late into the night, and the postmaster then felt too sleepy to cook. There would be some vegetable curry left over from midday, and Ratan would quickly light the fire and cook some chapati: they made their supper out of that.

Occasionally, sitting on a low wooden office-stool in a corner of his large hut, the postmaster would speak of his family – his younger brother, mother and elder sister – all those for whom his heart ached, alone and exiled as he was. He told this illiterate young girl things which were often in his mind but which he would never have dreamt of divulging to the indigo employees – and it seemed quite natural to do so. Eventually Ratan referred to the postmaster's family – his mother, sister and brother – as if they were her own. She even formed affectionate imaginary pictures of them in her mind.

It was a fine afternoon in the rainy season. The breeze was softly warm; there was a smell of sunshine on wet grass and leaves. Earth's breath – hot with fatigue – seemed to brush against the skin. A persistent bird cried out monotonously somewhere, making repeated and pathetic appeals at Nature's midday durbar. The postmaster had hardly any work: truly the only things to look at were the smooth, shiny, rain-washed leaves quivering, the layers of sun-whitened, broken-up clouds left over from the rain. He watched, and felt how it would be to have a close companion here, a human object for the heart's most intimate affections. Gradually it seemed that the bird was saying precisely this, again and again; that in the afternoon shade and solitude the same meaning was in the rustle of the leaves. Few would believe or imagine that a poorly paid sub-postmaster in a small village could have such feelings in the deep, idle stillness of the afternoon.

Sighing heavily, the postmaster called for Ratan. Ratan was at that moment stretched out under a guava tree, eating unripe guavas. At the sound of her master's call she got up at once and ran to him.

'Yes, Dadababu, you called?' she said, breathlessly.

'I'm going to teach you to read, a little bit each day,' said the postmaster. He taught her daily at midday from then on, starting with the vowels but quickly progressing to the consonants and conjuncts.

During the month of Śrābaṇ, the rain was continuous. Ditches, pits and channels filled to overflowing with water. The croaking of frogs and the patter of rain went on day and night. It was virtually impossible to get about on foot – one had to go to market by boat. One day it rained torrentially from dawn. The postmaster's pupil waited for a long time at the door, but when the usual call failed to come, she quietly entered the room, with her bundle of books. She saw the postmaster lying on his bed: thinking that he was resting, she began to tip-toe out again. Suddenly she heard him call her. She turned round and quickly went up to him saying, 'Weren't you asleep, Dadababu?'

'I don't feel well,' said the postmaster painfully. 'Have a look – feel my forehead.'

He felt in need of comfort, ill and miserable as he was, in this isolated place, the rain pouring down. He remembered the touch on his forehead of soft hands, conch-shell bangles. He wished his mother or sister were sitting here next to him, soothing his illness and loneliness with feminine tenderness. And his longings did not stay unfulfilled. The young girl Ratan was a young girl no longer. From that moment on she took on the role of a mother, calling the doctor, giving him pills at the right time, staying awake at his bedside all night long, cooking him convalescent meals, and saying a hundred times, 'Are you feeling a bit better, Dadababu?'

Many days later, the postmaster got up from his bed, thin and weak. He had decided that enough was enough: somehow he would have to leave. He wrote at once to his head office in Calcutta, applying for a transfer because of the unhealthiness of the place.

Released from nursing the postmaster, Ratan once again took up her normal place outside his door. But his call did not come for her as before. Sometimes she would peep in and see the postmaster sitting distractedly on his stool or lying on his bed. While she sat expecting his summons, he was anxiously awaiting a reply to his application. She sat outside the door going over her old lessons numerous times. She was terrified that if he suddenly summoned her again one day, the conjunct consonants would all be muddled up in her mind. Eventually, after several weeks, his call came again one evening. With eager heart, Ratan rushed into the room. 'Did you call, Dadababu?' she asked.

'I'm leaving tomorrow, Ratan,' said the postmaster.

'Where are you going, Dadababu?'

'I'm going home.'

'When are you coming back?'

'I shan't come back again.'

Ratan did not question him further. The postmaster himself told her that he had applied for a transfer, but his application had been rejected; so he was resigning from his post and returning home. For several minutes, neither of them spoke. The lamp flickered weakly; through a hole in the crumbling thatched roof, rain-water steadily dripped on to an earthenware dish. Ratan then went slowly out to the kitchen to make some chapati. She made them with none of her usual energy. No doubt her thoughts distracted her. When the postmaster had had his meal, she suddenly asked, 'Dadababu, will you take me home with you?'

'How could I do that!' said the postmaster, laughing. He saw no need to explain to the girl why the idea was impossible.

All night long, whether dreaming or awake, Ratan felt the postmaster's laugh ringing in her ears. 'How could I do that!'

When he rose at dawn, the postmaster saw that his bath-water had been put out ready for him (he bathed according to his

Calcutta habit, in water brought in a bucket). Ratan had not been able to bring herself to ask him what time he would be leaving; she had carried the bath-water up from the river late at night, in case he needed it early in the morning. As soon as he finished his bath, the postmaster called her. She entered the room softly and looked at him once without speaking, ready for her orders. 'Ratan,' he said, 'I'll tell the man who replaces me that he should look after you as I have; you mustn't worry just because I'm going.'

No doubt this remark was inspired by kind and generous feelings, but who can fathom the feelings of a woman? Ratan had meekly suffered many scoldings from her master, but these kindly words were more than she could bear. The passion in her heart exploded, and she cried, 'No, no, you mustn't say anything to anyone – I don't want to stay here.' The postmaster was taken aback: he had never seen Ratan behave like that before.

A new postmaster came. After handing over his charge to him, the resigning postmaster got ready to leave. Before going, he called Ratan and said, 'Ratan, I've never been able to pay you anything. Today before I go I want to give you something, to last you for a few days.' Except for the little that he needed for the journey, he took out all the salary that was in his pocket. But Ratan sank to the ground and clung to his feet, saying, 'I beg you, Dadababu, I beg you – don't give me any money. Please, no one need bother about me.' Then she fled, running.

The departing postmaster sighed, picked up his carpet-bag, put his umbrella over his shoulder, and, with a coolie carrying his blue-and-white-striped tin trunk on his head, slowly made his way towards the boat.

When he was on the boat and it had set sail, when the swollen flood-waters of the river started to heave like the Earth's brimming tears, the postmaster felt a huge anguish: the image of a simple young village-girl's grief-stricken face seemed to speak a great inarticulate universal sorrow. He felt a sharp desire to go back: should he not fetch that orphaned girl, whom the world had abandoned? But the wind was filling the sails by then, the swollen river was flowing fiercely, the village had been left behind, the riverside burning-ground was in view. Detached by the current of the river, he reflected philosophically that in life there are many separations, many deaths. What point was there in going back? Who belonged to whom in this world?

But Ratan had no such philosophy to console her. All she could do was wander near the post office, weeping copiously. Maybe a faint hope lingered in her mind that Dadababu might return; and this was enough to tie her to the spot, prevent her from going far. O poor, unthinking human heart! Error will not go away, logic and reason are slow to penetrate. We cling with both arms to false hope, refusing to believe the weightiest proofs against it, embracing it with all our strength. In the end it escapes, ripping our veins and draining our heart's blood; until, regaining consciousness, we rush to fall into snares of delusion all over again.

Profit and Loss [1]

When a daughter was born, after five sons, her parents dotingly named her Nirupama.[2] Such a high-flown name had never been heard in the family before. Usually names of gods and goddesses were used – Ganesh, Kartik, Parvati and so on.

The question of Nirupama's marriage now arose. Her father Ramsundar Mitra searched and searched without finding a groom he really liked; but in the end he procured the only son of a grand Raybahadur. The ancestral wealth of this Raybahadur had diminished considerably, but the family was certainly noble. They asked for a dowry of 10,000 rupees, and many additional gifts. Ramsundar agreed without a thought – such a groom should not be allowed to slip through one's fingers. But no way could he raise all the money. Even after pawning, selling, and using every method he could, he still owed 6,000 or 7,000 rupees; and the day of the wedding was drawing near.

The wedding-day came. Someone had agreed to lend the rest of the money at an extortionate rate of interest, but he failed to turn up on the day. A furious scene broke out in the marriage-room. Ramsundar fell on his knees before the Raybahadur, implored him not to bring bad luck by breaking off the ceremony, insisted he would pay him in full. 'If you can't hand the money to me, now,' replied the Raybahadur, 'the bridegroom will not be brought here.'

The women of the house wept and wailed at this disastrous upset. The root cause of it sat mutely in her silk wedding-dress and ornaments, her forehead decorated with sandal-paste. It cannot be said that she felt much love or respect for her prospective husband's family.

Suddenly the impasse was resolved. The groom rebelled against

1. *denāpāonā* in Bengali, meaning 'debit and credit' or 'investment and return', but also a deal, claim, transaction etc.
2. 'Peerless one'.

his father, saying firmly, 'This haggling and bartering means nothing to me. I came here to marry, and marry I shall.'

'You see, sir, how young men behave these days,' said his father to everyone he turned to.

'It's because they have no training in morality or the Shastras,' said some of the oldest there. The Raybahadur sat despondent at seeing the poisonous fruits of modern education in his own son. The marriage was completed in a gloomy, joyless sort of way.

As Nirupama left for her in-laws' house her father clasped her to his breast and could not hold back his tears. 'Won't they let me come and visit you, father?' she asked. 'Why shouldn't they, my love?' said Ramsundar. 'I'll come and fetch you.'

Ramsundar often went to see his daughter, but he had no honour in his son-in-law's house. Even the servants looked down on him. Sometimes he saw his daughter for five minutes in a separate outer room of the house; sometimes he was not allowed to see her at all. To be disgraced so in a kinsman's house was unbearable. He decided that somehow or other the money would have to be paid, but the burden of debt on his shoulders was already hard to control. Expenses dragged at him terribly; he had to resort to all sorts of petty subterfuges to avoid running into his creditors.

Meanwhile his daughter was treated spitefully at every turn. She shut herself into her room and wept – a daily penance for the insults heaped on her family. Her mother-in-law's assaults were especially vicious. If anyone said, 'How pretty the girl is – it's a pleasure to look at her,' she would burst out, 'Pretty indeed! Pretty as the family she came from!' Even her food and clothing were neglected. If a kind neighbour expressed concern, her mother-in-law would say, 'She has more than enough,' – implying that if the girl's father had paid full price she would have received full care. Everyone treated her as if she had no rights in the household, and had entered it by deceit.

Naturally news of the contempt and shame his daughter was suffering reached Ramsundar. He decided to sell his house. He did not, however, tell his sons that he was making them houseless: he intended to rent the house back after selling it. By this ploy, his sons would not know the true situation till after his death. But his sons found out. They came and protested vigorously. The three elder boys, particularly, were married and probably had children:

their objections were so forceful that the sale was stopped. Ramsundar then started to raise money by taking out small loans from
various quarters at high interest – so much so, that he could no
longer meet household expenses.

Nirupama understood everything from her father's expression.
The old man's grey hair, pallid face and permanently cowering
manner all indicated poverty and worry. When a father lets down
his own daughter, he cannot disguise the guilt he feels. Whenever
Ramsundar managed to get permission to speak to his daughter
for a few moments, it was clear at once even from his smile how
heart-broken he was.

She longed to return to her father's house for a few days to
console him. To see his sad face made it awful to be away. One
day she said to Ramsundar, 'Father, take me home for a while.'

'Very well,' he replied – but he had no power to do so, the
natural claims that a father has to his daughter had been pawned
in place of a dowry. Even a glimpse of his daughter had to be
begged for meekly, and if on any occasion it was not granted he
was not in a position to ask a second time. But if his daughter
herself wished to come home, how could he not bring her?

It is better not to tell the story of the indignity, shame and hurt
that Ramsundar had to endure in order to raise the 3,000 rupees
that he needed for an approach to his daughter's father-in-law.
Wrapping the banknotes in a handkerchief tied into a corner of
his chadar, he went to see him. He began breezily with local
news, describing at length a daring theft in Harekrishna's house.
Comparing the abilities and characters of Nabinmadhab and
Radhamadhab, he praised Radhamadhab and criticized Nabinmadhab. He gave a hair-raising account of a new illness in town.
Finally, putting down the hookah, he said as if in passing, 'Yes,
yes, brother, there's still some money owing, I know. Every day I
remember, and mean to come along with some of it, but then it
slips my mind. I'm getting old, my friend.' At the end of this
long preamble, he casually produced the three notes, which were
really like three of his ribs. The Raybahadur burst into coarse
laughter at the sight of them. 'Those are no use to me,' he said,
making it plain by using a current proverb that he did not want to
make his hands stink for no reason.

After that, to ask to bring Nirupama home seemed out of the

question, though Ramsundar wondered what good he was doing to himself by observing polite forms. After sitting in heart-stricken silence for a long time, he did at last softly raise the matter. 'Not now,' said the Raybahadur, giving no reason; then he left, to go about his work.

Unable to face his daughter, hands trembling, Ramsundar tied the three banknotes back into the end of his chadar and set off home. He resolved never to return to the Raybahadur's house until he had paid the money in full; only then could he lay claim to Nirupama confidently.

Many months passed. Nirupama sent messenger after messenger, but her father never appeared. In the end she took offence, and stopped sending. This grieved Ramsundar sorely, but he still would not go to her. The month of Āśvin came. 'This year I shall bring Nirupama home for the *pūjā* or *else!*' he said to himself, making a fierce vow.

On the fifth or sixth day of the *pūjā*-fortnight, Ramsundar once again tied a few notes into the end of his chadar and got ready to go out. A five-year-old grandson came and said, 'Grandpa, are you going to buy a cart for me?' For weeks he had set his heart on a push-cart to ride in, but there had been no way of meeting his wish. Then a six-year-old granddaughter came and said tearfully that she had no nice dress to wear for the *pūjā*. Ramsundar knew that well, and had brooded over it for a long time as he smoked. He had sighed to think of the women of his household attending the *pūjā* celebrations at the Raybahadur's house like paupers receiving charity, wearing whatever miserable ornaments they had; but his thoughts had no result other than making the old man's lines on his forehead even deeper.

With the cries of his poverty-stricken household ringing in his ears, Ramsundar arrived at the Raybahadur's house. Today there was no hesitation in his manner, no trace of the nervous glances with which he had formerly approached the gatekeeper and servants: it was as if he was entering his own house. He was told that the Raybahadur was out–he would have to wait a while. But he could not hold back his longing to meet his daughter. Tears of joy rolled down his cheeks when he saw her. Father and daughter wept together; neither of them could speak for some moments. Then Ramsundar said, 'This time I shall take you, my dear. Nothing can stop me now.'

Suddenly Ramsundar's eldest son Haramohan burst into the room with his two small sons. 'Father,' he cried, 'have you really decided to turn us out on the streets?'

Ramsundar flared up. 'Should I condemn myself to hell for your sakes? Won't you let me do what is right?' He had sold his house: he had gone to great lengths to conceal the sale from his sons, but to his anger and dismay it appeared that they had found out all the same. His grandson clasped him round his knees and looked up, saying, 'Grandpa, haven't you bought me that cart?' When he got no answer from the now crestfallen Ramsundar, the little boy went up to Nirupama and said, 'Auntie, will you buy me a cart?'

Nirupama had no difficulty in understanding the whole situation. 'Father,' she said, 'if you give a single paisa more to my father-in-law, I swear solemnly you will never see me again.'

'What are you saying, child?' said Ramsundar. 'If I don't pay the money, the shame will be forever on my head – and it will be your shame too.'

'The shame will be greater if you pay the money,' said Nirupama. 'Do you think I have no honour? Do you think I am just a money-bag, the more money in it the higher my value? No, Father, don't shame me by paying this money. My husband doesn't want it anyway.'

'But then they won't let you come and see me,' said Ramsundar.

'That can't be helped,' said Nirupama. 'Please don't try to fetch me any more.'

Ramsundar tremblingly pulled his chadar – with the money tied into it – back round his shoulders, and left the house like a thief again, avoiding everyone's stare.

It did not, however, remain a secret that Ramsundar had come with the money and that his daughter had forbidden him to hand it over. An inquisitive servant, a listener at keyholes, passed the information on to Nirupama's mother-in-law, whose malice towards her daughter-in-law now went beyond all limits. The household became a bed of nails for her. Her husband had gone off a few days after their wedding to be Deputy Magistrate in another part of the country. Claiming that Nirupama would be corrupted by contact with her relatives, her in-laws now completely forbade her from seeing them.

She now fell seriously ill. But this was not wholly her mother-in-law's fault. She herself had neglected her health dreadfully. On chilly autumn nights she lay with her head near the open door, and she wore no extra clothes during the winter. She ate irregularly. The servants would sometimes forget to bring her any food: she would not then say anything to remind them. She was forming a fixed belief that she was herself a servant in the household, dependent on the favours of her master and mistress. But her mother-in-law could not stand even this attitude. If Nirupama showed lack of interest in food, she would say, 'What a princess she is! A poor household's fare is not to her liking!' Or else she would say, 'Look at her. What a beauty! She's more and more like a piece of burnt wood.'

When her illness got worse, her mother-in-law said, 'It's all put on.' Finally one day Nirupama said humbly, 'Let me see my father and brothers just once, Mother.'

'Nothing but a trick to get to her father's house,' said her mother-in-law.

It may seem unbelievable, but the evening when Nirupama's breath began to fail was when the doctor was first called, and it was the last visit that he made too.

The eldest daughter-in-law in the household had died, and the funeral rites were performed with appropriate pomp. The Raychaudhuris were renowned in the district for the lavishness with which they performed the immersion of the deity at the end of *Durgā-pūjā*, but the Raybahadur's family became famous for the way Nirupama was cremated: such a huge sandalwood pyre had never been seen. Only they could have managed such elaborate rites, and it was rumoured that they got rather into debt as a result.

Everyone gave Ramsundar long descriptions of the magnificence of his daughter's death, when they came to condole with him. Meanwhile a letter from the Deputy Magistrate arrived: 'I have made all necessary arrangements here, so please send my wife to me quickly.' The Raybahadur's wife replied, 'Dear son, we have secured another girl for you, so please take leave soon and come home.'

This time the dowry was 20,000 rupees, cash down.

Housewife

When we were two years or so below the scholarship class, our teacher was Shibanath. He was clean-shaven, with closely cropped hair except for a short pigtail. The very sight of him scared boys out of their wits. In the animal world, creatures that sting do not bite. Our teacher did both. His blows and slaps were like hailstones pounding saplings, and his sarcasm, too, burnt us to the core.

He complained that the relationship between pupils and teacher was not what it was in times past; that pupils no longer revered their teacher like a god. Then he would hurl his power down on to our heads, like a slighted god, roaring thunderously; but his roaring was mixed with so many coarse words that no one could have taken it for a thunderbolt. His ordinary Bengali appearance, too, belied the noise he made, so no one confused this god of the second stream of the third year with Indra, Chandra, Varuna or Kartik. There was only one god like him: Yama, god of death; and after all these years there is no harm in admitting that we often wished he would go, there and then, to Yama's home. But clearly no god can be more malevolent than a man-god. The immortal gods cause nowhere near so much trouble. If we pick a flower and offer it to them, they are pleased; but they do not harass us if we don't offer it. Human gods demand far more; if we fall the slightest bit short, they swoop, red-eyed with fury, not at all godlike to look at.

Our teacher had a weapon for torturing boys that sounds trivial but which was actually terribly cruel. He would give us new names. Although a name is nothing but a word, people generally love their names more than their own selves; they will go to tremendous lengths to further their names; they are willing to die for them. If you distort a man's name, you strike at something more precious than life itself. Even if you change someone's ugly name to a pretty one – 'Lord of ghosts', say, to 'Lotus-lover' – it's unbearable. From this we derive a principle: that the abstract is worth more to us than the material, fees to the goldsmith seem dearer than gold, honour means more than life, one's name more than one's self.

Because of this deep law of human nature, Shashishekhar ('Moon-crown') was intensely distressed when Shibanath gave him the name 'Bhetaki' ('Flat-fish'). His misery was doubled by the knowledge that the name was precisely pointed at his looks; yet all he could do was sit quietly and suffer silently.

Ashu was given the name 'Ginni' ('Housewife'), but there was a story behind this.

Ashu was the goody-goody of the class. He never complained to anyone: he was very shy – maybe he was younger than the others. He smiled gently at anything that was said to him; he studied hard; many were keen to make friends with him, but he never played with any other boy, and as soon as we were released from class he would go straight home. At one o'clock every day a servant-girl would bring him a few sweets wrapped up in a leaf, and a little bell-metal pot of water. Ashu was very embarrassed by this; he could not wait for her to go home again. He did not want his classmates to think of him as anything more than a schoolboy. The people at home – his parents, brothers and sisters – everything about them was very much a private matter, which he did his utmost to conceal from the boys at school.

So far as his studies were concerned he could not be faulted in any way, but every now and then he was late to school and could give no good answer when Shibanath questioned him. His disgrace on these occasions was appalling: the teacher made him stand by the steps to the building, bent double with his hands on his knees. His misery and shame were thus displayed to four whole classes of boys.

A day's holiday came (to mark an eclipse). The next day Shibanath took his place on his stool as usual and, looking towards the door, saw Ashu entering the class with his slate and school-books wrapped in an ink-stained cloth. He was even more hesitant than usual.

'Here comes the Housewife!' said Shibanath, laughing drily. Later, when the class was over, just before he dismissed the boys, he called out, 'Listen to this, everyone.'

It was as if the whole of Earth's gravity were dragging young

Ashu down, but all he could do was sit with his legs and the end of his dhoti dangling down from the bench, while all the boys stared at him. There were many years to come in Ashu's life, many days of joy, sorrow and shame more significant than this – but none could compare with what his young heart suffered on this occasion. Yet the background to it was very ordinary, and can be explained in a very few words.

Ashu had a little sister. She had no friend or cousin of her own age, so Ashu was her only playmate. Ashu's home had a covered porch, with a gate and railings in front. The holiday had been cloudy and very wet. The few people who continued to pass by, shoes in their hands, umbrellas over their heads, were in too much of a hurry to look round. Ashu played all day with his sister, seated on the steps of the porch, while clouds darkened the sky and the rain pattered.

It was the wedding-day of his sister's doll. Ashu was giving solemn and scrupulous instructions to his sister about the preparations for the wedding. A problem then arose about who would be the priest. The little girl suddenly jumped up, and Ashu heard her ask someone, 'Please, will you be the priest at my doll's wedding?' Turning round, he saw a bedraggled Shibanath standing under the porch, folding his wet umbrella. He had been walking along the road, and had taken shelter from the rain there. It was Shibanath whom the little girl had asked to be priest at her doll's wedding.

Ashu dashed straight into the house when he saw him, abandoning the game and his sister. His holiday had been utterly ruined.

This was what Shibanath described with withering amusement the following day, to account for his calling Ashu 'Housewife' in front of everyone. At first the boy smiled gently, as he did to everything he heard, and tried to join in a little with the merriment all around him. But then one o'clock struck, the classes were dismissed, the servant-girl from home was standing at the gate with two sweets in a *śāl*-leaf and some water in a shining bell-metal pot, and Ashu's smile gave way to a deep red blush around his face and ears. The veins in his aching forehead began to throb; he could no longer hold back the flood of tears in his eyes.

Shibanath took a light meal in his rest-room, and settled down for a smoke. The boys danced round Ashu, boisterously chanting,

'Housewife, housewife!' He realized that to play with your little sister on a school holiday was the most shameful thing in the world, and he could not believe that people would ever forget what he had done.

Little Master's Return

Raicharan was twelve when he first came to work in the house. He was from Jessore district and had long hair and large eyes; a slender boy with gleaming dark skin. His employers, like him, were Kaisthas. His main duty was to help with looking after their one-year-old son – who in time progressed from Raicharan's arms to school, from school to college, and from college to being munsiff in the local court. Raicharan had remained his servant. But now there was a mistress as well as a master in the household, and most of the rights that Raicharan had hitherto had over Anukul Babu passed to her.

Although his former responsibilities were diminished by her presence, she largely replaced them with a new one. A son to Anukul was soon born, and was won over completely by the sheer force of Raicharan's devotion. He swung him about with such enthusiasm, tossed him in the air with such dexterity, cooed and shook his head in his face so vigorously, chanted so many meaningless random questions for which there could be no reply, that the very sight of Raicharan sent the little master into raptures.

When the boy learnt to crawl stealthily over a door-sill, giggling with merriment if anyone tried to catch him, and speedily making for somewhere safe to hide, Raicharan was entranced by such uncommon skill and quickness of decision. He would go to the child's mother and say admiringly, '*Mā*, your son will be a judge when he grows up – he'll earn a fortune.' That there were other children in the world who could at this young age dart over a door-sill was beyond Raicharan's imagination; only future judges could perform such feats. His first faltering steps were amazing too, and when he began to call his mother 'Ma', his *pisimā* 'Pishi', and Raicharan 'Channa', Raicharan proclaimed these staggering achievements to everyone he met. How astonishing it was that he should not only call his mother 'Ma',

his aunt 'Pishi', but also Raicharan 'Channa'! Really, it was hard
to understand where such intelligence had sprung from. Certainly
no adult could ever show such extraordinary intelligence, and
people would be unsure of his fitness to be a judge even if he
could.

Before long, Raicharan had to put a string round his neck and
pretend to be a horse; or he had to be a wrestler and fight with
the boy – and if he failed to let himself be defeated and thrown to
the ground, there would be hell to pay. By now, Anukul had been
transferred to a Padma river district. He had brought a push-
chair from Calcutta for his son. Raicharan would dress him in a
satin shirt, gold-embroidered cap, golden bangles and a pair of
anklets, and take the young prince out in his push-chair twice a
day for some air.

The rainy season came. The Padma began to swallow up
gardens, villages and fields in great hungry gulps. Thickets and
bushes disappeared from the sandbanks. The menacing gurgle of
water was all around, and the splashing of crumbling banks; and
swirling, rushing foam showed how fierce the river's current had
become.

One afternoon, when it was cloudy but did not look like rain,
Raicharan's capricious young master refused to stay at home. He
climbed into his push-chair and Raicharan gingerly pushed it to
the river-bank beyond the paddy-fields. There were no boats on
the river, no people working in the fields: through gaps in the
clouds, the sun could be seen preparing with silent fiery ceremony
to set behind the deserted sandbanks across the river. Suddenly
peace was broken by the boy pointing and calling, 'Fowers,
Channa, fowers!' A little way off there was a huge *kadamba* tree
on a wet, muddy stretch of land, with some flowers on its upper
branches: these were what had caught the boy's attention. (A few
days previously, Raicharan had strung some flowers on to sticks
and made him a '*kadamba*-cart'; he had had such fun pulling it
along with a string that Raicharan did not have to put on reins
that day – an instant promotion from horse to groom.)

'Channa' was not very willing to squelch through the mud to
pick the flowers. He quickly pointed in the other direction and
said, 'Look, look at that bird – flying – now it's gone. Come, bird,
come!' He pushed the chair forward fast, burbling on in this way.

But it was futile to try to distract by so simple a device a boy who would one day become a judge – especially as there was nothing particular to attract his attention anywhere, and imaginary birds would not work for very long. 'All right,' said Raicharan, 'you sit in the chair and I'll get you the flowers. Be good now, don't go near the water.' Tucking his dhoti up above his knees, he headed for the *kadamba* tree.

But the fact that he had been forbidden to go near the water immediately attracted the boy's mind away from the *kadamba*-flowers and towards the water. He saw it gurgling and swirling along, as if a thousand wavelets were naughtily, merrily escaping to a forbidden place beyond the reach of some mighty Raicharan. The boy was thrilled by their mischievous example. He gently stepped down from his chair, and edged his way to the water. Picking a long reed, he leant forward, pretending the reed was a fishing-rod: the romping gurgling wavelets seemed to be murmuring an invitation to the boy to come and join their game.

There was a single plopping sound, but on the bank of the Padma river in monsoon spate many such sounds can be heard. Raicharan had filled the fold of his dhoti with *kadamba*-flowers. Climbing down from the tree, he made his way back towards the push-chair, smiling – but then he saw that the child was not there. Looking all around, he saw no sign of him anywhere. His blood froze: the universe was suddenly unreal – pale and murky as smoke. A single desperate cry burst from his breaking heart: 'Master, little master, my sweet, good little master!' But no one called out 'Channa' in reply, no childish mischievous laugh came back. The Padma went on rushing and swirling and gurgling as before, as if it knew nothing and had no time to attend to the world's minor occurrences.

As evening fell the boy's mother grew anxious and sent people out to search with lanterns. When they reached the river-bank, they found Raicharan wandering over the fields like a midnight storm-wind, sobbing, 'Master, my little master!' At last he returned home and threw himself at his mistress's feet, crying in reply to all her questions, 'I don't know, *Mā*, I don't know.'

Although everyone knew in their hearts that the Padma was the culprit, suspicion fell on a group of gypsies encamped at the edge of the village. The mistress of the house even began to suspect that Raicharan had stolen the boy – so much so that she called him and entreated, 'Bring back my child! I'll give you whatever money you want.' But Raicharan could only beat his brow, and she ordered him from her sight. Anukul Babu tried to dispel his wife's unfounded suspicion: what motive could Raicharan have had for so vile an act? 'What do you mean?' said his wife. 'The boy had gold ornaments on him.'

II

Raicharan went back to his home village. His wife had not borne him a child, and he had long ceased to hope for one. But it so happened that before the year had ended his ageing wife gave birth to a son – and then soon afterwards died.

At first Raicharan had nothing but hatred for the newly born child, who he felt had somehow taken the little master's place by deceit. It seemed a deadly sin to delight in his own son after allowing his master's only son to be washed away. If his widowed sister had not been there, the child would not have breathed Earth's air for long.

Amazing it was, but after a few months the child began to crawl over the door-sill and show a merry ability to evade all sorts of restrictions. He chuckled and wailed just as the little master had done. Sometimes when Raicharan heard him cry his heart missed a beat; it was just as if the little master were crying somewhere for his lost Raicharan. Phelna – that was what Raicharan's sister called the boy – began in due course to call her 'Pishi'. When Raicharan heard that familiar name one day, he suddenly thought, 'The little master cannot do without my love: he has been born again in my house.'

There were several convincing proofs in favour of this belief. First, there was the short interval between the death and the birth. Second, his wife could not, at so advanced an age, have conceived a son merely through her own fecundity. Third, the child crawled, toddled and called his aunt 'Pishi' just as the little master had done. There was much to indicate that he too would grow up to become a judge. Raicharan then remembered the strong suspicions the mistress of the house had had, and he realized with astonishment that her maternal instinct had rightly told her that someone had stolen her son. He now felt deeply ashamed of the way he had neglected the child: devotion took hold of him again. From now on he brought him up like a rich man's son. He bought him satin shirts and a gold-embroidered cap. His dead wife's ornaments were melted down to make bangles and bracelets for him. He forbade him from playing with the local children; all day long he himself was the child's sole playmate. Whenever they got the chance, the local boys would mock Phelna for being a 'prince', and the villagers marvelled at Raicharan's odd behaviour.

When Phelna was old enough to go to school, Raicharan sold his land and took the boy to Calcutta. With great difficulty he found a job, and sent Phelna to a high-class school. He skimped and scraped to get the boy good food and clothing and a decent education, saying to himself, 'If it was love for me that brought you into my house, dear child, then you must have nothing but the best.'

Twelve years passed in this way. The boy did well at his studies and was fine to behold: sturdily built, with a dark, glossy complexion. He took great trouble over his hair; his tastes were refined and cultured. He could never think of his father quite as his father, because Raicharan treated him with a father's affection but a servant's devotion. To his discredit, Phelna never told anyone that Raicharan *was* his father. The students in the hostel where Phelna lived were always making fun of the rustic Raicharan; and it cannot be denied that when his father was not present Phelna joined in the fun. But everyone was fond of the mild, doting Raicharan, and Phelna also loved him – but (to repeat) not quite as his father: affection was mixed with condescension.

Raicharan grew old. His employer was perpetually finding fault with him. His health was deteriorating, and he could not concentrate on his work: he was getting forgetful. But no employer who pays full wages will accept old age as an excuse. Moreover, the cash that Raicharan had raised by selling off his possessions was nearly at an end. Phelna was always complaining now that he was short of proper clothes and luxuries.

III

One day Raicharan suddenly resigned from his job, and giving Phelna some money said, 'Something has happened – I need to go back to the village for a few days.' He then set off for Barasat, where Anukul Babu was now munsiff.

Anukul had had no other child. His wife still grieved for her son.

One evening Anukul was resting after returning from the court, while his wife, at great expense, purchased from a *sannyāsi* a holy root and a blessing that would bring her a child. A voice was heard in the yard: 'Greetings, *Mā*.'

'Who's there?' said Anukul Babu.

Raicharan appeared. 'I am Raicharan,' he said, taking the dust of his former master's feet.

Anukul's heart melted at the sight of the old man. He asked him numerous questions about his present circumstances, and invited him to work for him again.

Raicharan smiled weakly and said, 'Let me pay my respects to *Māṭhākrun*.'

Anukul Babu took him through to the inner rooms of the house. His wife was not nearly so pleased to see Raicharan, but Raicharan took no notice of this and said with clasped hands, 'Master, *Mā*, it was I who stole your son. It was not the Padma, it was no one else, it was I, ungrateful wretch that I am.'

'What are you saying?' said Anukul. 'Where is he?'

'He lives with me,' said Raicharan. 'I'll bring him the day after tomorrow.'

That was Sunday, and the courts were closed. Husband and wife watched the road anxiously from dawn. At ten o'clock, Raicharan arrived with Phelna.

Anukul's wife without thought or question drew him on to her lap, touched him, sniffed him, eyed his face intently, cried and laughed nervously. Truly, the boy was fine to look at – nothing in his looks or dress suggested a poor background. There was a very loving, modest, bashful expression in his face. At the sight of him, Anukul's heart too swelled with love. But keeping his composure, he asked, 'What proof have you?'

'How can such an act be proved?' said Raicharan. 'Only God knows that I stole your son; no one else in the world knows.'

Anukul thought the matter over and decided that since his wife had embraced the boy as her own with such fervour it would not be appropriate to search for proof now; whatever the truth might be, it was best to believe. In any case, how could Raicharan have acquired such a boy? And why should the old servant wish to mislead them now? Questioning the boy, he learnt that he had lived with Raicharan from an early age and had called him Father, but that Raicharan had never behaved towards him like a father – he had been more like a servant. Driving all doubt from his mind, Anukul said, 'But, Raicharan, you must not darken our door again now.'

With clasped hands and quavering voice Raicharan replied, 'I am old now, master. Where shall I go?'

'Let him stay,' said the mistress of the house. 'I have forgiven him. Let our son be blessed.'

'He cannot be forgiven for what he has done,' said the righteous Anukul.

'I didn't do it,' cried Raicharan, embracing his master's feet. 'God did it.'

Even angrier now that Raicharan should lay the blame for his own sin on to God, Anukul said, 'One should not place trust in someone who has betrayed trust so heinously.'

Rising from Anukul's feet, Raicharan said, 'It was not I, Master.'

'Then who was it?'

'It was my Fate.'

No educated man could be satisfied by such an explanation.

'I have no one else in the world,' said Raicharan.

Phelna was certainly rather annoyed that Raicharan had stolen him – a munsiff's son – and dishonourably claimed him as his own. But he said generously to Anukul, 'Father, please pardon him. If you won't let him stay in the house, then give him a monthly allowance.

Raicharan, saying nothing, looked once at his son and made an obeisance to all; then he went out through the door and disappeared into the world's multitude. At the end of the month, when Anukul sent a small sum to Raicharan at his village address, the money came back. No one of that name was known there.

The Divide

Genealogical investigation would reveal that Banamali and Himangshumali were actually distant cousins: the relationship was complicated, but possible to trace. Their families, however, had been neighbours for a long time, with only a garden dividing them; so however remote their blood-relationship, they knew each other very well.

Banamali was much older than Himangshu. Before Himangshu had cut his teeth or could talk, Banamali would carry him around in the garden to enjoy the morning or evening air; he would play with him, dry his tears, lull him to sleep; indeed he did everything an intelligent grown-up person is supposed to do to entertain a child – shaking his head at him, shrieking with dismay, expressing babyish excitement or fearsome enthusiasm. He had little education: he liked to garden, or be with his young cousin. He nurtured him like a rare and precious creeper, which he watered with all his love; and as the creeper grew, pervading the whole of his inner and outer life, Banamali counted himself blessed.

There may not be many, but there are some people who will easily sacrifice themselves completely to a small fancy or a little child or an undeserving friend. Their love may be tiny compared to the vastness of the world, but it is to them a business in which they happily sink all that is vital to them. They will then live contentedly on a pittance, or else one morning sell their remaining property and take to begging in the streets.

As Himangshu grew, he formed a firm friendship with Banamali, despite their difference in age and remoteness of blood-relationship. Age seemed of no consequence. There was a reason for this. Himangshu learned to read and write, and had by nature a strong desire for knowledge. He would sit and read any book that came his way: he would read many worthless books, no doubt, but his mind matured in all directions as a result of his reading. Banamali listened to him with great admiration. He took his advice, discussed every problem with him, small or large, never ignored him on any subject just because he was a child. Nothing is more cherished in this world than a person whom one has brought up with utmost love, and whose knowledge, intelligence and goodness inspire respect.

Himangshu also loved gardening. But there was a difference here between the two friends. Banamali loved it with his heart; Himangshu with his intelligence. For Banamali, raising plants was an instinctive occupation: they were like children to him, only more so, in their softness and unawareness, in the way they never asked to be cared for but would grow up like children if given loving care.[1] For Himangshu, plants were a subject of curiosity. The sowing of seeds, the sprouting of seedlings, the buds, the blooms all aroused his attention. He was full of advice about planting, grafting, manuring, watering and so on, and Banamāli gladly followed it. Whatever nature or nurture could do, in the combining or separating of plants, was achieved by the two friends in that modest patch of garden.

There was a small cement patio just inside the gate to the garden. At four o'clock Banamali would come there, lightly dressed, with a crimped chadar round his shoulders, and sit in the shade with his hookah. He was quite alone, and had no book or newspaper with him. He would sit and smoke, with a distracted meditative air, glancing with half-closed eyes to right or to left, letting time float by like coils of smoke from the hookah as they slowly drifted and broke and disappeared, leaving no trace.

At last Himangshu returned from school, and after a snack and a wash came into the garden. Banamali immediately dropped the stem of the hookah and stood up. His eagerness made it perfectly plain whom he had been patiently waiting for all this time. Then the two of them strolled in the garden, talking. When it became dark they sat on a bench, while the southern breeze stirred the leaves in the trees. On some days there was no wind: the trees would be as still as a picture, and the sky above would be full of brightly shining stars.

Himangshu talked, and Banamali listened quietly. Even what he did not understand, he enjoyed. Things that would have

1. *banamāli* means 'woodland gardener' or 'wearing a garland of wild flowers', and is a name for Krishna.

irritated him greatly coming from anyone else were amusing when spoken by Himangshu. Himangshu's powers of expression, recollection and imagination gained from having such an admiring, grown-up listener. He sometimes spoke of things he had read, sometimes things he had thought, sometimes whatever came into his head – supplying with his imagination whatever his knowledge lacked. He said much that was correct and much that was not correct, but Banamali listened solemnly. Sometimes he put in a word of his own, but accepted any objections that Himangshu made; and next day, sitting in the shade again, puffing at his hookah, he would ponder over what he had heard, marvelling at it.

Meanwhile a dispute had arisen. Between Banamali's garden and Himangshu's house there was a drainage ditch; at a point along this ditch a lime tree had grown. When the fruits ripened, Banamali's family servant tried to pick them, while Himangshu's family servant stopped him – and they began to argue so fiercely that if the insults they rained on each other had been made of something material, the whole ditch would have been choked with them. From this, a heated quarrel developed between Banamali's father Harachandra and Himangshu's father Gokulchandra, and they went to court over the ownership of the ditch. A long verbal war began between champion lawyers and barristers fighting on one side or the other. The money that was spent on each side exceeded even the floods that flowed through the ditch during the month of Bhādra.

In the end Harachandra won; it was proved that the ditch was his and no one else had a claim to the fruit of the lime tree. There was an appeal, but the ditch and the lime tree remained with Harachandra.

While the court-case was going on, the friendship between Banamali and Himangshu was not affected. Indeed, so anxious was Banamali not to let the dispute cast a shadow over either of them, that he tried to bind Himangshu ever more closely to him, and Himangshu showed not the slightest loss of affection either.

On the day that Harachandra won the case, there was great rejoicing in his house, especially in the women's quarters; but Banamali lay sleepless that night. The next afternoon, when he took his place on the patio in the garden, his face was sad and anxious, as if he alone had suffered an immense defeat that meant nothing to anyone else.

The time when Himangshu usually came elapsed; at six o'clock there was still no sign of him. Banamali sighed heavily and gazed at Himangshu's house. Through the open window he could see his friend's school-clothes hung up on the *ālnā*; many other familiar signs showed that Himangshu was at home. Banamali left his hookah and paced up and down, looking dejectedly towards the window again and again, but Himangshu did not come into the garden.

When the lamps were lit in the evening, Banamali slowly walked up to Himangshu's house. Gokulchandra was cooling himself by an open door. 'Who is it?' he said.

Banamali started. He felt like a thief who had been caught. 'It's me, Uncle,' he said nervously.

'What do you want?' he said. 'There's no one at home.'

Banamali returned to the garden and sat mutely there. When it was dark, he watched the window-shutters of Himangshu's house being closed for the night one by one. Lamplight inside the house shone through cracks round the doors; later, most of the lamps were extinguished. In the darkness of the night, Banamali felt that the doors of Himangshu's house were totally closed to him, and all he could do was remain alone in the darkness outside.

The next day he went again and sat in the garden, hoping that today Himangshu might come. His friend had come every day for so long that he never imagined that he might not come again. He never supposed that the bond between them could be torn; he had taken it so much for granted, that he had not realized how totally wrapped up in it his life had become. He had learnt now that the bond had indeed been torn, but so sudden a disaster was quite impossible to take in.

Every day that week he went on sitting in the garden at his usual time, in case Himangshu chanced to come. But alas, the meetings that used to occur by agreement failed to recur by chance. On Sunday he wondered if Himangshu would come to his house in the morning for lunch, as he had always done in the past. He did not exactly believe that he would, but he could not stop hoping. Mid-morning came, but Himangshu did not. 'He'll come after lunch,' said Banamali to himself – but he did not come after lunch. So he thought, 'Today perhaps he is taking a siesta. He'll come when he wakes up.' Whatever time Himangshu might have woken from his siesta, he did not come.

Evening fell again, then night; Himangshu's doors closed one by one, and the lights in his house went out one by one.

When Fate had taken each of the seven days from Monday to Sunday away from Banamali, leaving no day on which to pin his hopes, he turned his tearful eyes towards Himangshu's shuttered house, appealed to it from the depths of his distress. 'Dear God,'[1] he cried, gathering all his life's pain into the words.

---

1. *dayāmaya,* lit., 'full of kindness', a name for God.

Taraprasanna's Fame[1]

Like most writers, Taraprasanna was rather shy and retiring in nature. To go out amongst other people was an ordeal for him. Sitting at home and writing all the time had weakened his eyesight, bent his back, and given him little experience of the world. Social pleasantries did not come easily to him, so he did not feel very safe outside his home. Others thought him a bit stupid, and they could not be blamed for this. A distinguished gentleman on first meeting Taraprasanna might say warmly, 'I cannot tell you what pleasure it gives me to meet you.' Taraprasanna would not respond: he would stare, tongue-tied, at his right palm, as if to imply, 'It is possible that you are very pleased, but I wonder how I can be so false as to say that I am pleased.' Or he might be invited to someone's house one afternoon: his wealthy host might – as dusk fell and food was served – deprecate his own hospitality with such words as 'Nothing special – just our ordinary humble fare – a poor man's crust – not worthy of you at all, I'm afraid.' Taraprasanna would say nothing, as if it were impossible to disagree with what his host was saying. Sometimes some good-natured person averred that scholarship as profound as Taraprasanna's was rare in this age, that Sarasvati had deserted her lotus-seat to dwell in Taraprasanna's throat. He made no objection to this – choked, so it seemed, by Sarasvati's presence in his throat. He should have known that those who praise a man to his face, and disparage themselves, deliberately exaggerate because they expect to be contradicted. If the person they are speaking to takes in everything without blenching, they feel let down. They are pleased to be told that their statements are false.

Taraprasanna behaved quite differently with the people in his own home – so much so that even his wife Dakshayani could not beat him in an argument. She was forced to say, 'All right, all right, I give in. I've got things to do now.' Very few husbands have the skill or luck ever to get their wives to admit defeat in a verbal battle!

1. *Kīrti*, 'feat', 'accomplishment', but also used to mean fame or renown.

Taraprasanna lived contentedly. Dakshayani firmly believed that no one equalled her husband in learning or intellect, and she did not hesitate to say so. He would reply, 'You don't have any other husband to compare me with' – which made her very cross. Her only complaint was that her husband had never displayed his extraordinary talents to the outside world – had never made any effort to do so. Nothing that he had written had been published.

Sometimes she asked to hear her husband's writing, and the less she understood it the more it astonished her. She had read Krittibas's *Ramayana*, Kashidas's *Mahabharata* and Kabikankan's *Chandimangal*, and had heard them being recited. They were all as clear as water – even illiterate people could easily understand them; but she had never encountered writing like her husband's, so brilliant that it was unintelligible. She thought to herself, 'When these books are printed and no one understands a word, how amazed everyone will be!' Again and again she told her husband, 'You should get your writings printed.'

'With regard to the printing of books,' he replied, 'the great Manu has said: "It is a natural activity for created beings, but abstention brings great rewards."'[1]

Taraprasanna had four children – all daughters. Dakshayani regarded this as a failing in herself, and therefore felt unworthy of so talented a husband. To be married to a man who produced, at the drop of a hat, such formidable tomes, and yet to have nothing but female offspring, was shameful incompetence on her part.

When Taraprasanna's eldest daughter reached his chest in height, his carefree contentment ended. He now remembered that one by one his four daughters would have to be married, and this would cost an enormous amount of money. His wife said confidently, 'Just apply your mind a bit, and I'm sure we won't need to worry.'

'You really think so?' said Taraprasanna rather anxiously. 'All right, what do you suggest?'

'Go to Calcutta,' said Dakshayani, without hesitation or doubt. 'Have your books printed, get yourself known to everyone. The money will soon roll in.'

1. Laws of Manu V.56. Manu's *caveat* actually relates to 'eating, liquor-drinking and sexual intercourse'. See Manu in the Glossary.

Taraprasanna was gradually encouraged by his wife, and decided that what he had written to date was enough to pay for the wedding of every girl in the village. But now a big dilemma arose about his visit to Calcutta. Dakshayani could not bear to let her innocent, helpless, pampered husband go away on his own. Who would feed him, dress him, remind him of his daily chores, protect him from the various hazards of the world? Her inexperienced husband, however, was equally unhappy about taking his wife to a strange place. In the end Dakshayani engaged a worldly-wise man from the village to go in her stead, giving him countless instructions about her husband's daily needs. She extracted numerous vows from him as she saw him off, and loaded him with charms and amulets; and she threw herself to the ground weeping when he had gone.

In Calcutta Taraprasanna, with the help of his astute minder, published his book *The Radiance of Vedanta*. Most of the money he had raised by pawning his wife's jewellery was spent on this.

He sent *The Radiance of Vedanta* to bookshops; and to every editor, however important or unimportant, he sent copies for review. He also sent one to his wife, by registered mail. He was afraid that otherwise it would be stolen by the postman.

On the day that Dakshayani first saw the book, with her husband's name printed on the title page, she invited all the women she knew in the village round for a meal. She left the book open near to where she asked them to sit, and when everyone was seated she said, 'Oh dear, who's dropped that book over there? Annada, dear, could you pick it up? I'll put it away.' Annada was the only one who could read. The book was put back on the shelf. For a few minutes Dakshayani busied herself with something else; then she said to her eldest daughter, 'Do you want to read your father's book, Shashi? Go ahead, child, read it. Don't be shy.' But Shashi showed no interest in it, so a little later her mother said crossly, 'Don't spoil your father's book! Give it to Kamaladidi to put back on top of that cupboard.' If the book had been conscious of anything, it would have felt like the *death* of Vedanta after such a day of torment.

One by one reviews appeared in the papers. What Dakshayani had anticipated turned out to be largely correct: reviewers throughout the land, unable to understand a single word of the book, were mightily impressed by it. With one voice they said: 'No book of such substance has been published before.' Critics who never touched a book beyond Bengali translations of Reynolds' *London Mystery*[1] wrote with great enthusiasm: 'If instead of sackfuls of plays and novels more books like this could come out, Bengali literature would really attract readers.' Men who for generations had never heard of Vedanta wrote: 'We do not concur with Taraprasanna Babu on every point – lack of space prevents us from saying where. On the whole, however, our views are in agreement with the author's.' On the basis of that statement, if true, the book 'on the whole' should have been thrown to the flames.

From wherever there were libraries or no libraries, librarians wrote to Taraprasanna asking for the book, buying it with their official letter-heads rather than with money. Many wrote, 'Your thoughtful book has met a great need in our country.' Taraprasanna was not quite sure what they meant by 'thoughtful', but he proudly posted *The Radiance of Vedanta* to every library at his own expense.

Just when his pleasure at all these words of praise had reached its height, a letter came from Dakshayani: she was expecting a fifth child very soon. He and his custodian now went round to the shops to collect the money the book had earned – but the shopkeepers all said the same: not a single copy had been sold. Only in one place did he hear that someone had written from the country asking for the book: it was sent cash-on-delivery and returned – no one had taken it. The bookseller had to pay for the postage, so he angrily insisted on returning all the copies to the author there and then.

Taraprasanna went back to his lodgings, thinking and thinking but finding it impossible to comprehend what had happened. The more he thought about his 'thoughtful' book the more worried he became. At last he set off home, making do with the tiny amount of money he had left.

He greeted his wife with an elaborate show of cheerfulness. She was smiling in anticipation of good news. He threw a copy of *The Bengal Messenger* on to her lap. As she read it, she bestowed inexhaustible blessings on the editor, made mental *pūjā*-offerings to his pen. Then she turned to her husband again: he took out a

1. See Glossary, p. 309.

copy of *New Dawn*. Dakshayani read this too with immense
delight, and again turned her tender, expectant gaze on her
husband. He now took out *The New Age*; then *India's Fortune*;
then *The Happy Awakening*; then *The Sun's Light* and *The Wave
of News*; then *Hope*, *The Dawn*, *Uplift*, *Blossom*, *The Companion*,
The Sita Gazette, *The Ahalya Library Journal*, *Pleasant News*,
The Guardian, *World Judge*, *Jasmine-creeper*. The smiling Dakshayani wept tears of joy. Then, drying her eyes, she looked at
her husband once more – at the light of fame in his beaming face.

'There are lots more journals,' he said.

'I'll look at them this afternoon,' said Dakshayani. 'Now give
me the other news.'

'Just as I was leaving Calcutta,' said Taraprasanna, 'I heard
that the Governor-General's wife had brought out a book – but
she didn't mention *The Radiance of Vedanta* in it.'

'I don't want to hear about that,' said Dakshayani. 'Tell me
what else you have brought.'

'I have a few letters,' said Taraprasanna.

Then Dakshayani said straight out, 'How much money have
you brought?'

'Five rupees borrowed from Bidhubhushan,' said Taraprasanna.

When at last Dakshayani had heard the whole story, all her
trust in the honesty of the world was completely destroyed. The
booksellers had clearly cheated her husband, and all the book-
buyers of Bengal had conspired to cheat the booksellers. Finally
she concluded that Bidhubhushan, the man she had sent with her
husband to deputize for her, had secretly been in league with the
booksellers; and come to think of it, Bishvambhar Chatterjee
from across the village – her husband's chief enemy – had surely
had a part in the plot. Yes, two days after her husband had left
for Calcutta, she had seen Bishvambhar talking to Kanai Pal
under the banyan tree: it did not occur to her that Bishvambhar
quite often chatted to Kanai Pal, for the conspiracy was now as
clear as daylight to her.

Dakshayani's domestic worries continued to grow. The failure
of this one simple way of earning money redoubled her shame
that she had so sinfully borne only daughters. Neither Bishvambhar, Bidhubhushan, nor all the inhabitants of Bengal could be
held responsible for this: the shame rested on her alone, though

she also blamed her daughters themselves – those that she had and those that she might yet have. She had not a moment's peace of mind, day or night.

Her state of health, as her confinement approached, became so bad that everyone was very alarmed. The helpless, distraught Taraprasanna went to Bishvambhar and said, '*Dādā*, if you could take fifty or so of my books as a pledge for a loan, I could send for a good midwife from town.'

'Don't worry, my friend,' said Bishvambhar, 'I'll give you the money you need – you keep the books.' He then persuaded Kanai Pal to lend him some money, and Bidhubhushan went to Calcutta at *his* own expense to fetch the midwife.

Impelled by something, Dakshayani called her husband into her room and said, making him vow to her, 'Whenever that pain of yours gets bad, don't forget to take your Dream Medicine – and never take off the amulet the *sannyāsī* gave you.' Taking her husband's hands, she secured his promise on countless other minor matters. She also told him not to put any trust in Bidhubhushan, who had ruined him, so that now there was no question of putting her husband – medicine, amulet, blessings and all – into his hands. She repeatedly warned her husband – her trusting, forgetful, Shiva-like husband – about the heartless and crooked conspirators of this world. Finally, in a whisper, she said, 'When my baby daughter is born, if she lives, see that she is called Vedantaprabha, "The Radiance of Vedanta". Later you can call her simply "Prabha".' She took the dust of her husband's feet. In her mind was the thought, 'I came into his house to give him nothing but daughters. Perhaps his misfortunes will end now.'

When the midwife cried out, '*Mā*, look here, what a beautiful little girl you have,' Dakshayani took one look and then closed her eyes, saying faintly, 'Vedantaprabha'. She had no time to say any more in this world.

Wealth Surrendered

I

Brindaban Kunda was furious. He announced to his father, 'I'm leaving – right now.'

'You ungrateful scoundrel,' said Yajnanath Kunda. 'All I've spent feeding and clothing you over the years, with not a paisa back – and now see how you turn on me.'

In fact, the amount spent on food and clothing in Yajnanath's house had never been great. The sages of old survived on impossibly little; Yajnanath presented an equally noble example. He could not go quite as far as he liked, partly because of the demands of modern life, partly because of the unreasonable rules for keeping body and soul together which Nature imposes. His son had put up with this while he was unmarried; but after marrying, his standards of food and dress began to clash with his father's extreme austerity. Brindaban's standards were material rather than spiritual. His requirements were in line with society's changing response to cold, heat, hunger and thirst. There were frequent rows between father and son, and matters came to a head when Brindaban's wife fell seriously ill. The *kabirāj* wanted to prescribe an expensive medicine for her, but Yajnanath questioned his competence and dismissed him. Brindaban pleaded with his father at first, then grew angry, but to no avail. When his wife died, he accused his father of murdering her. 'What do you mean?' said Yajnanath. 'Do you suppose that no one who takes medicine dies? If expensive medicine were the answer, kings and emperors would be immortal. Why should your wife die with any more pomp than your mother or grandmother?'

Truly if Brindaban had not been blinded with grief and seen things objectively, he would have found much consolation in this thought. Neither his mother nor grandmother had taken medicine when they were dying. It was an ancient custom in the household not to do so. But modern people do not want to die according to ancient rules. (I am speaking of the time when the British had newly arrived in this country, but the behaviour of the younger generation was already causing consternation among their elders.)

This was why up-to-date Brindaban quarrelled with old-fashioned Yajnanath and said, 'I'm leaving.'

Giving him instant permission to go, his father said for all to hear that to give his son a single paisa would be as sinful as shedding a cow's blood. Brindaban, for his part, said that to take any of his father's money would be like shedding his mother's blood. They then parted company.

After so many undisturbed years, the people of the village were rather excited by this mini-revolution. And because Brindaban had been deprived of his inheritance, they all tried – as hard as they could – to distract Yajnanath from remorse at the rift with his son. They said that to quarrel with one's father over a mere wife could happen only in this day and age. After all, if a wife goes she can quickly be replaced by another – but if a father goes a second father cannot be found for love or money! This was a sound argument; but in my view (Brindaban being what he was) it would have cheered him somewhat rather than making him penitent.

It is unlikely that Yajnanath felt much distress at his son's departure. It was a considerable financial saving, and furthermore it removed a dread that had plagued him constantly – that Brindaban might one day poison him: what little food he ate was tainted by this morbid notion. It lessened somewhat when his daughter-in-law died; and now that his son had left he felt much more relaxed.

Only one thing pained him. Brindaban had taken his four-year-old son Gokulchandra with him. Gokul had cost relatively little to feed and clothe, so Yajnanath had felt quite easy towards him. (Despite his regret at the boy's removal, however, he could not help making some rapid calculations: how much he would save each month now that they had both gone, how much each year, and how much capital would earn an equivalent amount of interest.) It became difficult living in an empty house, without Gokul's mischief to disturb it. Yajnanath missed having no one to pester him during the *pūjās*, no one pinching his food at meal-times, no one running away with the inkpot when he did his accounts. Washing and eating with no one to disturb him was a melancholy business. Such undisturbed emptiness was what people gained after death, he thought. It tugged at his heart to see, in his bedding and quilt, holes made by his grandson, and, on the mat he sat on, ink-blots made by the same artist. For making his dhoti unfit to wear in less than two years, the pampered boy had been severely scolded by his grandfather. Now Yajnanath felt tears in his eyes when he saw that dhoti in Gokul's bedroom, dirty, torn, abandoned, knotted all over. Instead of using it to make wicks for lamps or for some other domestic purpose, he carefully stored it in a trunk, and promised that if Gokul returned and ruined a dhoti in even a single year, he would not scold him. But Gokul did not return. Yajnanath seemed to be ageing much faster than before, and the empty house felt emptier every day.

Yajnanath could not stay peacefully at home. Even in the afternoon, when all high-born people take a siesta, he roamed about the village with a hookah in his hand. During these silent afternoon walks, the village-boys would abandon their games and, retreating to a safe distance, bellow out locally composed rhymes about Yajnanath's miserliness. They none of them dared – in case their next meal was spoiled by so bad an omen – to utter his real name: they gave him names of their choosing. Old folk called him 'Yajnanash';[1] why exactly the boys should have called him 'Bat' is hard to explain. Perhaps they saw some resemblance in his pale, sickly skin.

II

One day Yajnanath was wandering along mango-tree-shaded paths in this way, when he saw a boy he had not previously seen taking command of the others and directing them in entirely new sorts of mischief. The boys were quite carried away by his forceful character and fresh imagination. Instead of retreating like them at the sight of the old man, the new boy went smartly right up to Yajnanath, and shaking out his chadar released a chameleon, which ran over Yajnanath's body and off into the bushes – leaving him quivering and smarting at the shock. The boys roared with amusement. A few paces on, Yajnanath's

1. 'Destroyer of sacrifice' as opposed to 'lord of sacrifice' (Yajnanath).

gāmchā was suddenly whipped off his shoulders, to reappear as a turban on the new boy's head.

Yajnanath was rather impressed by this novel kind of courtesy from a young stranger. He had not had such daring familiarity from any boy for a long time. By much shouting and coaxing, he managed to bring him to heel.

'What's your name?' he asked.

'Nitai Pal.'

'Where are you from?'

'Shan't tell you.'

'Who's your father?'

'Shan't tell you.'

'Why won't you tell me?'

'I've run away from home.'

'Why?'

'My father wanted to send me to school.'

Yajnanath felt immediately that to send such a boy to school would be a waste of money and that his father must be a fool.

'Will you come and live in my house?' he asked.

Raising no objection, the boy came along and settled in there as easily as under the shade of a roadside tree. Not only that, he issued barefaced orders for food and dress as if paid for in advance – and roundly disputed such matters with the master of the house. It had been easy to win arguments with his own son; but with someone else's, Yajnanath had to give in.

III

The villagers were amazed at the unprecedented affection that Yajnanath showed for Nitai Pal. 'The old man has not got much longer to live,' they thought, 'and this strange boy will inherit all his wealth.' They were all very envious of him, and were determined to do him down. But the old man hid him as closely as the ribs of his chest.

Sometimes the boy fretted and talked of leaving. Yajnanath would appeal to his greed, saying, 'You'll get all my wealth when I die.' The boy was still young, but he knew the measure of this promise.

Then the villagers started to search for Nitai's father. 'How

sore his parents must be about him!' they said. 'What a wicked
boy he is!' They hurled unrepeatable abuse at him – but their
feelings were fired more by selfish malice than moral outrage.

One day Yajnanath heard from a passer-by that a man called
Damodar Pal was looking for his lost son, and was on his way to
the village. Nitai was alarmed at this news – he was about to
abandon his prospects and flee; but Yajnanath reassured him,
saying, 'I'll hide you where no one will be able to find you. Not
even the people in this village.'

'Show me where,' said the boy, very intrigued.

'If I show you now, we'll be found out,' said Yajnanath. 'I'll
show you tonight.'

Nitai was excited by this promise of a new adventure. He
vowed that as soon as his father had gone, having failed to find
him, he would use the place to challenge his friends in a game of
hide-and-seek. No one would find him! It would be great fun. It
amused him greatly that his father had scoured the whole country
for him and had failed to find him.

At midday Yajnanath locked the boy into the house and went
out somewhere. When he returned, Nitai pestered him with
questions; and as soon as dusk fell he asked if they could go.

'It's not night yet,' said Yajnanath.

A little later Nitai said, 'It's night now, Dādā – let's go.'

'People are not asleep yet,' said Yajnanath.

'They're asleep now – let's go,' said Nitai a few moments later.

The night wore on. Though he was doing his utmost to stay
awake, Nitai began to nod as he sat. At one in the morning,
Yajnanath took Nitai by the hand and led him along the dark
paths of the sleeping village. There was no sound anywhere,
except for a dog barking from time to time, answered loudly by
other dogs near and far. Sometimes nocturnal birds, startled by
the sound of footsteps, flapped away through the forest. Nitai
nervously clasped Yajnanath's hand.

After crossing several fields, they came at last to a tumbledown,
god-forsaken temple surrounded by jungle. 'Here?' said Nitai,
rather crossly. It was not at all as he had imagined. There was no
mystery here. He had sometimes had to spend nights in ruined
temples like this after he had run away from home. The place was
not bad for hide-and-seek, but not totally beyond discovery.

Yajnanath lifted up a slab in the middle of the temple. The boy saw that beneath it there was a kind of cellar, with a lamp flickering. He was surprised and intrigued by this, but rather frightened too. Yajnanath climbed down a ladder into the cellar, and Nitai nervously followed him.

Down in the cellar, there were brass water-pots everywhere. There was a mat for a deity in the midst of them, with vermilion, sandal-paste, garlands and other *pūjā*-materials laid out in front. Nitai noticed with amazement that the pots were full of rupee-coins and gold *mohar*s.

'Nitai,' said Yajnanath, 'I told you that I would give you all my money. I haven't got much – just these few pitcherfuls. Today I place it all in your hands.'

Nitai jumped. 'All? Aren't you going to keep a single rupee for yourself?'

'It would bring leprosy to my hand if I took any of it. But one more thing: if my long-lost grandson Gokulchandra, or his son or grandson or great-grandson or any of his descendants come, then all this money must be given to him or to them.'

Nitai decided that Yajnanath had gone mad. 'All right,' he agreed.

'Now sit on this *āsan*,' said Yajnanath.

'Why?'

'You must be worshipped.'

'Why?'

'It is the custom.'

The boy sat on the *āsan*. Yajnanath smeared sandalwood on his forehead, and a spot of vermilion, and put a garland round his neck. Then, sitting before him, he began to mutter mantras. Nitai was terrified at finding himself worshipped as a god; terrified by the mantras. '*Dādā*,' he cried.

Yajnanath continued reading the mantras, without replying. At length he dragged the heavy pitchers, one by one, in front of the boy and dedicated them, making him say each time: 'I count and bequeath this money to Gokulchandra Kunda son of Brindaban Kunda son of Yajnanath Kunda son of Paramananda Kunda son of Prankrishna Kunda son of Gadadhar Kunda son of Yudhisthira Kunda; or to Gokulchandra's son or grandson or great-grandson or any of his true descendants.'

The repetition of this formula over and over again had a stupefying effect on the boy. His tongue gradually lost all movement. By the time the ceremony was over, the air of the little cave-like room was thick with smoke from the lamp and the breath of the two of them. Nitai's palate was dry; his arms and legs were feverishly hot; he was finding it difficult to breathe. The lamp guttered and went out. In the darkness, the boy sensed Yajnanath climbing up the ladder.

'Where are you going, *Dādā*?' he cried in alarm.

'I'm leaving you,' said Yajnanath. 'You stay here: no one will find you. But remember Gokulchandra son of Brindaban son of Yajnanath.'

He climbed out of the cellar and pulled the ladder up after him. '*Dādā*,' gasped Nitai, barely able to speak, 'I want to go back to my father.'

Yajnanath put the slab back into place, and straining his ears just managed to hear Nitai gasping the word, 'Father.' Then there was a thud, and after that no sound at all.

Consigning his wealth in this way to the care of a *yakṣa*, Yajnanath pressed some soil over the slab, and heaped it over with sand and broken bricks from the temple. He covered the heap with clumps of grass, and heeled in bushes from the forest. The night was almost over, but he could not bring himself to leave the place. Every now and then he put his ear to the ground. He imagined that he heard a crying from the innermost depths of the Earth; that the night sky was filled with that one sound; that all the people asleep in the world had been woken by it, and were sitting on their beds, listening. The old man went on frenziedly piling up more and more soil, as if trying to stop Earth's mouth. But somebody called out, 'Father' – and Yajnanath thumped the ground and hissed, 'Be quiet, everyone will hear you.'

Again, somebody called out, 'Father.'

The old man noticed dawn arriving. Fearfully he left the temple and emerged into open country. Even there someone was calling, 'Father.' He turned in great alarm: there in front of him was his son Brindaban.

'Father,' said Brindaban, 'I hear that my son has been hiding in your house. Give him back to me.'

The old man lurched towards Brindaban. His eyes and face

were horribly distorted as he leant forward and said, '*Your* son?'

'Yes,' said Brindaban, 'Gokul. Now his name is Nitai Pal and my name is Damodar. You have a bad name with everyone round about, so we changed our names – otherwise no one would have talked to us.'

The old man clawed at the sky with all his fingers, as if struggling to clasp the air; then fell to the ground, fainting. When he came round again, he hurried Brindaban to the temple. 'Can you hear the crying?' he asked.

'No,' said Brindaban.

'If you strain your ears, can't you hear someone crying "Father"?'

'No,' said Brindaban.

The old man seemed relieved at this. From then on he would go round asking everyone 'Can you hear the crying?' – and they all laughed at his madman's words.

About four years later, Yajnanath was on his death-bed. When the world's light grew dim in his eyes and breath began to fail, he suddenly sat up in delirium; groping with both hands, he murmured, 'Nitai – someone has taken my ladder away.' When he found no ladder out of the vast, lightless, airless cellar he was in, he slumped back against the pillows. Then he vanished, to the place which no one playing hide-and-seek on earth can discover.

Skeleton

There was a whole skeleton hanging on the wall of the room next to the one where the three of us slept when we were young. At night the bones used to clatter as the breeze stirred them. During the day we ourselves had to stir them: we were, at that time, studying *meghnād-badh kābya* with a pundit, and anatomy with a student from the Campbell Medical School. Our guardian wanted us to become instant experts in all fields of learning. To reveal how far his wishes were fulfilled would be superfluous to those who know us and unwise to those who do not.

This was all a long time ago. Meanwhile the skeleton disappeared from the room, and anatomical knowledge from our heads – heaven knows where.

A few days ago there was, for some reason, a shortage of space in the house and I had to spend the night in the room. Unused to being there, I couldn't sleep. I tossed and turned, and heard the big bell of the church clock nearly every time it struck. The oil-lamp in the corner of the room guttered, and five minutes later went out completely. Recently there had been a couple of deaths in our household – so the extinction of the lamp easily aroused morbid thoughts. The flame of a lamp could fade into eternal darkness at one in the morning; the little flame of a man's life could also go out one day or night and be forgotten. Gradually the memory of the skeleton came to me. As I imagined the life of the person whose skeleton it was, I suddenly felt a kind of live presence groping along the wall and circling round my mosquito-net, breathing audibly. It seemed to be looking for something, pacing rapidly round the room as it failed to find it. I knew perfectly well that this was all fabricated by my sleepless over-heated brain: it was the blood throbbing in my head that sounded like rapid footsteps. Nevertheless, I felt very odd. Trying to break out of my senseless fear, I called, 'Who's there?' The footsteps stopped right next to my mosquito-net and I heard an answer: 'Me. I've come to see where my skeleton might have gone.'

I decided I really could not show such fear to a creature of my imagination; so, clutching my pillow grimly, I said in a cheery voice as if speaking to an old friend, 'The right sort of task for the middle of the night! You still need that skeleton?'

From the darkness right against the mosquito-net the reply came, 'How could I not? My breast-bone was part of it – my twenty-six-year-old youth flowered around it. How could I not wish to see it again?'

'I understand what you mean,' I replied hastily. 'Finish searching and then go. I'm trying to get some sleep.'

'You're alone, I see,' said the voice. 'Then let me sit down a little. Let me talk to you. Thirty-five years ago I too sat next to men and chatted with them. For thirty-five years I have wandered about, moaning with the wind of cremation-grounds. Today I want to sit next to you and talk like a human being again.'

I sensed that someone had sat down next to my mosquito-net. Seeing no way out, I said brightly, 'Fine. Talk about whatever would make you feel better.'

'The most amusing story I have,' she said, 'is the story of my life.'

The church clock struck two.

'When I was alive and young there was someone I feared like death. My husband. I felt like a fish caught on a hook. That is, a completely unknown animal had hauled me up on a hook, snatched me out of the cool, deep, protective waters of my home, with no chance of escape. Two months after my marriage, my husband died. The grief that was expected of me was supplied in full by my in-laws. My father-in-law, pointing to numerous signs, told my mother-in-law that I was what the Shastras called a "poison-bride". I remember that distinctly. Are you listening? Are you enjoying the story?'

'Very much,' I said. 'It's very amusing so far.'

'Then listen. I returned joyfully to my father's house. I grew up. People tried to disguise it from me, but I well knew that women as beautiful as I was are rare. Do you agree?'

'Quite possibly. But I have never seen you.'

'Never seen me? Why? You saw my skeleton! But I mustn't tease you. How can I prove to you that in those empty eye-sockets there were big, wide, black eyes; that the skeleton's hideous toothy grin bore no comparison with the sweet smile that played on my red lips? It would be both amusing and annoying to describe to you the grace, the youth, the firm unblemished fullness that ripened day by day on those long dry pieces of bone! The anatomy of that body of mine was beyond even the greatest doctors! Indeed a doctor once said to his best friend that I was a "golden lotus"; meaning that anatomy and physiology could be learnt from any other human body, but I was unique – a miraculous flower. Does a golden lotus have a skeleton inside? When I moved, I knew that I was like a diamond sparkling in all directions when you turn it – such waves of natural beauty broke forth on all sides with my every gesture. I would sometimes gaze at my arms – arms that could have sweetly subdued the world's most passionate men like a horse's bridle. Do you remember Subhadra when she scooped up Arjuna and proudly drove him in her chariot astonishing heaven, earth and the nether world? Equal to hers were those delicate, shapely arms of mine, those pink palms, those beautifully tapered fingers. But that shameless, naked, unadorned skeleton bore false witness to me. I was speechless and helpless then, and angrier with you than anyone else in the world. I longed to stand before you as I was at sixteen, in the living, youthful flush of my beauty; to rob you of sleep; to disrupt your anatomy-learning and drive it away.'

'If you had a body,' I said, 'I would touch it and swear that not a trace of that learning remains in my mind. Your world-enchanting youthful beauty is all I am aware of now, radiantly etched against the night's dark background – nothing but that!'

'I had no female friend to keep me company. My elder brother had resolved not to get married. There were no other women in the house. I used to sit under a tree in the garden and imagine that the whole of Nature was in love with me, that all the stars were eyeing me, that the wind was sidling past me sighing deeply, that the grass on which my legs were stretched out would, were it conscious, quickly swoon to unconsciousness again. I supposed that all the world's young men were silently assembled round my feet like a clump of grass. What senseless anguish I felt!

'When my brother's friend Shashishekhar passed out of medical college, he became our family doctor. I had previously often observed him secretly. My brother was a very peculiar person – he seemed never to look at the world with his eyes open: as if there were never enough space in the world for him, and he therefore had to retreat to the outermost edge of it. Shashishekhar was his only friend, so of all the young men outside he was the one I watched most often. And when in the evening I sat like an empress at the foot of my flowering tree, all the world's young men sat at my feet in Shashishekhar's image. Are you listening? What are you thinking?'

'I'm thinking,' I said with a sigh, 'that I should have liked to have been born as Shashishekhar.'

'Listen to the whole story first. One day in the rainy season I caught a fever. The doctor came to see me. It was our first meeting. I turned my face towards the window, so that the red light of evening might mask my pallor. When the doctor came into the room and looked at my face, I imagined that I myself was the doctor looking at my face. In the evening light it was as delicate as a slightly wilted flower laid on a soft pillow; unkempt strands of hair had fallen on to my forehead, and my shyly lowered eyelashes cast shadows on to my cheeks. The doctor, speaking in a low, gentle voice, told my brother he would need to feel my pulse. I slid my rounded, listless arm out from underneath the coverings. Glancing at it, I reflected that it would have looked better with blue glass-bangles on it. As the doctor felt my sickly pulse, he was more unsettled than any doctor I had known. His fingers trembled most incompetently. He could feel the heat of my fever; I also had a sense of how his own pulse was racing. Don't you believe me?'

'I don't see any reason for disbelieving you,' I said. 'A man's pulse varies according to circumstances.'

'Gradually, after three or four more periods of illness and recovery, I found that at my imaginary evening court the millions of men in the world had reduced themselves to one. My world was almost deserted – a single doctor and a single patient were all that were left. I would surreptitiously put on a light-orange-coloured sari, plait a string of *bel*-flowers into my hair, and sit in the garden with a mirror in my hand. Why? For the pleasure one gets from looking at oneself? But in fact I was not looking at myself, for it was not I who did so. I had become two people, as I sat alone. I saw myself as the doctor saw me; I loved and worshipped and was enraptured; yet within me deep sighs heaved like the moaning evening wind.

'From that time on I was no longer alone. When I walked, casting my eyes down to look at the way my toes pressed the ground, I wondered how our newly qualified doctor would like my footsteps; in the afternoon, when the heat shimmered outside the window, and there was no sound except the cry of a kite flying high in the sky or toy-sellers outside our garden-fence calling, "Toys for sale, bangles for sale", I would spread out a clean sheet and lie down. I would stretch a naked arm casually across my soft bed and pretend that a certain someone had seen my arm and the way I stretched it out, had lifted it up in both hands, had planted a kiss on my pink palm and had crept out again. What would you think of the story if it ended here?'

'Not bad,' I replied. 'Still a bit incomplete – but I would happily spend the rest of the night finishing it off in my mind.'

'But it would be a very serious story then! What about the ironic twist at the end? What about the skeleton within, with all its teeth showing? Listen to what happened next. The doctor's practice built up, and he was able to open a small surgery on the ground floor of our house. I would sometimes jokingly ask him about medicines, poisons, what would make a man die quickly, and so on. The doctor spoke freely about his profession. As I listened, Death became as familiar as a relative. Love and Death were the only things that were real to me.

'My story is almost finished – there is not much more of it.'

'And the night is almost over too,' I murmured.

'After a while I noticed that the doctor had become distracted, seemingly embarrassed in my company. Then one day I saw him all dressed up, asking if he could borrow my brother's carriage – he was going somewhere that night. I could not bear to remain in ignorance. I went to my brother and eventually managed to ask, "Tell me, *Dādā*, where is the doctor going to tonight in the carriage?"

' "To die," said my brother laconically.

' "No, tell me truly," I said.

' "To get married," he said, more openly than before.

'"You don't say!" I said, laughing loudly.

'Bit by bit I discovered that the doctor would get 12,000 rupees from the marriage. But what was his purpose in shaming me by keeping his plans secret? Had I fallen at his feet and told him I would die of heart-break if he married? Men can never be trusted. I learnt this in one fell swoop, from the only man I cared about in the world.

'Just before dusk, when the doctor came into the room after seeing his patients, I laughed raucously and said, "Well, Doctor – so today you're getting married?"

'The doctor was not only embarrassed at my frankness, he became extremely glum.

'"Isn't there going to be any band or music?" I asked.

'"Is marrying a matter for such rejoicing?" he said with a slight sigh.

'I became quite overcome with laughter. I had never heard such a thing. "That won't do," I said. "There must be a band, there must be lights."

'I got my brother so worked up that he immediately set about organizing festivities on a grand scale. I chatted on about what would happen when the bride came into the house, what I would do. I asked, "Well, Doctor – will you go around feeling lady-patients' pulses now?" Although human thoughts, especially a man's thoughts, cannot be directly perceived, I can nevertheless swear that my words struck the doctor like a spear in the chest.

'The ceremony was fixed for the middle of the night. That evening the doctor sat out on the roof with my brother drinking a glass or two of liquor. It was their habit to do this. The moon rose slowly in the sky. I went to them and said, still laughing, "Has the Doctor Babu forgotten? The show is about to start!"

A minor detail here: I had, beforehand, gone secretly into the doctor's surgery to collect some powder, and had taken my chance to mix a small part of it into the doctor's glass, unseen by anyone. I had learnt from the doctor which powders were fatal. The doctor swallowed the drink in one gulp, and looking at me piteously said in a slightly choked and husky voice, "I must be off now."

'Flute-music began to play. I put on a Benares sari, and all the ornaments from my jewellery-chest; and I smeared vermilion liberally into my parting. Then I spread out my bedding under my favourite *bakul* tree. It was a beautiful night. Full, pure moonlight. A south wind blew away the tiredness of a sleeping world. The whole garden was fragrant with *bel*-blossoms and jasmine. When the sound of the flute had faded into the distance; when the moonlight had begun to fade, and the whole world around me – trees, sky, my life-long home – seemed unreal, I closed my eyes and smiled.

'My wish was that when people came and found me, that slight smile would still be intoxicatingly present on my red lips. My wish was that when I slowly entered my bridal-chamber of Eternal Night, I would take that smile with me. But where was the bridal-chamber? Where was my bridal attire? Woken by a clattering sound within me, I found three boys learning anatomy from me. In a breast that had throbbed with joy and sorrow, where, daily, the petals of youth had unfolded one by one, a teacher was pointing out with his cane which bone was which. And what trace was there now of the final smile I had formed with my lips?'

'How did you find my story?'
  'Hilarious,' I replied.
  The first crow cawed. 'Are you still there?' I asked.
  There was no reply. Dawn-light was entering the room.

A Single Night

I went to school with Surabala, and we played 'getting married' games together. Surabala's mother was very affectionate towards me whenever I went to their house. Seeing us as a pair, she would murmur to herself, 'They're meant for each other!' I was young, but I understood her drift fairly well. The feeling that I had a greater than normal claim to Surabala fixed itself in my mind. I became so puffed up with this feeling that I tended to boss her about. She meekly obeyed all my orders and endured my punishments. She was praised in the neighbourhood for her beauty, but beauty meant nothing to my barbarous young eyes: I merely knew that Surabala had been born to acknowledge my lordship over her – hence my inconsiderate behaviour.

My father was the chief rent-collector on the Chaudhuris' estate. His hope was that he would train me in estate-management when I was grown up, and find me a job as a land-agent somewhere. But I didn't like that idea at all. My ambitions were as high as our neighbour's son Nilratan's, who ran away to Calcutta to study and had become chief clerk to a Collector. Even if I didn't become that, I was determined to be at least Head Clerk in a magistrate's court. I had always noticed how respectful my father was towards legal officers of that kind. I had known since childhood that it was necessary, on various occasions, to make offerings to them of fish, vegetables and money; so I gave a specially privileged position in my heart to court employees, even to the peons. They were the most venerated of Bengal's deities, new miniature editions of her millions of gods. In pursuing prosperity, people placed greater trust in them than in bountiful Ganesh himself – so all the tribute that Ganesh formerly received now went to them.

Inspired by Nilratan's example, I also took my chance to run away to Calcutta. First I stayed with an acquaintance from my home village; later my father began to give me some help towards my education. My studies proceeded along conventional lines.

In addition, I attended meetings and assemblies. I had no doubt that it would soon become necessary for me to lay down my life for my country. But I had no idea how to accomplish so momentous an act, and no one to look to for an example. I was not, however, short of enthusiasm. We were village-boys, and had not learnt to ridicule everything like the smart boys of Calcutta; so our zeal was unshakeable. The leaders at our meetings gave speeches, but we used to wander about from house to house in the heat of the day, without lunch, begging for subscriptions; or we stood by the roadside giving out handbills; or we arranged benches and chairs before meetings. We were ready to roll up our sleeves and fight at the slightest word against our leaders. But to the smart boys of Calcutta, all this merely demonstrated our rural naïvety.

I had come to qualify myself to be a Head Clerk or Superintendent; but I was actually preparing to become Mazzini or Garibaldi. Meanwhile my father and Surabala's father agreed that I should be married to her. I had run away to Calcutta at the age of fifteen, when Surabala was eight; now I was eighteen. In my father's opinion my marriageable age was elapsing. But I vowed I would never marry: I would die for my country instead. I told my father I would not marry until my studies were completely finished.

Two or three months later I heard that Surabala had been married to the lawyer Ramlochan Babu. I was busy collecting subscriptions for down-trodden India, so I attached no importance to the news.

I passed into college, and was about to take my second-year exams when news came of my father's death. I was not the only one in the family – I had my mother and two sisters. So I had to leave college and search for work. With great difficulty I managed to get a post as assistant master in a secondary school in a small town in Naukhali District. I told myself I had found the right sort of work. My guidance and encouragement would raise each pupil to be a leader of the new India.

I started work. I found that the coming exam was much more demanding than the new India. The headmaster objected if I breathed a single word to the pupils outside Grammar and Algebra. In a couple of months my enthusiasm had faded away. I became one of those dull individuals who sits and broods when he is at home; who, when working, shoulders his plough with his head bowed, whipped from behind, meekly breaking up earth; content at night to stuff his belly with cattle-fodder; no energy or enterprise in him at all.

For fear of fire, one of the teachers had to live on the school premises. I was unmarried, so this duty fell upon me. I lived in a hut adjoining the large, thatched school-building. The school was rather isolated; it stood next to a big pond. There were betel-nut, coconut and coral trees all around; a pair of huge old *nim* trees – adjacent to each other and to the schoolhouse itself – gave shade.

There is something which I haven't mentioned so far and which for a long time I didn't think worthy of mention. The government lawyer here, Ramlochan Ray, lived quite near our schoolhouse, and I knew that his wife – my childhood companion Surabala – was there with him.

I became acquainted with Ramlochan Babu. I'm not sure if he was aware that as a child I had known Surabala, and when we met I did not think it appropriate to mention this. I did not particularly think about the fact that Surabala had at one time been involved with my life.

One day, during a school holiday, I went along to Ramlochan's house for a chat. I can't remember what we talked about – probably India's present plight. Not that he was very well-informed or concerned about the subject, but it was a way of passing an hour-and-a-half or so, smoking, and indulging in pleasurable gloom. As we talked I heard in the next room the soft tinkling of bangles, the rustle of garments, the sound of footsteps; it wasn't hard to deduce that inquisitive eyes were observing me through the half-open window. Suddenly I remembered those eyes – large eyes full of trust, simplicity and childish devotion: black pupils, dark eyelashes, an ever-calm gaze. Something seemed to clench my heart, and an anguish throbbed within me.

I returned to my hut, but the pain remained. Writing and reading were no distraction from it; it oppressed me like a huge weight in my chest, thudding in my veins. In the evening I calmed down a little and asked myself why I should be in such a state. The inner answer came, 'You are wondering why you lost your Surabala.'

I replied, 'But I gave her up willingly. I couldn't let her wait for me for ever.'

Someone within me said, 'You could have got her if you had wanted then, but now nothing whatever you can do will give you the right even to see her. However close the Surabala of your childhood lives to you now, however often you hear the tinkle of her bangles or feel the scent of her hair brushing past you, there will always be a wall keeping you apart.'

'No matter,' I said, 'who is Surabala to me?'

The reply came: 'Surabala is not yours today, but think what she could have been to you!'

That was true. Surabala could have been mine. She could have been my closest, most intimate companion; she could have shared all my sorrows and joys; but now she was so far away, so much someone else's, seeing her now was forbidden, it was a fault to speak to her, a sin to think about her. And a certain Ramlochan Babu, who was nobody before, was suddenly in the way. By mouthing a few mantras, he had whisked Surabala away from everyone else in the world.

I am not about to propose a new social morality; I do not wish to break convention or tear away restrictions. I am merely expressing my real feelings. Are all the feelings that arise in one's mind reasonable? I could not drive from my mind the conviction that the Surabala who reigned behind Ramlochan's portals was more mine than his. I admit this feeling was highly illogical and improper, but it was not unnatural.

I was now unable to concentrate on my work. At midday, as pupils burbled over their books, and everything outside shimmered, and a soft warm breeze brought the scent of the flowers of the *nim* trees, I yearned – what I yearned for I don't know – but this much I can say: I did not want to spend the rest of my life correcting the grammar of India's future hopefuls. I hated sitting alone in my large room after school hours, yet I couldn't bear anyone coming to see me. At dusk I listened to the meaningless rustle of the betel-nut and coconut trees by the pond, and reflected on life. What a baffling tangle! No one thinks of doing the right thing at the right time; instead, wrong and unsettling desires come at the wrong time. You, worthless though you are, could have been Surabala's husband and lived out your days in contentment. You wanted to be Garibaldi, but look what you became – an assistant master in a village school! And the lawyer Ramlochan Ray, why did *he* need to be Surabala's husband? She was nothing to him, right up to the wedding: he married her without giving her a thought, became a government lawyer and was earning nicely, thank you! He ticked her off if the milk smelled of smoke, and when he was in a good mood he ordered some jewellery for her. He was plump, wore a long coat, was perfectly pleased with life, never spent his evenings sitting by the pond staring at the stars and regretting the past.

Ramlochan had to go away for a few days on a big court-case. Surabala must have been as lonely in her house as I was in mine.

It was Monday, I remember. The sky had been cloudy since dawn. At ten, rain began to patter down gently. Seeing the look of the sky, the headmaster closed the school early. Large chunks of black cloud rolled across the sky all day, as if grandly preparing for something. The next day torrential rain started in the afternoon, and a storm blew up. It rained harder and harder through the night and the wind blew more and more fiercely. At first it had blown from the east, but it gradually swung round to the north and north-east.

It was pointless trying to sleep that night. I remembered that Surabala was alone in her house. The schoolhouse was much sturdier than hers. I several times thought of fetching her over to the school – I could spend the night on the raised bank of the pond. But I could not bring myself to do this.

At about one or one-thirty in the morning the roar of flood-waters became audible – a tidal wave was approaching from the sea. I left my room and went outside. I made my way to Surabala's house. The bank of the pond was on my way – I managed to wade as far as that, up to my knees in water. I scrambled up on to the bank, but a second wave dashed against it. Part of the bank was about six or seven feet high. As I climbed up on to it, someone else was climbing from the other side. I knew with every fibre of my being who that person was; and I had no doubt that she knew who *I* was.

We stood alone on an island nine feet long, everything around us submerged in water. It was like the end of the world – no stars in the sky, all earthly lamps extinguished. There would have been no harm in saying something, but no word was spoken. I didn't even ask if she was all right, nor did she ask me. We just stood, staring into the darkness. At our feet, deep, black, deadly waters roared and surged.

Surabala had abandoned the world to be with me now. She had no one but me. The Surabala of my childhood had floated into my life from some previous existence, from some ancient mysterious darkness; she had entered the sunlight and moonlight of this crowded world to join me at my side. Now, years later, she had left the light and the crowds to be with me alone in this terrifying, deserted, apocalyptic darkness. As a young budding flower, she had been thrown near me on to the stream of life; now, as a full-bloomed flower, she had again been thrown near me, on the stream of death. If but one more wave had come, we would have been shed from our slender, separate stems of existence and become one. But better that the wave did not come. Better that Surabala should live in happiness with her husband, home and children. Enough that I stood for a single night on the shore of the apocalypse, and tasted eternal joy.

The night was nearly over. The wind died down; the waters receded. Surabala, without saying a word, returned home, and I also went silently to my room. I reflected: I did not become a Collector's chief clerk; I did not become Court Clerk; I did not become Garibaldi; I became an assistant master in a run-down school. In my entire life, only once – for a brief single night – did I touch Eternity. Only on that one night, out of all my days and nights, was my trivial existence fulfilled.

Fool's Gold [1]

Adyanath and Baidyanath Chakrabarti were co-legatees; but Baidyanath was much the worse off of the two. His father Maheshchandra had no head for money, and left the management of his affairs to his elder brother Shibanath. In return, Shibanath, with many a soothing word, appropriated the inheritance to himself. Some Company Bonds were all that was left to Baidyanath, and were his only security in the rough ocean of life. After much searching, Shibanath managed to marry his son Adyanath to a rich man's only daughter, thereby giving himself a further opportunity to increase his wealth. Maheshchandra gave his son to the eldest of the seven daughters of a poor Brahmin he had taken pity on, and asked for not a paisa in dowry. He would have taken all seven daughters into his home; but he had only one son – and besides, the Brahmin didn't request this. But he gave him more than enough help with the cost of marrying them off.

After his father's death, Baidyanath was perfectly happy and satisfied with the Company Bonds. He gave no thought to earning a living. He occupied himself by cutting branches off trees and carefully carving them into walking-sticks. If young men or boys pressed him for one of these, he gave it away. He also spent many hours making – out of sheer generosity – fishing-rods, kites and reels. These required a great deal of careful carving and smoothing; and though the labour and time were of little benefit to his family, handiwork of this kind gave him enormous satisfaction. At times when, under every sacred *candimandap*, the air became thick with village feuds and intrigues, Baidyanath would often be seen alone on his verandah, working from dawn to afternoon and between siesta-time and evening, with a penknife and a piece of wood.

1. 'Golden deer' (*svarṇamṛg*) in Bengali, which has come to be the equivalent of 'fool's gold' because of the famous episode in the *Rāmāyaṇa* when Ravana's minister Maricha takes the form of a golden deer to entice Rama away from his forest hermitage, so that Ravana can abduct Sita.

Through the grace of Shashti – and in defiance of his enemies – Baidyanath produced two sons and one daughter.

His wife Mokshada, however, grew daily more dissatisfied. Why did they not have the home comforts that Adyanath's family enjoyed? It was against all reason that Mokshada should be deprived of the ornaments, Benares saris, refined conversation and imperious manners that Adyanath's wife Bindhyabasini had! They were the same family, after all. This higher standard of living had been achieved by cheating a brother out of his inheritance. The more she heard about her father-in-law, the more resentful Mokshada felt towards his only son. Nothing in her own house pleased her. Everything was inconvenient and humiliating. The beds were not fit for carrying a corpse on; the walls were so decayed that even an orphaned titmouse would not want to live in them, and the furnishings would make a saint weep. Men are too cowardly to oppose such exaggerated complaints. All Baidyanath could do was sit on his verandah and scrape at sticks with doubled concentration.

But to keep silence is not a permanent way of avoiding trouble. Sometimes Mokshada would interrupt her husband's wood-carving and call him into the house. Solemnly, looking away from him, she said, 'Stop the milkman from delivering milk.'

Baidyanath would be silent for a moment and then say, head bowed, 'How can I stop the milk? What will the children drink?'

'Stale rice-water,' his wife replied.

Or else, on other days, she would try a different tack: she would call him and say, 'I give up. You do what needs to be done.'

'What needs to be done?' Baidyanath asked wearily.

'You buy the food this month,' she replied. Then she gave him a shopping list worthy of a royal ceremonial feast. If Baidyanath plucked up courage to ask, 'Do we really need all this?', she answered, 'I suppose if the children didn't eat and they died and I too, you'd be able to run the house on your own, nice and cheaply!'

Baidyanath gradually realized he could not go on carving walking-sticks. Some solution would have to be found. But employment or business seemed out of the question. He needed to discover a short cut that would take him straight to Kubera's treasure-house.

One night he lay in bed and prayed passionately: 'O Mother Durga, if only you could reveal in a dream a patent medicine for a serious illness! I'd take care of advertising it in the papers.' But that night he dreamed his wife had furiously vowed she would 'marry again when she was widowed'. Baidyanath had objected to this by asking her where she would find – in their present state of poverty – the necessary ornaments. She refuted his objection by saying that widows didn't need ornaments to get married. He was groping vainly for some kind of clinching rejoinder, when he woke up and saw that it was morning; and on realizing why it was truly not possible for his wife to remarry, he felt rather dejected.

The next day, after his morning rites and ablutions, he was sitting alone making a kite-string, when a *sannyāsī* arrived at his door, chanting blessings. Instantly Baidyanath had a brilliant vision of future wealth. He invited the *sannyāsī* in, and fed and welcomed him lavishly. He managed, with difficulty, to establish that the *sannyāsī* could make gold, and was willing to impart his method.

Mokshada was enthralled. Like people with jaundice finding that everything looks yellow, the world seemed full of gold to her. As her imagination magically turned beds, furnishings and the walls of the house to gold, she mentally invited Bindhyabasini for a visit. The *sannyāsī*, meanwhile, consumed two seers of milk a day and one-and-a-half seers of *mohanbhog*; and by extracting the Company Bonds from Baidyanath raised large sums of money.

The seekers of fishing-rods, sticks and reels had to go away disappointed when they knocked on Baidyanath's door. His children might not get their meals on time, might fall and bruise their foreheads, might shake the heavens with their howls, but neither parent took notice. They sat stock-still in front of the *sannyāsī*'s cauldron – unblinking, speechless. The restless flames, casting reflections, turned the pupils of their eyes into touchstones. Their gaze grew red and fiery as a setting sun.

When two of the Company Bonds had become burnt offerings to that gold-creating fire, the *sannyāsī* said encouragingly, 'Tomorrow the gold colour will come.'

They couldn't sleep that night: husband and wife lay building a city of gold in their minds. Sometimes they argued over details, but were so happy that they quickly reached agreement. They were perfectly willing to forgo their individual views, so deep was their marital harmony that night.

The next day the *sannyāsī* was nowhere to be found. The gold all around them was obliterated: even the rays of the sun fell dark. Beds, furnishings and walls looked four times poorer and shabbier. If Baidyanath now offered some sort of trivial opinion on a domestic matter, his wife would say sweetly, 'You've shown how intelligent you are. Why not leave off for a bit?' He was utterly crushed. Mokshada acted superior, as if she had not believed for a minute in the golden mirage.

The crestfallen Baidyanath tried to think of ways to please his wife. One day he produced a present in a square packet, and smiling broadly, nodding his head sagely, said, 'Guess what I've brought you.'

Concealing her curiosity she said casually, 'How should I know? I'm not a soothsayer.' Without further ado, Baidyanath slowly untied the knots in the string, blew the dust off the wrapping-paper, and gingerly unfolded the paper to reveal an 'Art Studio' coloured print of the ten forms of Durga. Turning it to the light, he held it up before his wife. She immediately thought of the English oil-paintings hanging in Bindhyabasini's bedroom. In a tone of excessive indifference she said, 'Well, I never. You can hang it in your sitting-room and admire it there. It's not my style.' Baidyanath glumly realized that, along with other skills, God had denied him the difficult art of pleasing his wife.

Meanwhile Mokshada was consulting fortune-tellers of every kind, showing them her palms or getting them to study her horoscope. They all said her husband would outlive her. Although she was not very enthused by that joyous prospect, her curiosity remained unabated. She heard that her childbearing chances were good, that the house would soon be full of sons and daughters: she was not overjoyed about that. Eventually, however, an astrologer told her he would burn every one of his scrolls if Baidyanath failed to find hidden treasure within a few years. So powerful an oath convinced Mokshada of the truth of his prediction. The

astrologer took his leave, lavishly rewarded, but life now became
unbearable for Baidyanath. There were several common-
or-garden routes to wealth, such as farming, employment, theft or
deception. But there was no standard way of finding hidden
treasure. So the more Mokshada urged him and scolded him the
less he could see which road to take. He could not decide where
to begin digging, which pond to dredge, which wall in the house
to demolish.

Greatly annoyed, Mokshada told her husband that she never
knew a man could have dung instead of brains in his head. 'Get
moving!' she said. 'Do you think the sky will rain money if you
sit gaping like that?' She was right, and Baidyanath too was
desperate to make some sort of move; but where and by what
means, no one could tell him. So he continued to sit on the
verandah carving sticks.

It was the month of Āśvin, and the *Durgā-pūjā* was drawing
near. From the fourth of the month on, boats were arriving at the
ghāṭ. People were returning home. They brought baskets of
arum, pumpkins, dry coconuts; trunkfuls of clothes, umbrellas
and shoes for the children; perfume, soap, new story-books and
sweet-smelling coconut-oil for their loved ones. Autumn sunshine
filled the wide, cloudless sky like a festive smile; ripening paddy-
fields rippled; glossy, rain-washed leaves rustled in the fresh cool
breeze; and returning villagers, in raw-silk China-coats, made
their way home along field-paths. Each had an umbrella over his
head, and a twisted chadar swinging from his shoulder.

Baidyanath sat and watched, and sighed from the bottom of his
heart. He compared his joyless home with the atmosphere of
festivity and homecoming in so many other houses, and said to
himself, 'Why did God make me so useless?'

His sons rose at dawn to see the image of Durga being made in
Adyanath's yard. At meal-times the maid had to go and drag
them home. Baidyanath sat and reflected on the fruitlessness of
his life amidst such universal festivity. Rescuing his two sons
from the maid, he took them on to his lap and hugged them, and
asked the elder one, 'Well, Abu, tell me what you would like for
the *pūjā*?'

'I'd like a model boat, Father,' said Abinash at once.

The younger one, not wanting to be inferior to his brother in any respect, said, 'I'd like a boat too, Father.'

Sons worthy of their father! All he could do was make useless things, so that was what they wanted. 'Very well,' he said.

Meanwhile a paternal uncle of Mokshada's — a lawyer — had returned home from Benares for the *pūjā*-holidays. Mokshada visited his house several days running. One day she said to her husband, 'I think you should go to Benares.' Baidyanath immediately imagined that his death was near, that astrologers had discovered the date in his horoscope. His partner-in-life had found out, and was making preparations for his life beyond death. She told him, however, that there were rumours about a house in Benares where hidden treasure might be found: he must go and buy the house and bring home the treasure.

'Heaven forbid,' said Baidyanath. 'I can't go to Benares.' He had never been away from home. Women — so say the writers of the ancient Shastras — know instinctively how to make a family man adopt a life of asceticism. Mokshada's rhetoric filled the house like chilli-smoke; but it only made poor Baidyanath's eyes water: it failed to make him go to Benares.

Two or three days went by. Baidyanath sat cutting, carving and gluing pieces of wood to make two model boats. He fitted them with masts; cut up cloth to fix as sails; gave each a red cotton pennant; added oars and rudders. He even gave them passengers and a tiny helmsman. In all this he showed great care and astonishing skill. There is no boy alive whose heart would not have skipped a beat at the sight of such boats. So when Baidyanath gave them to his sons on the eve of the seventh day of the *pūjā*, they danced for joy. Even the shell of a boat would have been sufficient, but these had rudders, sails, boatmen in position: they were wonderful.

Attracted by the whoops of delight from the boys, Mokshada came and saw their indigent father's *pūjā* presents. At the sight, she raged, sobbed and beat her brow; then she snatched the two boats and threw them out of the window. Others were getting gold necklaces, satin shirts, embroidered caps: this miserable husband of hers had fobbed his sons off with two toy boats! Not a paisa had been spent on them; he'd made them himself!

The younger boy wailed loudly. 'Stupid boy,' she said, giving him a clout. The elder boy forgot his own distress when he saw his father's face. Trying to seem cheerful, he said, 'I'll look for the boats early tomorrow morning, Father, and bring them back.'

The next day Baidyanath agreed to go to Benares. But where was the necessary money? His wife sold some jewellery to raise cash: jewellery from his grandmother's era. Heavy, pure gold ornaments like that are unobtainable today. Baidyanath felt he was going to his death. He embraced and kissed his children and left home with tears in his eyes. Even Mokshada wept.

The owner of the house in Benares was a client of Mokshada's uncle. Probably that was why it was sold at such a steep price. Baidyanath took sole possession of it. It was right on the river: water lapped against its foundations.

At night Baidyanath shivered all over. He lay in an empty room, wrapped in his chadar, with a lamp by his pillow – but he couldn't sleep. At dead of night, when all noise outside had stopped, he was roused by a clinking noise from somewhere. It was faint, but clear – as if the King of the Underworld's treasurer was sitting and counting money. Baidyanath was afraid, but was also curious and full of impossible hope. Carrying the lamp in his trembling hand, he went round the rooms of the house. If he went into one room the sound seemed to be coming from another; if he went to that room it seemed to be coming from the previous one. He spent the whole night wandering from room to room. When day came, the underground clinking blended with other sounds, and was no longer distinct.

The following night, at two or three o'clock, when the world was asleep, the noise started again. Baidyanath's heart was pounding. He could not decide where to go to trace the noise. In a desert the gurgle of water can sometimes be heard, but it is impossible to say where it is coming from: one is afraid of losing it completely by following a false path. The thirsty traveller stands stock still, straining his ears with all his might, his thirst growing and growing – Baidyanath was like that.

He spent many days in this state of uncertainty. Sleeplessness and futile anxiety spread deep furrows over his formerly serene and kindly face. His sunken eyes blazed like desert sand in the afternoon. Then, one night, at two o'clock, he locked all the doors in the house and started to tap the floors with a crowbar. The floor of a small side room sounded hollow. While the rest of the town slept, Baidyanath crouched alone, digging down into the floor. When it was nearly dawn, his excavations were complete. He saw that there was a sort of lower room – in the darkness of the night he was not brave enough to step down into it recklessly. He spread his bedding over the hole and lay down. But the clinking noise was so distinct now that he had to get up again – though he was not prepared to go away, leaving the room unprotected. Greed and fear pulled at him in two opposite directions, as the night came to an end.

The noise could now be heard in the daytime too. He stopped the servant from coming into the room, and had his dinner outside. Then he went back into the room and locked the door. With Durga's name on his lips, he removed the bedding from the mouth of the hole. A gurgling of water and the clinking of something metallic could be heard clearly. As he nervously hung his head down into the hole he saw that water flowed over the floor of the low underground room: it was too dark to see much else. Jabbing a stick down into the water he found it was not more than knee-deep. Clutching matches and a lamp, he lightly jumped down into the shallow room. He so feared the extinction of all his hopes that his hands trembled as he tried to light the lamp. He wasted many matches before it was lit.

The lamp revealed a huge copper jar attached to a thick, heavy chain; whenever the water surged, the chain knocked against the jar and made a clinking noise. Splashing through the water, Baidyanath quickly reached the jar. It was empty. He could not believe his eyes: he picked up the jar and shook it violently. There was nothing inside. He turned it upside down. Nothing fell out. He noticed that the neck of the jar was broken. It appeared that it had at one time been completely sealed, but someone had broken into it. He started to thrash around in the water with his hands, like a madman. He felt an object in the mud – he lifted it up and found it was a skull. This too he lifted up to his ears and shook – there was nothing inside it. He hurled it away. He searched everywhere, but all he found were a few human bones. He saw that part of the wall which backed on to the river was broken: water was coming in there, and someone whose horoscope had also predicted the discovery of hidden treasure had possibly come in through that hole.

In utter despair, Baidyanath gave a long, heart-rending groan – 'Mā-ā-ā!' – and the echo seemed to include the groans of many disappointed people from ages past, groans rising from deep underground with gloomy resonance. Then, covered with mud, he climbed out of the underground room.

The crowded world outside seemed a complete lie, as empty as that broken chained jar. He couldn't bear the thought of having to pack up his things, buy a ticket, get on to the train, return home, quarrel with his wife, carry on with his daily existence. He just wanted to slide and slump into the water, like the crumbling river-bank.

He did, even so, pack up his things, buy his ticket and climb on to the train. And one winter evening he arrived back at his house. On autumn mornings in Āśvin, Baidyanath had sat by his door and watched many people returning home, and had often sighed with envy at their joy at returning from afar: he never dreamed he would one day suffer an evening like this. He entered the house and sat on a wooden seat in the yard as if in a trance: he did not go indoors. The maid was the first to see him, and broke into shrieks of delight; the children then came running, and finally Mokshada sent someone to fetch him. Baidyanath felt as if he was coming out of a trance, waking up in his former, familiar world. With a pale face and weak smile he lifted up one of the boys, and taking the hand of the other went indoors. Lamps were alight, and though it was not yet fully dark the winter evening was as still as night. For a while Baidyanath said nothing; then he gently asked his wife, 'How are you?'

His wife did not reply, but asked, 'What happened?'

Baidyanath struck his brow with his palm, and said nothing. Mokshada's expression was grim. The children, sensing that something was very badly wrong, softly withdrew. They went to the maid and said, 'Tell us that story about the barber.' Then they went to bed.

Darkness fell, but no word passed between Baidyanath and his wife. An eerie silence reigned, and Mokshada's lips were tight shut, ominous as thunder. At last, still without a word, she slowly

went into her bedroom and locked the door from inside. Baidyanath waited silently outside. The night-watchman called out the
hours. The world sank exhausted into untroubled sleep. From his
family all the way up to the stars in the sky, no one had anything
to ask the sleepless, disgraced Baidyanath.

Very late at night, his eldest son, probably waking from a
dream, got up, tiptoed out on to the verandah and called, 'Father.'
His father was not there. Raising his voice, going right outside
the closed doors, he called, 'Father.' But no answer came. Fearfully, he went back to bed.

In the morning, the maid prepared Baidyanath's tobacco as she
had always done before, but she couldn't find him anywhere.
Later in the day, neighbours came to visit their recently returned
friend, but he was not there.

Holiday

Phatik Chakrabarti, leader of the gang, suddenly had a bright idea. Lying by the river was a huge *sāl*-tree log, just waiting to be made into a mast. Everyone must help to roll it along! Without giving a thought to the surprise, annoyance and inconvenience that would be caused to the person who needed the log for timber, all the boys fell in with this suggestion. They got down to the task with a will; but just then Phatik's younger brother Makhanlal came and solemnly sat on the log. The boys were rather non-plussed by his haughty, dismissive attitude.

One of them went up to him and nervously tried to push him off, but he refused to budge. Wise beyond his years, he continued to ponder the vanity of all childish games.

'You'll pay for this,' said Phatik, brandishing his fist. 'Clear off.'

But Makhanlal merely adjusted his perch and settled down even more immovably on the log.

In this kind of situation, Phatik ought to have preserved his supremacy over the other boys by delivering immediately a hearty slap on his wayward brother's cheek – but he didn't dare. Instead he assumed a manner implying that he could, had he so wished, have meted out this customary punishment, but he wasn't going to, because a more amusing idea had occurred to him. Why not, he proposed, roll the log over with Makhanlal on it?

Makhan at first saw glory in this; he did not think (nor did anyone else) that like other worldly glories it might carry dangers. The boys rolled up their sleeves and began to push – 'Heave ho! Heave ho! Over we go!' With one spin of the log, Makhan's solemnity, glory and wisdom crashed to the ground.

The other boys were delighted at such an unexpectedly quick outcome, but Phatik was rather embarrassed. Makhan immediately jumped up and threw himself on to him, hitting him with blind rage and scratching his nose and cheeks. Then he made his way home tearfully.

The game having been spoilt, Phatik pulled up a few reeds, and climbing on to the prow of a half-sunk boat sat quietly chewing them. A boat – not a local one – came up to the mooring-place. A middle-aged gentleman with a black moustache but grey hair stepped ashore. 'Where is the Chakrabartis' house?' he asked the boy.

'Over there,' replied Phatik, still chewing the reed-stalks. But no one would have been able to understand which direction to take.

'Where?' asked the gentleman again.

'Don't know,' said Phatik, and he carried on as before, sucking juice from the stalks. The gentleman had to ask others to help him find the house.

Suddenly Bagha Bagdi (a servant) appeared and said, 'Phatik-*dādā*, Mother's calling you.'

'Shan't go,' said Phatik.

He struggled and kicked helplessly as Bagha picked him up bodily and carried him home. His mother shouted furiously when she saw him: 'You've beaten up Makhan again!'

'I didn't beat him up.'

'How dare you lie to me?'

'I did *not* beat him up. Ask him.'

When Makhan was questioned he stuck to his earlier accusation, saying, 'He *did* beat me up.' Phatik could not stand this any more. He charged at Makhan and thumped him hard, shouting, 'So who's lying now?' His mother, taking Makhan's part, rushed and slapped Phatik's back several times heavily. He pushed her away. 'So you'd lay hands on your own mother?' she screamed.

At that moment the black-grey gentleman entered the house and said, 'What's going on here?'

'*Dādā!*' said Phatik's mother, overwhelmed with surprise and joy. 'When did you come?' She bent down and took the dust of his feet.

Many years previously her elder brother had gone to the west of India to work, and in the meantime she had had two children; they had grown, her husband had died – but all this time she had never seen her brother. At long last Bishvambhar Babu had returned home, and had now come to see his sister.

There were celebrations for several days. At length, a couple of days before his departure, Bishvambhar questioned his sister about the schooling and progress of her two sons. In reply, he was given a description of Phatik's uncontrollable wildness and inattention to study; while Makhan, by contrast, was perfectly behaved and a model student. 'Phatik drives me mad,' she said.

Bishvambhar then proposed that he take Phatik to Calcutta, keep him with him and supervise his education. The widow easily agreed to this. 'Well, Phatik,' he asked the boy, 'how would you like to go to Calcutta with your uncle?' 'I'd love to,' said Phatik, jumping up and down.

His mother did not object to seeing her son off, because she always lived in dread that Makhan might be pushed into the river by him or might split his head open in some terrible accident; but she was a little cast down by the eagerness with which Phatik seized the idea of going. He pestered his uncle with 'When are we going? When are we going?' – and couldn't sleep at night for excitement.

When at last the day to leave came, he was moved to a joyous display of generosity. He bestowed on Makhan his fishing-rod, kite and reel, with permanent right of inheritance.

When he arrived at his uncle's house in Calcutta, he first had to be introduced to his aunt. I cannot say she was over-pleased at this unnecessary addition to her family. She was used to looking after her house and three children as they were, and suddenly to loose into their midst an unknown, uneducated country boy would probably be most disruptive. If only Bishvambhar had insight commensurate with his years! Moreover, there is no greater nuisance in the world than a boy of thirteen or fourteen. There is no beauty in him, and he does nothing useful either. He arouses no affection; nor is his company welcome. If he speaks modestly he sounds false; if he speaks sense he sounds arrogant; if he speaks at all he is felt to be intrusive. He suddenly shoots up in height so that his clothes no longer fit him – which is an ugly affront to other people. His childish grace and sweetness of voice suddenly disappear, and people find it impossible not to blame him for this. Many faults can be forgiven in a child or a young man, but at this age even natural and unavoidable faults are felt to be unbearable.

He himself is fully aware that he does not fit properly into the world; so he is perpetually ashamed of his existence and seeks forgiveness for it. Yet this is the age at which a rather greater longing for affection develops in him. If he gets at this time love and companionship from some sympathetic person, he will do anything in return. But no one dares show affection, in case others condemn this as pampering. So he looks and behaves like a stray street-dog.

To leave home and mother and go to a strange place is hell for a boy of this age. To live with loveless indifference all around is like walking on thorns. This is the age when normally a conception forms of women as wonderful, heavenly creatures; to be cold-shouldered by them is terribly hard to bear. It was therefore especially painful to Phatik that his aunt saw him as an evil star. If she happened to ask him to do a job for her and – meaning well – he did more than was strictly necessary, his aunt would stamp on his enthusiasm, saying, 'That's quite enough, quite enough. I don't want you meddling any more. Go and get on with your own work. Do some studying.' His aunt's excessive concern for his mental improvement would then seem terribly cruel and unjust.

He so lacked love in this household, and it seemed he could breathe freely nowhere. Stuck behind its walls, he thought con-stantly of his home village. The fields where he would let his 'monster-kite' fly and flap in the wind; the river-bank where he wandered aimlessly, singing a *rāga* of his own invention at the top of his voice; the small stream in which he would jump and swim now and then in the heat of the day; his gang of followers; the mischief they would get up to; the freedom; above all his harsh, impetuous mother; all this tugged continually at his help-less heart. A kind of instinctive love, like an animal's; a blind longing to be near; an unspoken distress at being far; a heartfelt, anguished cry of '*Mā, Mā*' like a motherless calf at dusk; such feelings perpetually afflicted this gawky, nervous, thin, lanky, ungainly boy.

At school there was no one more stupid and inattentive than he. If asked a question he would just stare back vacantly. If the teacher cuffed him, he would silently bear it like a laden, ex-hausted ass. At break-time, he would stand at the window staring at the roofs of distant houses, while his classmates played outside.

If a child or two appeared for a moment on one of the roofs, in the midday sunshine, playing some game, his misery intensified.

One day he plucked up courage to ask his uncle, 'Uncle, when will I be going home to see Mother?'

'When the school holiday comes,' said his uncle. The *pūjā*-holiday in the month of Kartik – that was a long way off!

One day Phatik lost his school-books. He never found it easy to prepare his lessons, and now, with his books lost, he was completely helpless. The teacher started to beat and humiliate him every day. His standing in school sank so low that his cousins were ashamed to admit their connection with him. Whenever he was punished, they showed even greater glee than the other boys. It became too much to bear, and one day he went to his aunt and confessed like a criminal that he had lost his school-books. 'Well, well,' said his aunt, lines of annoyance curling round her lips, 'and do you suppose I can buy you new books five times a month?' He said no more. That he should have wasted *someone else*'s money made him feel even more hurt and rejected by his mother. His misery and sense of inferiority dragged him down to the very earth.

That night, when he returned from school, he had a pain in his head and was shivering. He could tell he was getting a fever. He also knew that his aunt would not take kindly to his being ill. He had a clear sense of what an unnecessary, unjustifiable nuisance it would be to her. He felt he had no right to expect that an odd, useless, stupid boy such as he should be nursed by anyone other than his mother.

The next morning Phatik was nowhere to be seen. He was searched for in all the neighbours' houses round about, but there was no trace of him. In the evening torrential rain began, so in searching for him many people got soaked to the skin – to no avail. In the end, finding him nowhere, Bishvambhar Babu informed the police.

A whole day later, in the evening, a carriage drew up outside Bishvambhar's house. Rain was still thudding down relentlessly, and the street was flooded to a knee's depth. Two policemen bundled Phatik out of the carriage and put him down in front of Bishvambhar. He was soaked from head to foot, covered with mud, his eyes and cheeks were flushed, he was trembling violently. Bishvambhar virtually had to carry him into the house.

'You see what happens,' snapped his wife, 'when you take in someone else's child. You must send him home.' But in fact the whole of that day she had hardly been able to eat for worry, and had been unreasonably tetchy with her own children.

'I was going to go to my mother,' said Phatik, weeping, 'but they brought me back.'

The boy's fever climbed alarmingly. He was delirious all night. Bishvambhar fetched the doctor. Opening his bloodshot eyes for a moment and staring blankly at the ceiling joists, Phatik said, 'Uncle, has my holiday-time come?' Bishvambhar, dabbing his own eyes with a handkerchief, tenderly took Phatik's thin, hot hand in his and sat down beside him. He spoke again, mumbling incoherently: 'Mother, don't beat me, Mother. I didn't do anything wrong, honest!'

The next day, during the short time when he was conscious, Phatik kept looking bewilderedly round the room, as if expecting someone. When no one came, he turned and lay mutely with his face towards the wall. Understanding what was on his mind, Bishvambhar bent down and said softly in his ear, 'Phatik, I've sent for your mother.'

Another day passed. The doctor, looking solemn and gloomy, pronounced the boy's condition to be critical. Bishvambhar sat at the bedside in the dim lamplight, waiting minute by minute for Phatik's mother's arrival. Phatik started to shout out, like a boatman, 'More than one fathom deep, more than two fathoms deep!' To come to Calcutta they had had to travel some of the way by steamer. The boatmen had lowered the hawser into the stream and bellowed out its depth. In his delirium, Phatik was imitating them, calling out the depth in pathetic tones; except that the endless sea he was about to cross had no bottom that his measuring-rope could touch.

It was then that his mother stormed into the room, bursting into loud wails of grief. When, with difficulty, Bishvambhar managed to calm her down, she threw herself on to the bed and sobbed, 'Phatik, my darling, my treasure.'

'Yes?' said Phatik, seemingly quite relaxed.

'Phatik, darling boy,' cried his mother again.

Turning slowly on to his side, and looking at no one, Phatik said softly, 'Mother, my holiday has come now. I'm going home.'

Kabuliwallah

My five-year-old daughter Mini can't stop talking for a minute. It only took her a year to learn to speak, after coming into the world, and ever since she has not wasted a minute of her waking hours by keeping silent. Her mother often scolds her and makes her shut up, but I can't do that. When Mini is quiet, it is so unnatural that I cannot bear it. So she's rather keen on chatting to me.

One morning, as I was starting the seventeenth chapter of my novel, Mini came up to me and said, 'Father, Ramdoyal the gatekeeper calls a crow a *kauyā* instead of a *kāk*. He doesn't know anything, does he!'

Before I had a chance to enlighten her about the multiplicity of languages in the world, she brought up another subject. 'Guess what, Father, Bhola says it rains when an elephant in the sky squirts water through its trunk. What nonsense he talks! On and on, all day.'

Without waiting for my opinion on this matter either, she suddenly asked, 'Father, what relation is Mother to you?'

'Good question,'[1] I said to myself, but to Mini I said, 'Run off and play with Bhola. I've got work to do.'

But she then sat down near my feet beside my writing-table, and, slapping her knees, began to recite '*āgḍum bāgḍum*' at top speed. Meanwhile, in my seventeenth chapter, Pratap Singh was leaping under cover of night from his high prison-window into the river below, with Kanchanmala in his arms.

My study looks out on to the road. Mini suddenly abandoned the '*āgḍum bāgḍum*' game, ran over to the window and shouted, 'Kabuliwallah, Kabuliwallah!'

Dressed in dirty baggy clothes, pugree on his head, bag hanging from his shoulder, and with three or four boxes of grapes in his hands, a tall Kabuliwallah was ambling along the road. It was hard to say exactly what thoughts the sight of him had put into

---

1. Lit. 'In my mind I said "sister-in-law".' See *śyālikā* in the Glossary.

my beloved daughter's mind, but she began to shout and shriek at him. That swinging bag spells trouble, I thought: my seventeenth chapter won't get finished today. But just as the Kabuliwallah, attracted by Mini's yells, looked towards us with a smile and started to approach our house, Mini gasped and ran into the inner rooms, disappearing from view. She had a blind conviction that if one looked inside that swinging bag one would find three or four live children like her.

Meanwhile the Kabuliwallah came up to the window and smilingly salaamed. I decided that although the plight of Pratap Singh and Kanchanmala was extremely critical, it would be churlish not to invite the fellow inside and buy something from him.

I bought something. Then I chatted to him for a bit. We talked about Abdur Rahman's efforts to preserve the integrity of Afghanistan against the Russians and the British. When he got up to leave, he asked, 'Babu, where did your little girl go?'

To dispel her groundless fears, I called Mini to come out. She clung to me and looked suspiciously at the Kabuliwallah and his bag. The Kabuliwallah took some raisins and apricots out and offered them to her, but she would not take them, and clung to my knees with doubled suspicion. Thus passed her first meeting with the Kabuliwallah.

A few days later when for some reason I was on my way out of the house one morning, I saw my daughter sitting on a bench in front of the door, nattering unrestrainedly; and the Kabuliwallah was sitting at her feet listening – grinning broadly, and from time to time making comments in his hybrid sort of Bengali. In all her five years of life, Mini had never found so patient a listener, apart from her father. I also saw that the fold of her little sari was crammed with raisins and nuts. I said to the Kabuliwallah, 'Why have you given all these? Don't give her any more.' I then took a half-rupee out of my pocket and gave it to him. He unhesitatingly took the coin and put it in his bag.

When I returned home, I found that this half-rupee had caused a full-scale row. Mini's mother was holding up a round shining object and saying crossly to Mini, 'Where did you get this half-rupee from?'

'The Kabuliwallah gave it to me,' said Mini.

'Why did you take it from the Kabuliwallah?' said her mother.

'I didn't ask for it,' said Mini tearfully. 'He gave it to me himself.'

I rescued Mini from her mother's wrath, and took her outside. I learnt that this was not just the second time that Mini and the Kabuliwallah had met: he had been coming nearly every day and, by bribing her eager little heart with pistachio-nuts, had quite won her over. I found that they now had certain fixed jokes and routines: for example as soon as Mini saw Rahamat, she giggled and asked, 'Kabuliwallah, O Kabuliwallah, what have you got in your bag?' Rahamat would laugh back and say – giving the word a peculiar nasal twang – 'An *elephant*.' The notion of an elephant in his bag was the source of immense hilarity; it might not be a very subtle joke, but they both seemed to find it very funny, and it gave me pleasure to see, on an autumn morning, a young child and a grown man laughing so heartily.

They had a couple of other jokes. Rahamat would say to Mini, 'Little one, don't ever go off to your *śvaśur-bāṛi*.' Most Bengali girls grow up hearing frequent references to their *śvaśur-bāṛi*, but my wife and I are rather progressive people and we don't keep talking to our young daughter about her future marriage. She therefore couldn't clearly understand what Rahamat meant; yet to remain silent and give no reply was wholly against her nature, so she would turn the idea round and say, 'Are *you* going to your *śvaśur-bāṛi*?' Shaking his huge fist at an imaginary father-in-law Rahamat said, 'I'll settle him!' Mini laughed merrily as she imagined the fate awaiting this unknown creature called a *śvaśur*.

It was perfect autumn weather. In ancient times, kings used to set out on their world-conquests in autumn. I have never been away from Calcutta; precisely because of that, my mind roves all over the world. I seem to be condemned to my house, but I constantly yearn for the world outside. If I hear the name of a foreign land, at once my heart races towards it; and if I see a foreigner, at once an image of a cottage on some far bank or wooded mountainside forms in my mind, and I think of the free and pleasant life I would lead there. At the same time, I am such a rooted sort of individual that whenever I have to leave my familiar spot I practically collapse. So a morning spent sitting at my table in my little study, chatting with this Kabuliwallah, was quite enough wandering for me. High, scorched, blood-coloured, forbidding mountains on either side of a narrow desert path; laden camels passing; turbaned merchants and wayfarers, some on camels, some walking, some with spears in their hands, some with old-fashioned flintlock guns: my friend would talk of his native land in his booming, broken Bengali, and a mental picture of it would pass before my eyes.

Mini's mother is very easily alarmed. The slightest noise in the street makes her think that all the world's drunkards are charging straight at our house. She cannot dispel from her mind – despite her experience of life (which isn't great) – the apprehension that the world is overrun with thieves, bandits, drunkards, snakes, tigers, malaria, caterpillars, cockroaches and white-skinned marauders. She was not too happy about Rahamat the Kabuliwallah. She repeatedly told me to keep a close eye on him. If I tried to laugh off her suspicions, she would launch into a succession of questions: 'So do people's children never go missing? And is there no slavery in Afghanistan? Is it completely impossible for a huge Afghan to kidnap a little child?' I had to admit that it was not impossible, but I found it hard to believe. People are suggestible to varying degrees; this was why my wife remained so edgy. But I still saw nothing wrong in letting Rahamat come to our house.

Every year, about the middle of the month of Māgh, Rahamat went home. He was always very busy before he left, collecting money owed to him. He had to go from house to house; but he still made time to visit Mini. To see them together, one might well suppose that they were plotting something. If he couldn't come in the morning he would come in the evening; to see his lanky figure in a corner of the darkened house, with his baggy pyjamas hanging loosely around him, was indeed a little frightening. But my heart would light up as Mini ran to meet him, smiling and calling, 'O Kabuliwallah, Kabuliwallah,' and the usual innocent jokes passed between the two friends, unequal in age though they were.

One morning I was sitting in my little study correcting proof-sheets. The last days of winter had been very cold, shiveringly so. The morning sun was shining through the window on to my feet below my table, and this touch of warmth was very pleasant. It must have been about eight o'clock – early morning walkers, swathed in scarves, had mostly finished their dawn stroll and had returned to their homes. It was then that there was a sudden commotion in the street.

I looked out and saw our Rahamat in handcuffs, being marched along by two policemen, and behind him a crowd of curious boys. Rahamat's clothes were blood-stained, and one of the policemen was holding a blood-soaked knife. I went outside and stopped him, asking what was up. I heard partly from him and partly from Rahamat himself that a neighbour of ours had owed Raha-mat something for a Rampuri chadar; he had tried to lie his way out of the debt, and in the ensuing brawl Rahamat had stabbed him.

Rahamat was mouthing various unrepeatable curses against the lying debtor, when Mini ran out of the house calling, 'Kabuliwal-lah, O Kabuliwallah.' For a moment Rahamat's face lit up with pleasure. He had no bag over his shoulder today, so they couldn't have their usual discussion about it. Mini came straight out with her 'Are *you* going to your *śvaśur-bāṛi*?'

'Yes, I'm going there now,' said Rahamat with a smile. But when he saw that his reply had failed to amuse Mini, he bran-dished his handcuffed fists and said, 'I would have killed my *śvaśur*, but how can I with these on?'

Rahamat was convicted of assault, and sent to prison for several years. He virtually faded from our minds. Living at home, carry-ing on day by day with our routine tasks, we gave no thought to how a free-spirited mountain-dweller was passing his years behind prison-walls. As for the fickle Mini, even her father would have to admit that her behaviour was not very praiseworthy. She swiftly forgot her old friend. At first Nabi the groom replaced him in her affections; later, as she grew up, girls rather than little boys became her favourite companions. She even stopped coming to her father's study. And I, in a sense, dropped her.

Several years went by. It was autumn again. Mini's marriage had

been decided, and the wedding was fixed for the *pūjā*-holiday.
Our pride and joy would soon, like Durga going to Mount
Kailas, darken her parents' house by moving to her husband's.

It was a most beautiful morning. Sunlight, washed clean by
monsoon rains, seemed to shine with the purity of smelted gold.
Its radiance lent an extraordinary grace to Calcutta's back-streets,
with their squalid, tumbledown, cheek-by-jowl dwellings. The
sānāi started to play in our house when night was scarcely over.
Its wailing vibrations seemed to rise from deep within my rib-
cage. Its sad Bhairavī *rāga* joined forces with the autumn sunshine, in spreading through the world the grief of my imminent
separation. Today my Mini would be married.

From dawn on there was uproar, endless coming and going. A
canopy was being erected in the yard of the house, by binding
bamboo-poles together; chandeliers tinkled as they were hung in
the rooms and verandahs; there was constant loud talk.

I was sitting in my study doing accounts, when Rahamat
suddenly appeared and salaamed before me. At first I didn't
recognize him. He had no bag; he had lost his long hair; his
former vigour had gone. But when he smiled, I recognized him.

'How are you, Rahamat?' I said. 'When did you come?'

'I was let out of prison yesterday evening,' he replied.

His words startled me. I had never confronted a would-be
murderer before; I shrank back at the sight of him. I began to feel
that on this auspicious morning it would be better to have the
man out of the way. 'We've got something on in our house today,'
I said. 'I'm rather busy. Please go now.'

He was ready to go at once, but just as he reached the door he
hesitated a little and said, 'Can't I see your little girl for a moment?'

It seemed he thought that Mini was still just as she was when
he had known her: that she would come running as before, calling
'Kabuliwallah, O Kabuliwallah!'; that their old merry banter
would resume. He had even brought (remembering their old
friendship) a box of grapes and a few nuts and raisins wrapped in
paper – extracted, no doubt, from some Afghan friend of his,
having no bag of his own now.

'There's something on in the house today,' I said. 'You can't
see anyone.'

He looked rather crestfallen. He stood silently for a moment longer, casting a solemn glance at me; then, saying 'Babu salaam', he walked towards the door. I felt a sudden pang. I thought of calling him back, but then I saw that he himself was returning.

'I brought this box of grapes and these nuts and raisins for the little one,' he said. 'Please give them to her.' Taking them from him, I was about to pay him for them when he suddenly clasped my arm and said, 'Please, don't give me any money – I shall always be grateful, Babu. Just as you have a daughter, so do I have one, in my own country. It is with her in mind that I came with a few raisins for your daughter: I didn't come to trade with you.'

Then he put a hand inside his big loose shirt and took out from somewhere close to his heart a crumpled piece of paper. Unfolding it very carefully, he spread it out on my table. There was a small handprint on the paper: not a photograph, not a painting – the hand had been rubbed with some soot and pressed down on to the paper. Every year Rahamat carried this memento of his daughter in his breast-pocket when he came to sell raisins in Calcutta's streets: as if the touch of that soft, small, childish hand brought solace to his huge, homesick breast. My eyes swam at the sight of it. I forgot then that he was an Afghan raisin-seller and I was a Bengali Babu. I understood then that he was as I am, that he was a father just as I am a father. The handprint of his little mountain-dwelling Parvati reminded me of my own Mini.

At once I sent for her from the inner part of the house. Objections came back: I refused to listen to them. Mini, dressed as a bride – sandal-paste pattern on her brow, red silk sari – came timidly into the room and stood close by me.

The Kabuliwallah was confused at first when he saw her: he couldn't bring himself to utter his old greeting. But at last he smiled and said, 'Little one, are you going to your *svaśur-bāṛi*?'

Mini now knew the meaning of *svaśur-bāṛi*; she couldn't reply as before – she blushed at Rahamat's question and looked away. I recalled the day when Mini and the Kabuliwallah had first met. My heart ached.

Mini left the room, and Rahamat, sighing deeply, sat down on the floor. He suddenly understood clearly that his own daughter would have grown up too since he last saw her, and with her too he would have to become re-acquainted: he would not find her exactly as she was before. Who knew what had happened to her these eight years? In the cool autumn morning sunshine the *sānāi* went on playing, and Rahamat sat in a Calcutta lane and pictured to himself the barren mountains of Afghanistan.

I took out a banknote and gave it to him. 'Rahamat,' I said, 'go back to your homeland and your daughter; by your blessed reunion, Mini will be blessed.'

By giving him this money, I had to trim certain items from the wedding-festivities. I wasn't able to afford the electric illuminations I had planned, nor did the trumpet-and-drum band come. The womenfolk were very displeased at this; but for me, the ceremony was lit by a kinder, more gracious light.

The Editor

While my wife was alive I didn't give much thought to Prabha. I was more involved with her mother than with her. I was happy to watch her play and laugh, to listen to her half-formed speech and respond to her affection; I would, whenever I was in the mood, romp around with her; but the moment she started to cry I would return her to her mother's arms and make a speedy escape. I never considered what care and effort were needed to bring up a child.

But with the sudden and untimely death of my wife, Prabha's upbringing passed to me, and I clasped her warmly. I don't quite know whose concern was the stronger: mine to bring up my motherless daughter with double affection, or hers to look after her wifeless father. But from the age of six, she took charge of the house. It was plain to see that this little girl was trying to be her father's sole guardian.

It tickled me to put myself entirely into her hands. I noticed that the more useless and helpless I was, the more she liked it; if I picked up my clothes or umbrella myself, she reacted as if I had infringed her rights. She had never before had a doll as big as her father; she revelled all day in feeding him, dressing him, settling him down to sleep. Only when I took her through her arithmetic book or the first part of her poetry reader did my paternal responsibility come slightly alive.

From time to time I remembered that to marry her to a suitable groom would cost a lot of money – but where was I to get that money? I was educating her as well as I could: it would be awful if she ended up in some nincompoop's hands.

I gave my attention to the need to earn money. I was too old to get a job in a government office, and there was no way I could get into any other office either. After much pondering, I started to write books.

If you punch holes in a hollow bamboo stick, it doesn't become a receptacle; you can't keep oil or water in it; it can't be put to any practical use. But if you blow into it, it makes an excellent cost-free flute. I had the idea that anyone who was unfortunate enough to be useless at any practical work would certainly write good books. Confident of this, I wrote a satirical farce. People said it was good, and it was performed on stage.

The dangerous result of my sudden taste of fame was that I now couldn't stop writing farces. With knotted brow, I spent all day writing them.

Prabha would come and ask, with a loving smile, 'Won't you have your bath, Father?'

'Leave me alone,' I snapped. 'Don't bother me now.'

Probably the girl's face darkened like a lamp suddenly blown out; but I never even noticed her silent, pained withdrawal from the room.

I flared up at the maid, and cuffed the male servant; if a beggar came calling for alms I would drive him away with a stick. If an innocent passer-by spoke through my window to ask the way (my room looked on to the street), I would tell him to go to hell. Why couldn't people understand that I was, at that moment, writing a hilarious farce?

But the money I earned was not at all proportionate either to the hilarity of my farces or to my fame. Nor, at the time, was the money uppermost in my mind. Meanwhile, in unthought-of places, grooms suitable for Prabha were growing up who would set other fathers free from their duty to their daughters, and I failed to notice. Probably only starvation would have brought me to my senses; but now a new opportunity came my way. The zamindar of Jahir village invited me to be the salaried editor of a paper he was starting. I accepted, and within a few days I was writing with such fervour that people used to point me out in the street, and in my own estimation I was as blindingly brilliant as the afternoon sun. Next to Jahir was Ahir village. The zamindars of the two villages were bitter enemies. Previously their quarrels had led to brawls – but now the magistrate had bound them over to keep the peace, and the zamindar of Jahir had engaged poor me in place of his murderous *lāṭhiyāl*s.

Everyone told me I discharged my duties most honourably. The Ahir villagers were utterly cowed by my pen. The whole of their history and ancestry was blackened by it.

This was a good time for me. I became quite fat. There was a perpetual smile on my face. I fired devastating verbal sallies at the people of Ahir and their ancestors, and everyone in Jahir split their sides at my wit. I was blissfully happy.

In the end, Ahir village also brought out a paper. They didn't mince their words. They hurled insults with such zeal and in such crude and vulgar language that the very letters on the page seemed to shriek before one's eyes. The people of both villages knew exactly what was intended. But I, as was my custom, attacked my opponents with humour, subtlety and irony, so that neither my friends nor my enemies could understand what I meant. The result was that though I had won the argument everyone thought I had lost. I then felt compelled to write a sermon on good taste – but I found that this too was a grave mistake, for whereas it is easy to ridicule what is good, it is not so easy to ridicule what is already ridiculous. The sons of Hanu can happily make fun of the sons of Manu, but the sons of Manu can never be so successful at pillorying the sons of Hanu: whose snarls, therefore, drove good taste out of town.

My employer cooled towards me. I was not welcome at public gatherings. When I went out, no one hailed me or spoke to me. People even began to laugh when they saw me. My farces, meanwhile, were completely forgotten. I felt like a spent match; I had flamed for a minute, and then burned out. I was so disheartened that however hard I scratched my head, not a line of writing would come. I began to feel there was no point in living any more.

Prabha was now scared of me. She did not dare approach unless she was invited. She had come to see that a clay doll was a much better companion than a father who wrote satires.

One day it became apparent that the Ahir paper had started to concentrate on me rather than on the zamindar. Vile things were written. My friends each brought me the paper and read it out with great amusement. Some of them said that whatever the content, the language was superb: by which they meant that the slanders it contained were easy to understand. I heard this same opinion throughout the day.

There was a small plot of garden in front of my house. One evening I was pacing there alone, utterly sick at heart. As the

birds returned to their nests and stopped their singing, freely
consigning themselves to the peace of the evening, I was taken
with the thought that there are no satirists' cliques among birds,
no arguments about good taste. But I was still preoccupied with
how I could best reply to my slanderers. One of the drawbacks of
refinement is that not every sort of person understands it. Boorish
language is relatively commonplace, so I decided I would write a
reply in appropriately boorish style. I would not give in! At that
moment I heard a small, familiar voice in the darkness of the
evening, and next I felt a tender, hot hand touch mine. I was so
worried and distracted that even though the voice and touch were
known to me, they did not sink in. But a moment later the voice
was gently sounding in my ears, and the delicate touch was
intensifying. A little girl was beside me, and was softly calling,
'Father.' When she got no answer she lifted my right hand and
pressed it lightly against her cheek; then she slowly went indoors.

Prabha had not called me like this for a long time – had not, of
her own accord, come and showed that sort of affection. So her
tender touch this evening went straight to my heart.

A little later I returned to the house and saw Prabha lying on
the bed. She looked worn out, and her eyes were slightly closed;
she lay like a flower, shed at the end of the day. I felt her brow: it
was very warm; her breath was hot too; the veins in her temple
were throbbing. I realized now that the girl, distressed by the
onset of illness, had gone to her father longing with all her heart
for his care and affection; and her father had at the time been
engrossed in thinking up a scorching reply for the Jahir paper to
print.

I sat down next to her. Saying nothing, she pulled my hand
into the feverishly warm palms of her hands and, placing her
cheek on it, lay quietly.

I made a bonfire of all the Jahir and Ahir papers. I never wrote
my riposte. And giving up like that gave me greater happiness
than I had ever known.

When her mother died, I held Prabha in my lap. Now, after
cremating her stepmother – my writing – I lifted her into my
arms again and carried her indoors.

Punishment

I

When the brothers Dukhiram Rui and Chidam Rui went out in the morning with their heavy farm-knives, to work in the fields, their wives were already quarrelling and shouting. But the people near by were as used to the uproar as they were to other customary, natural sounds. As soon as they heard the shrill screams of the women, they would say, 'They're at it again' – that is, what was happening was only to be expected: it was not a violation of Nature's rules. When the sun rises at dawn, no one asks why; and whenever the two wives in this *kuri*-caste household let fly at each other, no one was at all curious to investigate the cause.

Of course this wrangling and disturbance affected the husbands more than the neighbours, but they did not count it a major nuisance. It was as if they were riding together along life's road in a cart whose rattling, clattering, unsprung wheels were inseparable from the journey. Indeed, days when there was no noise, when everything was uncannily silent, carried a greater threat of unpredictable doom.

The day on which our story begins was like this. When the brothers returned home at dusk, exhausted by their work, they found the house eerily quiet. Outside, too, it was extremely sultry. There had been a sharp shower in the afternoon, and clouds were still massing. There was not a breath of wind. Weeds and scrub round the house had shot up after the rain: the heavy scent of damp vegetation, from these and from the waterlogged jute-fields, formed a solid wall all around. Frogs croaked from the pond behind the cowshed, and the buzz of crickets filled the leaden sky.

Not far off the swollen Padma looked flat and sinister under the mounting clouds. It had flooded most of the grain-fields, and had come close to the houses. Here and there, roots of mango and jackfruit trees on the slipping bank stuck up out of the water, like helpless hands clawing at the void for a last fingerhold.

That day, Dukhiram and Chidam had been working at the zamindar's office-building. On the sandbanks opposite, paddy had ripened. The paddy needed to be cut before the sandbanks were washed away; the poorest villagers were busy there either in their own fields or in other people's fields; but a bailiff had come from the office and forcibly engaged the two brothers. As the office roof was leaking in places, they had to mend that and make some new wickerwork panels: it had taken them all day. They couldn't come home for lunch; they just had a snack from the office. At times they were soaked by the rain; they were not paid normal labourers' wages; indeed, they were paid mainly in insults and sneers.

When the two brothers returned at dusk, wading through mud and water, they found the younger wife, Chandara, stretched on the ground with her sari spread out. Like the sky, she had wept buckets in the afternoon, but had now given way to sultry exhaustion. The elder wife, Radha, sat on the verandah sullenly: her eighteen-month son had been crying, but when the brothers came in they saw him lying naked in a corner of the yard, asleep.

Dukhiram, famished, said gruffly, 'Give me my food.'

Like a spark on a sack of gunpowder, the elder wife exploded, shrieking out, 'Where is there food? Did you give me anything to cook? Must I walk the streets to earn it?'

After a whole day of toil and humiliation, to return – raging with hunger – to a dark, joyless, foodless house, to be met by Radha's sarcasm, and especially by that last insinuation, was suddenly unendurable. 'What?' he roared, like a furious tiger, and then, without thinking, plunged his knife into her head. Radha collapsed into her sister-in-law's lap, and in minutes she was dead.

'What have you done?' screamed Chandara, her clothes soaked with blood. Chidam pressed his hand over her mouth. Dukhiram, letting the knife drop, fell to his knees with his head in his hands, stunned. The little boy woke up and started to wail in terror.

Outside there was complete quiet. The herd-boys were returning with the cattle. Those who had been cutting paddy on the opposite side of the river were crossing back five or six to a boat, with a couple of bundles of paddy on their heads as payment, and were now nearly all home.

Ramlochan Chakrabarti, pillar of the village, had been to the post office with a letter, and was now back in his house, placidly smoking. Suddenly he remembered that his sub-tenant Dukhiram was very behind with his rent: he had promised to pay some today. Deciding that the brothers must be home by now, he threw his chadar over his shoulders, took his umbrella, and stepped out.

As he entered the Ruis' house, he felt uneasy. There was no lamp alight. On the dark verandah, the dim shapes of three or four people could be seen. In a corner of the verandah there were fitful, muffled sobs: the little boy was trying to cry for his mother, but was stopped each time by Chidam.

'Dukhi,' said Ramlochan nervously, 'are you there?'

Dukhiram had been sitting like a statue for a long time; now, on hearing his name, he burst into tears like a helpless child.

Chidam quickly came down from the verandah into the yard, to meet Ramlochan. 'Have the women been quarrelling again?' Ramlochan asked. 'I heard them yelling all day.'

Chidam, all this time, had been unable to think what to do. Various impossible stories occurred to him. All he had decided was that later that night he would move the body somewhere. He had never expected Ramlochan to come. He could think of no swift reply. 'Yes,' he stumbled, 'today they were quarrelling terribly.'

'But why is Dukhi crying so?' asked Ramlochan, stepping towards the verandah.

Seeing no way out now, Chidam blurted, 'In their quarrel, *Choṭobau* struck at *Baṛobau*'s head with a farm-knife.'

When immediate danger threatens, it is hard to think of other dangers. Chidam's only thought was of how to escape from the terrible truth – he forgot that a lie can be even more terrible. A reply to Ramlochan's question had come instantly to mind, and he had blurted it out.

'Good grief,' said Ramlochan in horror. 'What are you saying? Is she dead?'

'She's dead,' said Chidam, clasping Ramlochan's feet.

Ramlochan was trapped. *'Rām, Rām,'* he thought, 'what a mess I've got into this evening. What if I have to be a witness in court?' Chidam was still clinging to his feet, saying, *'Ṭhākur,* how can I save my wife?'

Ramlochan was the village's chief source of advice on legal matters. Reflecting further he said, 'I think I know a way. Run to the police station: say that your brother Dukhi returned in the evening wanting his food, and because it wasn't ready he struck his wife on the head with his knife. I'm sure that if you say that, she'll get off.'

Chidam felt a sickening dryness in his throat. He stood up and said, '*Ṭhākur*, if I lose my wife I can get another, but if my brother is hanged, how can I replace him?' In laying the blame on his wife, he had not seen it that way. He had spoken without thought; now, imperceptibly, arguments that would serve his own interest were forming in his mind.

Ramlochan took the point. 'Then say what actually happened,' he said. 'You can't protect yourself on all sides.'

In no time after he had hurried away, the news spread round the village that Chandara Rui had, in a quarrel with her sister-in-law, split her head open with a farm-knife. Police charged into the village like a river in flood. Both the guilty and the innocent were equally afraid.

II

Chidam decided he would have to stick to the path he had chalked out for himself. The story he had given to Ramlochan Chakrabarti had gone all round the village; who knew what would happen if another story was circulated? But he realized that if he kept to the story he would have to wrap it in five more stories if his wife was to be saved.

Chidam asked Chandara to take the blame on to herself. She was dumbfounded. He reassured her: 'Don't worry – if you do what I tell you, you'll be quite safe.' But whatever his words, his throat was dry and his face was pale.

Chandara was not more than seventeen or eighteen. She was buxom, well-rounded, compact and sturdy – so trim in her movements that in walking, turning, bending or squatting there was no awkwardness at all. She was like a brand-new boat: neat and shapely, gliding with ease, not a loose joint anywhere. Everything amused and intrigued her; she loved to gossip; her bright, restless, deep black eyes missed nothing as she walked to the *ghāṭ*, pitcher on her hip, parting her veil slightly with her finger.

The elder wife had been her exact opposite: unkempt, sloppy and slovenly. She was utterly disorganized in her dress, housework, and the care of her child. She never had any proper work in hand, yet never seemed to have time for anything. The younger wife usually refrained from comment, for at the mildest barb Radha would rage and stamp and let fly at her, disturbing everyone around.

Each wife was matched by her husband to an extraordinary degree. Dukhiram was a huge man – his bones were immense, his nose was squat, in his eyes and expression he seemed not to understand the world very well, yet he never questioned it either. He was innocent yet fearsome: a rare combination of power and helplessness. Chidam, however, seemed to have been carefully carved from shiny black rock. There was not an inch of excess fat on him, not a wrinkle or pock-mark anywhere. Each limb was a perfect blend of strength and finesse. Whether jumping from a river-bank, or punting a boat, or climbing up bamboo-shoots for sticks, he showed complete dexterity, effortless grace. His long black hair was combed with oil back from his brow and down to his shoulders – he took great care over his dress and appearance. Although he was not unresponsive to the beauty of other women in the village, and was keen to make himself charming in their eyes, his real love was for his young wife. They quarrelled sometimes, but always made peace again, for neither could defeat the other. There was a further reason why the bond between them was firm: Chidam felt that a wife as nimble and sharp as Chandara could not be wholly trusted, and Chandara felt that her husband had roving eyes – that if she didn't keep him on a tight rein he might go astray.

A little before the events in this story, however, they had a major row. Chandara found that her husband used work as an excuse for travelling far and for staying extra days away, yet brought no earnings home. Finding this ominous, she too began to overstep the mark. She kept going to the *ghāṭ*, and returned from wandering round the village with rather too much to say about Kashi Majumdar's middle son.

Something now seemed to poison Chidam's life. He could not settle his attention on his work. One day he bitterly rebuked his sister-in-law, laying the blame on her: she threw up her hands and said in the name of her dead father, 'That girl runs before the storm. How can I restrain her? Who knows what ruin she will bring?'

Chandara came out of the next room and said sweetly, 'What's the matter, *Didi*?' and a fierce quarrel broke out between them.

Chidam glared at his wife and said, 'If I ever hear that you've been to the *ghāṭ* on your own, I'll break every bone in your body.'

'That would be a blessed release,' said Chandara, starting to leave. Chidam sprang at her, grabbed her by the hair, dragged her back to the room and locked her in.

When he returned from work that evening he found the doors open, the house empty. Chandara had fled three villages away, to her maternal uncle's house. With great difficulty Chidam persuaded her to return, but now he had to give in. It was as hard to restrain his wife as to hold a handful of mercury; she always slipped through his fingers. He did not use force any more, but there was no peace in the house. Ever-fearful love for his elusive young wife wracked him with intense pain. He even once or twice wondered if it would be better if she were dead: at least he would get some peace then. Human beings can hate each other more than death.

It was at this time that the crisis hit the house.

When her husband asked her to admit to the murder, Chandara stared at him, stunned; her black eyes burnt him like fire. Then she slowly shrank from him, as if to escape his devilish clutches. She turned her heart and soul quite away. 'You've nothing to fear,' said Chidam. He taught her repeatedly what she should say to the police and the magistrate. Chandara paid no attention – sat like a wooden idol whenever he spoke.

Dukhiram relied on Chidam for everything. When he told him to lay the blame on Chandara, Dukhiram asked, 'But what will happen to her?' 'I'll save her,' said Chidam. His burly brother was content with that.

III

This was what Chidam instructed his wife to say: 'The elder wife was about to attack me with the vegetable-slicer. I picked up a farm-knife to stop her, and it somehow cut into her.' This was all Ramlochan's invention. He had generously supplied Chidam with the proofs and embroidery that the story would require.

The police came to investigate. The villagers were sure now

that Chandara had murdered her sister-in-law, and all the witnesses confirmed this. When the police questioned Chandara, she said, 'Yes, I killed her.'

'Why did you kill her?'

'I couldn't stand her any more.'

'Was there a brawl between you?'

'No.'

'Did she attack you first?'

'No.'

'Did she ill-treat you?'

'No.'

Everyone was amazed at these replies, and Chidam was completely thrown off balance. 'She's not telling the truth,' he said. 'The elder wife first –'

The inspector silenced him sharply. Subjecting Chandara to a thorough cross-examination, he repeatedly received the same reply: Chandara would not accept that she had been attacked in any way by her sister-in-law. Such an obstinate girl was never seen! She seemed absolutely bent on going to the gallows; nothing would stop her. Such fierce, disastrous pride!¹ In her thoughts, Chandara was saying to her husband, 'I shall give my youth to the gallows instead of to you. My final ties in this life will be with them.'

Chandara was arrested, and left her home for ever, by the paths she knew so well, past the festival carriage, the market-place, the *ghāṭ*, the Majumdars' house, the post office, the school – an ordinary, harmless, flirtatious, fun-loving village wife; carrying a stigma that could never be obliterated. A bevy of boys followed her, and the women of the village, her friends and companions – some of them peering through their veils, some from their doorsteps, some from behind trees – watched the police leading her away and shuddered with embarrassment, fear and contempt.

To the Deputy Magistrate, Chandara again confessed her guilt, claiming no ill-treatment from her sister-in-law at the time of the murder. But when Chidam was called to the witness-box he broke down completely, weeping, clasping his hands and saying,

---

1. *abhimān*: there is no single English word for this emotion. It includes hurt pride, bruised feelings, and rejection by someone we love. Chandara is *abhimān* incarnate.

'I swear to you, sir, my wife is innocent.' The magistrate sternly told him to control himself, and began to question him. Bit by bit the true story came out.

The magistrate did not believe him, because the chief, most respectable, most educated witness – Ramlochan Chakrabarti – said: 'I appeared on the scene a little after the murder. Chidam confessed everything to me and clung to my feet saying, "Tell me how I can save my wife." I did not say anything one way or the other. Then Chidam said, "If I say that my elder brother killed his wife in a fit of fury because his food wasn't ready, will she get off?" I said, "Be careful, you rogue: don't say a single false word in court – there's no worse offence than that."' Ramlochan had previously prepared lots of stories that would save Chandara, but when he found that she herself was bending her neck to receive the noose, he decided, 'Why the hell should I run the risk of giving false evidence now? I'd better say what little I know.' So Ramlochan said what he knew – or rather said a little more than he knew.

The Deputy Magistrate committed the case to a sessions trial. Meanwhile in fields, houses, markets and bazaars, the mirth and grief of the world carried on; and just as in previous years, torrential monsoon rains fell on to the new rice-crop.

Police, defendant and witnesses were all in court. In the civil court opposite hordes of people were waiting for their cases. A Calcutta lawyer had come on a suit about the sharing of a pond behind a kitchen; the plaintiff had thirty-nine witnesses. Hundreds of people were anxiously waiting for hair-splitting judgements, certain that nothing, at present, was more important. Chidam stared out of the window at the constant throng, and it seemed like a dream. A *koel*-bird was hooting from a huge banyan tree in the compound: no courts or cases in *his* world!

Chandara said to the judge, 'Sir, how many times must I go on saying the same thing?'

The judge explained, 'Do you know the penalty for the crime you have confessed?'

'No,' said Chandara.

'It is death by the hanging.'

'Then please, please give it to me, sir,' said Chandara. 'Do what you like – I can't take any more.'

When her husband was called to the court, she turned away. 'Look at the witness,' said the judge, 'and say who he is.'

'He is my husband,' said Chandara, covering her face with her hands.

'Does he not love you?'

'Like crazy.'

'Do you not love him?'

'Madly.'

When Chidam was questioned, he said, 'I killed her.

'Why?'

'I wanted my food and my sister-in-law didn't give it to me.'

When Dukhiram came to give evidence, he fainted. When he had come round again, he answered, 'Sir, I killed her.'

'Why?'

'I wanted a meal and she didn't give it to me.'

After extensive cross-examination of various other witnesses, the judge concluded that the brothers had confessed to the crime in order to save the younger wife from the shame of the noose. But Chandara had, from the police investigation right through to the sessions trial, said the same thing repeatedly – she had not budged an inch from her story. Two barristers, of their own volition, did their utmost to save her from the death-sentence, but in the end were defeated by her.

Who, on that auspicious night when, at a very young age, a dusky, diminutive, round-faced girl had left her childhood dolls in her father's house and come to her in-laws' house, could have imagined these events? Her father, on his deathbed, had happily reflected that at least he had made proper arrangements for his daughter's future.

In gaol, just before the hanging, a kindly Civil Surgeon asked Chandara, 'Do you want to see anyone?'

'I'd like to see my mother,' she replied.

'Shall I call your husband?' asked the doctor. 'He wants to see you.'

'To hell with him,'[1] said Chandara.

---

1. 'maraṇ!' Lit. 'death!' – a common ironic expression particularly among village-women. The complex implications here include Chandara's rejection of the husband she still loves, the abhimān that prevents her from backing down, and a shy reluctance to display her true marital feelings in public.

A Problem Solved

I

Krishnagopal Sarkar of the village of Jhinkrakota handed over the running of his estate and his other responsibilities to his elder son, and set off for Benares. His humble tenants wept bitterly at losing him: so liberal and pious a landlord was rare indeed in the age of Kali.

His son Bipinbihari was a modern, sophisticated BA. He had a beard, wore glasses, and did not mix much with others. He was highly virtuous: he never even smoked or played cards. His manner was courteous and affable – but in fact he was a very hard man, and his tenants quickly felt the effect of this. The old landlord had been lenient with them; but with his son there was no hope of a paisa's exemption from debt or rent, on whatever grounds. They had to pay on the nail, without a single day's leeway.

When Bipinbihari took over, he found that his father had frequently released land to Brahmins free of rent, and many people had had their rent reduced. If anyone came with a plea of some kind, he was never able to refuse it: this was his weakness.

'It won't do,' said Bipinbihari. 'I can't let half the estate go rent-free.' He reached two separate conclusions. Firstly, workshy people who sat at home growing fat on rent from land they had sublet were in most cases useless and deserved no pity. Charity to the likes of them simply gave refuge to idlers. Secondly, it was much harder to ensure an income than in his father and grandfather's time. There was much more scarcity. It cost four times as much to preserve a gentleman's dignity as it had in the past. His father's open-handed, happy-go-lucky scattering of assets would not do now; on the contrary, they should now be retrieved and expanded. Bipinbihari began to do what his conscience told him – that is, he began to act according to 'principle'.[1] Whatever had

1. The English word is used.

gone out of the house, bit by bit came in again. He allowed very few of the rent-free tenancies to continue, ensuring that even these would not be permanent.

In Benares, Krishnagopal heard, through letters, of his tenants' distress: some of them actually went and appealed to him personally. He wrote to Bipinbihari saying that what he was doing was deplorable. Bipinbihari replied that formerly when gifts had been made various things were received in return. There had been a reciprocal relationship between zamindar and tenants. Recently laws had been passed that banned anything being given in return other than straightforward rent: a zamindar's rights and privileges, other than rent, had been abolished. So what else could he do but keep a close eye on his dues? If the tenants gave him nothing extra, why should he give extra to them? The landlord–tenant relationship was now purely commercial. He would go bankrupt if he went on being so charitable: it would be impossible to maintain either his property or his ancestral dignity.

Krishnagopal pondered deeply on the way that the times had so greatly changed, and concluded that the rules of his own era no longer applied to what the younger generation had to do. If one tried to interfere from a distance, they would say, 'Take back your property then; we can't manage it in any other manner.' What was the point? It was better to devote what was left of one's life to God.

II

Things went on like this. After a great deal of litigation, wrangling and argument, Bipinbihari had arranged nearly everything as he wanted. Most tenants were afraid to resist his pressure; Mirja Bibi's son Achimaddi Bisvas was the only one who refused to give in.

Bipinbihari's attacks on him were the most severe of all. Land given away to a Brahmin could be justified by tradition, but it was impossible to see why this son of a Muslim widow should be given land free or nearly free. True, he had won a scholarship and learnt a little at school, but this did not give him the right to be so above himself. Bipin learnt from the older staff on the estate that the family had received favours from the landlord for a long time – they did not know exactly why. Maybe the widow had gone to him with tales of woe, and he had taken pity on her. But to Bipin the favours seemed highly inappropriate. Never having seen the family's former poverty, he looked at their prosperity and arrogance and felt they had cheated his soft-hearted, unsuspecting father – had stolen some of the zamindar's wealth.

Achimaddi was a very confident young man. He was determined not to budge an inch from his rights, and a fierce contest developed. His widowed mother urged repeatedly that it was stupid to take on the zamindar: they had been protected so far – it was best to have faith in that protection, and give the landlord what he wanted. 'You don't understand these things, Mother,' said Achimaddi.

Achimaddi lost at each stage as the case went through the courts. But the more he lost, the more his tenacity increased. He staked all he had on keeping all that he had.

One afternoon Mirja Bibi came with a small present of garden vegetables and met Bipinbihari privately. Casting her plaintive eyes on him as if caressing him with her motherly gaze, she said, 'You are like my son – may Allah preserve you. Do not ruin Achim, my dear – there'll be no virtue in that. I consign him to you: think of him as an unruly younger brother. Son, do not begrudge him a tiny piece of your untold wealth!'

Bipin was furious with the woman for impertinently using the privilege of age to speak so familiarly to him. 'You're a woman,' he said, 'you don't understand these things. If you've anything to tell me, send your son.' Mirja Bibi had now been told by another's son as well as her own that she didn't understand these things. Praying to Allah, dabbing at her eyes, the widow returned to her house.

III

The case went from the criminal court to the civil court, from the civil court to the district court, from the district court to the High Court. It continued for nearly eighteen months. By the time that Achimaddi was awarded a partial victory in the appeal court, he was up to his neck in debt. Moreover, he had escaped from the tiger on the river-bank only to be assailed by the crocodile in the river. The money-lenders chose this moment to put the court's decree into action. A day was fixed for the auctioning of all that Achimaddi had.

The day was Monday, market-day on the bank of a small river near by. The river was high during the monsoon, so some of the trading was on the bank, some of it in boats: the hubbub was continuous. Among the produce of the season, jackfruit was especially plentiful, and there was lots of hilsa-fish too. The sky was cloudy: many of the traders, fearing rain, stuck bamboo-poles into the ground and stretched canopies over their stalls.

Achimaddi had also come to do some shopping, but without a paisa in his hand: no one would sell to him even on credit. He had brought a kitchen-chopper and a brass plate, hoping to raise money by pawning them.

Bipinbihari had strolled out to take the evening air, attended by a couple of bodyguards with *lāṭhis*. Attracted by the crowd, he decided to visit the market. He was just – out of interest – questioning Dvari the oil-man about his earnings, when Achimaddi came at him charging and roaring like a tiger, brandishing his chopper. The stallholders intervened and quickly disarmed him. He was soon handed over to the police, and the trading in the market continued as before.

It cannot be said that Bipinbihari was unhappy at this turn of events. For a hunted animal to turn and have a go at the hunter is an atrocious breach of etiquette; but never mind, the fellow would receive his due punishment. The women of Bipin's household were outraged by the episode. The fellow was an impudent scoundrel! The prospect of his punishment, though, consoled them.

Meanwhile, that same evening, Mirja Bibi's house – foodless, childless – grew darker than death. Everyone forgot what had happened, had their dinner and went to bed: only for one old woman was it more significant than anything else, yet there was no one in the whole world to fight against it except for her: a few old bones and a frightened, bitter heart in an unlit hut!

IV

Three days passed. On the next there was to be a hearing before the Deputy Magistrate. Bipin himself was to give evidence. He had no objection, even though the zamindar had never appeared in the witness-box before. That morning at the appointed time, he put on a turban and watch-chain and with great ostentation was carried in a palanquin to the court. The court-room was packed: there had not been such a sensational case for a long time.

Just before the case was to be heard, an attendant came up to Bipinbihari and said something in his ear: somewhat flustered, saying he was needed outside, he left the court-room. Outside, he saw his aged father standing a little way off under a banyan tree. He was barefoot, wore a *nāmābali*, and carried a Krishna-rosary: his slender body seemed to glow with kindness; calm compassion for the world shone from his brow. In his chapkan, *jobbā* and tight fitting pantaloons, Bipin had difficulty in doing obeisance to his father. His turban slipped over his nose, and his watch fell out of his pocket. Fumbling to replace them, he invited his father to step into a lawyer's house near by. 'No,' said Krishnagopal, 'what I need to say can be said here.'

Bipin's attendants drove curious bystanders away. 'Everything must be done to release Achim,' said Krishnagopal, 'and the property taken from him should be returned.'

'Have you come all the way from Benares just to say this?' asked Bipin, amazed. 'Why do you favour him so much?'

'What would be the point of telling you why?' said Krishnagopal.

Bipin was insistent. 'I've managed to retrieve gifts of land from many whom I felt were unworthy of them, Brahmins among them – and you didn't turn a hair. So why have you gone to such lengths over this Muslim fellow? If, having gone so far, I release Achim and hand back everything, what shall I say to people?'

Krishnagopal was silent for a while. Then, fiddling nervously with his rosary, he said in a quavering voice, 'If a frank explanation is necessary, tell them that Achimaddi is your brother – my son.'

'By a Muslim mother?' said Bipin in horror.

'Yes, my boy,' said Krishnagopal.

Bipin was flabbergasted. At length he said, 'You can tell me everything later. Please come home now.'

'No,' said Krishnagopal, 'I shall not live at home ever again. I'm returning to Benares at once. Please do whatever your conscience permits.' Blessing him, fighting back tears, unsteady on his feet, Krishnagopal set off back.

Bipin could not think of what to say or do. He stood in silence. But at least he understood now what morals were like in the old days! How superior he was to his father in education and character! This was what happened when people had no 'principles'! As he walked back to the court, he saw Achim waiting outside – drained, exhausted, pale, white-lipped, red-eyed – captive between two guards, clad in dirty rags. And this was Bipin's brother!

Bipin was friendly with the Deputy Magistrate. The case was dismissed on a technicality, and within a few days Achim was restored to his former circumstances. But he did not understand the reason, and other people were surprised too.

It soon got about, however, that Krishnagopal had appeared at the time of the trial. All sorts of rumours circulated. Shrewd lawyers guessed the truth of the matter. Among them, the lawyer Ramtaran had been brought up and educated at Krishnagopal's expense. He had all along suspected – and now he could see clearly – that if you looked carefully, even the most respectable could be caught out. However much a man might finger his rosary, he was probably as much of a rogue as anyone else. The difference between the respectable and the unrespectable was that the former were hypocrites and the latter were not. In deciding, however, that Krishnagopal's famous generosity and piety were a sly façade, Ramtaran found that an old and difficult problem had been solved and, in addition, felt – through what logic I do not know – that the burden of gratitude was lifted from his shoulders. What a relief!

Exercise-book

As soon as she learnt to write, Uma caused tremendous trouble. She would write 'Rain patters, leaves flutter' on every wall of the house with a piece of coal – in great, childish, curving letters. She found the copy of *The Secret Adventures of Haridas* that her elder brother's wife kept beneath her pillow and wrote in pencil, 'Black water, red flower'. Most of the stars and planets in the new almanac that everyone in the house used were, so to speak, eclipsed by her huge scribbles. In her father's daily account-book, in the middle of his calculations, she wrote:

> He who learns to write
> Drives a horse and cart.

Up to now she had not been interrupted in these literary endeavours; but at last she met with a dire mishap.

Uma's elder brother Gobindalal had a very benign look about him, but he wrote perpetually for the newspapers. None of his friends or relatives supposed from his conversation that he was a thinker, and indeed one could not justly accuse him of thinking on any subject. Nevertheless he wrote – and his opinions were in tune with most readers in Bengal. He had recently, for example, completed an elegant essay demolishing – by the spirit of his attack and the exuberance of his language rather than by logic – some gravely false ideas about anatomy that were current in European science.

In the quiet of the afternoon, Uma took her brother's pen and ink and wrote on the essay in bold letters:

> So well-behaved is young Gopal
> Whatever you give he eats it all.[1]

I don't believe she meant this to be a dig at the readers of

1. See Ishvarchandra Vidyasagar in the Glossary.

Gobindalal's essay, but he was beside himself with rage. First he smacked Uma; then he took away her pencil-stub, her ink-smeared blunted pen and all her other carefully accumulated writing implements. The little girl, quite unable to understand the reason for such disgrace, sat in a corner and cried her heart out.

When her punishment was finished, Gobindalal softened a little. He returned the confiscated items, and tried to dispel the little girl's distress by giving her a well-bound, nicely ruled exercise-book.

Uma was seven years old at the time. From then on, this exercise-book was under her pillow every night, and in her lap or under her arm all day long. When with her hair plaited Uma was taken along by the maid to the girls' school in the village, the exercise-book went too. Some of the girls were intrigued by the book, some coveted it, and some begrudged her it.

In the first year that she had the exercise-book, she neatly wrote in it: 'Birds are singing, Night is ending.'[1] She would sit on the floor of her bedroom embracing the exercise-book, chanting out loud and writing. She accumulated many snatches of prose and rhyme in this way.

In the second year, she wrote some things of her own: very short but very much to the point: no introduction or conclusion. For example, at the end of 'The Tiger and the Crane' – a story in *kathāmālā* – a line was added which is not to be found in that book or anywhere else in Bengali literature. It was this: 'I love Yashi very much.'

Let no one suppose that I am about to concoct a love-story! Yashi was not an eleven- or twelve-year-old local boy: she was an old house-servant, whose actual name was Yashoda. But this one sentence should not be taken as firm proof of Uma's feelings towards her. Anyone wanting to write an honest account of the matter would find that the sentence was fully contradicted two pages later in the exercise-book.

This was not just a stray example: there were blatant contradictions in Uma's writings at every step. In one place one could read of her life-long rift with Hari (not Hari meaning Krishna, but a girl at school called Haridashi). But something a few lines below

1. The first line of a popular poem by Madanmohan Tarkalankar. See Glossary.

suggested there was no one in the world whom she loved more than Hari.

The next year, when Uma was nine years old, a *sānāi* began to play one morning. It was her wedding-day. The groom was called Pyarimohan, one of Gobindalal's fellow-writers. Although he was still quite young and had acquired some education, modern ideas had not penetrated him at all. He was therefore the darling of the neighbourhood. Gobindalal adopted him as a model, though not with complete success.

Dressed in a Benares sari, her little face covered with a veil, Uma left tearfully for her father-in-law's house. Her mother said, 'Do what your mother-in-law tells you, my dear. Do the house-work, don't spend your time reading and writing.' And Gobind-alal said, 'Mind that you don't go scratching on walls; it's not that sort of house. And make sure you don't scrawl on any of Pyarimo-han's writings.'

Uma's heart trembled. She realized there would be no mercy in the house where she was going; she would have to learn after endless scoldings what things were regarded there as mistakes and faults.

The *sānāi* sounded on that day too, but I doubt if anyone in that crowd of wedding-guests really understood what the girl felt in her trembling heart, behind her veil, Benares sari and ornaments.

Yashi went along with Uma. She was supposed to settle her into her in-laws' house, then leave her there. The tender-hearted Yashi, after much reflection, took Uma's exercise-book along too. The book was a piece of her parental home: a much-loved memento of her short residence in the house of her birth; a brief record of parental affection, written in round childish letters. It gave her, in the midst of domestic duties that had come too early, a taste of the cherished freedom that is a young girl's due.

For the first few days that she was in her in-laws' house she did not write anything – she had no time. But the time came for Yashi to return; and on the day that she left, Uma shut the door of her bedroom at midday, took her exercise-book out of her tin box, and tearfully wrote: 'Yashi has gone home, I shall go back to Mother too.'

Nowadays she had no leisure in which to copy out passages from *Easy Reader* or *The Dawn of Understanding*; maybe she had no inclination either. So there were no long passages dividing her own childish writings. Below the sentence mentioned above was written: 'If only *Dādā* could take me home again, I would never spoil his writings again.'

Word had it that Uma's father sometimes tried to invite her home for a bit; but Gobindalal and Pyarimohan joined forces to prevent this. Gobindalal said that now was the time to learn her duties towards her husband: bringing her back to the old atmosphere of affection would disturb her quite unnecessarily. He wrote such a shrewd and witty essay on the subject, that his like-minded readers could not but agree. Uma got wind of what was happening, and wrote in her exercise-book: '*Dādā*, I beg you, take me home again just once – I promise not to annoy you.'

One day she was in her room with the door closed, writing something similarly pointless. Her sister-in-law Tilakmanjari, who was very inquisitive, decided she must find out what Uma got up to behind her closed door. When she peeped through a crack and saw her writing, she was amazed: the Goddess of Learning[1] had never before made so secret a visitation to the female quarters of the house. Her younger sister Kanakmanjari came and peeped too; and her youngest sister Anangamanjari – precariously standing on tiptoe to peer at the mysteries within.

Uma, as she wrote, suddenly heard three familiar voices giggling outside the room. Realizing what was afoot, she hastily shut the exercise-book in her box and buried her face in the bedclothes.

Pyarimohan was most perturbed when he was told about what had been seen. Reading and writing, once started, would lead to play- and novel-writing, and household norms would be endangered. As he thought further about the matter, he worked out a most subtle theory. Perfect marriage was produced by a combination of female and male power. But if through women's education female power was weakened, then male power would prevail unchecked; and the clash between male and male would be so destructive that marriage would be annihilated, and women would be widowed. As yet, no one had been able to challenge this theory.

1. Sarasvati. See Glossary.

That evening Pyarimohan came to Uma's room and gave her a
thorough scolding, and ridiculed her too, saying: 'So the wife
wants to go to an office with a pen behind her ear? We'll have to
get her a *śāmlā*!' Uma could not understand what he meant. She
had never read his articles, so she hadn't learnt to appreciate his
wit. But she was deeply humiliated, and wished that the earth
would swallow her up.

For a long time after she wrote nothing. But one autumn
morning she heard a beggar-woman singing an *āgamanī* song.
She listened quietly, resting her chin on the bars of the window.
The autumn sunshine brought back so many memories of childhood; hearing an *āgamanī* song as well was too much to bear.

Uma could not sing; but ever since she learnt how to write, her
habit had been to write down songs, to make up for not being
able to sing them. This was what the beggar-woman sang that
day:

> The citizens say to Uma's[1] mother,
> 'Your lost star has returned.'
> The Queen runs, madly weeping,
> 'Where is Uma, tell me?
> My Uma has returned –
> Come, my darling,
> Let me clasp you to me!'
> Stretching her arms,
> Hugging her mother's neck,
> Uma chides her, sore at heart:
> 'Why did you not send for me?'

With the same soreness of heart, Uma's eyes filled with tears.
She furtively called the singer over and, shutting the door of her
room, began to make a strangely spelt copy of the song in her
exercise-book.

Tilakmanjari, Kanakmanjari and Anangamanjari saw this
through the crack in the door and shouted out, clapping their
hands: '*Baudidi*, we've seen everything, *Baudidi*!' Uma opened
the door and said in great distress, 'Dear sisters, don't tell anyone,
please, I beg you. I won't do it again, I won't write again.' Then

---

1. See Durga in the Glossary.

she saw that Tilakmanjari had her eye on the exercise-book. She ran over to it and clasped it to her breast. Her sisters-in-law struggled to snatch it from her; failing to do so, Ananga called her brother.

Pyarimohan came and sat down on the bed sternly. 'Give me that book,' he thundered. When his command was not obeyed, he growled in an even deeper voice, 'Give it to me.'

The girl held the exercise-book to her breast and looked at her husband, entreating him with her gaze. When she saw that Pyarimohan was about to force it from her, she hurled it down, covered her face with her hands, and fell to the floor.

Pyarimohan picked up the exercise-book and loudly read out from her childish writings. As she listened, Uma tried to clutch the nethermost depths of the earth. The other girls collapsed into peals of laughter.

Uma never got the exercise-book back again. Pyarimohan also had an exercise-book full of various subtly barbed essays, but no one was philanthropic enough to snatch *his* book away and destroy it.

Forbidden Entry

One morning two young boys were standing by the roadside laying bets on an extremely daring enterprise. They were debating whether it was possible to take some flowers from the *mādhabī*-creeper in the temple compound. One of the boys was saying that he would be able to do it, and the other was saying, 'You never will.' To understand why this was easy to talk about but not so easy to do requires a fuller explanation.

Jaykali Devi, widow of the late Madhabchandra Tarkabachaspati, was the guardian of the temple, which was dedicated to the Blessed Lord Krishna. Her husband had been given the title 'Tarkabachaspati' ('Master of Debate') in his capacity as teacher at the village *ṭol*, but had never been able to prove to his wife that he deserved it. Some pundits were of the opinion that, because talking and arguing were his wife's preserve, he amply merited the title by virtue of being her 'Master'.[1] Actually, Jaykali did not say very much; she could stop even the mightiest verbal torrents with a couple of words or by saying nothing at all.

Jaykali was a tall, strong, sharp-nosed, tough-minded woman. Through her husband's mismanagement, property endowed to them for the maintenance of the temple had almost been lost. His widow, by collecting all the arrears, fixing new limits, and recovering claims that had lapsed for many years, had managed to get everything straight again. No one could do her out of a single paisa.

Because this woman had many of the qualities of a man, she had no female friends. Women were terrified of her. Gossip, small talk and tears were all anathema to her. Men were afraid of her too, because she could rebuke the bottomless idleness of the men of the village with a stare so fierce and silently contemptuous that it pierced their fat inertia, cut them to the quick. She had a remarkable capacity for contempt and a remarkable capacity for conveying contempt. Anyone she judged to be at fault, she could

1 A pun on *pati,* which means both 'husband' and 'master'.

blast with her manner and expression, with a word or with no word. She kept close tabs on everything that happened in the village, good or bad. She effortlessly dominated all its affairs. Wherever she went she was in charge: neither she nor anyone doubted it.

She was expert in nursing the sick, but her patients feared her as much as death. If anyone broke the treatment or diet she prescribed, her anger was hotter than the fever itself. Her tall, strict presence hung over the village like the Judgement of God; no one loved her, yet no one dared to defy her. She knew everyone, yet no one was as isolated as she.

The widow had no children, but she had taken on the upbringing of two orphaned nephews. No one could say that the lack of a male parent had deprived them of discipline, or that they had been spoilt by blind affection from their aunt. The elder of them was now eighteen. From time to time the question of his marriage arose, and the boy was not averse to the bonds of love. But his aunt's mind was shut to that happy prospect. Unlike other women, she did not find the blooming of love in a young married couple particularly pleasing to contemplate. On the contrary, it was to her unpleasantly likely that, like other married men, her nephew would sit about the house, growing fatter by the day as his wife pampered him. No, she said, Pulin had better start earning – then he could bring a wife into the house. Neighbours were shocked by her harsh words.

The temple was Jaykali's most precious possession. She was never remiss in tending, dressing and bathing the deity. The two attendant Brahmins feared her far more than the god himself. Formerly the god had not received his full rations, because there was another object of worship living secretly in the temple, a 'temple-maid' called Nistarini. Offerings of ghee, milk, curds and butter were shared between heaven and hell. But under Jaykali's iron rule, offerings were enjoyed in full by the deity. Lesser gods had to find means of support elsewhere.

The widow made sure that the courtyard of the temple stayed spotlessly clean – not a blade of grass anywhere. On a trellis to one side there was a *mādhabī*-creeper: whenever it shed dry leaves, Jaykali removed them. She could not bear the slightest invasion of the sanctity, cleanliness and orderliness of the temple.

Previously local boys playing hide-and-seek had hidden inside the courtyard, and sometimes baby goats came and chewed at the bark of the *mādhabī*. There was no chance of that now. Except on festival-days, boys were not permitted to enter the courtyard, and hungry little goats, beaten by sticks, had to run bleating to their mothers.

Irreverent persons, even if they were close relatives, were not allowed to enter the temple yard. Her brother-in-law, who liked eating chicken-meat cooked by Muslims, had come to the village once to see his relations, and had wanted to visit the temple; Jaykali objected so violently, there had nearly been a complete rift between her and her elder sister. The excessive zeal with which the widow watched over the temple seemed quite crazy to ordinary people.

Whereas in other spheres Jaykali was harsh and haughty and independent, in her care of the temple she surrendered herself completely. To the image inside it she was mother, wife and slave: she treated it with watchfulness, tenderness, grace and humility. The stone temple with its stone image was the only thing that brought out her femininity. It was her husband and son: her entire world.

Readers will now appreciate what limitless courage was required to steal *mādhabī*-blossoms from the temple courtyard. The boy concerned was Nalin, the younger of her nephews. He knew what his aunt was like, but discipline had not tamed him. He was drawn to anything risky, and was always eager to break restrictions. It was said that in childhood his aunt had been like that too.

Jaykali was, at the time, sitting on her verandah telling her rosary, gazing with motherly love and devotion at the image of the deity. The boy crept up from behind and stood underneath the *mādhabī*. He found that the flowers on the lower branches had all been used for *pūjā*. So he gingerly started to climb the trellis. Seeing some buds on a high branch, he stretched with the whole length of his body and arm to pick them; but the strain on the frail trellis was too great, and it noisily collapsed. Boy and creeper fell sprawling on the ground together.

This glorious feat brought Jaykali running: she grabbed him by the arms and wrenched him up from the ground. He had been

knocked badly by his fall, but one could not call this a punishment, because it had not come from a living thing. So now
Jaykali's living punishment rained down on the boy's bruised
body. He suffered it in silence, without a single tear. His aunt
then dragged him into a room and bolted the door. He was given
no food that afternoon. Hearing this, the servant-girl Mokshada
begged – tearfully and with trembling voice – that the boy be
forgiven. Jaykali would not be moved. No one in the house dared
give food to the hungry boy behind Jaykali's back.

The widow sent for men to repair the trellis, and once again
took her seat on the verandah with her rosary in hand. A little
later Mokshada came up to her and said timorously, '*Ṭhākurmā*,
the young master is weeping with hunger: shall I give him some
milk?'

'No,' said Jaykali with her face set. Mokshada withdrew again.
From the room in the hut near by Nalin's plaintive whimpering
gradually swelled into wails of anger – until, much later, he was
too exhausted to go on, and only an occasional panting sob
reached the ears of his aunt as she sat telling her rosary.

Nalin's distress had subsided into exhausted near-silence when
the sounds of another unhappy creature – mixed with the distant
noise of people running and shouting – loudly disturbed the road
outside the temple. Suddenly footsteps were heard in the temple
yard. Jaykali turned and saw something heaving under the
creeper. 'Nalin!' she shouted furiously. No one replied. She
thought that Nalin must have somehow escaped from his prison
and was trying to enrage her again. She stepped down into the
yard, with her lips grimly clenched. 'Nalin!' she shouted again as
she neared the creeper. There was still no answer. Lifting up a
branch, she saw an extremely dirty and frightened pig lurking in
the thick foliage.

The creeper that was a modest substitute, in this brick-built
courtyard, for the groves of Vrindavan, the scent of whose blossoms recalled the fragrant breath of the *gopī*s and evoked a gorgeous
dream of dalliance along the banks of the Yamuna – to think that
the sacredness of it, tended by the widow with total devotion, had
been suddenly desecrated by this sordid event! An attendant
Brahmin came with a stick to drive out the pig, but Jaykali
rushed to stop him, and bolted the gate of the temple from inside.

A short while later a crowd of drunken Ḍoms arrived at the temple gate and began to clamour for the animal they intended to sacrifice. 'Clear off, you scum,' shouted Jaykali from behind the closed gate. 'Don't you dare besmirch my temple.'

The crowd dispersed. Even though they had as good as seen it with their own eyes, it was beyond belief that *Mā* Jaykali had given asylum to an unclean animal inside her Krishna temple.

The great god of all mortal creatures was delighted at this odd little episode, even if the petty god of mean and narrow social custom was mightily outraged.

In the Middle of the Night

'Doctor! Doctor!'

Someone pestering me! In the middle of the night! I opened my eyes to see our local zamindar, Dakshinacharan Babu. I scrambled to my feet, dragged out my broken-backed armchair for him, sat him down, and looked anxiously into his face. It was half past two by my watch.

His face was pale and his eyes were staring as he spoke: 'The same trouble again tonight – your medicine hasn't worked.'

'Perhaps you've been drinking again,' I said, hesitantly.

He flared up. 'You're quite wrong there – it isn't drink. Unless I tell you the whole story from beginning to end, you'll never know the reason.'

The small tin kerosene lamp on the shelf was guttering, and I raised the wick. It shone a little more brightly and made lots of smoke. I tucked up my dhoti and sat cross-legged on a packing-case covered with newspaper. Dakshinacharan Babu began.

'You don't find many housewives like my first wife. But I was young then, and susceptible, and always immersed in poetry, so undiluted housewifery didn't appeal to me much. Those lines of Kalidasa kept coming to me:

> A wife is a counsellor, friend and lover;
> In the fine arts, it's a joy to teach her.

But I didn't get much joy in my efforts to teach my wife, and if I tried to address her in terms of a lover she would burst out laughing. Like Indra's elephant floundering in the Ganges, the finest gems of poetry and fondest endearments were swept away instantly by her laughter. She was marvellously good at laughing.

'Four years went by, and then I fell terribly ill. I had boils on my lips; I was delirious with fever; I was fighting for my life. No one thought I would survive. Things got so far, that the doctor gave me up for lost. But then a relative of mine brought a monk from somewhere: he gave me a root mixed with ghee – and, whether through the power of this medicine or through Fate, I recovered.

'While I was ill my wife didn't rest for a minute. Death's envoys gathered at the door for those few days, and a feeble woman fought them continuously with mere human strength and the utmost power of feeling. She seemed to clutch and press my unworthy life to her breast as if it were her child, giving all her love and care. She didn't eat, or sleep; she had no thought for anything else in the world.

'Like a vanquished tiger, Death dropped me from its jaws and went away; but as he went, he dealt my wife a heavy blow with his paw. She was pregnant at the time, and after a short time gave birth to a dead baby. Various complicated illnesses began after that. I had to look after her. This used to embarrass her. "What are you doing?" she would say. "What will people think? Don't keep coming in and out of my room like this all the time!"

'At night, when she was feverish, if I tried to fan her by pretending I was fanning myself, a tug-of-war for the fan would ensue. If sometimes my nursing took me ten minutes past my meal-time, I had to beg and coax her to accept it. The slightest attention seemed to do more harm than good. She would say, "It's not right for a man to do all this."

'I dare say you've seen our house at Baranagar. There's a garden in front, between the house and the Ganges. On the south side of the house, just beneath our bedroom, my wife enclosed a small plot with a henna hedge and made a garden of her own. Out of all the garden, that plot was the most unostentatious and natural. That is to say, colour did not take precedence over scent, or botanical variety over blooms; and there were no tags with Latin names next to nondescript plants in tubs. Instead, there were roses, jasmine, gardenia, oleander and tuberose in wild abundance. A seat of white marble had been made round the base of a huge *bakul* tree. Before her illness, my wife herself stood at it twice a day, scrubbing it clean. On summer evenings, when her housework was finished, she sat there. She could watch the Ganges, but Babus, in company-yachts, could not see her.

'After many days of being confined to bed, she suddenly said one moonlit Caitra evening, "I'm sick of being shut up indoors; today I shall go and sit in my garden for a while."

'I slowly and gingerly guided her to the stone seat under the *bakul* tree, and laid her down there. I would have been quite happy to have her head resting on my knee, but I knew she would find this odd; so I brought a pillow for her instead.

'Full-blown *bakul*-flowers floated down in ones and twos, and shadowy moonlight shone through gaps in the branches on to her wasted face. It was still and peaceful all around; and as I sat beside her in the fragrant shadows and looked at her face, tears came to my eyes.

'I slowly edged towards her and took her hot, emaciated hand in mine. She made no objection. After sitting in silence like this for a while, my heart swelled and I burst out, "I shall never forget your love!" At once I realized I should not have said that. My wife laughed. In that laugh there was modesty, pleasure, and some disbelief; but also a considerable dose of the keenest mockery. She offered not a word of argument, but her laughter said, "You'll *never* forget? That's impossible and I don't expect it either."

'For fear of this sweet piercing laugh, I never dared use amorous words with my wife. Whatever came to my mind when I was alone seemed utterly stupid if I tried to come out with it to her face. To this day, I cannot understand why words which, when I saw them in print, made my eyes stream with tears, seemed so ludicrous when spoken.

'Arguments deal in words, but you cannot argue with a laugh; so all I could do was stay silent. The moonlight grew brighter; a *koel*-bird was calling more and more impatiently. I sat and wondered if, even on a moonlit night like this, the female *koel*-bird was deaf.

'Despite every medical effort my wife's illnesses showed no sign of recovery. The doctor said, "Why not try a change of air?" I took her to Allahabad.'

Dakshinacharan Babu suddenly stopped at this point. He eyed me suspiciously, and then sat thinking with his head in his hands. I also kept silent. The kerosene lamp on the shelf was dim now, and the whining of the mosquitoes could be heard clearly in the still room. Suddenly he broke his silence and began again:

'At Allahabad my wife was treated by Dr Haran. He spent a long time treating her, but finally he too said what I and my wife already knew: that her condition could not be cured. She would be ill for the rest of her life.

'One day she said to me, "I shan't get better and neither can I hope for a speedy death. Why should you spend your life with a living corpse? You should marry again."

'She saw this as a logical and rational solution: she had not the slightest sense of anything great or heroic or peculiar in it. Now it was my turn to laugh – had I had any of her talent for laughter. Like the hero of a novel, I gravely and pompously started: "For as long as there is life in my body –"

'"Come, come," she interrupted. "Don't go on! Hearing you talk like that is enough to kill me!"

'"I shall not be able to love anyone else –" I continued, refusing to give in. My wife laughed loudly at this, so I had to stop.

'I don't know if I ever admitted it to myself at the time, but I can now see I was wearying of all this nursing with no hope of recovery. I never imagined I would back out of it; but I was dismayed by the prospect of spending my whole life with an incurable patient. When as a young man I had looked ahead, my whole future seemed packed with the magic of love, the lure of pleasure, the charm of beauty. But that was all a mirage now, and a hopeless, barren desert stretched out in front of me.

'My wife must have perceived this inner tiredness in my nursing of her. I did not know it at the time, but I am sure she could read me as easily as the unjoined letters of a child's first reader. So when I cast myself in the role of a romantic hero, and solemnly mouthed my poeticisms, she laughed with affection, but also with helpless merriment. I still want to die with shame when I think of her godlike insight into my innermost thoughts.

'Dr Haran was of the same caste as ourselves. I was often invited to his house. After a few days of going there, he introduced me to his daughter. The girl was unmarried; she was about fifteen. The doctor told me she was not yet married because he had not found a groom to his liking. But from others I heard a rumour of some kind of scandal in the family. She could not, though, be faulted in any other respect. She was as accomplished as she was beautiful. We talked of many things, and sometimes I returned home late – past the time for my wife's dose of medicine. She knew I had gone to Dr Haran's house, but never asked the reason for my lateness.

'I began to see a new mirage in the desert. Bursting with thirst, I saw clear, overflowing water lapping and purling before me. However hard I tried, I could not turn my mind from it, and my wife's sick-room became doubly unattractive to me. My nursing and doses of medicine began to fail in their regularity.

'Dr Haran said to me sometimes that death was best for those whose illnesses could not be cured, because they could take no pleasure in being alive and were a misery to others. General statements like this are permissible: he should not, however, have said such a thing with reference to my wife. But doctors become so indifferent to human mortality that they don't always understand people's feelings.

'Suddenly one day I heard my wife saying in the next room, "Doctor, why are you swelling your earnings by making me swallow all these useless medicines? Since my life has become so wretched, give me something to carry me off!"

'"Come, come," said the doctor. "You mustn't talk like that."

'It cut me to the quick to hear such a thing. As soon as the doctor had gone, I went to my wife's room and sat on the edge of her bed, slowly stroking her forehead. "It's very hot in this room," she said. "You go out. It's time for your walk. If you don't go, you won't feel hungry in the evening."

'Going for a walk meant going to the doctor's house. I had told my wife that I needed to be out for some of the day in order to work up an appetite. I'm certain now that she saw through this deception. I was stupid, so I thought she was stupid too.'

Dakshinacharan was silent again after this, with his head in his hands. At last he said, 'Give me a glass of water.' He drank the water and went on:

'One day the doctor's daughter Manorama expressed a desire to meet my wife. I wasn't exactly pleased with this proposal, but I had no reason to refuse it. So one evening she came along to where we were staying.

'My wife was in even greater pain than usual. On days when the pain was bad, she would lie totally still and silent: only when she clenched her fist or looked blue in the face could one tell what agony she was in. There was no movement at all in the room that evening; I sat quietly on the edge of the bed. Maybe she had no strength to tell me to go for my walk, or maybe she wanted me to stay with her at a time of such suffering. The kerosene light was by the door, in case it hurt her eyes. All that could be heard in the hushed darkness was a heavy sigh from my wife whenever the pain abated.

'Manorama appeared at the door, and the light from the kerosene lamp fell on to her face. She lingered in the doorway, making out nothing at first in the mixture of light and dark. My wife started and clutched my hand. "Who's she?" she said. Frightened in her weakened state by the sight of an unknown person, she muttered two or three times, "Who's she? Who's she? Who's she?"

'Like a fool, I first replied, "I don't know." But something seemed to lash me like a whip as I spoke, and I quickly said, "Oh – she's Dr Haran's daughter."

'My wife looked up at me; I couldn't bring myself to look at her. Then she murmured to the visitor, "Come in", and to me, "Hold up the light." Manorama came in and sat down. She talked with my wife for a bit.

'Then the doctor appeared. He had brought two bottles with him from his dispensary. He showed them to my wife and said, "You should rub on the lotion in the blue bottle and take the other by mouth. Make sure you don't mix them up, for the massage-lotion is very poisonous."

'Warning me too to be very careful, he put the bottles on the bedside table; and as he said goodbye he called his daughter to come with him. "Why can't I stay, Father?" she said. "There's no other woman to help with the nursing."

'"No, no, please don't trouble yourself," said my wife in alarm. "We have an old servant – she looks after me like a mother."

'"How good your wife is!" said the doctor with a laugh. "She's nursed others for so long that she can't stand anyone nursing *her*!"

'As the doctor turned to leave with his daughter, my wife said, "Dr Haran, my husband has been sitting in this closed room for too long. Take him out with you."

'"Come," said the doctor to me, "come with us for a walk by the river."

'I did not demur for long. As we left, the doctor once again warned my wife about the two bottles.

'I ate at the doctor's house that night. It was late when I returned, and my wife was tossing and turning. Stabbed with remorse, I asked, "Is the pain worse?"

'She stared at me, speechlessly, too choked to reply. I ran to fetch the doctor again. For a long time, the doctor could not make out what was wrong. Eventually he asked, "Is the pain worse? Why not rub on the lotion?" He picked up the bottle from the table and, finding it empty, asked, "Did you drink this medicine by mistake?" By a silent nod, my wife answered that she had. The doctor immediately rushed back to his house in a tonga to fetch a stomach-pump. I fell half-senseless on to my wife's bed.

'Then, like a mother soothing a child, she pulled my head on to her breast and by the touch of her hands tried to convey what she felt. By the sad touch of her hands, she assured me again and again: "Don't grieve, it's for the best – you'll be happy, and that makes me die happily."

'When the doctor returned, my wife's torments were over.'

Complaining of the heat, Dakshinacharan took another drink of water. Then he stepped outside and walked up and down the verandah a few times before coming in and sitting down again. He did not seem to want to go on talking: it was as though I myself was extracting the words from him by a kind of sorcery. He began again:

'I married Manorama and returned to Bengal. She had married me with her father's permission; but whenever I spoke affectionately to her, whenever I tried to win her with loving words, she remained solemn and unsmiling. There were misgivings, perhaps, at the back of her mind that I didn't quite fathom. It was at this time that my drinking got out of hand.

'One evening early in autumn I was walking with Manorama in our garden at Baranagar. It was eerily dark. There was no sound even of birds fluttering their wings in their nest – just the rustling of shadowy *jhāu* bushes on either side as we walked.

'Feeling tired, Manorama reached the white stone seat at the base of the *bakul* tree, and lay down with her head on her arms. I sat down next to her. The darkness was even denser there, though the bits of sky that were visible were covered with stars. The crickets under the trees were stitching, as it were, a narrow border of sound along the edge of the robe of silence that had slipped down from the sky. I had been drinking that afternoon, and my mind was in a fluid, maudlin state. As the darkness pressed my eyes, the shadowy shape of my wife's languid body, the dim pallor of her loose sari, stirred me with inexorable passion. But she seemed like a shadow herself – impossible to hold in my arms.

'Suddenly the darkness over the *jhāu* bushes seemed to catch fire: a thin, yellow crescent moon climbed slowly into the sky above the trees, lighting the face of the woman slumped in her white sari on the white stone seat. I could hold back no longer. I moved and clasped her hand and said, "Manorama, you don't believe me, but I do love you. I shall never be able to forget you."

'I winced in alarm at my own words, remembering I had once spoken in the very same way to someone else. And that very moment, above the *bakul* tree, over the tops of the *jhāu* bushes, under the yellow slice of the moon, right from the eastern to the far western bank of the Ganges, a laugh sped swiftly, a rolling laugh. I cannot describe that heart-rending laugh, the way it seemed to split the sky. I lost consciousness, and fell from the stone seat.

'When I came round, I found I was lying on my bed indoors. My wife was saying, "Why did you pass out like that?"

'"Didn't you hear?" I replied, trembling. "Didn't you hear that laughter, the way it filled the sky!"

'"Laughter, you call it?" said my wife, laughing herself. "A huge flock of birds flew past, I heard the noise of their wings. Do you get frightened by so little?"

'In the light of day I could understand that it was indeed a

flock of birds in flight – ducks from the north coming to feed on
the river sandbanks. But by the evening, I could not believe that
any more: I felt that loud laughter was lying in wait to fill the
darkness: at the slightest opportunity it would burst out, splitting
the dark and enveloping the sky. Things reached such a pitch that
after dusk each day I was frightened even to speak to Manorama.

'I decided to take her on a boat-trip, away from the Baranagar
house. My fears faded in the river's late autumn breezes. For a
few days we were happy. Lured by the beauty around her,
Manorama at last opened slowly the locked door of her heart.

'We sailed beyond the Ganges and Kharia and reached the
Padma. The awesome river had started her long winter sleep,
lifeless and inert as a hibernating snake. To the north, barren
banks of sand stretched bleakly towards the horizon; and in the
villages on the steep southern banks, mango-groves quaked and
pleaded in the face of the river's demonic power. From time to
time the Padma rolled over sleepily, and pieces of the crumbling
shore slapped and splashed as they broke away. We found a good
mooring and tied up the boat.

'One day we wandered far from the boat. As the golden shadows
of the sunset faded, a clear full moon rose up before our eyes; and as
a great, unchecked flood of moonlight spread right up to the
horizon, over vast white sandbanks, I felt as if we alone were
wandering in a boundless dream-world, empty as the moon. Manorama was swathed in a red shawl, flowing down from her head,
wound round her face, covering her whole body. As the silence
thickened, and nothing showed but an infinite, directionless white-
ness and emptiness, Manorama slowly brought out her hand and
gripped mine; she edged close and seemed to rest the whole of
her mind and body, youth and existence on me. My heart raced,
and I wondered if love could ever be fulfilled indoors. Where is
there room for lovers except where the sky is open and naked and
endless like this? We seemed without home, without doors, without anywhere to return to, free to wander without constraint
through this moonlit emptiness, hand in hand, heading nowhere.

'Walking like this, we came to a pool of water in the middle of
the sand: the Padma had changed her course and the water had
been left trapped. A long bar of moonlight lay as if in a swoon
across that waveless, sleeping, desert-pool. We stood on the edge

together: as Manorama gazed at me pensively, her shawl slipped from her head. I lifted her face – gleaming in the moonlight – and kissed her.

'At once a voice resounded through the empty waste, saying three times, "Who's she? Who's she? Who's she?" I started in alarm, and my wife shuddered too. But the next moment we realized it was not a human voice, not a supernatural one either – just the call of the water-birds scouring the sandbanks. They had been startled by the sight of people approaching their safe retreat.

'Shaken by our fear, we hurried back to the boat. We lay on our beds: Manorama was exhausted and quickly fell asleep. But someone came and stood by my mosquito-net in the dark, and pointing once at Manorama with a long, thin, bony finger whispered ever so softly and indistinctly into my ear, "Who's she? Who's she? Who's she?"

'I sat up and struck a match for the lamp. Instantly a gale of laughter swept the shadowy figure away, shaking my mosquito-net, rocking the boat, turning the blood of my sweat-soaked body to ice as it sped through the dark night. Over the Padma it went, over the sandbanks, over the sleeping fields and villages and towns, travelling on and on across countries and peoples, gradually becoming fainter as it shrank into the distance; leaving even the realm of life and death; becoming thinner than the point of a needle, till it was too faint to hear, too faint to imagine; yet there seemed to be endless sky inside my head whose borders the sound could never cross however far it travelled. It went on till I could bear it no more: I decided I'd have to turn out the light or I'd never sleep – but as soon as I did so and lay down again, immediately that strangulated voice returned to the darkness next to my mosquito-net, close to my ear: "Who's she? Who's she? Who's she?" To the same rhythm as the blood in my heart it continued: "Who's she? Who's she? Who's she? . . . Who's she? Who's she? Who's she?" In the depth of the night, on that silent boat, my round clock seemed to come to life too, its hands pointing from the shelf at Manorama, and saying with its tick-tock, "Who's she? Who's she? Who's she? . . . Who's she? Who's she? Who's she?"'

Dakshinacharan Babu had turned yellow as he spoke, and his

voice was hoarse. 'Drink some more water,' I said, touching him. My kerosene lamp guttered and went out. I noticed that it was getting light outside. The crows were cawing. Magpie-robins were whistling. An ox-cart creaked past on the road in front of my house. Dakshinacharan's expression changed: there was no sign of fear any more. He seemed ashamed that the sorcery of the night and the frenzy of his imaginary fears had made him tell me so much. I felt that he blamed it on me. Without a single civil word, he abruptly rose and left the house.

The next night, half-way through, there was a knocking at my door again, and the sound of 'Doctor! Doctor!'

Unwanted

Towards evening the storm grew steadily worse. What with the lashing of the rain, the claps of thunder and flashes of lightning, it was like war between gods and demons in the sky. Great black clouds rolled hither and thither like banners proclaiming world-destruction; rebellious waves danced across the river, crashing on the shore; huge trees in the garden groaned as their branches heaved and thrashed to right and left.

Meanwhile in a bungalow in Chandernagore, in a shuttered room lit only by an oil-lamp, a husband and wife sat on bedding spread out on the floor by a bed and talked.

'In a little while,' Sharat Babu was saying, 'you'll be quite recovered, and we can go back home.'

'I'm better already,' said Kiranmayi. 'It won't hurt me to go home now.'

Any married person will know that the conversation was not actually so brief. The question was simple, but the argument to and fro fell short of a solution. It spun faster and faster like a boat without oars, till it seemed in danger of sinking in floods of tears.

'The doctor says,' said Sharat Babu, 'you should stay a bit longer.'

'Does the doctor know everything?' said Kiran.

'You must know,' said Sharat, 'that this is the season back home in which it's easy to catch infections. You should wait for another month or so.'

'Are you saying there are no infections here?' said Kiran.

What had happened was this. Kiran was loved by everyone in the household, even by her mother-in-law. When she fell badly ill, they were all alarmed; and when the doctor advised a change of air, her husband and mother-in-law were pleased to take her, gladly abandoning work and household. Village wiseacres questioned whether recovery would necessarily arise from the change: wasn't it rather modish and excessive to make such a fuss about a young wife – as if no one else's wife got ill sometimes, or people were immortal in Chandernagore? Was there any place where the prescriptions of Fate did not apply? But Sharat and his mother paid no heed. The life of their darling Kiranmayi was more important than the collective wisdom of the village. When a loved one is threatened, people are often irrational.

Sharat took a bungalow in Chandernagore, and Kiran recovered from her illness: she was just still rather weak. There was a touching feebleness in her face and eyes, so that anyone looking at her felt, with quaking heart, that she'd had a most narrow escape.

But Kiran was jolly by nature, gregarious. She didn't like being alone in this place. She had nothing to do in the house, no neighbours or friends; simply nurturing her health all day bored her to death. The dose of medicine every hour, the watching of her temperature and diet – it was all very irksome. This was why husband and wife were quarrelling in a shuttered room this stormy night.

So long as Kiran came up with replies, the argument proceeded equally; but in the end she resorted to silence. She sat with her head bowed and her face turned away from Sharat, who now found himself weak and weaponless. He was just about to give up the fight, when the Bearer was heard loudly calling from outside. Sharat opened the door. He was told that a young Brahmin boy had been shipwrecked – he'd swum ashore to their garden. Kiran's anger and misery disappeared when she heard this, and at once she sent some dry clothes from the ālnā. In no time she had warmed a pan of milk and called for the boy to come in.

He had long hair, large round eyes, and no sign of a moustache. Kiran sat with him as he ate, and asked him about himself. She heard that he belonged to a band of travelling players, and his name was Nilkanta. They'd been engaged to perform at the Sinhas' house near by, but had been shipwrecked, and who knew what had happened to the others in the troupe? The boy was a good swimmer, so he'd saved himself. Here he was! Kiran felt a surge of tenderness towards him as she realized how easily he could have died.

'This will be a good thing,' thought Sharat to himself. 'Kiran has something new to do – it will keep her going for a while.' His mother, too, welcomed the merit to be gained from caring for a

Brahmin boy; and Nilkanta himself was pleased to escape from death and his former master into the arms of this rich family.

Before very long, Sharat and his mother began to change their minds. They felt that the boy had stayed long enough – there'd be trouble if they didn't get rid of him soon. Nilkanta had begun to smoke Sharat's hookah in secret, puffing away grandly. On rainy days he would shamelessly take Sharat's favourite silk umbrella and strut around the village making new friends. A dirty stray dog he had petted brazenly frequented Sharat's finely furnished room, leaving pawprints on the spotless floor-cover to record its gracious visits. A large circle of young admirers formed round Nilkanta, and the village mangoes were given no chance to ripen that year.

Kiran was far too lavish with the boy – there was no doubt of that. Her husband and mother-in-law often took her to task for this, but she ignored them. She decked him out like a Babu, giving him Sharat's old shirts and socks, and new shoes, dhoti and chadar. She would call him at whim, to satisfy her need to show affection as well as her sense of fun. She would sit smiling on the bed, *pān*-box beside her, with a maidservant combing and drying her long wet hair, while Nilkanta acted with flamboyant gestures the story of Nala and Damayanti. This way, the long afternoon passed quickly. She tried to get Sharat to come and watch the performance, but this annoyed him, and in any case in front of Sharat Nilkanta's talent failed to shine. Sometimes Kiran's mother-in-law came, attracted by the gods in the story; but her customary afternoon sleepiness soon defeated her piety – she would end up lying on her back.

Nilkanta was often subjected to cuffs and boxes on the ear from Sharat, but used as he was from birth to even harsher methods of discipline he didn't feel either hurt or dishonoured. He firmly believed that just as the world was divided between sea and land, so human life was divided between food and beatings – and beatings were the larger part of it.

It was difficult to tell exactly how old he was. If he was fourteen or fifteen, one would say his face had matured beyond his years; if he was seventeen or eighteen, one would call him underdeveloped. He was younger than he looked, or else he looked younger than he was. Because he had joined the troupe of

players at an early age, he acted Radha, Damayanti, Sita, and
'Vidya's confidante'. The needs of his master and the will of God
coincided, and his growth stopped. Everyone thought of him as
small, and he thought of himself as small: he was never treated as
befitted his true age. Through such causes natural and unnatural,
by the time he was seventeen, he looked more like an overde-
veloped fourteen-year-old than an underdeveloped seventeen-
year-old. His lack of moustache added to this false impression.
Whether from smoking tobacco, or from using language ill-suited
to his years, his lips had an adult curl to them; but his eyes, with
their large pupils, were simple and childish. One could say that
inside he was a child, but his *yātrā*-life had made him adult on the
surface.

Nature's relentless laws, however, worked on him as he stayed
on in Sharat Babu's Chandernagore bungalow. Held back at the
threshold for so long, he quietly crossed it at last. His seventeen
or eighteen years of growth attained their proper ripeness.

The change was not evident from the outside, but it was there
in the way Nilkanta felt hurt and embarrassed when Kiran continued to treat him like a boy. One day she frivolously asked him
to dress as a female *sakhī*: her request was suddenly awkward for
him, though he couldn't see why it was so. These days, if she
asked him to imitate a *yātrā*-performance, he would run from
her sight. He was no longer willing to think of himself as a
juvenile member of a sordid *yātrā*-troupe. He had even made up
his mind to try to learn to read and write with the manager of the
bungalow. But because Nilkanta was Kiran's pet, the manager
couldn't stand him; and so unaccustomed was he to concentrated
study that the letters swam before his eyes. He would sit for
hours on the river-bank leaning against a champak tree, with a
book open on his lap: the water gurgled gently, boats floated past,
fidgety birds on the branches made their irrelevant chirping
comments, and Nilkanta kept his eyes on the book – but what he
was thinking he alone knew, or maybe he didn't. He could hardly
move from one sentence to another, but he liked to feel he was
reading a book. Whenever a boat passed, he would hold up the
book impressively, mutter, and make a great show of reading; but
as soon as the spectators had gone, his enthusiasm waned again.

Formerly he sang *yātrā*-songs mechanically; but now their

melodies caused a strange disturbance in his mind. The words were utterly trivial, full of meretricious wordplay: their meaning was impenetrable – but when he sang,

> O swan, swan, Brahmin twice born,[1]
> Why are you so heartless?
> Say for what good, in this wild wood,
> Do you threaten the life of a princess?

he was suddenly now transported to a different life and world. The familiar scene around him and his insignificant life were transformed into song, took on a new appearance. The swan and the princess created extraordinary pictures in his mind: who he thought he was he couldn't exactly say, but he forgot he was an orphan boy from a *yātrā*-troupe. Just as a miserable grubby child in a wretched hovel somewhere listens at night to the story of 'The Prince, the Princess and the Ruby', and in the dimly lit darkness of his dingy home is released from deprivation, finding in a fairy-tale world in which anything is possible a new beauty, a brighter aspect, a matchless power; so this *yātrā*-boy was able to see, through the tunes of these songs, both himself and his world in a new light. The sound of the water, the rustling of leaves, the call of birds, the smiling face of the kind woman who had given this friendless boy her protection, her loving bangle-laden arms, her preciously beautiful lotus-pink feet – all were transformed into music by who knows what miraculous magic! But another time this musical mirage was swept away: the *yātrā*-boy with his long shaggy hair was rediscovered, and Sharat – informed by the owner of a mango-orchard – was upon him, thwacking him with slaps on his cheeks; and Nilkanta would flee to his band of devoted followers to seek new excitement on land or in water or the branches of trees.

Meanwhile Sharat's brother Satish had come to stay in the house for his Calcutta college-holiday. Kiran was delighted – now she had something new to occupy her. He was equal to her in age: in her dress, manners, or in serving him at meals she teased him at every turn. Sometimes she smeared her palms with vermilion

1. There is a pun here on *dvija*, which can mean either a Brahmin or a bird, because both are 'twice-born': a Brahmin through the sacred-thread ceremony in adolescence, a bird when it hatches from an egg.

and pressed them over his eyes; sometimes she wrote 'monkey' on the back of his shirt; sometimes she bolted his door from outside and ran off merrily. Satish was not a man to be outdone: he would get his own back by stealing her keys, putting chillies in her *pān*, or slyly tying the end of her sari to her bed. Thus they spent the day teasing and chasing and laughing – or quarrelling, weeping, entreating and then making up again.

Something got into Nilkanta now. He could not think of a reason for quarrelling with anyone, yet was full of bitterness and unease. He began to be needlessly nasty to the boys who followed him around; he gave his pet dog undeserved kicks, so that it yelped noisily; he violently slashed at weeds with a stick as he walked along.

Kiran loved to see people eat well, to sit and serve them with their food. Nilkanta was a good eater: it was not hard to get him to take more and more of whatever he liked. So Kiran would often call him and serve him herself – it gave her special pleasure to watch him enjoying his food. But now that Satish was here, Kiran often did not have time to sit with Nilkanta as he ate. Formerly his appetite had not been affected by her absence: he would even rinse the milk-pan and drink the water. But now if she didn't call him he was sick at heart and felt a bitter taste in his mouth: he would rise without finishing, telling the maid in a husky voice that he wasn't hungry. He hoped that Kiran would send for him if she heard about this, entreat him to take some food; he resolved that he would not give in, would go on saying he wasn't hungry. But no one told her, and she didn't send for him: the maidservant finished up the food that was left. He would then turn out the lamp in his room, throw himself down on the dark bed, sobbing and choking and pressing his face into the pillow. But what use was this? Who took any notice? Who came to give him comfort? Eventually sleep – kindest of nurses – came with her gentle touch to bring relief to this sad, motherless boy.

Nilkanta was convinced that Satish was running him down before Kiran. On days when she was silent for no reason, he was sure she was angry with him because of something that Satish had said. He often now prayed to the gods fiercely, 'May I be Satish in another life, and may Satish be me.' He knew that a curse delivered by a Brahmin with full concentration never failed, and he therefore as good as burnt himself with passion as he put the fire of Brahma on to Satish, while peals of merry laughter – Satish's laugh mixed with Kiran's – came down from the room above.

Nilkanta did not dare to come out in open enmity with Satish, but took every opportunity to cause him minor inconveniences. If Satish left his soap on the steps down to the Ganges while he went for a dip, Nilkanta would swoop and run off with it, so that when Satish returned it was no longer there. Once when swimming he suddenly saw his best embroidered shirt floating away: he assumed it had flown in the wind, but there didn't seem to be any wind blowing.

One day Kiran, wanting to entertain Satish, called Nilkanta and asked him to sing some *yātrā*-songs. Nilkanta made no reply. Surprised, she asked what had happened. Again Nilkanta was silent. She asked once more. 'I've forgotten them,' he said, and went out.

At last it was time for Kiran to return home. Everyone started to get ready: Satish too was to go back with them. But no one said anything to Nilkanta. No one seemed even to consider whether he would go or stay. Kiran eventually proposed to take him; but when her mother-in-law, husband and brother-in-law all objected with one voice, Kiran too abandoned her resolve. Finally two days before they were due to leave, she called the boy and gently advised him to return to his village.

To hear her speak tenderly to him again after such long neglect was too much for Nilkanta, and he burst out crying. Kiran's eyes, too, filled with tears. She realized with great distress how wrong she had been temporarily to encourage affection in a person she would have to leave.

Satish was near by at the time. Infuriated by the sight of a grown boy weeping, he snapped, 'Good God! At the drop of a hat, overcome with snivelling!' Kiran rebuked him for this heartless remark. 'You don't understand, *Baudi*,' said Satish. 'You believe in everyone too much. You knew nothing about him, yet you let him live here like a king. He's frightened of being small fry again – that's why he's making such a scene. He knows that a couple of tears will sway you.'

Nilkanta rushed out of the room. In his mind he was stabbing an image of Satish with a knife, piercing him with needles, setting him on fire. Satish's actual body remained unscathed: the only blood that flowed was from Nilkanta's heart.

Satish had brought from Calcutta a fancy inkstand he had purchased, with two shell-boats on either side to hold the ink, and a German silver swan in the middle with its wings spread and beak open to hold the pens. Satish prized this greatly; he would even sometimes polish it carefully with a silk handkerchief. Kiran would often jokingly tap the swan's beak with her finger and sing,

> O swan, swan, Brahmin twice born,
> Why are you so heartless?

– and joking arguments would follow between her and her brother-in-law about it.

The morning before their departure, Satish could not find the inkstand. Kiran laughed and said, 'Your swan has flown away to search for your Damayanti!' But Satish was incensed. He was certain that Nilkanta had stolen the thing – he could even find witnesses who had seen him loitering near Satish's room the previous night. The accused was brought before Satish. Kiran was present too. Satish asked straight out, 'Where have you put the inkstand that you stole from me? Give it back!'

Nilkanta had often received beatings from Sharat for various offences and also for no offences, and had borne them all stoically. But when the theft of the inkstand was ascribed to him in front of Kiran, his large eyes burnt like fire, his chest heaved and choked his throat, and if Satish had said one more word the boy would have pounced like a furious kitten and gouged him with all ten fingernails.

Kiran called him into the next room and asked him in kind, soft tones, 'Nilu, if you have that inkstand, give it me quietly and no one will say anything to you.' Heavy tears welled from his eyes: he covered his face with his hands and wept. Kiran came out of the room and said, 'Nilkanta did not steal your inkstand.'

Sharat and Satish both insisted, 'No one but him could have stolen it.'

'It wasn't him,' said Kiran firmly.

Sharat wanted to fetch Nilkanta to interrogate him, but Kiran said, 'No. I forbid you to ask him anything about the theft.'

'We should search his room and his box,' said Satish.

'If you do that,' said Kiran, 'I shall have nothing more to do with you. You shouldn't cast suspicion on the innocent.'

As she spoke, tears collected in her eyelids. The appeal of those tears in her sad eyes ensured that no further action was taken against Nilkanta. But the unjust treatment of an innocent orphan boy sent a surge of sympathy through Kiran's heart. That evening she entered Nilkanta's room with a fine matching dhoti and chadar, two shirts, a pair of new shoes and a ten-rupee note. Her plan was to put these loving gifts inside his box without telling him. The tin box too had been given by her. Taking her bunch of keys from the end of her sari, she quietly opened the box. But she couldn't fit her presents into it. Cotton-reels, bamboo-twigs, polished shells for cutting green mangoes, the bottoms of broken glasses, and various similar articles were heaped inside it. She decided that if she carefully rearranged these things, everything would go in. She began to empty the box. First of all the cotton-reels, spinning-tops and knives came out; then some clean and dirty clothes, and then, right at the bottom, Satish's precious swan inkstand.

Amazed and flushed, Kiran sat pondering for a long time with the inkstand in her hand. When Nilkanta came into the room from behind her, she never even noticed. He saw everything: realized that Kiran had herself come like a thief to confirm his thieving, and that he had been caught. But how could he explain that he had not stolen like a common thief out of greed, that he'd done it in retaliation, that he'd meant to throw the thing into the river, and only in a moment of weakness had he not thrown it away but had buried it in his box? He was *not* a thief, he was *not* a thief! But then what was he? How could he say what he was? He had stolen something but he was not a thief! The fact that Kiran had suspected him – it was the cruel injustice of this that he would never be able to explain, never be able to bear.

With a long sigh, Kiran put the inkstand back into the box. Like a thief herself, she pressed the dirty clothes on top of it, then those boyish things – cotton-reels, twigs, spinning-tops, shells, pieces of glass; then she arranged her presents and the ten-rupee note.

The next day there was no sign of the Brahmin boy. The villagers said they had not seen him; the police said he was missing. 'We must look at his box now,' said Sharat.

'Not on any account,' said Kiran adamantly.

Later, she fetched the box into her own room, took out the inkstand and secretly threw it into the Ganges.

Sharat and his family went home; the house and garden lay empty. Only Nilkanta's village dog remained. It wandered along by the river, forgetting to eat, searching, searching and howling.

Elder Sister

I

'If you want my opinion,' said Shashi's neighbour Tara after describing in detail how one of the husbands in the village ill-treated his wife, 'husbands like that should have burning coals shoved down their throats.'

Shashi, wife of Jaygopal, was appalled by such a remark. It did not do credit to a wife to wish anything other than the fire of a cheroot to be in a husband's mouth, whatever the circumstances. But when she expressed her dismay, the hard-hearted Tara said with doubled venom, 'Better to be widowed in seven successive lives than have a husband like that.' And ending the conversation there, she went on her way.

'I can't imagine any fault in a husband so bad that one could feel such dreadful things about him,' said Shashi to herself. As she reflected on this, her soft heart swelled with tender feelings towards her own absent husband. She stretched her arms over the part of the bed where he normally slept, kissed the vacant pillow, sensed a whiff of her husband's hair, and then, closing the door, took from a wooden box an almost forgotten photograph of him and some of his letters. She sat alone in her room through the still afternoon, musing and reflecting, tearfully pining for him.

Shashikala and Jaygopal were not recently married. They had been married as children, and now they had children of their own. They had been together for a long time, and lived normally and straightforwardly. There had never been signs of exceptional passion between them. But when, after nearly sixteen years in which they had never been separated, her husband's work had suddenly taken him away, Shashi felt a much more intense love for him. His absence pulled at her heart, tightening the knot of love; feelings whose existence she had never previously known tugged and twinged within her. So despite her years, and despite being a wife and mother, Shashi sat on her lonely bed, day-dreaming like a fresh young bride. The love that had, unbeknown to her, flowed through her life like a river, suddenly woke her with its murmur: she began to see a succession of golden cities and flowering arbours along its banks, whose promise of pleasure was now beyond her reach, a thing of the past. She said to herself, 'When I get my husband back I shall never again let life be dull, or the spring fruitless.' Why had she argued so often with her husband over footling matters? Now, in her intensity of love, she resolved never to be impatient again, never to oppose his wishes or commands. She would meekly and lovingly accept his activities whether good or bad, because nothing was more precious or divine than a husband.

For many years Shashikala had been her parents' beloved only child. So although Jaygopal earned little, he was not anxious about the future. He would inherit from his father-in-law Kaliprasanna enough to live like a prince, in village terms. But very unexpectedly, at an advanced age, Shashikala's parents produced a son. Truth to tell, Shashi was rather scandalized that her parents should have done something so inappropriate to their years; and Jaygopal was not too happy either.

Her parents' love for this child of their old age became extreme. Unknowingly, this new-born, suckling, sleepy brother-in-law robbed Jaygopal of his hopes, seized them in his tiny fists. Hence this job in an Assam tea-garden. Everyone had urged him to look for work nearer home, but whether out of grudge or from the notion that he would quickly rise high there, Jaygopal listened to no one. Leaving Shashi and their children in her father's house, he went off to Assam. It was the first time he had ever been away from her.

Shashikala was very angry with her baby brother for causing this. A grievance that cannot be expressed openly always festers. *He* just sucked at the breast comfortably and shut his eyes in sleep, but his big sister resented having to warm his milk or cool his rice, making her own son late for school. Her resentment upset the whole household.

Within a short time the boy's mother was dead. Before she died she entrusted her baby son to her daughter's care.

It was not long before the motherless infant conquered his

sister's heart. He would leap with a shriek on to her lap and greedily gobble her face and eyes and nose with his toothless little mouth; he would grab her hair in his fist and refuse to let go; he would wake before dawn, snuggle close, tickle her gently and babble; whatever he did she was helpless! Soon he was calling her '*Jiji*' and '*Jijimā*',[1] getting up to mischief when she worked or rested, eating what was forbidden, going where he was forbidden – she gave in totally to this wilful little scallywag. Because he had no mother, his hold on her was all the greater.

II

The boy's name was Nilmani. When he was two years old, his father fell seriously ill. A letter was sent to Jaygopal, telling him to come at once. With great difficulty Jaygopal managed to get leave: when he arrived, Kaliprasanna was dying.

Before he died, he entrusted his little son to the guardianship of Jaygopal and left a quarter of his estate to his daughter. Jaygopal therefore had to resign from his job and return to manage the estate.

Husband and wife were reunited after a long time. If a material thing gets broken it can be dovetailed together again; but there are no clean edges along which two people who have been apart for a long time can be stuck together. This is because the mind is a living substance, changing and ripening with every moment. For Shashi, to be reunited was a new emotional experience. It was as if she were marrying her husband again. The staleness that the habits of a long-standing marriage bring about had been dispelled by absence; she felt she was receiving her husband back more fully than before. She promised herself: 'Whatever the future may bring, however long I live, I shall never let this bright new love for my husband grow dim.'

But Jaygopal's feelings at the reunion were different. When they had lived together before, all his interests and habits had been bound up with Shashi: she had grown to be a permanent feature in his life – if ever he was without her, gaps were made in his daily routine. So when he first went away, Jaygopal found himself at a loss. But gradually the gaps were patched over with

1. i.e., '*Didi*' and '*Didimā*'. See Glossary.

new routines. Not only that. Formerly, his life had been leisurely and serene; but now, over the last two years, he had become so ambitious to improve his circumstances that he thought of little else. Compared to this, his old way of life seemed thin as a shadow. In women, the greatest changes are worked by love; in men, by ambition.

Jaygopal did not get his wife back after two years exactly as she had been before. His little brother-in-law had added a new dimension to her life – one which was completely unknown to him, one in which he had no part. His wife tried to get him to share her love for the boy, but I cannot say she was successful. She would bring Nilmani in her arms and smilingly hold him up to her husband: Nilmani would cling to her, bury his face in her shoulder, would not acknowledge any kinship with him. She wanted her little brother to show Jaygopal his tricks – but Jaygopal was not very interested, and the boy was not keen either. Jaygopal could not for the life of him understand why this skinny, large-headed, solemn, dark-complexioned child deserved such affection.

Women are never slow to perceive real feelings. Shashi soon saw that Jaygopal was not enamoured of Nilmani. She then became very protective: doing her utmost to keep him away from her husband's withering stare. The child became her secret treasure, the object of her love alone. Everyone knows that the more love is secretive, the more it grows.

When Nilmani cried, Jaygopal was extremely irritated, so Shashi would clasp him to her breast trying with all the force of her embrace to soothe him. And when her husband's sleep was disturbed by Nilmani's crying, and he shouted out in fury, full of aggression towards him, Shashi herself felt guilty and embarrassed. She swept him out of earshot, and soothed him to sleep again with meek and adoring repetitions of 'My treasure, my jewel, my precious'.

Quarrels between children can flare up for various reasons. Formerly on such occasions Shashi would punish her own children, taking her brother's part because he had no mother. But now a change of judge had brought about a change in the penal code. Nilmani had to suffer harsh punishments, unfair and undeserved. The injustice of it cut his sister to the quick: she would take her disgraced little brother to her room, give him sweets and toys, caress him and kiss him, do everything she could to heal the child's wounded feelings.

The result was this: the more Shashi doted on Nilmani the more Jaygopal resented him, and the more dislike Jaygopal showed towards Nilmani the more Shashi adored him. Jaygopal never actually ill-treated his wife, and Shashi continued to serve him with silent, meek devotion; it was only Nilmani who was a concealed but ever-growing bone of contention between them. Silent animosity and jealousy of this kind is harder to bear than open conflict.

III

Nilmani's head was out of proportion to his body. It was as if the Creator had blown a bubble on the end of a stick. Doctors were afraid sometimes that the boy would be as fragile and short-lived as a bubble. It took him a long time to learn to talk and walk. His mournful, solemn face made one think that his parents had piled their elderly worries on to this little child's head. But his big sister's careful nurturing got him through the dangerous years, and he reached the age of six.

In the month of Kārtik, Shashi dressed Nilmani up as a little gentleman in a red-bordered dhoti and performed the *bhāiphõṭā* ceremony, marking his forehead with sandal-paste. Tara – the blunt-speaking neighbour mentioned earlier – appeared then, and picked a quarrel with Shashi. 'What good will the paste do,' she said, 'when in fact you've been secretly ruining him?'

Shashi was thunderstruck. The rumour was – so Tara told her – that she and her husband had defaulted on the payment of duty on Nilmani's estate, so that they could buy it back at auction in the name of Jaygopal's cousin. Shashi cursed those who put about such slanders: they deserved to catch leprosy.

She then went tearfully to her husband and told him what people were saying. 'You can't trust anyone these days,' said Jaygopal. 'Upen is my cousin: I was entirely happy to leave the management of Nilmani's property to him. I had no idea he had secretly defaulted on payment of duty, and bought the estate at Hasilpur himself.'

'Aren't you going to sue him?' said Shashi in amazement.

'How can I sue my cousin?' said Jaygopal. 'And there'd be no point – it would just be a waste of money.'

To trust her husband's word was Shashi's highest duty, but she had no faith in him now. Her happy family, her loving home, now seemed monstrously ugly. What had been a haven was suddenly a cruel trap, squeezing both her and her brother on all sides. How could she, a woman, on her own, protect the hapless Nilmani? What refuge was there? The more she thought, the more her heart filled with horror, and the more it filled with love for her little brother in his plight. She wondered if there was a way in which she could appeal to the Governor-General: maybe she could even write to the Queen of England to restore her brother's inheritance. The Queen would never have allowed the Hasilpur estate – which brought in 758 rupees a year for Nilmani – to be sold. She went on thinking about how she would appeal to the Queen to secure full restitution from her husband's cousin; but suddenly now Nilmani developed a fever, and started to have convulsions.

Jaygopal called the local Indian doctor. When Shashi begged him to call a better doctor he said, 'Why, is Matilal such a bad one?'

Shashi fell at his feet, implored him. 'All right,' said Jaygopal, 'I'll bring the doctor from town.'

Shashi clasped Nilmani to her, lay down clutching him to her breast. Nilmani too never took his eyes off her; held on to her lest she should slip away while he was not looking. Even when he fell asleep, he continued to grasp her sari.

In the evening, after a whole day of this, Jaygopal returned and said, 'I couldn't get the town doctor – he's gone to see a patient out of town somewhere. I've got to leave today to attend a court-case. I've told Matilal to visit the patient regularly.'

That night Nilmani began to rave in his sleep. In the morning Shashi, without pausing to consider the matter, boarded a boat with her sick brother and travelled all the way to the doctor's house. The doctor was at home – he had not left to go anywhere. Seeing that Shashi was of good family, he arranged accommodation for her, with an elderly widow in attendance, and started to treat the boy.

The next day Jaygopal arrived. Blazing with anger, he ordered his wife to return with him at once. 'Wild horses couldn't drag

me back,' she said. 'You and your people want to kill Nilmani: he
has no mother, no father, no one but me. I'll protect him.'

'Then stay here,' roared Jaygopal, 'and never set foot in my
house again.'

'*Your* house!' said Shashi, incensed too. 'It's my brother's house!'

'We'll see about that,' said Jaygopal.

For a few days, local people raised an uproar about these
events. The neighbour Tara said, 'If a woman wants to quarrel
with her husband, she should do it comfortably at home. There's
no need to move out. After all, a husband *is* a husband!'

By spending all the money she had with her, and by selling her
ornaments, Shashi managed to save her brother from death. She
then heard that the large piece of land her family owned at Dvari
village, on which their house stood, and which, all told, brought
in an annual income of nearly 1,500 rupees, had been appropriated
by Jaygopal in his own name and in collusion with the zamindar.
The property now belonged to him, not to her brother.

When he had got over his illness and was up again, Nilmani said
piteously, '*Didi*, let's go home.' He missed his playmates – Shashi's
own children. 'Please, *Didi*, let's go home,' he said, over and over
again. His sister could only weep and say, 'Where is our home now?'
But there was no point in weeping. Nilmani had no one in the world
now but his big sister. When this had sunk in, Shashi dried her eyes
and went to see the wife of Tarini Babu, the Deputy Magistrate.

The Deputy Magistrate knew Jaygopal. He was annoyed that a
wife of good family should want to leave her home and quarrel
with her husband over property. Soothing her down, he wrote
urgently to Jaygopal – who came at once, forced his wife and
brother-in-law on to a boat and took them home.

For the second time, husband and wife were reunited after a
separation. Fated to be united!

Nilmani was delighted to be back playing with his friends. It
broke Shashi's heart to see his carefree happiness.

IV

In the winter the English District Magistrate went out on tour
and pitched his tent in the village, hoping to do some hunting
there. Nilmani met the Magistrate on a village-path. The other

boys made scarce, giving him as wide a berth as Chanakya recommends for animals with sharp nails, teeth or horns. But the solemn Nilmani stayed to examine the *sāheb* with calm curiosity.

'Do you go to school?' asked the Magistrate pleasantly.

The boy silently nodded, 'Yes.'

'What texts are you reading?' asked the *sāheb*.

Not understanding the meaning of the word 'text', Nilmani went on staring at the Magistrate. Later, he enthusiastically described this meeting with the Magistrate to his sister.

That afternoon Jaygopal dressed himself up in chapkan, pantaloons and turban, and went to pay his respects to the honourable Magistrate. Petitioners, defendants, messengers and constables crowded round. To escape the heat, the *sāheb* had emerged from his tent and was sitting at a camp-table in the shade outside. Offering Jaygopal a stool he questioned him about local affairs. Jaygopal swelled with pride to be given this privileged position in front of the villagers, and thought, 'If only the Chakrabartis and Nandis could see me now!'

It was then that a veiled woman appeared, bringing Nilmani with her, and stood before the Magistrate. '*Sāheb*,' she said, 'I entrust this orphaned little brother of mine to you: please look after him.'

Seeing for the second time this serious, large-headed little boy, with a woman who was clearly of good family, the *sāheb* stood up and said, 'Come into the tent.'

'I shall say right here what I have to say,' said the woman. Jaygopal went pale and began to fidget. The curious villagers closed in avidly; but withdrew when the *sāheb* raised his cane.

Holding her brother's hand Shashi told his whole story from beginning to end. From time to time Jaygopal tried to interrupt, but the Magistrate, flushed with anger, snapped at him to shut up and, pointing with his cane, directed him to stand up from his stool. Jaygopal stood in silence, inwardly fuming at Shashi. Nilmani pressed against his sister and listened open-mouthed.

When Shashi had finished her account the Magistrate asked Jaygopal some questions, and after hearing his replies fell silent. Then, addressing Shashi, he said, 'My dear, although I can't hear this case myself, you can rest assured that I shall do what needs to be done. You can return home with your brother without fear.'

'So long as he cannot get back the house which is his by rights,' said Shashi, 'I shall not dare to take him there. Only if you keep Nilmani yourself will he be safe.'

'Where will you go?' asked the *sāheb*.

'I shall return to my husband's house. *I* have nothing to fear.'

With a slight smile, the *sāheb* gave in. He agreed to take away this skinny, dark, serious, calm, gentle, amulet-wearing Bengali boy.

As Shashi said goodbye, the boy clung to her sari. 'Don't worry, little chap,' said the *sāheb*. 'Come with me.'

With tears streaming behind her veil, Shashi said, 'Darling brother, go now – you'll see your *Didi* again.' Then she embraced him, stroked his head and back, somehow extricated the end of her sari from his grasp and swiftly walked away. The *sāheb* put his left arm round Nilmani, but he cried out, *'Didi, Didi!'* Shashi turned once and waved at him with her right hand, trying to send him silent consolation. Then, heart-broken, she continued on her way.

Once again husband and wife were reunited in their long-familiar home. Fated to be united! But this reunion did not last long. For not long afterwards the villagers heard one morning that Shashi had been smitten with cholera during the night and had been cremated that very night. No one made any comment on this. The neighbour Tara would sometimes shout out what she thought, but people told her to shut up.

When she said goodbye to her brother, Shashi said that he would see her again. I do not know if that promise has been fulfilled.

Fury Appeased

I

Gopinath Shil's wife Giribala lived on the top floor of Ramanath Shil's three-storey house. There were tubs of *bel*-flowers and roses outside the southern door of her bedroom. The roof had a high parapet around it, with spaces between the bricks so that one could look at the view. The bedroom was hung with engravings of foreign ladies in various states of dress and undress; but the reflection of the sixteen-year-old Giribala in the large mirror opposite the door was not inferior to any of the pictures on the wall.

Giribala's beauty was like a sudden ray of light, a surprise, an awakening, a shock. It could be quite overwhelming. One felt on seeing her, 'I was not prepared for this. She is absolutely different from what I see around me all the time.' And she herself was thrilled by her own beauty. Her body seemed brimful of youth, like foaming wine in a beaker − overflowing in her dress and ornaments, movements, gestures, the tilt of her neck, the dance of her steps, the jingle of her bracelets and anklets, her laugh, her sharp retorts, her brilliant glances.

She was drunk with the wine of her beauty. She was often seen restlessly pacing on her roof, draped in brightly coloured clothes: as if she wished to dance with every limb to an unexpressed tune in her mind. She had a kind of joy, driving and hurling her body into movement; she seemed to receive from the various facets of her beauty a strange pulsation, a throbbing in her blood. She would tear a leaf off a plant, raise it high and release it on the breeze: the graceful curve of her arm soared towards the clouds like an unseen bird released from a cage, while her bangles tinkled and her sari slipped from her shoulder. Or else she would pick up a clod from a tub and pointlessly scatter it about; or standing on tiptoe glance through the spaces in the wall at the great world beyond; or spin her sari-end around her, so that the keys that were tied to it jingled. Maybe she would go to the mirror, unbind her hair and whimsically plait it again – tying the hair at the root with a string, holding the end of the string in her jasmine-white teeth, and lifting her arms behind her head to coil the plaits up tightly. With nothing to do next, she would spread herself out on the soft bed, like moonlight shining through leaves.

She had no children; nor in this wealthy home did she have any housework. Alone every day like this, it was becoming impossible for her to contain herself. She had a husband, but he was outside her control. It had somehow escaped his notice that she had grown out of her childhood so fully.

She had, on the contrary, received his affection when she *was* a child. He had played truant from school, evaded his dozing guardians, to come and flirt with his girlish young bride. Even though they lived in the same house, he wrote her letters on fancy notepaper, showing them proudly to his schoolfriends. His feelings were amorous enough to be ruffled by clashes with his wife over small or imaginary matters.

Since then, his father had died and Gopinath had himself become master of the house. Unseasoned planks are soon attacked by woodworm. Gopinath had gained independence early: there were many pests to fasten themselves on to him. His visits to the inner part of the house became rarer as he roved further and further afield.

To be a leader is exciting; society can be a potent drug. The desire that Napoleon had to extend his influence over men and history can be felt on a smaller scale in the drawing-room. It is marvellously exciting to create and bind together with crude wit an admiring circle of cronies, to lord it over them and win their applause. Many are willing to embrace debt and scandal and ruin to obtain this.

Gopinath found it thrilling to be a leader. Each day, new feats of wit brought him ever greater glory. In the eyes of his followers, his repartee was unparalleled. Blinded by vanity and excitement to all other duties and feelings, he abandoned himself completely to a ceaseless social whirl.

Meanwhile Giribala, imperiously beautiful, ruled a realm without subjects from her bedroom's desolate throne. She knew that God had given her a sceptre; she knew she could conquer with a glance the vast world she could see through the gaps in the parapet – yet no one in the world was hers.

She had a pert and witty servant called Sudhamukhi – Sudho for short – who could sing, dance, make up verses, celebrate Giribala's beauty and rail that it was wasted on so boorish a husband. Giribala leant on her utterly. She would wallow in Sudho's praise of her face, figure and complexion; sometimes she demurred, took pleasure in rebuking her for flattery – but when Sudho swore by her opinion, Giribala easily believed her. When Sudho sang, 'I have signed myself in bondage at your feet', Giribala took this as a hymn to her own flawless, lac-painted feet, and imagined a lover rolling before them. But alas, despite the victorious jingle of her anklets as she strode to and fro on her empty roof, no lover came to enslave himself to those feet.

Gopinath, however, was enslaved to Labanga, who acted at the theatre. She was wonderful at swooning on stage, and whenever she broke into artificial tears, nasally sobbing 'Lord of my life, Lord of my soul', the audience in their long stockings and waistcoats worn over dhotis would roar, 'Excellent, excellent.'[1]

Giribala had often heard descriptions of Labanga's extraordinary talent from her husband (he still came to her occasionally). She did not know the full extent of his infatuation, but she felt jealous all the same. She could not bear to think that another woman had charms and accomplishments which she lacked. She frequently asked, with jealous curiosity, to be taken to the theatre; but her husband refused.

Finally one day she gave Sudho some money and sent her there. When she came back, she spoke of the actresses with disgust, frowning, screwing up her nose. Really, in God's name, they should be beaten on the brow with a broomstick, and men who fell for their ugly figures and phoney movements deserved the same treatment! This reassured Giribala a little. But with her husband virtually cut off from her now, her doubts returned. She voiced them to Sudho, who swore on her life that Labanga was as ugly as a burnt stick dressed in rags. Giribala, unable to see what her husband saw in the actress, smarted with this blow to her pride.[2]

In the end one evening she secretly went to the theatre with

1. In English.
2. *abhimān:* see p. 131, n. 1.

Sudho. Forbidden acts are thrilling! The soft throbbing in her
arteries made the brightly lit, crowded stage – filled with music,
surrounded by spectators – all the more wondrous to behold.
Instead of her lonely, cheerless room, here was a festive world,
gorgeous, beautiful. It was like a dream.

The musical play 'Fury Appeased'[1] was being performed that
day. The warning bell rang, the band stopped playing, the eager
spectators fell silent for a moment, the footlights brightened, the
curtain rose, a troupe of girls beautifully dressed as the milkmaids
of Vraj danced to musical accompaniment, the theatre resounded
with bursts of clapping and roars of approval from the audience –
and Giribala's youthful blood surged. The rhythm of the music,
the lights, the brilliant costumes and the bursts of applause made
her forget for a moment her whole domestic world. She had
found a place of beautiful, unfettered liberty.

Sudho edged up to her at intervals and whispered nervously,
'Bauṭhākrun, it's time to go home. If the Master finds out, we'll be
done for!' Giribala took no notice. Nothing frightened her now.

The performance neared its climax. Radha was in an almighty
huff; Krishna was thrashing hopelessly – his moans and appeals
were getting him nowhere. Giribala seethed with outrage, felt as
exultant as Radha herself at Krishna's discomfiture. No one ever
assailed *her* like this – neglected, deserted wife that she was; but
how thrilling it was to realize that she too could make a lover
groan! She had heard that beauty could be ruthless, had guessed
how it might be so: now, in the light and music of the stage, she
saw its power in action. It set her brain on fire.

At last the curtain fell, the gas lights dimmed, the audience
started to leave; Giribala sat in a trance. She had no thought of
leaving the theatre to return home. The performance would
surely go on for ever! The curtain would rise again, Krishna
would be crushed by Radha; nothing else was conceivable. 'Bauṭhākrun,' said Sudho, 'what are you doing? Come on! They're
turning out the lights!'

Late that night Giribala returned to her room. A lamp flickered
in a corner; there was not a soul or a sound – just an old
mosquito-net stirring in the breeze above the empty bed. Life

---

1. *mānbhañjan* (the title of the story). See Krishna in the Glossary.

seemed horribly mean and trivial. Where was that brightly lit musical realm, where she could reign at the world's centre, dispensing her greatness, where she would no longer be merely an unknown, unloved, insignificant, ordinary woman.

From now on she went to the theatre each week. Gradually the rapture of her first visit faded: she could now detect the make-up of the actors and actresses' faces, the lack of real beauty, the falseness of the acting; but she remained addicted to it. Like a warrior thrilling to the sound of martial music, her heart leapt each time the curtain went up. For an Empress of Beauty, what throne was more magical than this high, enchanting stage, separate from the world, lettered in gold, adorned with scene-paintings, strung with a fabulous web of music and poetry, pressed by enraptured spectators, pregnant with off-stage mysteries, revealed to all by garlands of brilliant lights?

On the night that she first saw her husband at the theatre, loudly appreciating one of the actresses, how she despised him! She decided bitterly that if the day came when her husband, lured by her beauty, were to fall at her feet like a scorched insect, enabling her to walk away grandly, her very toenails shining with contempt, only then would her wasted beauty and youth be avenged! But how could such a day come? She hardly saw him now. She had no idea of his movements, where he went to with his gang of followers, driving them on like dust before a storm.

On a night of full moon in Caitra, Giribala, dressed in the light-orange colours of the spring, sat on her roof, the end of her sari floating in the breeze. Though her husband never came to her, Giribala had not given up her constant changes of clothes and ornaments. Jewels created a stunning effect when she wore them – a gleaming, tinkling aura around her. Today she wore armlets, a necklace of rubies and pearls, and a sapphire ring on her left little finger. Sudho sat by her and sometimes stroked her soft, perfect lotus-pink feet, saying with artless eagerness, 'O *Bauṭhākrun*, if I were a man I would clasp these feet to my breast and die!' Giribala laughed haughtily and said, 'You would die before that, for I'd kick you away! Stop blabbering. Sing me that song.' On the quiet and moonlit roof-top, Sudho sang:

> I have signed myself in bondage at your feet.
> Let all in Vrindavan witness it!

It was ten o'clock at night. Everyone had finished their dinner and gone to bed. Suddenly Gopinath appeared, smeared with pomatum, silk scarf flowing; and Sudho, mightily flustered, hastily pulled down her veil and fled.

'My day has come,' thought Giribala to herself. She did not look up. She sat as still as Radha, proud and dignified. But the curtain did not rise, Krishna did not roll at her feet in his head-dress of peacock feathers, no one burst out singing, 'Why darken the moon by hiding your face?' In a gruff and tuneless voice, Gopinath said, 'The key please.'

On a moonlit spring night like this, after so long a separation, that these should be his first words! Was all that was written in poems, plays and novels utterly false? On the stage, the lover would have come with a song and fallen at his lady-love's feet; her husband as a member of the audience would have melted at the scene – but here he was on a roof on a spring night, saying to his matchless young wife, 'The key please.' No music, no love, no magic, no sweetness – it was so utterly *banal*!

The breeze sighed heavily now – pained, so it seemed, by this insult to all the world's poetry. Fragrance spread across the roof from the tubs of *bel*-flowers; Giribala's unbound tresses blew across her face and eyes; her scented spring-coloured sari fluttered uneasily. She swallowed her pride and stood up. Taking her husband's hand, she said, 'Come into the bedroom – I'll give you the key.' Today her crying *would* make him cry, her lonely fantasies *would* be fulfilled, her divine weapons *would* be used and would triumph! She was *sure*. 'I haven't got long to wait,' said Gopinath. 'Give me the key.'

'I'll give you the key and everything it locks,' said Giribala. 'But tonight I shan't let you go out.'

'That's impossible,' said Gopinath. 'I've got to go.'

'Then I shan't give you the key,' said Giribala.

'You'll give it or else!' said Gopinath. 'Just you try not to give it to me.' He noticed then that there were no keys tied to the end of her sari. He went into the bedroom, pulled open the dressing-table drawer: no keys there either. He broke open her hair-dressing box, found collyrium, vermilion, hair-string and other things – but no key. He rumpled the bedding, upturned the mattress, smashed the cupboard, ransacked the whole room.

Giribala stood in silence, gripping the door and looking out at the roof. Seething with rage and frustration, Gopinath shouted, 'I'm telling you to give me the key, or there'll be trouble.' She made no reply. He then grabbed hold of her, wrenched off her armlets, her necklace and rings, kicked her, and left.

No one in the house woke up; no one near by knew anything; the moonlit night remained as still as ever; peace seemed to reign unbroken. But if the pounding in Giribala's heart could have been heard outside, the serene and moonlit Caitra night would have been split through and through with a fierce howl of agony. Such total silence; such fearful heart-break!

All nights end, even this. Giribala could not reveal – even to Sudho – her shame and defeat. She thought of killing herself, of tearing to shreds her incomparable beauty, to avenge her loveless state. But she realized that nothing would be gained by that: the world would remain unaffected, no one would feel the loss. There was no pleasure in living, but no consolation in dying.

'I shall go back to my parents,' said Giribala. Her parents' house was a long way from Calcutta. Everyone told her not to go, but she listened to no one and took no one with her. And meanwhile Gopinath too went off on a boat-trip with his cronies – no one knew where.

II

Gopinath attended nearly every performance at the Gandharva Theatre. Labanga was playing the title-role in *Manorama*; and Gopinath and his followers sat in the front row and cheered and threw pouches of money on to the stage. The noise they made was sometimes very annoying to the rest of the audience. But the theatre-managers never had the courage to stop them.

One day Gopinath, rather the worse for drink, got into the Green Room and caused complete uproar. He somehow thought he had been slighted by one of the actresses, and was now assaulting her. The whole theatre was aroused by the actress's screams and Gopinath's stream of abuse. This was more than the managers could stand. The police were called to throw him out.

Gopinath was determined to get his own back for this insult. A month before the *pūjā*-holiday, the managers announced – with great publicity – further performances of *Manorama*. Calcutta was festooned with playbills; it was as if the goddess of the city was wearing a *nāmābali* with the author's name inscribed. But meanwhile Labanga, the leading actress in the play, disappeared, whisked away on a boat-trip by Gopinath.

The theatre-managers were completely flummoxed. They waited for some days, but eventually had to rehearse a new actress in the role of Manorama, delaying the opening night. Not that this did much harm. The theatre was full to bursting. Hundreds of people had to be turned away at the door. The critics were ecstatic – and news of this reached Gopinath, far away though he was. He could not keep away any longer. Consumed with curiosity, he returned to Calcutta to see the play.

In the first half, the curtain rose on Manorama in her in-laws' house, meanly dressed like a servant, going about her housework in furtive, cowed, timid fashion, saying nothing and hiding her face. In the second, her greedy husband had sent her back to her parents' house so that he could marry a millionaire's daughter. On examining his new bride after the wedding, he found she was Manorama again, this time dressed not as a servant but as a princess: her incomparable beauty, decked in jewels and finery, shone all around. In childhood she had been stolen from her rich parents' home and brought up in poverty. Many years later, her father had found her again, and brought her back to his house. Now, with new lavishness, she was married to her husband for the second time. A post-wedding 'Fury Appeased' scene now began.

But all hell had broken loose in the audience. While Manorama's face had been hidden by a servant's dirty veil, Gopinath had sat quietly. But when she stood up in the bridal chamber, in all her beauty, unveiled, dressed in red, glittering with jewels, inclining her head with indescribable *hauteur*, directing at all, but especially at Gopinath, a fiercely contemptuous stare, sharp as lightning, so that all the hearts of the audience leapt and the whole theatre rocked with a barrage of applause: it was then that Gopinath jumped up and yelled, 'Giribala, Giribala!' He ran and tried to leap on to the stage – but the musicians restrained him.

Outraged by this interruption to their pleasure, the audience shouted in English and Bengali, 'Get him out, throw him out.'

Choking like a madman, Gopinath screamed, 'I'll kill her, I'll kill her.'

The police came and dragged him from the theatre. All of Calcutta continued to feast their eyes on Giribala's performance; all except for Gopinath.

Ṭhākurdā

I

The zamindars of Nayanjor were at one time regarded as true gentlemen – 'Babus' – a title that in those days was not at all easy to achieve. Today, no one can be called 'Raja' or 'Raybahadur' without the ritual of dances, dinners, horse-races, flattery and connections; likewise in those days great efforts were needed to win from the public the name of 'Babu'.

The 'Babus' of Nayanjor used to tear off the borders of their Dhaka muslins before they wore them, because the borders were too coarse for their aristocratic skins; they spent lakhs of rupees on marrying their pet kittens; and on one particular festive occasion they were said to have turned night into day not only by the number of lights but by showering real silver tinsel to simulate the sun's rays. Such grandeur could obviously not be handed down intact to their heirs. Like oil in a multi-wicked lamp, it was soon burnt away.

Our friend Kailaschandra Raychaudhuri was a burnt-out scion of the famous Nayanjor Babus. At his birth, the lamp was nearly out of oil; with his father's death, it spluttered in a final show of funereal excess and then went out completely. Assets were sold to pay off debts; the remainder was far too little to keep up the name of the family. So Kailas Babu left Nayanjor and came with his son to Calcutta; but before long his son too abandoned a faded existence in this world for the world beyond, leaving an only daughter.

We were neighbours of Kailas Babu. Our own history was entirely different. My father had earned his wealth through his own efforts, counting every paisa, economizing even in the length of his dhoti,[1] and never aspiring to be a 'Babu'. As his only son, I was grateful to him. I was proud to have acquired some education,

1. Traditionally gentlemen in Bengal wear the dhoti long, reaching to their ankles. To 'wear it short' is a metaphor for miserliness or ill-breeding.

to have enough means to hold my head high without too much effort. It's better to inherit Company Bonds in a small iron box than an empty store of ancestral glories.

Probably this is why I was so irritated when Kailas Babu tried to draw hefty cheques on the failed bank of his ancestry! I felt that he somehow despised my father for earning his own money. It made me furious – who was he to despise us? A man who had sacrificed a lot, resisted many temptations, had no desire to be famous; who had through effort and care, intelligence and skill beaten all obstacles, seizing every chance to make his pile, building it with his own hands: *he* was not to be despised because he didn't wear his dhoti below his knees!

I was young then, this was why I reacted like this, fumed like this. Now I'm older, and it doesn't bother me any more. I'm well off; I lack for nothing. If a man who has nothing gets pleasure from sneering, it doesn't cost me a penny, and maybe the poor fellow gets some consolation from it.

It was striking that no one found Kailas Babu irritating except me, for he had a rare sort of innocence. He involved himself totally in the feelings and activities of his neighbours. He had smiles for them all, from the youngest to the eldest; he took pleasure in inquiring kindly about everyone, whoever they were and wherever they were. At every encounter he would launch into a stream of questions: 'How are you? How is Shashi? Is your father well? I hear that Madhu's boy has fever – is he better now? I haven't seen Haricharan Babu for a long time now – has he been ill? How about Rakhal? Is everyone at home well?' – and so on.

He was always beautifully dressed. He didn't own many clothes, but he daily aired them in the sun: his waistcoat, chadar and shirt – together with his pillowcase, mat and ancient bedspread – were brushed and hung on a line, then folded and placed neatly on the *ālnā*. He seemed when one saw him to be always out in his Sunday best. His room, though poorly furnished, was spotless; he appeared to be better off than he was. For lack of servants, he would shut the door of his room and neatly crimp his dhoti himself, and carefully press his chadar and shirt-sleeves. He had lost his family's huge estates, but had managed to keep from the jaws of poverty a valuable rose-water spray, a pomatum-pot, a gold saucer, a silver hookah, an expensive shawl, an old-fashioned pair of pyjamas, and a turban. If occasion arose, he would get these out and revive the glory and world-wide fame of the Babus of Nayanjor.

Gentle and natural though he was, he could sometimes be conceited – but only out of loyalty to his ancestors. People indulged this: they found it rather charming. They called him 'Ṭhākurdā' – Grandfather – and constantly gathered at his house. But lest the cost of tobacco became too much for his slender means, someone would bring some along and say, 'Ṭhākurdā, have a taste of this – it's beautiful.' Ṭhākurdā would take a few puffs and say, 'Not bad, not bad at all', then speak of tobacco that cost 60 or 65 rupees an ounce: would anyone like to try it? But to say 'yes' would mean a hunt for the key, or the assertion that his old servant Ganesh, that rascal, must have put the tobacco heaven knows where – a charge that Ganesh accepted serenely – till everyone chorused, 'Don't worry, Ṭhākurdā, it wouldn't have agreed with us: this tobacco will be fine.'

Ṭhākurdā smiled at this, and didn't repeat his offer. When people got up to leave, he would say, 'Well then, when are you coming to have a bite with me?' 'We can fix that another time,' they would answer. 'Fine,' said Ṭhākurdā, 'let it rain a bit, and get a bit cooler. We can't have a proper blow-out in this heat.' When the rain came, no one reminded him of his promise; and if ever the subject came up, everyone said, 'Better wait till the rains are over.'

His friends would agree that it did not befit him to live in such a small place, that it must be very trying for him; but it was so difficult to find a decent place in Calcutta! It could take five or six years to find a good-sized rented house. 'Never mind that, my friends,' said Ṭhākurdā, 'it's a pleasure to live so near you. I have a big house at Nayanjor, but I don't feel at home there.' I'm sure that Ṭhākurdā knew that everyone understood his true position; and when he pretended that the defunct estate at Nayanjor still existed, and everyone played along with this, he knew in his heart that this mutual deception was just an expression of friendship.

But I found it disgusting! When one is young one wants to stamp on vanity, however harmless, and foolishness is less forgivable than many more serious sins. Kailas Babu was not exactly stupid; everyone sought his help and advice; but concerning the glories of Nayanjor, he had no sense at all. People loved him too much to object to the nonsense he spoke, so he gave it free rein; and if anyone sang the praises of Nayanjor, he happily swallowed the lot, never suspecting for a moment that others might doubt it.

Often I wished I could openly knock down, with a couple of cannon-shots, the old and false fortress in which he lived, which he thought to be permanent. If a hunter sees a bird conveniently perched on a nearby branch, he wants to shoot it; if a boy sees a hanging boulder on a mountainside, he wants to send it rolling down with a kick. To give a final push to a thing which is just on the point of falling, but which still hangs on, is a satisfying act and brings applause from spectators. Kailas Babu's lies were so simple-minded, so slenderly based; they danced so wantonly before the guns of Truth, that I longed to destroy them in a trice: only my laziness and deference to convention held me back.

II

In so far as I can analyse my past state of mind, I think there was another deep-seated reason for my malice towards Kailas Babu. This needs some explanation.

Although I was a rich man's son, I passed my MA on time; and despite my youth, I did not indulge in low pleasures or company. Even after my parents' death, I was not corrupted by becoming master of the family. As regards my appearance, to say I was handsome would be conceited, but it would not be untrue. So my value in the marriage-market of Bengal was certainly high, and I was determined to capitalize on it fully. A beautiful, educated, only daughter of a rich man was what I wanted.

Proposals came from far and wide, offering dowries of 10,000 or 20,000 rupees. I weighed them up carefully and objectively, but none of them seemed quite right. I found myself agreeing with Bhababhuti:

> Who knows if my equal can be born?
> The world is wide and life is long –

but I wondered if so rare an article would ever be found within Bengal's modest confines.

Parents fulsomely sang my praises, and offered me various *pūjā*s; and this (whether I liked their daughters or not) was quite congenial to me. A decent fellow like me deserved their *pūjā*s! In the Shastras one reads that whether the gods grant favours or not, they are angry if they don't receive their proper *pūjā*s: regular offerings to me gave me equally high ideas.

I have mentioned that Ṭhākurdā had an only granddaughter. I had often seen her, but had never considered her beautiful. I had therefore no thought of marrying her. I expected, though, that Kailas Babu – personally or through some intermediary – would have made an offering to me, with his granddaughter's marriage in mind, simply because I was a good catch. But he didn't do that. I heard that he had said to some friend that the Babus of Nayanjor never on any account made the first move: even if it meant that his granddaughter remained unmarried, he would never break this rule. I was very offended by this, and my anger lasted for a long time. It was only my good breeding that made me keep quiet about it.

My nature was such, however, that in my anger there was a spark of humour, like lightning linked to thunder. I could not do outright injury to the old man, but I was tempted by an amusing plan. I described earlier how people used to come out with all sorts of fibs in order to please him. A retired Deputy Magistrate living nearby often said, 'Ṭhākurdā, whenever I met the Lieutenant-Governor he always asked about the Babus of Nayanjor – he said that the Rajas of Burdwan and the Babus of Nayanjor were the only really noble families in Bengal.' Ṭhākurdā was very chuffed at this, and if he met the retired Deputy Magistrate would ask amidst other pleasantries, 'How is the Lieutenant-Governor? And the *memsāheb*? And are all their children well?' He intended to visit the Lieutenant-Governor one day soon. But the Deputy Magistrate knew that many Lieutenant-Governors and Governor-Generals would come and go before the famous four-horse coach of Nayanjor would be ready for the visit.

One morning I went to Kailas Babu and, taking him aside, said confidentially, 'Ṭhākurdā, yesterday I was at the Lieutenant-Governor's levee. He started talking about the Babus of Nayanjor, and I told him that Kailas Babu of Nayanjor was living in

Calcutta. He was very sorry that he had not been to see you all this time, and said that he would visit you privately today at noon.'

Anyone else would have seen the absurdity of this, and even Kailas Babu himself would have laughed if he had heard it told about anyone else; but applied to himself he did not doubt the news in the slightest. He was both delighted and flustered: where would he seat the Lieutenant-Governor? What should he do for him? How should he welcome him? How should he keep up the honour of Nayanjor? He had no idea! On top of that he did not know English, so conversation would be a problem.

'Don't worry about that,' I said. 'He'll have an interpreter with him. But the Lieutenant-Governor is particularly keen that no one else should be present.'

In the afternoon, when most inhabitants of the area were at their offices, or snoozing at home indoors, a carriage and pair drew up outside Kailas Babu's residence. Liveried footmen announced, 'His Excellency the Lieutenant-Governor.' Ṭhākurdā was ready, dressed in old-fashioned white pyjamas and turban; the old servant Ganesh was dressed in his master's dhoti, chadar and shirt. As soon as he heard the announcement, Ganesh ran panting and trembling to the door, and, bowing low in repeated salaams, showed into the room a close friend and contemporary of mine, dressed in English clothes.

Spreading his one valuable shawl on to a stool, and seating the bogus Lieutenant-Governor there, Kailas Babu delivered a long and excessively humble speech in Urdu. He then presented, on a gold plate, one of his carefully preserved heirlooms: a string of Moghul gold coins. Ganesh meanwhile stood at the ready with the rose-water sprinkler and pomatum-pot.

Kailas Babu repeatedly expressed regret that His Excellency had not visited him in his home at Nayanjor, where he would have been able to offer him proper hospitality. In Calcutta he was an exile, a fish out of water: he couldn't do anything properly – and so on.

My friend shook his top-hatted head gravely. He should, according to English custom, have removed his hat indoors; but he tried to keep himself covered as much as possible in case he was found out. No one other than Kailas Babu and his besotted old servant would have fallen for the young Bengali's disguise for a moment.

After ten minutes my friend bowed and made his exit. Footmen, well-rehearsed, took into the impostor's carriage the string of coins on the gold plate, and the shawl from the stool; then, from Ganesh's hands, the rose-water sprinkler and pomatum-pot. Kailas Babu assumed this was the Lieutenant-Governor's custom. I watched all this from the next room, and my ribs were close to cracking with suppressed laughter.

Finally, unable to bear any more, I ran into a room a bit further away: but no sooner had I collapsed into laughter when I saw a girl slumped on a low bed, sobbing. She stood up at once when she saw me. Choking with tears, darting fiery glances from her large, black eyes, she snapped, 'What has my grandfather done to you? Why have you come to trick him? Why have you come?' Then, unable to manage any more, she buried her face in her sari and burst into tears again.

So much for my fit of laughter! All this time it had not entered my head that there was anything other than humour in what I had done. Now I saw I had hit a very tender spot; the revolting cruelty of my action was glaringly exposed; and I slunk out of the room, ashamed and embarrassed, like a kicked dog. What harm had the old man done me? His innocent conceit had never harmed anyone! Why had my own conceit been so malicious?

My eyes were opened to something else as well. For a long time I had thought of Kusum as an item of merchandise waiting on the shelf till some unmarried man's notice was attracted. She was there because I didn't want her: let anyone who wanted have her! Now I understood that here in this house there was a girl with a human heart inside her, a heart whose array of feelings encompassed a land of mystery: to the east an imponderable past, to the west an unknowable future. Did anyone who had such a heart deserve to be picked by the size of her dowry or the shape of her nose and eyes?

I didn't sleep at all that night. The next morning I crept like a thief to Ṭhākurdā's house, carrying all the valuable things we had taken from the old man; I intended to hand them back to the servant without saying anything.

Flummoxed at not finding him, I heard the old man and his granddaughter talking somewhere inside the house. The girl was asking, with sweet affection, 'Grandfather, what did the Lieutenant-

Governor say to you yesterday?' Ṭhākurdā cheerfully spun a long panegyric to the ancient house of Nayanjor, supposedly delivered by the Lieutenant-Governor. The girl received it eagerly.

My eyes filled with tears at the tender, maternal deception played by this young girl on her aged guardian. I sat silently for a long time; when at last Ṭhākurdā had finished his story and gone, I went up to his granddaughter with the things I had deceitfully stolen, placed them before her, and left without a word.

When I saw the old man again, I did *praṇām* to him (previously, in accordance with modern custom, I had not offered any salutation). He presumably thought this sudden show of respect was prompted by the Lieutenant-Governor's visit. He excitedly described it to me, and I happily fell in with his account. Others who were there listening knew that it was all made up, but merrily accepted it.

When everyone had gone I nervously and humbly made a proposal. I said that although my own lineage was in no way comparable to the Babus of Nayanjor, yet . . .

When I had finished, the old man clasped me to his breast and said joyfully, 'I am poor – I never imagined I would have good fortune like this, my friend – my Kusum must have won great merit in heaven for you to favour us now.' He wept as he spoke. This was the first time that Kailas Babu forgot his duty to his noble ancestors and admitted he was poor, admitted it would not do damage to the house of Nayanjor to accept me. I had plotted to humiliate the old man, while he had longed for me, heart and soul, as the worthiest possible groom for his granddaughter.

Guest

I

Matilal Babu, zamindar of Kathaliya, was returning home with his family by boat. One afternoon he moored the boat near a riverside market so that their meal could be prepared. A Brahmin boy came over and asked, 'Where are you going, Babu?' The boy was not more than fifteen or sixteen.

'Kathaliya,' replied Matilal Babu.

'Could you drop me at Nandigram on the way?'

Matilal consented. 'What's your name?' he asked.

'Tarapada,' said the boy.

The fair-skinned boy was beautiful to look at. His smile and his large eyes had the grace of youth. His body – bare except for a stained dhoti – was free of any excess: as if lovingly carved by a sculptor, or as if in a previous life he had been a young sage whose pure religious devotion had removed all grossness, honed him to gleaming, Brahminical perfection.

'Come and wash, *bābā*,' said Matilal Babu tenderly. 'You can eat with us.'

'Leave that to me,' said Tarapada, and without a moment's hesitation he joined in the cooking. Matilal's servant was Hindusthani: he was not very good at cutting up fish.[1] Tarapada took over, and soon had the dish ready, and had cooked some vegetables too with practised skill. He then took a dip in the river, and, opening his bundle, produced a clean white garment and a small wooden comb. He sleeked his long hair away from his forehead and down to his neck, adjusted his glistening sacred thread, and stepped on to the boat.

Matilal Babu invited him into the cabin. His wife and his nine-year-old daughter were there. His wife Annapurna was tenderly attracted to the boy when she saw him, and wondered, 'Whose child is he? Where has he come from? How could his mother bear

1. Fish is eaten much less in North India than in Bengal.

to abandon him?' She placed mats for Matilal and the boy to sit on, side by side. The boy was not a big eater. Annapurna felt he must be shy, and tried to get him to eat this or that; but when he had finished, he would not be tempted to more. He clearly did everything according to his own wishes – but with such ease that there was nothing assertive about him. He was not at all shy.

When everyone had eaten, Annapurna sat him next to her and asked him about his background. She didn't gather much. All she could establish was that the boy had run away from home of his own volition at the age of seven or eight.

'Isn't your mother alive?' asked Annapurna.

'She is,' said Tarapada.

'Doesn't she love you?' asked Annapurna.

Tarapada seemed to find this question peculiar. 'Why shouldn't she love me?' he said, laughing.

'Then why did you leave her?' said Annapurna.

'She has four more sons and three daughters,' said Tarapada.

Pained by this odd reply, Annapurna said, 'What a thing to say! Just because I have five fingers, does it mean that I want to chop one off?'

Tarapada was young, so his life-story was brief; but the boy was a complete original. He was his parents' fourth son, and was still a baby when his father died. Despite there being so many in the house, Tarapada was the darling of all; mother, brothers, sisters and neighbours doted on him. So much so, that his tutor never beat him – everyone would have been appalled if he had. There was no reason for him to leave. Half-starved boys who constantly stole fruit from trees and were thrashed by the owners of the trees – *they* never strayed from the village or their scolding mothers! But this darling of everyone joined a touring *yātrā*-troupe and left his village without a thought.

Search-parties went out and he was brought back. His mother pressed him to her breast and drenched him with tears; his sisters wept too. His elder brother tried to perform his duty as guardian; but he soon abandoned his feeble attempts at discipline, and welcomed him back with open arms. Women invited him to their houses, plied him with even greater displays of affection. But he would not accept ties, even ties of love: his stars had made him a wanderer. If he saw strange boats on the river, or a *sannyāsi*

from a distant region under the local peepul tree, or if gypsies sat
by the river, making mats or wicker baskets, his heart would stir
with longing to be free, to explore the outside world. And after he
had run away two or three times, family and villagers gave up
hope of him.

Again he joined a *yātrā*-troupe at first. But when the master of
the troupe began to treat him almost as a son, and the members
of the troupe, young and old, had all fallen for him – and even the
people in the houses where they performed (especially the women)
began to make a special fuss of him – one day, without saying a
word, he disappeared, and could not be found.

Tarapada was as wary of ties as a young fawn, and was also like
a deer in his love of music.[1] The songs of the *yātrā* were what
had first lured him away from home. Melodies sent a trembling
through his veins, and rhythms made his body swing. Even as a
baby he had shown such solemn, grown-up attention at musical
gatherings, sitting and swaying and forgetting himself, that his
elders could hardly restrain their amusement. Not only music:
when the rains of Śrābaṇ fell on the thick leaves, when the clouds
thundered, when the wind moaned in the woods like a motherless demon-child, his heart was swept away. The call of a kite
high in the sky in the still heat of noon, the croaking of frogs
on rainy evenings, the howling of jackals at night, all entranced
him. Impelled by this passion for music, it was not long before
he had joined a group of *pā̃cāli*-singers. The leader of the group
carefully taught him songs and trained him to recite *pā̃cāli*
by heart. He too began to love him as his own. Like a pet cage-
bird, Tarapada learnt a few songs, and then one morning flew
away.

Finally he joined a troupe of gymnasts. From Jyaiṣṭha to Āṣāṛh
a fair toured the district. *Yātrā*-troupes, *pā̃cāli*-singers, bards,
dancers and stallholders travelled by boat from one site to another.
For the second year running this round of entertainment included
a small gymnastics-troupe from Calcutta. At first Tarapada joined
the stallholders – sold *pān* at the fair. But then his natural
curiosity drew him to the wonderful skills of the gymnasts, and
he joined their troupe. He had taught himself to play the flute

1. There is a traditional belief in India that deer are musical. In Rajput
paintings, deer are shown dumbstruck before a musician.

very well: during the gymnastic display he had to play Lucknow *ṭhumri*s at top speed on the flute – this was his only task.

It was from this troupe that he had most recently absconded. He had heard that the zamindars at Nandigram had founded, on a lavish scale, an amateur *yātrā*-group, so he tied up his bundle and headed for the place, meeting Matilal Babu on the way.

Despite these connections with various groups, his nature had not been corrupted by any. He was, deep down, entirely detached and free. The foul language he had heard, the dreadful sights he had seen, had not fixed themselves in his mind. They passed him by. He remained unbound by any kind of habit or custom. He swam in the murky waters of the world with pure white wings, like a swan. However many times his curiosity made him dive in, his wings could not be soaked or soiled. There was a pure and natural innocence in this runaway boy's expression. So much so, that the worldly-wise Matilal Babu invited him in without doubt or question, and with great tenderness.

II

In the afternoon the boat set sail. Annapurna continued to ask the boy kind questions about his home and family; he answered laconically, and then went out on deck to escape. The monsoon river, swollen to maximum fullness, seemed to harry the earth with its reckless turbulence. In the cloudless sunshine, the half-sunk reeds along the bank, the fields of succulent sugar-cane beyond, and the far-off bluey-green woods kissing the horizon, seemed transformed by the touch of a golden wand into new beauty. The speechless sky gazed down in wonder: everything was alive, throbbing, awash with confident light, shiny with newness, bursting with plenty.

Tarapada took refuge on the roof of the boat in the shade of the sail. Sloping pastures, flooded jute-fields, green, rippling late-autumn paddy, narrow paths leading from the *ghāṭ*s, and villages shaded by encircling foliage, came one by one into view. To this water, earth and sky, this movement of life and sound, these varied levels and vast vistas, to this huge, immovable, mute, unblinking, natural world, the boy was intimately linked. Yet not for a moment did it try to hold him with its loving embrace.

Calves running on the banks with tails up-raised; ponies grazing and hopping about with hobbled legs; kingfishers swooping from fishing-net poles to plop into the water to catch fish; boys splashing; women shrilly chatting as they stood chest-deep, floating their saris out in front to rub them clean; fish-wives with baskets, saris tucked up, buying fish from the fishermen: all of this Tarapada watched with unflagging curiosity – never were his eyes sated.

As he sat, he soon got talking with the helmsman and oarsmen. Sometimes he took the *lagi* and punted the boat himself. When the helmsman needed a smoke, he would take the tiller; when the sail needed to be turned, he helped skilfully.

Just before dusk Annapurna called Tarapada and asked, 'What do you like to eat at night?'

'Whatever I get,' said Tarapada. 'I don't eat every day.'

She felt disturbed by this beautiful Brahmin boy's indifference to her hospitality. She longed to feed, clothe and give succour to him. But she could not discover how to please him. She ostentatiously sent her servants to buy milk and sweets: Tarapada ate the sweets willingly enough, but he would not touch the milk. Even the taciturn Matilal urged him to drink it, but he simply replied, 'I don't like it.'

Three days passed. Tarapada expertly joined in everything, from the cooking and shopping to the sailing of the boat. Anything he saw interested him; any work that he did absorbed him. His sight, his hands and his mind were ever-active: like Nature herself he was always serene and detached, yet always busy. People usually dwell in a fixed place, but Tarapada was like a joyous wave on life's unending stream: past or future meant nothing – moving forward was the only thing that mattered.

By mixing with various groups, he had learnt all sorts of delightful accomplishments. Things were stamped on his mind with astonishing ease, unclouded as it was by any kind of worry. He knew *pãcāli*, folk-tales, *kīrtan*, and long pieces from *yātrā*s. Matilal Babu habitually read the *Rāmāyaṇa* to his wife and daughter. One evening he had just got to the story of Kush and Lab when Tarapada, unable to restrain himself, came down from the roof of the boat and said, 'Put the book away. I know a song about Kush and Lab – listen!'

He began a *pãcāli*. Dashu Ray's verse, sweet as a flute, flowed

on swiftly; the helmsman and oarsmen came and peered through
the door of the cabin; as dusk fell, a stream of laughter, pathos
and music spread through the evening air: the banks became
alert, and people in passing boats were lured for a moment and
strained their ears to listen. When the *pācāli* had finished,
everyone sighed deeply, wishing it would last forever. The tearful
Annapurna longed to take the boy and press him to her breast
and bury her face in his hair. Matilal Babu thought, 'If I could
somehow keep this boy, he would make up for my having no
son.' The little girl Charushashi, though, was full of envy and
jealousy.

III

She was her parents' only child, sole claimant on their affection.
There was no end to her wilfulness and obstinacy. She had her
own opinions about food, clothes and hair-styles, but there was
no consistency in them. Whenever she was invited out, her
mother was terrified that she would make impossible demands
over dress. If her hair-style displeased her, to do and redo it
made no difference, and merely led to a tantrum. She was like
this with everything. But if she was in a good mood, she was
amenable to anything – and would show excessive love for her
mother, hugging her, kissing her, laughing in an unbalanced way.
The girl was a puzzle.

But now her volatile feelings began to concentrate in fierce
animosity towards Tarapada, and she caused exceptional trouble
to her parents. At meals she scowled and pushed her plate away:
she would complain about the cooking, slap the maid, and object
to everything. The more that Tarapada's accomplishments impressed her and others, the more angry she became. She would
not admit that he had any virtues at all; undeniable evidence of
them made her even more critical. On the night that Tarapada
sang about Kush and Lab, Annapurna thought, 'Wild animals
can be tamed by music, so perhaps my daughter will soften.'
'How did you like it, Charu?' she asked. She gave no answer,
merely tossed her head, implying: 'I didn't like it at all and shall
never like it.'

Realizing that Charu was jealous, her mother stopped showing

affection for Tarapada in front of her. After dark, when Charu
had gone to bed after eating early, Annapurna would sit by the
door of the cabin and Matilal Babu and Tarapada would sit
outside, and at Annapurna's request Tarapada would sing. With
his singing, the goddess of the sleeping, darkened homes on the
bank would sink into a trance, and Annapurna's heart swelled
with love and appreciation. But Charu would get up and shout
tearfully and angrily, 'Mother, I can't get to sleep with this
noise!' She found it quite unbearable to be sent to bed on her
own while her parents sat and listened to Tarapada singing.

The natural fierceness of this fiery black-eyed girl fascinated
Tarapada. He would tell her stories, sing her songs, play her the
flute, make great efforts to win her round – but with no success at
all. Only in the afternoons when he bathed in the swollen river,
sporting his fair, pure body in a swimming display worthy of a
young water-god – only then could she not help being attracted
just a little bit. She would watch him then. But she didn't reveal
her interest to anyone, and – born actress that she was – carried
on knitting a woollen scarf with apparent indifference to Tarapada's water-sports.

IV

Tarapada took no notice of Nandigram when they passed it. The
large boat – sometimes with its sails up, sometimes towed –
proceeded slowly on down rivers and tributaries, and the days of
the passengers too flowed with a soft and easy pace through the
peace and beauty of the scene. No one was in any kind of hurry;
long afternoons were spent bathing and eating; and as soon as
dusk fell the boat was moored at a village *ghāṭ*, by trees buzzing
with crickets and aglow with fireflies.

After about ten days of this the boat arrived at Kathaliya.
Ponies and a palanquin were sent from the house to receive the
zamindar; a guard of honour (with bamboo *lāṭhis*) fired rounds
of blanks – raucously echoed by the village crows.

Meanwhile Tarapada slipped off the boat and quickly looked
round the village. Calling one villager *Dādā*, another *Khuṛā*,
another *Didi*, and another *Māsī*, he established friendly relations
with everyone in a couple of hours. Because he had no normal

ties, he could get to know people with amazing ease and speed. Within a few days he had won all hearts.

He mixed with everyone on equal terms. He was unconventional, yet able to adapt to any situation or work. With boys he was a boy, yet somehow separate and special; with older people he was not a boy, yet not too precocious either; with herders he was a herder, yet also a Brahmin. He joined in with things as if used to them all his life. He'd be chatting in the sweet-shop: the sweet-maker would say, 'Could you mind the shop for a while? I shan't be long.' Cool as a cucumber, Tarapada sat there keeping the flies off the *sandeś* with a *śāl*-leaf. He could even make sweets himself, knew something of weaving, and was not completely ignorant of how to turn a potter's wheel.

Tarapada reigned over the whole village; there was just one young girl whose hatred he simply could not overcome. Perhaps it was because this girl so fiercely wished him to leave that he stayed on so long. But Charushashi now proved how hard it is to fathom even a juvenile female mind.

Bāmunṭhākrun's[1] daughter Sonamani had been widowed at the age of five; she was Charu's playmate. She had been ill for a while, and had not been able to go out to see her friend. When she was recovered and came to see her again, a rift between them came about for almost no reason.

Charu had been speaking at length about Tarapada: she hoped, by saying what a precious asset he was, to astonish and intrigue her friend. But when she discovered he was known to Sonamani, that he called Bāmunṭhākrun *Māsī* and that Sonamani called him *Dādā*; when she heard that he not only treated mother and daughter to *kīrtan*-tunes on his flute but had, at Sonamani's request, made her a bamboo flute; that he'd picked her fruits from high branches and flowers from thorny ones; when she heard all this, darts of fire stabbed her. She had thought of Tarapada as *their* Tarapada – guarded closely, so that ordinary people might glimpse him yet never be able to grasp him: they would admire his beauty and talents from a distance, and Charushashi's family would gain glory thereby. Why should Sonamani have such easy contact with this singular, divinely favoured Brahmin boy? If Charu's family had not taken him in, had not looked

1. A title rather than a name, often given to Brahmin widows.

after him so, how would Sonamani ever have seen him? Sonamani's *Dādā* indeed! She burned all over at the thought.

Why was the Charu who had tried to strike the boy down with
arrows of hatred so anxious to claim sole rights over him? Understand this who will.

Later that day Charu had a serious rift with Sonamani over
another trivial matter. She marched into Tarapada's room, found
his beloved flute, and callously jumped and stamped on it. She
was still doing so when Tarapada came in. He was amazed by the
image of destruction that the girl presented.

'Charu, why are you smashing my flute?' he asked.

'I *want* to smash it! I'm *going* to smash it!' shouted Charu with
red eyes and flushed face; and, stamping unnecessarily on the
already smashed flute, she burst into loud sobs and ran from the
room. Tarapada picked up the pieces, turned them this way and
that, but it was useless. To wreak destruction on his old, innocent
flute was so absurd that he burst out laughing. Charushashi
intrigued him more every day.

He was also intrigued by the English illustrated books in
Matilal Babu's library. Tarapada had considerable knowledge of
the world, but he could not enter the world of these pictures at
all. He tried to do so in his imagination, but found no satisfaction
in this. Seeing his interest in these books, Matilal said one day,
'Would you like to learn English? You'll understand these pictures
then.'

'I *would* like to learn it,' he replied at once.

Matilal Babu happily engaged the headmaster of the village
secondary school – Ramratan Babu – to teach the boy English
each evening.

V

Tarapada set about learning English with great concentration and
retention. It released him into a hitherto inaccessible realm,
unconnected with his former world. The local people saw no
more of him; at dusk, when he went to the empty riverside to
pace swiftly up and down reciting his lessons, his boyish devotees
mournfully watched from a distance; they dared not disturb his
studies.

Charu too did not see much of him now. Formerly Tarapada ate in the women's quarters, under Annapurna's loving gaze; but because this could take a long time he asked Matilal Babu to arrange for him to eat outside them. Annapurna was hurt by this and objected, but Matilal was so pleased by Tarapada's keenness to learn that he agreed to the new arrangement.

Charu now insisted that she too wanted to learn English. At first her parents were amused by their wayward daughter's new idea, lovingly laughed at it; but its absurdity was soon washed away by tears. Doting parents that they were, they were forced to give in, and she started to study alongside Tarapada with the same tutor.

Study, however, was alien to her restless nature. She learned nothing herself – merely disrupted Tarapada's learning. She fell far behind, couldn't learn anything by heart, but couldn't bear to be behind! If Tarapada overtook her and moved on to a new lesson, she was furious and burst into tears. When he finished an old book and bought a new one, she had to buy the new book too. In his spare time he would sit in his room learning and writing his lessons: the jealous girl couldn't stand this – she would secretly come and pour ink on his exercise-book, steal his pen, even tear from the book the passage he had been set to learn. Tarapada bore most of this with amusement: if she went too far he slapped her, but he was quite unable to control her.

A chance occurrence saved him. One day, truly annoyed, he tore up his ink-spilled exercise-book and sat gloomily. Charu came to the door, and prepared herself for a beating. But nothing happened: Tarapada went on sitting in silence. The girl went in and out of the room. Several times she came so close that Tarapada could, if he had wished, easily have thwacked her on the back. But he did not do that, and remained solemn. The girl was in a quandary. How to ask for forgiveness was something she had never learnt; yet she was extremely anxious for forgiveness. Finally, seeing no other way, she took a piece of the torn exercise-book, sat down next to Tarapada and wrote in large round letters, 'I will never pour ink on your exercise-book again.' She then made elaborate efforts to attract his attention. At this Tarapada could not contain himself any more, and he burst out laughing. The girl dashed from the room, overcome with shame and anger.

Only if she had been able to expunge from all time the paper on which she had humbled herself, would her fury have been eased.

During this period Sonamani had once or twice, with her heart in her mouth, lurked outside the lesson-room. She was close to her friend Charushashi in most matters, but with regard to Tarapada she feared and distrusted her. At moments when Charu was in the women's quarters, she would stand timidly outside Tarapada's door. He would look up from his book and say tenderly, 'What is it, Sona, what's up? How is *Māsī*?' Sonamani would say, 'You haven't been to see us for a long time – Mother wishes you would sometime. She has backache, so she can't come to you.'

Charu would perhaps now appear. Sonamani was flustered: she felt like a thief. Charu would scowl and shriek at her, 'Well, Sona – coming to disturb our studies! I'll tell my father!' As if she herself was Tarapada's guardian, whose sole object was to watch him day and night in case his studies were disturbed! But God was not unaware of what her actual motive was in coming to Tarapada's room at this odd time, and Tarapada also knew it well. Poor Sonamani fumbled for false explanations; when Charu venomously called her a liar she withdrew, sick at heart, defeated. The kindly Tarapada would call her and say, 'Sona, I'll come to your house this evening.' Charu hissed back like a snake, 'How can you go? What about your lessons? I'll tell *Māṣṭārmaśāy*!'

Undaunted by Charu's threat, Tarapada spent a couple of evenings at Bāmunṭhākrun's house. On the third day Charu, without further warning, quietly bolted his door; and, fetching the padlock from her mother's spice-box, locked him in. She kept him prisoner for the whole evening, only opening the door when it was time to eat. Tarapada was angrily silent, and was about to go out without eating. Then the passionate, overwrought girl clasped her hands and cried out repeatedly, 'I promise you – cross my heart – that I won't do it again. Please, I beg you, eat before you go!' When even this had no effect she began to wail, and he was forced to turn back and eat.

Charu many times promised herself that she would behave properly towards Tarapada, that she would not annoy him again; but when Sonamani and others turned up it put her into such a rage that she could not control herself. If she was good for a few days, Tarapada would steel himself for another tempest. No one could say how the attack would come or on what grounds. There would be a mighty storm, and floods of tears to follow, and after that peace and affection again.

VI

Almost two years passed like this. Tarapada had never moored himself to anyone for so long. Maybe his studies had a hold on him; or maybe he was changing as he grew up, and a stable existence in a comfortable house had more appeal than before. Maybe the beauty of his study-companion – even if she had been constantly bad-tempered – was exerting unconscious influence.

Meanwhile Charu had reached the age of eleven. Matilal Babu had sought out two or three good marriage-offers. Now that she had reached marriageable age, he placed a ban on English books and outside visits. She kicked up a terrible fuss at these new restrictions.

Then one day Annapurna called Matilal and said, 'Why search outside for a groom? Tarapada would make a fine husband. And your daughter likes him.'

Matilal Babu was astonished at this suggestion. 'That's impossible,' he said. 'We don't know anything about his family. She's my only daughter: I want to marry her well.'

Some people came from the zamindar's house at Raydanga to look at the girl. Efforts were made to dress Charu up: she shut herself in her room and refused to come out. Matilal Babu begged and rebuked her from outside, but without result. Finally he had to lie to the delegation from Raydanga: his daughter had suddenly fallen ill, and could not be seen today. They assumed from this lame excuse that the girl had some kind of defect.

Matilal Babu started to reflect that Tarapada was indeed good to look at, good in every outward aspect; he could keep him at home, so his only daughter would not have to go to someone else's house. He realized that his truculent daughter's foibles, which he and his wife could smile at, would not be received so well by in-laws.

After lengthy discussion, Matilal and Annapurna sent a man to Tarapada's village to find out about his family. The information came that it was poor, but high-caste. Matilal Babu then sent a marriage-proposal to the boy's mother and brothers. They were well-pleased, and agreed to it at once.

Back at Kathaliya, Matilal and Annapurna discussed the day and hour of the wedding, but the naturally cautious Matilal kept the whole matter secret.

Charu, though, could not be restricted. She sometimes burst into Tarapada's room like a cavalry-charge, disturbing his studies with crossness, eagerness or scorn. Sometimes, detached and independent though he was, he felt a strange stirring in his heart at this, a sort of electrical impulse. Till now he had floated lightly and serenely without impediment on Time's stream: sometimes now he was snared by strange distracting day-dreams. He would leave his studies and go into Matilal Babu's library and flick through the pages of the illustrated books; the imaginary world which he mixed with these pictures was much changed – much more highly-coloured than before. He could not laugh at Charu's strange behaviour quite as he had done in the past. When she was bad he never thought of beating her now. This deep change, this powerful feeling of attraction, was like a new dream.

Matilal Babu fixed the wedding for the month of Śrābaṇ, and sent word to Tarapada's mother and brothers; but he did not inform Tarapada himself. He told his *moktār* in Calcutta to hire a trumpet-and-drum band, and he ordered everything else that would be needed for the wedding.

Early monsoon clouds formed in the sky. The village-river had been dried up for weeks; there was water only in holes here and there; small boats lay stuck in these pools of muddy water, and the dry river-bed was rutted with bullock-cart tracks. But now, like Parvati returning to her parents' home, gurgling waters returned to the empty arms of the village: naked children danced and shouted on the river-bank, jumped into the water with voracious joy as if trying to embrace the river; the villagers gazed at the river like a dear friend; a huge wave of life and delight rolled through the parched village. There were boats big and small with cargoes from far and wide; in the evenings the *ghāṭ* resounded with the songs of foreign boatmen. The villages along the river had spent the whole year confined to their own small worlds: now, with the rains, the vast outside world had come in its earth-coloured watery chariot, carrying wondrous gifts to the villages, as if on a visit to its daughters. Rustic smallness was temporarily subsumed by pride of contact with the world; everything became more active; the bustle of distant cities came to this sleepy region, and the whole sky rang.

Meanwhile at Kurulkata, on the Nag family estate, a famous chariot-festival was due to be held. One moonlit evening Tarapada went to the *ghāṭ* and saw, on the swift flood-tide, boats with merry-go-rounds and *yātrā*-troupes, and cargo-boats rapidly making for the fair. An orchestra from Calcutta was practising loudly as it passed; the *yātrā*-troupe was singing to violin accompaniment, shouting out the beats; boatmen from lands to the west split the sky with cymbals and thudding drums. Such excitement! Then clouds from the east covered the moon with their huge black sails; an east wind blew sharply; cloud after cloud rolled by; the river gushed and swelled; darkness thickened in the swaying riverside trees; frogs croaked; crickets rasped like wood-saws. To Tarapada the whole world seemed like a chariot-festival: wheels turning, flags flying, earth trembling, clouds swirling, wind rushing, river flowing, boats sailing, songs rising! There were rumbles of thunder, and slashes of lightning in the sky: the smell of torrential rain approached from the dark distance. But Kathaliya village next to the river ignored all this: she shut her doors, turned out her lamps and went to sleep.

The following morning Tarapada's mother and brothers arrived at Kathaliya; and that same morning three large boats from Calcutta, laden with things for the wedding, moored at the zamindar's *ghāṭ*; and very early, that same morning, Sonamani brought some mango-juice preserve[1] in paper and some pickle wrapped in a leaf, and timidly stood outside Tarapada's room – but Tarapada was not to be seen. In a cloudy monsoon night, before love and emotional ties could encircle him completely, this Brahmin boy, thief of all hearts in the village, had returned to the unconstraining, unemotional arms of his mother Earth.

---

1. *āmsattva*; a great delicacy, made by drying mango-juice in the sun.

Wishes Granted

Subalchandra's son was called Sushilchandra. But people do not always suit their names.[1] Subalchandra was not strong, and Sushilchandra was not very well-behaved. He would go around annoying all the people of the neighbourhood. His father tried to chase after him, but he had rheumatism in his legs and the boy could run like a deer; so the cuffs, blows and slaps did not always fall in the right places. But whenever Sushilchandra *was* caught, he did not get off lightly.

Today was Saturday and school stopped at two o'clock, but Sushilchandra did not want to go to school at all. There were many reasons for this. One was that today there was to be a geography test; another was that tonight there was to be a firework display at the Boses' house near by. The preparations had started in the morning. Sushil wanted to spend the day there.

After a lot of thought, he lay down on his bed when it was time to go to school. His father Subal asked him, 'What's this? Lying on your bed? Aren't you going to school?'

'I've got a stomach-ache,' said Sushil, 'I can't go to school today.'

'Just you wait!' said Subal to himself, seeing right through him, and went on: 'Then you'd better not go out anywhere. I'll send Hari to watch the Boses' fireworks. I had bought some toffee for you today; you'd better not eat that either. You stay here quietly, and I'll make some herbal medicine for you.'

Bolting the door, he went and prepared an extremely bitter herbal medicine. Sushil was in a fix: he hated medicine quite as much as he loved toffee. He had been looking forward ever since yesterday night to going to the Boses' house, and now it was ruled out.

When Subal Babu returned to the room with a large bowl of medicine, Sushil jumped up from his bed saying, 'My stomach-ache is completely gone – I'll go to school.'

'Out of the question,' said Subal. 'Drink the medicine and rest

1. *subal* means 'strong' and *suśīl* means 'gracious', 'polite'.

quietly.' He forced him to drink the medicine and went out again, locking the door with a padlock.

As he lay on the bed weeping, Sushil kept thinking, 'If only I could be as old as Father! I could do as I liked and no one would be able to stop me!'

His father Subal was sitting alone outside the room and thinking, 'My parents spoilt me so – I never did any proper study. If only I could have my childhood back, I wouldn't waste any time – I'd do nothing but schoolwork.'

The Goddess of Desires[1] was passing by at that time. Seeing what father and son desired, she decided, 'Right – let their wishes be granted for a while.' So she said to the father, 'Your wish is fulfilled. From tomorrow you will be as young as your son.' To the boy she said, 'From tomorrow you will be as old as your father.' They were both delighted.

The elderly Subalchandra did not sleep well at night – he used to fall asleep towards dawn. But today what happened? He woke up bright and early, and positively sprang out of bed. He found he was very small; all his lost teeth had been restored; his beard and moustache had vanished. The dhoti and shirt he had gone to sleep in were so loose and baggy that the sleeves practically reached the floor, the neck reached down to his chest, and the bottom of the dhoti drooped so low that he tripped on it.

Sushilchandra normally got up early and ran around making mischief, but today he didn't wake up. When he was roused by Subalchandra's shouting, he found his clothes were so tight that they were in danger of bursting at the seams. His body had expanded all round; half his face was hidden by a pepper-and-salt beard; and when he felt his head, which formerly had a full shock of hair, he found a gleaming bald patch. He did not want to get out of bed. He yawned noisily, rolled over to this side and that; and at last – greatly annoyed by his father's shouts – he staggered to his feet.

Both had had their wishes fulfilled; but with very awkward consequences. Earlier I said that Sushilchandra had thought that if he could be big and free like his father Subalchandra, he would climb trees as he pleased, jump into water, eat green mangoes,

1. *Icchāṭhākrun*: a made-up deity, not a traditional Hindu goddess.

grab bird-chicks, and wander all over the fields. He would come home and eat when he liked, and no one would be able to stop him. But the extraordinary thing was that when he woke up this morning he had no wish to climb trees. When he saw the pond he felt he would catch his death of cold if he jumped into it. Instead, he spread out a mat on the verandah, and quietly sat down to think.

He decided that it would not be good to give up games completely; he ought to have a go. So he tried several times to climb an *āmrā* tree. The day before he would have climbed it as nimbly as a squirrel; but now with his old body he couldn't climb it at all. A slender branch low down broke under his weight and he thudded to the ground. Passers-by burst out laughing at the sight of an old man climbing a tree like a boy and falling. Hanging his head in shame, Sushilchandra returned to the mat on the verandah.

Calling the servant he said, 'Hey, go and buy me a rupee's worth of toffee!' He had a passion for toffee. There were various kinds displayed in a shop near the school; he bought them with the few odd paisa he got as pocket-money – and was determined that when he had money like his father he would stuff his pockets full of sweets and eat them all the time! Today the servant brought him a whole bagful: he took one, put it into his toothless mouth, and started to suck – but a child's sweets are not right at all for an old man. 'My father is now a little boy, so he can have them,' he thought to himself; but then he thought, 'No, I can't do that – it will make him ill to eat so many.'

Until yesterday all the local boys had played *kapāṭi* with Sushilchandra, but today when they came to look for him and found the elderly Sushilchandra, they ran off. He had thought, 'If I were free like my father I would spend all day playing *kapāṭi* with my chums – *ḍu-ḍu-ḍu-ḍu* all day long!' But today he didn't want to see Rakhal, Gopal, Akshay, Nibaran, Harish and Nanda – he wanted to sit quietly. Boys were too noisy.

I said earlier that his father Subalchandra used to sit on a mat on the verandah and think, 'When I was young I used to waste my time mucking about; if I could be young again I'd be a good boy – I'd sit indoors with the door closed and learn my lessons. I'd even stop listening to Grandmother's stories in the evening: instead I'd study till ten or eleven at night.'

But now that he *was* a boy again, Subalchandra didn't want to go to school at all. When Sushil irritably asked, 'Father, aren't you going to school?' Subal scratched his head, looked at his feet and murmured, 'I've got a stomach-ache today. I can't go to school.'

'Can't you indeed?' said Sushil angrily. 'I've also had stomach-aches like that at going to school. I know all about them.'

Indeed Sushil had shirked school on so many pretexts and so recently that there was no way his father could deceive him. He packed his little father off to school. As soon as he got back, he wanted to dash straight out and play, but the elderly bespectacled Sushilchandra was at that very time intoning to himself from a copy of Krittibas's *Rāmāyaṇa*, and Subal's noise and running about disturbed his reading. So he sat Subal down in front of him, put a slate into his hand and made him do sums. He devised such huge sums that it took his father an hour to complete just one of them. In the evening a crowd of old men gathered in Sushil's room to play chess. To keep Subal quiet at that time, Sushil engaged a tutor who taught him till ten at night.

Sushil was very strict about food, because when his father had been old his digestion had not been good – if he ate too much he suffered from acidity. Sushil remembered this well, so he was careful not to let him over-eat. But now that he was suddenly young again his father had such an appetite that he could have eaten a horse! Sushil gave him so little that he raged with hunger. He grew very thin – his bones stuck out all over. Thinking he was seriously ill, Sushil stuffed him with medicine.

But the elderly Sushil also had many difficulties. He could not bear what formerly he had liked. Before, if he heard of a *yātrā* anywhere, he would run out of the house, however cold or rainy, to watch it. When the elderly Sushil tried that, he got a cold and cough, pains in his head and limbs, and had to stay three weeks in bed. He had long been used to bathing in the village pond, but no sooner had he tried that now than the joints in his arms and legs swelled and he got terrible rheumatism: he had to be treated by a doctor for six months. After that he bathed in warm water only, at two-day intervals, and refused to let Subal bathe in the pond. Once he forgot his age and jumped out of bed with a single bound, jarring his bones terribly. When he stuffed a whole *pān* into his mouth, he found he had no teeth, and couldn't chew it. If he absent-mindedly combed or brushed his whole head, the scratching reminded him that most of it was bald. Sometimes he forgot he was as old as his father had been and lapsed into tricks such as chucking pebbles into old women's water-pots. When people drove him off, scandalized that an old man could behave like a child, he wanted to hide his face with shame.

Subalchandra also sometimes forgot that he was now a little boy. Imagining that he was as old as previously, he would go and join the old folks at their card-playing, sit down and chat to them as equals; at which everyone said, 'Run off and play, run along now! Who do you think you are?' And seizing him by the ears, they threw him out. Or he'd go to the schoolmaster and say, 'Have you got some tobacco to spare? I feel like a smoke.' The schoolmaster made him stand on one leg on a bench for this. Or he'd go to the barber and say, 'Why haven't you come to shave me for so long, you scoundrel?' 'Cheeky devil,' thought the barber, and answered, 'I'll come in ten years' time.' Sometimes he tried to beat his son Sushil as he had often done before. Sushil was incensed at this and said, 'Is that what school has taught you? To have a go at an old man, you little rascal!' People came running from all around to slap and beat and hurl abuse at him.

Then Subal started to pray fervently, 'If only I could be big and free like my son Sushil, I'd be out of this!' And Sushil said with clasped hands, 'O God, make me small like my father, so that I can play around as I like. My father has become so naughty that I cannot control him; it's getting me down.'

The Goddess of Desires came back and said, 'Well, have you got what you wanted?'

They both knelt and did *praṇām* to her and said, 'We assure you, Goddess, we have. Now make us what we were before.'

'All right,' said the Goddess of Desires, 'when you wake up tomorrow you'll be back to what you were.'

The next morning when Subal woke up he was as old as formerly; and Sushil when *he* woke up was a boy again. They both assumed they had woken from a dream. Subalchandra shouted out gruffly, 'Sushil, are you learning your grammar?'

'I think I've lost my book, Father,' said Sushilchandra, scratching his head.

False Hope

Darjeeling was swathed in rain and cloud when I arrived. I didn't want to go outside, but to stay indoors was even more unappealing. Straight after my hotel breakfast I put on heavy boots and a full-length mackintosh, and went out for a walk. It was drizzling intermittently, and the thick pall of cloud all around gave the impression that God was trying to erase the entire scene, mountains and all, with a rubber.

As I walked along the deserted Calcutta road, I hated these misty heights and wished I could grasp with all five senses Earth's busy variety and colour again. It was then that I heard the pathetic sound of a woman crying, not far off. Life is so tragic and troubled that the sound of crying is nothing out of the ordinary, and at any other time I doubt if I would have looked round; but here amidst the clouds the sound seemed like the cry of a whole vanished world. I could not ignore it.

I approached, and saw a woman sitting on a rock by the road, weeping. Her clothes were ochre-coloured, and her matted, light-coloured hair was scooped up into a top-knot. Hers was no recent grief: long suppressed exhaustion and misery had snapped under the weight of the clouds and desolation, and had burst out. 'This is odd,' I said to myself. 'I could base a brilliant story on this. I never thought to see a *sannyāsinī* sitting on a mountainside!' I could not tell which caste she was. I asked her kindly in Hindi, 'Who are you? What's happened to you?'

At first she did not answer, and merely glanced at me with fiery, tearful eyes. I spoke again: 'Don't be afraid – I'm a gentleman.' She smiled then and said in flawless Hindusthani, 'I've been beyond fear and terror for a long time now – shame, too. Once, Babuji, I lived in such purdah that even my own brother had to ask for permission to see me. But nothing hides me from the world now.'

I was rather annoyed. My clothes and manners were those of a *sāheb*. Yet this wretched woman addressed me, without hesitation, as 'Babuji'. I felt like ditching the story and stumping off in my best *sāheb*'s manner, nose in the air and puffing cigarette-smoke like a train. But curiosity got the better of me. I asked her, tilting my head haughtily, 'Can I help you? Do you need anything?'

She stared straight at me, and after a pause replied briefly, 'I am the daughter of Golamkader Khan, Nawab of Badraon.'

I had not the slightest idea where Badraon was or who Golamkader Khan was or why his daughter should be sitting by the Calcutta Road in Darjeeling and weeping. I didn't believe her, either, but decided I would not spoil the fun, or the chance of such a good story. So I made a lengthy and solemn salaam before her and said, 'Bibisaheb, forgive me, I did not know who you were.' (There are many logical reasons why I did not know her, the chief one being that I had never seen her before, and on top of that the mist was so thick it was hard to see one's own hands and feet.) 'Bibisaheb' did not take offence, and pointing to a rock next to her said pleasantly, 'Sit down.'

I could see she was used to giving orders. I felt surprisingly honoured at being allowed to sit on a wet, hard, mossy rock beside her. The daughter of Golamkader Khan of Badraon, the Princess Nurunni Shah or Meherunni Shah or whatever she was called, had graciously given me a muddy seat by the Calcutta Road in Darjeeling, next to her and at about the same height! When I set out from the hotel in my mackintosh, I never dreamt of such a lofty possibility.

It might seem like poetry: a man and a woman mysteriously conversing on a rocky mountainside. Hot from the pen of a poet, it would rouse in the reader's heart the sounds of streams gurgling in mountain caves, or the wonderful music of Kalidasa's *Meghadūta* or *Kumārasambhava*. Yet surely there must be few representatives of Young Bengal[1] who would *not* have felt ridiculous sitting in boots and mackintosh by the Calcutta Road on a muddy rock with a ragged Hindusthani lady! But we were wrapped in mist, there was no one to see us, no cause for embarrassment, no one but the Nawab of Badraon Golamkader Khan's daughter and I – a freshly minted Bengali *sāheb* – two people on two rocks, like relics of a totally destroyed world.

1. Progressive-minded products of English education in nineteenth-century Calcutta were known collectively as 'Young Bengal'.

The great absurdity of our incongruous meeting concerned only *our* destinies, no one else's.

'Bibisaheb,' I said, 'who put you into this state?'

The Princess of Badraon struck her forehead. 'How can I know how things are caused? Who is it who hides these huge, harsh mountains in flimsy clouds?'

I agreed with her, not wishing to start a philosophic debate. 'Yes indeed, who knows the mysteries of Fate? We crawl like worms before them.'

I would have argued, I would not have let Bibisaheb off so lightly – but my Hindi was insufficient. The little I had learnt from dealing with watchmen and bearers did not permit me to discuss Fate and Free Will with a Princess of Badraon or of any other place, sitting by the Calcutta Road.

Bibisaheb said, 'The extraordinary story of my life has only just finished. At your command I shall tell it to you.'

'Command?' I said, rather flustered. 'If you *favour* me with it I shall be highly honoured.'

No one should think that I spoke exactly like this, but in Hindi. I wanted to, but I was not capable of doing so. When Bibisaheb spoke, it was like a delicate morning breeze stirring a dewy golden cornfield: there was such easy meekness in her flow of sentences, such beauty. And I could only reply in blunt, barbarous, broken phrases. I had never known such effortless excellence of speech; as I talked to Bibisaheb I felt, for the first time, my own inadequacy.

'My father,' she said, 'had the blood of the Emperor of Delhi in his veins, and in order to preserve the honour of his family went to great lengths to find me a suitable husband. A proposal came from the Nawab of Lucknow: my father was dealing with this when the fighting broke out between the British and the sepoys over cartridge-biting, and Hindusthan turned dark with the smoke of cannon-fire.'[1]

I had never before heard Hindusthani spoken by a woman, let

---

1. The Indian Mutiny of 1857 was sparked off by the use of animal fat in cartridges which had to be 'bitten off' before use. Hindus suspected cow-fat; Muslims suspected pig-fat (taboo in each case).

alone by a high-born lady, and as I listened it was clear to me that
this was aristocrat's language and that the days of this language
were over. Everything today has been lowered, stunted, stripped
by the railways and telegraph, by the hurly-burly of work, by the
extinction of the nobility. As I listened to this nawab's language
amidst the thick mists of British-built, modern, stony Darjeeling,
an imaginary Mogul city arose in my mind, with huge white
marble palaces soaring into the sky, with long-tailed liveried
horses in the streets and elephants with gold-tasselled howdahs; a
city whose people wore many-coloured turbans, baggy shirts and
pyjamas of wool and silk and muslin, with brocade slippers curled
up at the toes, and scimitars tied to their waists; a leisured,
elegant, courteous way of life.

'Our fort,' said the Nawab's daughter, 'was on the bank of the
Yamuna. Our army-commander was a Hindu Brahmin, called
Keshar Lal.'

The woman seemed to pour all the music of her voice into that
one name 'Keshar Lal'. I laid my walking-stick on the ground
and settled myself into a bolt-upright position.

'Keshar Lal was a strict Hindu. When I got up in the morning
I would look from the window of the zenana and watch him
immerse himself up to the chest in the Yamuna, watch him
circumambulating with hands cupped in an offering to the rising
sun. He would sit with sopping clothes on the *ghāṭ*, recite
mantras devotedly, and then sing a hymn clearly and smoothly in
Rāg Bhairavī as he walked back to his house.

'I was a Muslim girl, but I had never been told about my
religion and I did not know its doctrines and practices. Among
our menfolk, religious rules had been weakened by indolence,
drinking and self-indulgence; and in the luxury of the zenana,
too, religion was not much alive.

'God probably implanted in me a natural thirst for religion – I
cannot see how else it was caused. Be that as it may, at the sight
of Keshar Lal performing his rituals in the pure dawn light on
the bare white steps down to the calm blue Yamuna, my hitherto
dormant feelings were seized by a sweet, unspoken devotion.

'With his regular, disciplined piety, and his fair and supple
body, Keshar Lal was like a smokeless flame: his Brahminical

sanctity and grace chastened the ignorant heart of a Muslim girl
with a strange reverence.

'I had a Hindu maid who did obeisance before Keshar Lal
every day and took the dust of his feet. The sight of this pleased
me but also made me jealous. On days when special rites were
observed, this maid would also sometimes lay on meals for Brahmins. I offered to help with the cost of this, saying, "Why not
invite Keshar Lal?" She answered in horror, "Keshar Lal does
not take food or gifts from anyone." It gnawed at my heart that I
could not make any direct or indirect expression of devotion to
Keshar Lal.

'One of my ancestors had abducted a Brahmin girl and married
her. As I sat inside the zenana, I felt her pure blood in my
veins and found some comfort in thinking I was linked to Keshar
Lal by that thread. I listened to everything my Hindu maid could
tell me about Hinduism, its customs and rules, its amazing tales
of gods and goddesses, its marvellous *Rāmāyaṇa* and *Mahābhārata*; as I listened, a wonderful picture of the Hindu world
unfolded before me. Statues and idols, the sounds of bells and
conches, gold-topped temples, the smoke of incense, the scent of
flowers and sandalwood, the unearthly powers of *yogī*s and *sannyāsī*s, superhuman Brahmins, the wiles and sports of gods in
human disguise: all combined to create a realm that was supernatural, distant, vast and immeasurably old. My heart was like a bird
without a nest, flying at dusk from room to room of a huge and
ancient palace. To my girlish mind, the Hindu world was an
enchanting fairy-tale kingdom.

'It was at this time that the fighting broke out between the
Company and the sepoys. Waves of revolt spread even to our
small fort. Keshar Lal said, "The pale-skinned cow-eaters must
be driven from Aryavarta! Hindu and Muslim kings must be
free again to gamble for power!"

'My father Golamkader Khan was a calculating man. "Those
damned English can do the impossible," he said. "The people of
Hindusthan can never match them. I'm not going to stake this
little fort of mine on so slender a chance. Don't ask me to fight
with the Honourable Company!"

'At a time when the blood of both Hindus and Muslims was on
fire, we were all enraged by my father's merchant-like prudence.

Even my mother and step-mothers were stirred. Soon Keshar Lal came with an armed troop, and said to my father, "Nawab-saheb, if you don't join us I shall take you prisoner while the fighting lasts and command the fort myself."

'"There is no need for that," said my father. "I'm on your side."

'"Give us some money from your treasury," said Keshar Lal.

'My father did not give much. "I'll give you more when you need it," he said.

'I took my whole array of ornaments, tied them up in a cloth and gave them to my Hindu maid to take to Keshar Lal. He accepted them. I tingled with pleasure at this, all over my denuded body.

'With the scraping and polishing of rusty guns and the sharpening of ancient swords, Keshar Lal began to get ready. But suddenly, one afternoon, the District Commissioner arrived: his red-shirted soldiers stormed into the fort, raising clouds of dust. My father Golamkader Khan had secretly given him news of the revolt.

'Keshar Lal commanded such loyalty in the Nawab's guard that they fought to the death with their broken guns and blunt swords.

'My traitorous father's house was like hell to me. I was bursting with grief and hatred, but I did not shed a single tear. I dressed in the clothes of my cowardly brother and escaped from the zenana, while no one was looking.

'Dust, gunpowder smoke, the shouting of soldiers and the noise of guns died down, and the terrible stillness of death settled over land and water and sky. The sun set, turning the Yamuna red, and a nearly full moon hung in the evening sky. The battlefield was strewn with hideous scenes of death. At any other time my heart would have been pierced by the pity of it, but instead I wandered around as if in a trance, trying to find Keshar Lal – no other aim had meaning for me. I searched until, in the middle of the night, in bright moonlight, not far from the battle-field, on the bank of the Yamuna, in the shade of a mango-grove, I came across the dead bodies of Keshar Lal and his loyal batman. I could see that – appallingly wounded – either master had carried servant or servant had carried master from the battle-

field to this place of safety, where they had quietly given themselves up to Death.

'The first thing I did was fulfil the craving I had had for so long to
abase myself before Keshar Lal. I fell to my knees beside him,
loosed my long tresses, and fervently rubbed the dust from his feet.
I raised his ice-cold soles to my feverish forehead, and kissed them;
months of suppressed tears welled up. But then his body moved,
and a weak groan emerged from his lips. I drew back in alarm at the
sound. With closed eyes and parched voice he murmured, "Water."

'I ran to the Yamuna – returned with my clothes soaking wet. I
wrung the water out over Keshar Lal's half-open lips, and tore
wet strips of cloth to bind the ghastly wound that had destroyed
his left eye. I brought him water a few more times in this way,
and as I moistened his face and eyes he slowly regained some
consciousness. "Shall I give you more water?" I asked.

'"Who are you?" said Keshar Lal.

'I could not hold back any more and said, "I am your humble,
devoted servant. I am the daughter of Golamkader Khan, the
Nawab." At least he would die knowing my devotion to him! No
one could deprive me of the joy of that feeling.

'But as soon as he heard who I was he roared out like a lion,
"Daughter of an arch-traitor! Heretic! You, a Muslim, have
profaned my religion by giving me water at my time of death!"
He struck me a heavy blow on my cheek with his right hand:
everything swam before my eyes and I nearly fainted.

'I was sixteen years old and this was the first time I had been
out of the zenana; the greedy heat of the sun had not yet stolen
the luscious pink of my cheeks; but this was the first greeting I
received from the outside world, from my one idol in the world!'

My cigarette had gone out. All this time I had sat like a figure in
a painting – so engrossed that I knew not whether it was words or
music that I heard. I had said nothing myself. But now at last I
burst out, 'Animal!'

'Animal?' said the Nawab's daughter. 'Would a dying animal
refuse a drop of water?'

Embarrassed, I said, 'Maybe not. He was a god, then.'

'What sort of god?' said the Princess. 'Would a god reject the
service of an eager and devoted heart?'

'Indeed not,' I said, and fell silent again.

'At first,' continued the Princess, 'I was devastated. I felt as if the world had collapsed over my head. But I quickly recovered myself, bowed from a distance before that harsh, cruel, high-minded Brahmin, and said to myself, "O Brahmin, you accept neither the service of the wretched, nor food from another's hand, nor the gifts of the wealthy, nor the youth of a girl, nor the love of a woman: you are separate, alone, aloof, distant. I have no right at all to offer my soul to you."

'I cannot say what Keshar Lal thought when he saw the daughter of the Nawab bowing down before him till her head touched the dust, but there was no surprise or change of expression in his face. He looked at me calmly; then, very slowly, stood up. I anxiously stretched out my arm to support him, but he silently refused it, and with great difficulty staggered to the bank of the Yamuna. A ferry was moored there. There was no one to cross and no one to take anyone across. Keshar Lal boarded the boat and untied the mooring-rope: the boat quickly drifted to the middle of the stream and gradually faded from view. I longed with all the force of my feelings, youth and unrequited devotion to make a last obeisance before that boat and drown: to end this futile life of mine in the waveless, moonlit Yamuna, in the still night, like a bud shed before it could bloom.

'But I could not do that. The moon in the sky, the dense black woods on the bank, the inky-blue unruffled waters, the towers of our fortress glittering above the mango-grove in the moonlight, sang together a silent, solemn song of death; heaven, earth and the nether world that night, by their moon-and-star-studded stillness, told me with one voice to die. But a frail invisible boat, on the calm breast of the Yamuna, dragged me from the moonlit night's soothing, ever-bewitching spell of death and back to the path of life. I followed the bank of the river like a sleep-walker, sometimes through clumps of reeds, sometimes over sandbanks, sometimes over rugged broken-up beaches, sometimes through scarcely penetrable thickets.'

She fell silent here. I also said nothing. After a long pause the Nawab's daughter said, 'What happened after this was very complicated. I don't know how to break it up and describe it clearly to you. I wandered through a thick forest, but I can't remember which path I took when. Where shall I begin? Where shall I end? What shall I leave out? What shall I keep in? How can I make the whole story clear so that it won't seem impossible or preposterous or unnatural?

'During this period of my life I realized that nothing is impossible or unattainable. To a young girl from a nawab's zenana the outside world might seem totally forbidding, but that is an illusion: if one once steps out, a way through will be found. This path is not a nawab's path; but it is a path by which people have always come. It is rugged, weird and uncharted, full of branchings and divisions, fraught with agony and ecstasy, obstacles and obstructions; but it *is* a path.

'An account of a princess's long, solitary journey along this inevitable path would not be pleasant to listen to, and even if it was I have no wish to tell it. In a word, I endured many trials and dangers and indignities; yet life was not unbearable. Like a firework, the more I burned the more wildly I moved; so long as I kept moving I did not feel I was burning. But now at last the flame of my pain and joy has gone out, and I find myself lying like a dumb thing in the roadside dust. My journey is over; my story is finished.'

With this the Nawab's daughter stopped. I mentally shook my head: the story was surely *not* yet over. I was silent for a while, then said in broken Hindi, 'Forgive my rudeness, but if you would speak a little more openly about the last part of your story my impudent curiosity would be greatly eased.'

The Nawab's daughter smiled. No doubt my broken Hindi helped. If I had been able to speak Hindi properly, she would not have been so frank with me: the fact that I knew so little of her mother tongue created a space between us, a protective veil.

She began again. 'I often got news of Keshar Lal, but in no way could I get to meet him. He had joined Tatya Tope's army,[1] and kept appearing and disappearing like a bolt of thunder from a sky that was still dark with revolt: sometimes to the east, sometimes

1. See Glossary.

to the west, sometimes to the north-east, sometimes to the south-west.

'I was by then dressed as a *yoginī*, and studying the Sanskrit Shastras in Benares with Shibananda Swami, my spiritual father. News from all over India reached him: I devotedly learnt the Shastras, and at the same time eagerly lapped up news of the war.

'Gradually the British Raj stamped out the flames of revolution in Hindusthan. There was no more news of Keshar Lal. All the heroic figures, right across India, who had been glimpsed in the bloody light of battle, were eclipsed. I could hold myself no longer. I left the protection of my guru, and went out in the world again, dressed as a devotee of Shiva. I wandered from road to road, shrine to shrine, to ashrams and temples, but found no news of Keshar Lal anywhere. Some who knew his name said, "He must have died in the fighting or been executed." My heart said, "That can never be: Keshar Lal cannot die. He is a Brahmin; that blazing invincible fire can never be put out; it is still burning brightly on a lonely, remote, ritual hearth, waiting for me to sacrifice myself to it."

'It is said in the Hindu Shastras that through meditation and austerity a Shudra can become Brahmin; there is no mention of a Muslim becoming a Brahmin, for the simple reason that there were no Muslims at that time. I knew it would be a long time before I could be united with Keshar Lal, because first I had to become a Brahmin. Thirty long years went by. I became a Brahmin inside and out; in habit and behaviour; in body, mind and speech. The blood of my Brahmin grandmother flowed through my body with unmixed energy; I acquired a strange mental fire, by abasing myself totally before the first and last Brahmin of my adolescence and youth, for me the only Brahmin in the world.

'I had heard a lot about Keshar Lal's heroism in the revolutionary war, but that was not what imprinted itself on my heart. What I saw was Keshar Lal floating out alone in a little boat into the calm central stream of the Yamuna, in the silent moonlight: *that* was the picture that obsessed me. I saw nothing but this, day and night: a Brahmin floating away on the empty stream towards some undefined mystery – with no companion, no servant, no need of anyone; immersed in the purity of his soul, complete in himself; with the planets, moon and stars watching him silently.

'Then I heard that Keshar Lal had escaped execution and taken refuge in Nepal. I went there. After living there for many months I heard that he had left Nepal a long time before and had gone nobody knew where.

'I wandered through the mountains. This was not a Hindu land: it was a land of Bhutanese and Lepchas with their weird beliefs; there was no orthodoxy in their diet and behaviour; their gods and styles of worship were completely alien; I was terrified of the slightest desecration of the holiness I had acquired through years of spiritual endeavour. I took great pains to avoid being touched by anything unclean. I knew that my boat was nearly at the shore, that my life's supreme goal was not far off.

'What shall I say of what happened next? The end of the story is very brief. When a lamp is about to go out it can be extinguished with a single puff. I need not elaborate. After thirty-eight years, I have arrived in Darjeeling. I saw Keshar Lal this morning.'

She fell silent again, so I asked her eagerly, 'What did you see?'

'I saw,' said the Nawab's daughter, 'an aged Keshar Lal in a Bhutanese village with his Bhutanese wife, sitting in a filthy yard with their grandchildren born of her, picking grain out of maize.'

Her story was finished. I thought I ought to offer some word of consolation. 'How can anyone,' I said, 'who has had to survive amidst strangers for thirty-eight years, stick to his religious rules?'

'You think I don't understand that?' said the Nawab's daughter. 'But why was I so deluded for so long? Why didn't I know that the Brahminism that stole away my young heart was nothing but custom and superstition? I thought it was *dharma*, unending and eternal. How else could I – after being so shamefully rejected when I offered on that moonlit night my freshly bloomed body and heart and soul, trembling with devotion, after leaving my father's house for the first time at the age of sixteen – how else could I have silently accepted the insult as a kind of initiation by a guru, and meekly dedicated myself to him with redoubled devotion? Alas, Brahmin, you exchanged one set of habits for another, but I gave away my life and youth, and how can I get them back again?'

The woman stood up and said, 'Namaskār, Babuji!' Then a moment later she said, as if correcting herself, 'Salaam Babusaheb!' With this Muslim valediction she took her leave, as it were, of the Brahminism whose foundations had crumbled to the dust. Before I could say anything, she disappeared like a cloud into the mists that swirled round these icy mountain-tops.

I shut my eyes for a while and let all she had described roll through my mind. I saw the young, sixteen-year-old Nawab's daughter sitting on a fine carpet in her room overlooking the Yamuna; I saw the statuesque figure of a yoginī rapt in ecstatic devotion during evening worship in a place of pilgrimage; and then I saw also an image of heart-broken disillusionment in an older woman, shrouded in mist, on the edge of the Calcutta Road in Darjeeling; and the poignant music of beautiful, pure Urdu, formed by the clash of Brahmin and Muslim blood flowing through this woman in opposite ways, reverberated in my mind.[1]

I opened my eyes. The clouds had parted, and the clear sky was bright with gentle sunshine. Englishwomen in hand-pushed carts and Englishmen on horseback were out taking the air. There were one or two Bengalis too, casting amused glances at me from faces swathed in scarves.

I got up quickly, and in the bright light of this sunny world I could no longer believe in the stormy story I had heard. My imagination had made it up, out of mist mixed with ample tobacco-smoke. That Muslim-Brahmin woman, that Brahmin hero, that fort on the bank of the Yamuna, had perhaps no truth in them at all.

---

1. There is a large area of overlap between Hindi and Urdu. Hindi uses the devanāgarī script and draws from Sanskrit for its higher vocabulary. Urdu uses the Persian script and a more Perso-Arabic vocabulary. In British India 'Hindusthani' was the name given to the colloquial language common to Hindi and Urdu; but the Princess's Hindusthani is clearly a highly refined hybrid, i.e. Urdu.

Son-sacrifice

Baidyanath was the shrewdest man in the village, and he always did everything with an eye to the future. When he married, he had a clearer vision of the son he hoped for than of the bride in front of him. So far-sighted a look at the moment of the first unveiling has rarely been seen.[1] He knew what he was about, and was therefore more concerned with the offering of oblations after his death than he was with love. 'One gets a wife to have a son': it was in this spirit that he married Binoda.

But even shrewd people can be cheated in this world. Though ripe for child-bearing, Binoda failed in her chief duty, and Baidyanath grew very alarmed when he saw the open gates of *punnām-narak* – the hell to which men without sons are condemned. Worried about who would inherit his wealth when he died, it became less of a pleasure to him now. As I have said, the future was more real to him than the present.

But how could one expect the youthful Binoda to look so far ahead? For her, poor girl, the worst thing was that her precious *present* life was being wasted: her budding youth was withering away through lack of love. The hunger of her heart in *this* world burned too strongly for her to care about the hunger of the spirit in the next. The Holy Laws of Manu, and her husband's psychical exposition of them, gave no relief to her craving.

Say what one may, at this age a woman finds her every joy in giving and receiving love, and has a natural tendency to value it more than duty. But instead of the delicate showers of new love, Fate decreed a stinging, roaring hailstorm, poured down by her husband and his lofty family hierarchy. They all accused her of being barren. Her wasted youth wilted, like a flowering plant kept indoors away from light and air.

Whenever she could bear the scolding and repression no longer,

---

1. The moment of *śubhadṛṣṭi* in Hindu weddings, when the bride is unveiled for the first time in front of her husband.

she would go to Kusum's house to play cards. She enjoyed this greatly. The terrible shadow of damnation lifted for a while, and jokes and laughter and chatter flowed freely. On days when Kusum had no female partner for the game, she would call in her young brother-in-law Nagendra, brushing aside any objection that either he or Binoda might make. Older people know how one thing can lead to another, how a game can become something more serious; but the young are not so aware of this. Nagendra's objections faded: soon he could hardly bear to wait for each card-playing session.

It thus happened that Binoda and Nagendra started to meet each other often, and he often now lost the game, because his eyes and mind were on something more vital than cards. Kusum and Binoda were both well aware of this (the real reason why he lost). As I have said, the young do not understand the consequences of their actions. Kusum found it highly amusing, and avidly watched the joke unfold. Young women delight in secretly watering the seeds of love.

Neither was Binoda unwilling. For a woman to wish to sharpen her weapons of conquest on a man may be wrong, but it is not unnatural. So as the games were won and lost and the cards were shuffled and dealt, the minds of two of the players came together in a way that only one other (apart from God) saw – and enjoyed.

One day at noon Binoda, Kusum and Nagendra were playing cards. After a while Kusum heard her young child (who was ill) crying, and went out of the room. Nagendra kept on chatting to Binoda, but he had no idea what he was saying: his heart galloped, and his blood surged through every vessel in his body. Suddenly youthful passion broke through the barriers of modesty: he seized Binoda's arms, wrenched her towards him, and kissed her. Shocked, angered, wounded, flustered by this affront, Binoda struggled to get free – but suddenly they noticed a third person in the room, a servant-woman. Nagendra looked at the ground, searching for an escape-route.

'*Bauṭhākrun,*' said the woman in a grim voice, 'your aunt is calling for you.' Tearfully, and with flashing glances at Nagendra, Binoda went out with her.

The servant-woman soon raised a storm in Baidyanath's house, making light of what she had seen but greatly elaborating what she had not. The plight that Binoda fell into is easier to imagine than to describe. She did not try to defend her innocence to anyone; she merely bowed her head.

Baidyanath, deciding that his chance of a son by her to offer funerary oblations was now extremely remote, turned on her with the words: 'Slut! Get out of my house.'

Binoda shut the door of her bedroom and lay on the bed, her tearless eyes blazing like a desert in the afternoon. When it was dark, and the crows in the garden stopped cawing, she looked up into the peaceful, star-studded sky and thought of her mother and father; only then did tears start to trickle down her cheeks.

That night, she left her husband's house. No one tried to find her. She did not know at that time that she had attained 'woman's greatest fortune': that her husband's salvation in the next world was secure in her womb.

Ten years passed, during which Baidyanath grew wealthier and wealthier. He had now left the village and bought a large house in Calcutta. But the more his wealth increased, the more anxious he became about who would inherit it.

He made two more marriages, each of which led only to dissension, not to a son. Soothsayers, healers and holy men filled his house: a stream of roots, amulets, magic waters and patent medicines. If the bones of all the goats he sacrificed at Kalighat had been piled high, they would have dwarfed Tamburlaine's victory-tower of skulls. But not even the tiniest of babies – not even the tiniest bundle of bones and flesh – arrived to inherit a corner of Baidyanath's palatial estate. He could hardly eat for worry about whose son it would be who would feed off his substance after his death.

Baidyanath married yet again, because human hope has no limits, and there is no shortage of parents with daughters to dispose of. Astrologers examined the girl's horoscope and pronounced that the auspicious conjunctions therein were such that Baidyanath's household would quickly increase its numbers; but six years went by in which those conjunctions failed to become active.

Baidyanath sank into despair. Finally, on the advice of pundits learned in the Shastras, he prepared an enormously costly fertility rite.[1] Scores of Brahmins were fed in connection with it.

Meanwhile, widespread famine was reducing Bengal, Bihar and Orissa to skin and bones. While Baidyanath sat amidst his abundant supplies and worried about who would one day eat them, an entire famished country looked at its empty platter and wondered *what* it would eat.

For four months Baidyanath's fourth wife drank water in which a hundred Brahmins had bathed their feet; and a hundred Brahmins, eating gross lunches and monstrous suppers, filled the municipal rubbish-carts with discarded earthenware cups and plates and banana-leaves smeared with curd and ghee. At the smell of the food, starving people crowded round the doors. Extra guards were employed to drive them away.

One morning, in Baidyanath's marble mansion, a pot-bellied *sannyāsī* was being served with two seers of *mohanbhog* and one-and-a-half seers of milk; and Baidyanath was watching this holy meal, sitting on the ground humbly and piously, hands clasped, chadar over his shoulder. An extremely thin woman with her emaciated child entered the room – she had somehow evaded the guards – and said piteously, 'Babu, give us a bite to eat.'

Baidyanath, in a flurry, shouted for his servant, 'Gurudoyal, Gurudoyal!' Fearing the worst, the woman said pathetically, 'Can't you give the child something? I don't want anything.'

Gurudoyal came and chased off the woman and her little boy. That starving unfed boy was Baidyanath's only son. A hundred well-nourished Brahmins and three stout *sannyāsī*s, enticing Baidyanath with the faint prospect of a son, went on guzzling his supplies.

---

1. This is the *yajña* of the story's title *putrayajña*, a rite (sacrifice) performed in order to acquire a son.

The Hungry Stones

I went away during the *pūjā* holiday, touring the country with a theosophist relative. It was on the train back to Calcutta that we met the man. He was a Bengali Babu, but his dress made us think at first that he was a Muslim from Northern India – and his conversation was even more surprising. He spoke on every subject with such authority, that one might have taken him for God's personal adviser. We had been quite content not to know about the world's secret happenings: how far the Russians had advanced, what the British were plotting, or the bungling machinations of the Native States. But our informant said with a slight smile, 'There happen more things in heaven and earth, Horatio, than are reported in your newspapers.' It was the first time we had been away from home, so the man's whole style was a revelation to us. He could jump, at the drop of a hat, from science to the Veda to recitations of Persian couplets; having no such command ourselves, we admired him more and more. So much so, that my theosophist relative grew sure there was supernatural aura around the man – a strange sort of magnetism, a divine power, an astral body, or something of that sort. He listened to every little thing he said with rapt attention, and made surreptitious notes. I suspected that our strange companion was not unaware of this, and was rather flattered.

The train came to a junction, and we sat in a waiting-room for a connection. It was half past ten at night. We heard that some kind of disruption on the line had delayed the train badly. I decided to spread my bed-roll out on the table and get some sleep, but it was then that the man began the following story. I got no more sleep that night . . .

'Because of some disagreements over policy, I left my employ in the state of Junagar and entered the service of the Nizam of Hyderabad. I was young and sturdy at that time, so I was first of all given the job of collecting the cotton-tax at Barich.

'Barich is a most romantic place. The Shusta river there (the name is derived from the Sanskrit *svacchatoyā*¹) flows through large forests with desolate mountains above, snaking its pebbly way over rocks like a skilful dancer picking her feet. A white marble palace stands alone on high rocks beneath the mountains, with 150 steep stone steps leading up from the river. There is no other house near by. The village of Barich with its cotton-market is a long way off.

'About 250 years ago Shah Mahmud II built the palace as a private pleasure-dome. In those days there were rose-scented fountains in the bathrooms: young Persian concubines sat in seclusion on cool marble, with their hair unplaited for bathing, dipping their soft, naked feet in pools of pure water, sitars in their laps, singing vineyard ghazals. Those fountains play no longer, the songs are heard no more, fair feet no longer fall on white stone: there is no one to inhabit the palatial emptiness of the place but a single, lonely tax-collector. But the old clerk in the office, Karim Khan, told me over and over again not to live there. "If you want, go there during the day," he said, "but don't ever spend a night." I scoffed at him. The servants, likewise, were willing to work there till dusk, but not to sleep there. "Suit yourselves," I said. The building had such a bad name that even thieves didn't venture there at night.

'At first the desolation of the palace oppressed me like a weight on my chest. I kept away from it as much as I could, working continuously, returning exhausted to my room to sleep. But after a few weeks, it began to exert a strange attraction. It is difficult to describe my state of mind and equally hard to convince people of it. The whole building seemed alive: it was sucking me in, its powerful stomach-juices were digesting me slowly. Probably it started to work on me from the moment I first set foot in it, but I clearly remember the day when I first became conscious of its power.

'It was the beginning of the summer: the market was sluggish, and I had little work to do. I had sat down in a comfortable chair by the river at the bottom of the steps, a little before sunset. The Shusta was depleted; its many sandbanks opposite were ruddy in the afternoon light; near me, pebbles glittered in the clear, shallow

1. 'Clear water.'

water at the bottom of the steps. There was not a breath of wind. The scent of wild basil, spearmint and aniseed in the hillside woods made the air oppressive.

'When the sun went down behind the crags, a long shadow fell, like a curtain abruptly ending the drama of the day. Here in this cleft between mountains there was no real dusk, no mingling of light and dark. I was about to mount my horse and ride away, when I heard footsteps on the stairway. I turned round – but there was no one there.

'Thinking that my senses were deceiving me, I settled in my chair again; but now lots of footsteps could be heard – as if a crowd of people were rushing down the steps together. Slight fear mixed with a peculiar pleasure filled my body. Even though there was no physical presence before me, I had a clear impression of a crowd of jubilant women rushing down the steps this summer evening to bathe in the Shusta. There was no actual sound this evening on the silent slopes and river-bank, or inside the empty palace, but I could none the less hear bathers passing me, chasing one another with merry laughter like the waters of a spring. They didn't seem to notice me. I was as invisible to them as they were to me. The river was as undisturbed as before, but I had a clear feeling that its shallow stream was being ruffled by jingling, braceleted arms, that friends were splashing each other and shriek-ing with laughter, that kicking swimmers were scattering spray like fistfuls of pearls.

'I felt a kind of trembling in my chest: I can't say if the feeling was of fear or delight or curiosity. I longed to see what was happening, but there was nothing in front of me to see. I felt that if I strained to listen, I would hear all that was spoken – but when I *did* try to listen, I only heard scraping crickets! I felt that a 250-year-old black curtain was dangling in front of me; if only I could lift one corner and peer behind it, what a splendid royal scene would be revealed! But in the deep darkness nothing could be seen.

'Suddenly the sultriness of the air was broken by a sharp gust of wind: the calm Shusta shook like the tresses of a nymph, and the whole shadowy forest stirred as if waking from a bad dream. Whether dream or not, the invisible pageant from a world of 250 years ago was whisked away in a trice. The magic women who brushed past me with bodiless footsteps and noiseless laughter to

jump into the Shusta did not return up the steps, wringing the
water from their clothes. The spring breeze blew them away like
a scent, in a single gust.

'Had the ruinous Goddess of Poetry landed on my shoulders,
finding me all on my own? Had she come to clobber me, for
being such a slave to tax-collection ? I decided I had better eat:
an empty stomach can play havoc with one's health. I called my
cook and ordered a full, spicy Moglai meal, swimming in ghee.

'The next morning the whole affair seemed ridiculous. I cheerfully trundled about, driving my pony-trap myself, wearing a
pith helmet like a *sāheb*, making routine inquiries. I had my tri-
monthly report to write, so I meant to stay late at my office. But
as soon as it was dusk, I found myself drawn to the palace. I
cannot say *who* was drawing me; but I felt it unwise to delay. I
felt I was expected. Instead of completing my report, I put on
my helmet again and returned to the huge, rock-bound palace, disturbing the deserted, shadowy path with my rattling pony-trap's
wheels.

'The room at the top of the steps was immense. Its huge
decorated, vaulted ceiling rested on three rows of pillars. It
echoed all the time with its own emptiness. Evening was well-
advanced, but no lamps had been lit. As I pushed open the door
and entered that vast room, I felt a tremendous upheaval, like a
court breaking up – people dispersing through doors, windows,
rooms, passages, verandahs. I stood astonished; there was nothing
I could *see*. I shuddered, went gooseflesh all over. A lingering
scent of age-old shampoo and *ātar* caught my nostrils. I stood
in the gloom between the pillars, and heard all round me the
gush of fountains on stone, the sound of a sitar (but what
the tune was I did not know), the tinkle of gold ornaments, the
jingle of anklets, the noise of a gong striking the hour, a distant *ālāp* on a *sānāi*, the chinking of chandeliers swinging in
the breeze, the song of a caged nightingale on the verandah, the
cry of tame cranes in the gardens: all combining to create the
music of the dead. I was transfixed: I felt that this impalpable,
unreal scene was the only truth in the world, that everything
else was a mirage. Was I really the Honourable Mr So-and-
So, eldest son of the late Mr So-and-So, earning 450 rupees
a month for collecting cotton-taxes? Did I really wear a pith

helmet and short kurta, drive a pony-trap to the office? It seemed so odd and absurd and false, that I burst out laughing as I stood in that great, dark room.

'My Muslim servant then came in with a flaming kerosene lamp. I don't know whether he thought I was mad – but I suddenly remembered that I *was* the Honourable Mr So-and-So, eldest son of the late Mr So-and-So. Our great poets and artists could maybe say whether disembodied fountains played eternally in this world or somewhere outside it, or whether endless *rāgas* were plucked on a magic sitar by invisible fingers, but this was true for sure, that I earned 450 rupees a month collecting taxes in the Barich cotton-market! Sitting at my lamplit camp-table with my newspaper, I recalled my strange hallucination of a little while ago, and laughed boisterously.

'I finished the newspaper, ate my Moglai food, turned out the lamp, and lay down in my small corner bedroom. Through the open window in front of me, a brilliant star above the darkly wooded Arali hills looked down from millions and millions of miles away at the Honourable Tax-collector on his measly camp-bed. I cannot say when I fell asleep, reflecting on the wonder and absurdity of that. And I don't know how long I slept. But suddenly I awoke with a start – not that there was any sound in the room, or any person that I could see. The bright star had set behind the dark hills, and the thin light of the new moon shone wanly through my window as if afraid to enter. I couldn't see anyone. But I seemed to feel someone gently pushing me. I sat up; whoever it was said nothing, but five ring-studded fingers pressed me firmly to follow.

'I stood up gingerly. Although there was not a soul but me in that palace with its hundreds of rooms and immense emptiness, where sound slept and only echoes were awake, I still walked in fear of waking someone. Most of the rooms in the palace were kept closed, and I had never been in them before; so I cannot say where and by which route I went that night, following with soundless steps and bated breath that urgent, unseen guide! I couldn't keep track of the narrow dark passages, the long verandahs, the huge solemn audience-chambers, the airless and obscure cells.

'Although I could not see my guide with my eyes, I had an

image of her in my mind. She was an Arab woman, whose marble-white hands emerged from voluminous sleeves – hard and flawless hands. A fine veil hung down from her head-dress; a curved knife was tied to her waist. It was as if a night had come floating from *One Thousand and One Nights*. I felt I was making my way through the narrow unlit alleyways of sleeping Baghdad, towards some dangerous assignation.

'At last my guide stopped before a dark blue curtain and seemed to point to something underneath. There was nothing there, but the blood in my chest froze with fear. In front of the curtain a fearsome African eunuch sat with drawn sword in his lap, legs sprawled out, dozing. The guide tiptoed over his legs and lifted a corner of the curtain. Behind it was a room spread with Persian carpets: I could not see who was sitting on the couch, but I saw two feet lazily resting on a pink velvet footstool, beautiful feet in brocade slippers peeping out of loose saffron pyjamas. On the floor near by was a bluish crystal bowl with apples, pears, oranges and grapes; and next to this there were two small goblets and a glass decanter of golden wine ready for a guest. From within the room, a strange intoxicating incense enthralled me.

'I was nerving myself to step over the sprawled legs of the eunuch, but he suddenly woke – his sword fell on to the stone floor with a clatter. There was then a horrible yell, and I found myself sitting on my camp-bed, soaked with sweat. It was dawn: the thin moon was pale as a sleepless invalid, and our local madman, Meher Ali, was walking as usual down the empty early-morning road shouting, "Keep away, keep away!"

'My first Arabian Night ended in this way – but a thousand more nights were to follow. A gulf between my days and my nights developed. During the day I would go about my work in a state of exhaustion, cursing my nights with their empty delusions and dreams; but at night it was my work-bound existence that seemed trivial, false and ridiculous. After dark I lived in a trance, in a maze of intoxication. I took on a strange *alter ego*, hidden in an unwritten history of hundreds of years ago. My short English jacket and tight trousers ill-befitted that person. So I dressed very carefully in baggy pyjamas, flower-patterned kurta, red velvet fez, a long silk choga; I perfumed my handkerchief with *ātar*; instead of cigarettes I smoked an enormous many-coiled hubble-bubble filled with rose-water; I sat in a large cushioned *kedārā* – waiting, it seemed, for a grand romantic tryst. But as darkness thickened a weird thing happened which I cannot describe. It was as if some torn pages from a marvellous story were blown by a sudden spring breeze to flutter around the various rooms of that vast palace. They could be followed so far, but never right to the end. I spent my nights wandering from room to room chasing those swirling torn pages.

'Amidst the swirling, tattered dreams, the whiffs of henna, the snatches of sitar-music, the gusts of wind spattered with scented water, I caught from time to time, like flashes of lightning, glimpses of a beautiful woman. She was dressed in saffron pyjamas; brocade sandals curving at the toe on her soft pink feet; a richly embroidered bodice tight round her breast; a red cap on her head with a fringe of golden tassels framing her forehead and cheeks. She made me mad. I spent my nethermost dreams each night wandering through the streets and dwellings of an intricate fantasy realm, in quest of her.

'On some evenings, I would light two lamps either side of a large mirror and carefully dress myself like a prince. Suddenly next to my own reflection in the mirror, the spectre of that same Persian girl appeared for a moment. She would bend her neck and direct her deep black eyes at me, full of a fierce, plaintive passion, while unspoken phrases hovered on her moist, beautiful lips. Then, nimbly twisting her buxom body round and up in a light and exquisite dance, she would vanish into the mirror – smile, gaze, ornaments, pain, longing, confusion flashing like a shower of sparks – whereupon a wild gust of wind, scented with woodland plunder, blew out my two lamps. I would undress and stretch myself on the bed next to my dressing-room, eyes closed, tingling with delight. The air all around me – laden with mixed scents from the Arali hills – swam with kisses and caresses; the touch of soft hands seemed to fill the secretive dark. I felt murmurs in my ear, perfumed breath on my brow, and the end of a delicate veil fragrantly brushing my cheeks. Ravishing, serpentine coils seemed to grip me ever more tightly – until, with a heavy sigh, limp with fatigue, I sank into deep slumber.

'One afternoon I decided to ride out – someone told me not to,

I forget who, but I insisted on going. My *sāheb*'s hat and jacket were hanging on a wooden hook: I snatched them and was going to put them on, but a tremendous whirlwind, sweeping before it sand from the Shusta banks and dry leaves from the Arali hills, whisked them away from me, and a sweet peal of laughter, hitting every note of mirth, driven higher and higher up the scale by the wind, soared to where the sun sets, and spiralled away.

'I did not go riding that day; and from then on I gave up wearing the short jacket and *sāheb*'s hat that had been so ridiculed. That night I sat up in bed and heard someone groaning and wailing: beneath the bed, under the floor, from within a dark tomb in the stone foundations of the palace, someone was crying, "Release me; break down the doors of futile fantasy, deep slumber, cruel illusion; lift me on to your horse, press me to your breast, carry me away through forests, over mountains, over rivers to your daylit abode!"

'Who was I? How could I rescue her? *Which* lovely, drowning projection of desire should I drag ashore from a whirlpool of swirling dreams? Divinely beautiful, where and when did you live? By which cool spring, and in which palm-shade, and to which desert nomad were you born? To which slave-market were you taken to be sold, crossing hot sands, riding on a lightning horse, torn from your mother's lap by a Bedouin brigand, like a flower from a wild creeper? Which royal servant studied your blooming bashful beauty, counted out gold *mudrā*s, took you overseas, placed you in a golden palanquin, gave you to his master's harem? What was your story there? Amidst the *sāraṅgī*-music, the tinkling anklets, the cruelly glittering wine, did there not lurk the flash of daggers, the bite of poisons, the savagery of covert glances! Unlimited wealth; eternal imprisonment! Two maids either side of you, waving fly-whisks, diamond bracelets twinkling! Kings and princes sprawling before the jewel-and-pearl-studded slippers encasing your fair feet! At the entrance-door, a Negro like Hell's messenger but in Heaven's garb, standing with sword unsheathed! Did you, O desert-flower, float away on that stream of wealth so horribly gleaming, so fraught with conspiracy, foaming with envy and smirched with blood, to meet a cruel death or to land on an even more regal, even more abominable shore?

'Suddenly Meher Ali, the madman, was shouting, "Keep away,

keep away! All is false! All is false!" I saw that it was dawn; the chaprassi was giving me the mail; the cook was salaaming and asking what he should cook today. "No," I announced, "I can't stay in this palace any more." That very day I moved all my things to the office. The old clerk Karim Khan smiled slightly when he saw me. Annoyed at his smile, I said nothing to him and settled down to my work.

'As the day wore on, the more distracted I became. I wondered what point there was in going anywhere. Tax-assessment seemed pointless; the Nizam and his government meant little; everything coming and going and happening around me was wretched, worthless, senseless!

'I threw aside my pen, slammed my ledger shut, and quickly climbed into my pony-trap. As if of its own accord it took me to the palace, arriving as dusk fell. I rapidly climbed the steps and went in.

'Today everything was still. The dark rooms seemed sullen. My heart was swelling with repentance, but nowhere was there anyone to speak to, anyone to ask for forgiveness. I roamed around the dark rooms blankly. I wished I could find a musical instrument, sing a song to someone. I would have sung, "O fire, the insect that tried to flee you has returned to die. Have pity on it now, burn its wings, shrivel it to ashes." Suddenly two tears fell on my forehead from above. That day thick clouds had gathered over the Arali hills. The dark forest and the inky Shusta seemed paralysed with dread. But now, water and land and sky shuddered; and a lightning-fanged storm unleashed itself through distant trackless forests, roaring and howling and rushing hither. Doors in the palace slammed; huge empty rooms boomed with a note of despair.

'The servants were all at the office; there was no one to light the lamps. I distinctly felt, on that cloudy moonless night, in the jet-black darkness of the rooms, that a woman was lying face-down on a carpet at the foot of a bed, tearing her unkempt hair with tight-clenched fists; blood was pouring from her pale brow; sometimes she was laughing fiercely and hysterically; sometimes she was sobbing wildly; she had ripped off her bodice and was beating her naked breasts; the wind was roaring through the window, driving in rain that soaked her to the skin.

'The storm went on all night, and the weeping too. I went on wandering through pitch-black rooms in fruitless remorse. There was no one anywhere; no one whom I could comfort. Who was it who was so distressed? Where was this inconsolable grief coming from?

'Once again the madman was shouting, "Keep away! Keep away! All is false! All is false!" I saw that it was dawn, and Meher Ali even on this storm-swept day was circling the palace shouting his usual cry. I wondered now if Meher Ali too had at one time lived in this palace; even though he was mad now and lived outside, he was daily lured by its monstrous stony charm, and every morning came to walk round it. I immediately ran up to the madman through the rain and asked, "Meher Ali, what is false?"

'He gave no answer, pushed me aside and, like a wheeling bird transfixed by the leer of a huge snake, continued to shout and wander round the palace, continued to warn himself over and over again with all his might, "Keep away! Keep away! All is false!"

'Dashing through the rain and storm like a man possessed, I returned to the office. I called Karim Khan and said, "Tell me what all of this means."

'The gist of what he told me was this. Once upon a time the palace had been churned by insatiable lust, by the flames of wild pleasure. Cursed by those passions, those vain desires, every stone now hungered and thirsted, strove like a vampire to consume every soul who came near. Of those who had stayed for more than three nights in the palace, only Meher Ali had emerged, with his wits gone. No one else till now had escaped its grasp.

'I asked, "Is there no escape for me?"

'The old man answered, "There is only one way and that is very hard. I can tell it to you, but first I must tell you the ancient story of one who lived there, a Persian slave-girl. A stranger and sadder tale was never heard."'

At that moment, the coolies came and told us that the train was coming. So soon? We rolled up our bedding, and the train arrived. A sleepy Englishman stuck his head out of a first-class compartment to read the name of the station. 'Hello,' he shouted, recognizing our companion, and he let him into his carriage. We got into the second class. We never found out who the gentleman was, and we never heard the end of the story either.

I said, 'The fellow took us for fools and was pulling our legs; he made the whole thing up.' My theosophist relative disagreed, and our dispute caused a rift which was never healed.

Thoughtlessness

I had to leave my homestead. I shall not tell you directly how this happened, only indirectly.

I was the native doctor in the village, and my house was opposite the police station. I was as intimate with the Police Inspector as I was with Death – aware, therefore, of the torments inflicted on humanity by Man *and* by his Protector.[1] And just as jewels and bangles, worn together, enhance each other, so the Inspector drew financial benefit from my interventions and I from his.

Yes, my friendship with Lalit Chakrabarti, Police Inspector, experienced fixer, was very special. It made me almost as vulnerable to his repeated suggestion that I and a spinster relative of his should marry as she was herself. But I could not bear to subject Shashi, my only daughter, motherless though she was, to a stepmother. Every year moments defined by the almanac as auspicious for a wedding passed by. I watched many worthy and not so worthy grooms climb into palanquins, and all I could do was join the groom's party, eat wedding-feasts in other people's houses, and return home with a sigh.

Shashi was twelve – nearly thirteen. I'd had some indication from a certain well-placed family that if I could get together a decent sum of money, I'd be able to marry her into it. And if *that* could be accomplished, I would then turn my attention to my own matrimonial arrangements.

I was brooding one day over this pressing need for money, when Harinath Majumdar of Tulsi village came to me in a state of desperation. What had happened was that his widowed daughter had suddenly died in the night, and enemies of his had written letters to the Police Inspector insinuating that she had died from an abortion. The police now wanted to examine her dead body.

The shame of this on top of his grief for his dead daughter was

1. *Nārāyaṇa*, a name for Vishnu as Protector, ironically doubling here as an epithet for the police.

more than he could bear. I was a doctor, and a friend of the Inspector: surely I could do something?

When the Goddess of Prosperity wishes to call, she comes sometimes through the front door, sometimes through the back. I shook my head and said, 'I'm afraid it's a complex matter.' I cited a couple of bogus precedents, and the trembling old Harinath wept like a child.

To cut a long story short, Harinath had to beggar himself in order to give his daughter her proper funeral rites.

My daughter Shashi came to me and asked me pitifully, 'Father, why did that old man come and weep before you like that?'

'Run along,' I said crossly. 'That's no business of yours.'

The path to finding a groom to whom I could give my daughter was now smoothed. The wedding-date was fixed. She being my only daughter, I planned the wedding-feast elaborately. I had no wife, so kind neighbours helped me. The penniless but grateful Harinath laboured for me night and day.

On the eve of the wedding – the day when bride and bridegroom are dabbed with turmeric – at three in the morning, Shashi suddenly went down with cholera, and quickly grew worse and worse. After every effort, after hurling bottle upon bottle of useless medicine to the ground, I rushed to Harinath and fell on my knees before him. 'Forgive me, *Dādā*,' I cried. 'Forgive me for my sin! She is my only daughter. I have no one else.'

'What are you doing, Doctor Babu, what are you doing?' said Harinath, greatly perplexed. 'I shall always be indebted to *you*! Don't kneel before me!'

'I ruined you, though you had done nothing wrong,' I said. 'Because of my sin, my daughter is dying.'

I started to shout to everyone, 'Oh, I ruined this old man, and am being punished for it! God, God, save my Shashi!'

I seized Harinath's sandal and started beating myself on the head with it. The old man, greatly embarrassed, snatched it back from me.

The next day at ten o'clock, with the turmeric still on her, Shashi bid farewell for ever to this world.

The very next day after that, the Inspector said, 'Well, why don't you get married now? You need someone to look after you.'

This kind of callous disrespect for a man's grief would have shamed even the Devil! But I had fallen in with the Inspector on so many other occasions that I could not bring myself to speak. How my friendship with him stung and shamed me now!

However pained the heart, life has to go on. One has to turn one's full energy again to the normal effort of finding food to eat, clothes to wear, wood for the stove, laces for one's shoes. In intervals from work, when I sat alone in my house, I would sometimes hear in my ear that pitiful question, 'Father, why was that old man weeping before you?' I rethatched Harinath's tumbledown house at my own expense, gave him my own milch-cow, and redeemed his plot of land from the money-lender.

Unbearably grief-stricken, alone in the evenings and sleepless at night, I could not stop thinking: 'My tender-hearted daughter – even though she has escaped this life – has found no peace in the next world from her father's cruel misdeeds. She seems to keep on returning in distress, asking, "Father, why did you do that?"'

For a while I was in such a state that I found it impossible to ask poor people for fees for medical treatment. If any young girl was ill, I felt it was my Shashi who was ill by proxy; I saw her in all the sick girls in the village.

The village was now awash with heavy rain. Fields and houses could be reached only by boat. The rain started early in the morning and went on all day.

A call came to me from the zamindar's office. The zamindar's boatman would not stand any delay and was agitating to leave at once.

Formerly, when I had to go out in such weather, there had been someone to open my ancient umbrella for me and see if there were any holes in it; and an anxious voice would ask me over and over again to be careful to protect myself from the damp wind and lashings of rain. Today as I looked for my umbrella in the empty, silent house, I paused for a moment to recall her loving face. I looked at her closed bedroom and wondered why God had arranged – for a person who gave no thought to the sorrows of others – such a supply of love. As I passed the door of that empty room, I felt a deep ache in my chest. But then, at the sound of the zamindar's servant irascibly shouting for me, I quickly suppressed my grief and went outside.

As I climbed into the boat I saw a small canoe tied to the police-station *ghāṭ*, with a farmer in it, soaking wet, wearing only a loin-cloth. I asked him what was up, and he told me that last night his daughter had been bitten by a snake – the wretched man had had to come all the way from a distant village to report it. I could see he had taken off his only garment to cover the dead body.

The impatient boatman from the zamindar's office untied the rope and we set off. At one o'clock I returned to my house and saw that the man was still sitting, soaked, with his knees huddled up to his chin; the Inspector Babu had not yet appeared. I sent him part of my midday meal. He refused to touch it.

After eating quickly I again had to set out to see the patient in the zamindar's office. In the evening when I returned the fellow was still sitting, in a nearly catatonic state. When I questioned him he was scarcely able to reply; he just stared at me. This river, village and police station; this drenched, cloudy, muddy world; to him it was as hazy as a dream. By repeated questioning I learnt that a constable had come out once to ask him if he had any money tucked into the loincloth. He had told him he was very poor – he had nothing. The constable had said, 'Wait, you rogue, sit and wait.'

I had often seen sights like this before, and never thought anything of them. But today I could not stand it. My Shashi's plaintive, silenced voice seemed to throb through the entire rainy sky. This speechless, daughterless farmer's unendurable grief seemed to beat against my own ribs.

The Inspector Babu was sitting comfortably on a wicker stool, smoking a hookah. An uncle – the one who had a daughter to dispose of – had recently arrived with me in mind: he was sitting on a mat and chatting. I burst in on them like a storm. I bellowed at them, 'Are you men or monsters?' and banged my whole day's earnings down in front of them saying, 'If you want money, take this: go to hell with it. Give that fellow outside a break now. Let him cremate his daughter.'

The love between the doctor and the Inspector, which the tears and torments of many others had nourished, crashed to the ground in that storm.

Not long after, I myself was on my knees before the Inspector, praising his greatness and bewailing my own stupidity; but I still had to leave my homestead.

The Gift of Sight

I have heard that these days many Bengali girls have to find their husbands through their own efforts. I have also had to find mine, but God has helped me. Maybe this is because of my many vows and *pūjā*s to Shiva, from an early age. I was not yet eight years old when I was married. But my sins in an earlier life stopped me from acquiring my husband fully. Three-eyed Mother Durga took away my two eyes. For the whole of the rest of my life she denied me the pleasure of seeing my husband.

My baptism of fire began in childhood. Before I was fourteen years old I gave birth to a dead baby, and I myself came close to death. But if a person is fated to suffer sorrow, she is not allowed to die too soon. A lamp that is meant to burn long has to have enough oil: it mustn't go out until night is over. I survived my illness, true, but whether through physical weakness, or mental distress, or for whatever reason, my eyes were affected.

My husband was at that time studying to be a doctor. With all the enthusiasm of a student, he leapt at a chance to try out his medical knowledge. He began to treat my eyes himself. My elder brother was at college that year, studying for his BL. He came to my husband one day and said, 'What are you doing? You'll destroy Kusum's eyes. Let a really good doctor examine her.'

'If a good doctor came,' said my husband, 'what new treatment could he give? I know about all the available medicines.'

My brother grew angry and said, 'So I suppose there is no difference between you and the top man at your college?'

'You are studying law,' said my husband. 'What do you know of medicine? When *you* get married, and have to go to law, say, over your wife's property, will you come to *me* for advice?'

'When kings fight,' I said to myself, 'ordinary folk had best keep out of the way. My husband is quarrelling with *Dādā*, but I'm the one who will pay for it.' I also felt that since I'd been given away in marriage, my brother and his friends no longer had a right to intervene. My sorrow and happiness, health and sickness were all in the hands of my husband.

Relations between my husband and brother became rather strained over this small matter of medical treatment. My flow of tears, already copious, now became even heavier – with neither my husband nor my brother understanding the true reason.

One afternoon when my husband was at college my brother suddenly appeared with a doctor. The doctor examined me and said that if care were not taken my eye-condition might get worse. He prescribed a new set of medicines, which my brother immediately sent someone to fetch. When the doctor had gone I said, '*Dādā*, I beg you, don't interfere with the treatment I am following at the moment.'

I had been in awe of my brother ever since childhood: to speak to him so bluntly was an odd thing for me to do. But I knew well that no good would come of the treatment that my brother had arranged behind my husband's back. My brother, too, was probably surprised at my boldness. He was silent for a while, then said, 'All right, I shan't bring a doctor again, but please try the medicines that are on their way.' When the medicines arrived, my brother explained how I should use them, and then left. Before my husband returned from college, I took the bottles, pill-box, brush and instructions and carefully disposed of them in the well in the courtyard of our house.

As if out of grudge towards my brother, my husband now treated my eyes with redoubled vigour. He changed medicines from one day to the next. I wore blinkers over my eyes, or spectacles; I put drops into them, or smeared them with powder; I even put up with the foul-smelling fish-oil he gave me to swallow and which made me want to vomit. My husband would ask me how I was feeling and I would say, 'Much better.' I even tried to persuade myself that my tears were a good sign; when the streaming stopped I decided I was on the road to recovery. But before long the pain was unendurable. My vision was blurred, and I was writhing with headache. I could see that even my husband was downcast. He was finding it difficult to think of a pretext for calling a doctor after so long.

'To set my brother's mind at rest,' I said, 'what harm would there be in calling a doctor? He's becoming so unreasonably angry – it's upsetting me. You can carry on treating me, but a doctor can be brought in too, for form's sake.'

'That's a good idea,' said my husband. That very day he returned with an English doctor. I don't know what exactly was said, but it seemed that the *sāheb* gave my husband quite a scolding – for he stood silently, hanging his head. When the doctor had gone, I took my husband's hand and said, 'Why did you bring that conceited white-skinned ass? A native doctor would have done. Why should that man understand my eye-condition better than you?'

'It has become necessary to operate on your eyes,' said my husband nervously.

I made a show of anger and said, 'If an operation is necessary, why did you not tell me so at the beginning? Did you think I was scared?'

My husband became more confident again, and said, 'How many men are so heroic that they wouldn't be scared at the prospect of having their eyes cut open?'

'Maybe they're only heroic to their wives,' I said jokingly.

'You're right,' said my husband, turning suddenly pale and solemn. 'Men are essentially driven by vanity.'

I dismissed his solemnity by saying, 'Do you want to match us in vanity too? We have the edge over you even in that.'

Meanwhile my brother had come, and I called him aside to say, '*Dādā*, by following all this time what the doctor of yours prescribed, my eyes have been getting much better, but by mistake the other day I smeared on to my eyes the medicine which I should have swallowed, and they've started to go fuzzy again. My husband says I shall have to have an operation.'

'I thought you were following your husband's treatment,' said my brother. 'I was annoyed, that's why I haven't been to see you.'

'No,' I said, 'I've secretly been following that doctor's prescription. I didn't tell my husband, in case *he* got angry.'

What lies women have to tell! I couldn't upset my brother, and I couldn't damage my husband's self-esteem either. A mother has to beguile her child; a wife has to keep her husband happy – women have to stoop to so many deceptions! But the result of my ploy was that before I finally became blind I was able to see a reconciliation between my husband and brother. My brother supposed that the damage was done by the treatment he arranged secretly; my husband felt that it would have been better to have listened to my brother's advice from the beginning. They both felt guilty, and thus longed for forgiveness and drew very close to each other. My husband came to my brother for guidance, and my brother sought my husband's opinion on all matters.

At last they mutually agreed to call an English doctor to come and operate on my left eye. In its weakened state, it failed to withstand the shock of surgery, and its dim remaining light went out. After that the other eye also little by little faded into darkness. A curtain was drawn forever over the sandal-decorated youthful image I had first seen in childhood, standing in front of me at the moment of the *śubhadṛṣṭi*.[1]

One day my husband came to my bedside and said, 'I shall not try to bamboozle you any more. It was I who destroyed your eyes.'

I could tell from his voice that he was close to tears. I pressed his right hand with both my hands and said, 'Don't worry, you took what belonged to you. Suppose my eyes had been destroyed by some other doctor's treatment – what comfort would there have been in that? If it was inevitable that no one could save my eyes, the one consolation of my blindness is that my eyes were taken by you. When he had insufficient flowers for a *pūjā* Rama tore out his own eyes and offered them to God. I too have given my eyes to a god – I have given to you my light of the full moon, my morning sunshine, my blue of the sky, my green of the earth. Describe to me anything you see that pleases you. I shall receive from you the grace of your gift of sight.'

I was not able to say all this – I could not find the words for it; but I had felt these things for a long time. Sometimes when weariness overcame me, when my faith started to ebb, when I started to regard myself as deprived or tragic or unfortunate, then I would speak to myself in these terms: I would try to lift myself out of my depression by relying on this solace, this devotion. That day, partly by what I said, partly by what I was not able to say, I think I conveyed my feelings to him. He said in turn, 'Kumu, I can never give you back what I destroyed through my

1. See p. 229, n. 1.

stupidity, but as far as I am able I shall make up for your loss of sight by staying by you.'

'There is no point in that,' I said. 'I shall never allow you to make your home a hospital for the blind. You must marry again.'

I was just about to explain in detail why it was so necessary for him to marry again, when I choked slightly. Before I could recover my breath, my husband blurted out: 'I may be stupid, I may be arrogant, but that is not to say that I am wicked too! I made you blind with my own hands; if I compound my error by deserting you and taking another wife, then I vow, by my *iṣṭa-devatā* Krishna, to count it a sin as wicked as patricide or the killing of Brahmins!'

I would not have let him make so terrible a vow – I would have stopped him; but tears were swelling my breast, throttling my throat, straining my eyes, preparing to stream down in torrents: I could not restrain them enough to allow myself to speak. As I listened to what he said, I buried my face in the pillow and wept tears of intense joy. I was blind, but he would not leave me! He would clutch me to his heart as a grieving man clings to his grief! I did not expect such blessings, but my mind, in its selfishness, revelled in them.

When my first shower of tears was over, I drew his face close to my breast and said, 'Why did you make such a dreadful vow? I did not tell you to marry again for your own happiness. It would be in *my* interest to have a co-wife. I could hand over to her work for you that my blindness makes impossible for me.'

'Housework can be done by servants,' said my husband. 'How can I marry a servant out of convenience and place her on the same seat as you, who are a goddess to me?' He lifted my face and placed a single, pure kiss on my forehead; that kiss seemed to open a third eye on my brow, to invest me with instant divinity. 'Fine,' I said to myself. 'Now that I am blind I cannot be a housewife any more in the outer, physical world, but instead – rising above that world – I can be a goddess working for my husband's good! No more lies, no more deceptions – I'm through with the meanness and deviousness that are the house-wife's lot.'

Yet for the whole of that day there was a conflict within me. I rejoiced in the deep-seated knowledge that my husband's awesome vow would prevent him from marrying again. Nothing could dislodge that joy. But the goddess I had found in myself that day said, 'Perhaps a time will come when remarriage will do your husband more good than adherence to the vow.' To which the woman in me answered, 'That may be so, but having made such a vow, no way can he marry again.' The goddess then said, 'Maybe – but there's no reason for you to be happy at that.' To which the woman answered, 'I understand what you are saying, but he did, after all, make the vow.' And so forth. The debate went on and on. The goddess then lapsed into silent disapproval, and my whole inner self was engulfed by a terrifying darkness.

My conscience-stricken husband put a ban on all servants, and was ready to run errands for me himself. At first I enjoyed my helpless dependence on him in every trivial matter, because in this way I kept him always near me. Because I couldn't see him with my eyes, my desire to keep him close grew overwhelming. That part of my pleasure in him that had belonged to my eyes was now shared out between my other senses – who fought to increase their share. Now, if ever my husband worked away from the house for long, I would feel lost, bereft, with nothing to hold on to. Previously when my husband went to college, if he was late coming back, I would open the window a bit and watch the road. I would let my eyes, as it were, bind to myself the world in which he moved. Now my whole sightless body tried to reach out to him. My main bridge between my world and his had collapsed. There was now an impassable darkness between him and me: I could only sit helplessly and anxiously, waiting for him to come from his shore to mine. Therefore, whenever he had to leave me for even a moment, my whole blind body longed to cling to him, desperately called out to him.

But such yearning and dependence is not healthy. A wife is burden enough on her husband, without adding the great weight of blindness as well. My all-consuming darkness was for me alone to bear. I fervently promised I would not use my blindness to bind my husband to me.

Within a short time I had learnt to carry out my customary tasks through sound and smell and touch. I even managed much of the housework with greater skill than formerly. I came to think that vision distracts as much as it helps us in our work. The eyes see far more than is necessary to do a job well. And when the eyes act as watchmen, then the ears become lazy; they hear much less than they should. Now, in the absence of those vigilant eyes, my other senses did their duty calmly and fully. I stopped allowing my husband to do my work, and restored to myself all the work I had done for him before.

'You're depriving me of my chance to make amends,' my husband said.

'I don't know about your making amends,' I said, 'but why should I add to my failings?' Whatever he might say, it was a great relief to him when I set him free. No man should have to make a lifelong vow of servitude to a blind wife.

My husband qualified as a doctor and took me off to a country district. To come to a village was like returning to my mother. I was eight years old when I left my village and came to the city. In the next ten years, my birthplace became as vague as a shadow in my mind. For as along as my sight lasted, Calcutta crowded out my memories. When I lost my sight, I realized that Calcutta had merely tricked my eyes; it could not fill my heart. As soon as I lost my sight, the village of my childhood grew as bright in my mind as a starry evening sky.

Towards the end of Agrahāyaṇ we went to Hasimpur. It was a new place for me – I did not know what it looked like; but it hugged me with the scents and sensations of my childhood. The dawn breeze from the newly ploughed, dew-soaked fields; the sweet pervasive scent of golden fields of mustard and pigeon-pea; the songs of the cowherds; even the clatter of bullock-cart wheels on broken roads; all thrilled me. The buried memories of my early life seemed to come alive, to surround me again with their inexpressible sounds and scents; my blind eyes were no obstacle to them. I returned to my childhood: only my mother had not been restored to me. I could see in my mind my *Didimā* letting her sparse hair hang loose down her back in the sun, and laying out rows of *bari*s in the yard; but I no longer heard, in her sweet old quavering voice, the lilting hymns of our village saint. The festival of the new rice-crop boisterously rang through the moist winter air; but among the crowd threshing the new paddy in the husking-shed, where were my village playmates? In the evening I heard the lowing of the cattle from some way off, and I remembered *Mā* with an evening lamp in her hand, on her way to place it in the cowshed. The smell of damp fodder and burning straw-smoke so entered my heart that I seemed to hear the cymbals and bells from the Bidyalankars' temple next to our village tank. It was as if someone had sifted through all the things I had known in my first eight years of life, and had wrapped me round with their quintessential flavour.

I also recalled my childhood religious devotion – the way I picked flowers at dawn to offer to Shiva. But alas, how Calcutta's hustle and bustle and chatter deform the mind! Religion loses its simplicity. A short time after I became blind I remember a friend from my old village came to me and said, 'Aren't you angry, Kumu? If I were in your shoes I wouldn't be able to stand the sight of your husband.' I replied, 'The sight of him has been stopped, true, and I'm cross with my useless eyes for that; but why should I blame my husband?' Labanya was angry with him for not having called a doctor in time, and was trying to make me angry too. I explained to her that if we live in this world, our wisdom and follies cause us – whether we like it or not – various kinds of pleasure and pain; but if we keep a firm faith within, we can have peace even amidst troubles – otherwise we spend our life in anger and rivalry and conflict. Being blind was burden enough; so why should I increase the burden by harbouring a grudge against my husband? Labanya was not pleased to hear such old-fashioned notions from a girl like me, and she went away, contemptuously shaking her head. But there can, I admit, be poison in words: no words are wholly without effect. A few sparks from her anger entered my mind; I stamped them out, but one or two burn-marks remained. This is why I say that there is too much talk, too much chatter in Calcutta; one can so quickly become harsh and entrenched in one's thinking.

When I came to the village, the cool scent of *śiuli*-flowers picked as an offering to Shiva revived my hopes and beliefs, made them bright and fresh as they were in childhood. My heart and home were filled with the Spirit of God. I bowed my head and said, 'O Lord, it is good that my eyes have gone, for you are mine.'

Alas, I was mistaken. To say of God 'You are mine' – even this is vanity. 'I am yours' is all we have a right to say. And a day was soon to come when God forced these words out of me: when nothing was left for me, yet I had to struggle on; when I had no claim on anyone, only on myself.

Life was happy for a while. My husband became quite a respected doctor. His income became respectable too. But money is not a good thing. It stunts the mind. When the mind is in control, it creates its own pleasure; but when wealth takes up the pursuit of pleasure, there is nothing for the mind to do. Where formerly the mind's pleasure reigned, possessions now stake their claim. Instead of happiness, we acquire nothing but *things*.

I cannot pin-point a particular remark or event, but whether because a blind person's powers of perception are intensified, or for whatever other reason, I was well able to see a change in my husband as his material prosperity increased. The deep concern he had had, when young, for justice and injustice, right and wrong, seemed to grow duller each day. I remember how at one time he used to say, 'I am not studying medicine only to earn a living, but to bring as much benefit as possible to the poor.' On the subject of doctors who turned up at the doors of the dying and would not even take a pulse without being paid in advance, he was almost speechless with disgust. But I could see that was not so now. A poor woman came and clung to his feet, begging him to save the life of her only son, and he shook her off; in the end I persuaded him to treat the boy, but his heart was not in it. I remember well my husband's attitude to corrupt earning in the days when we were short of money. Now there was lots of money in the bank, yet a rich man's secretary came and had two days of secret discussions with my husband – I don't know what about; but when he came to me afterwards talking breezily about other things, an uneasy feeling in my heart told me he was up to no good.

Where was the husband I saw for the last time before I went blind? He who had elevated me to a goddess by kissing me between my sightless eyes, what had become of him? Those who suddenly fall prey to a raging passion can pick themselves up again through another emotional impulse; but those who, day by day, moment by moment, harden from the marrow of their being, whose emotional capacities are throttled, steadily, by outward success – for them I see no way out.

The visual gulf that had arisen between my husband and me was nothing in itself; but I felt sick inside when I realized that where I was now, he was not. I was blind – sitting in an inner region devoid of the world's light, with my youthful love still fresh, my devotion still intact, my trust still unshaken: the dew of my gift of *śephālī*-flowers – arranged with girlish care, offered to God at the start of my life – had still not dried up; yet my husband had left my shaded, cool, eternally renewing world, and was lost in the desert of money-making! All the things I believed in, the faith I held to, all that I valued more than any worldly treasure, were now scorned and dismissed by him from afar. At one time there was no such rift; when we were young we had started along the same road; but then (neither he nor I knew exactly when) our paths divided, and now he was out of hearing when I called.

Sometimes I wondered if I made too much of things because I was blind. With eyes, I could have seen the world as it is.

My husband himself one day told me no less. That morning an old Muslim had come to ask him to treat his granddaughter for cholera. I heard the man say, 'I'm poor, sir, but Allah will bless you.' My husband said, 'Whatever Allah will do is not enough; tell me first what *you* will do for me.' When I heard this I thought, 'God has made me blind; why not deaf too?' The old man sighed, 'O Allah!' and took his leave. I at once got my maid to bring him to the back door of the women's quarters, and said, '*Bābā*, here is some money to pay for your granddaughter's treatment. Fetch Dr Harish from the village – and pray for my husband.'

All day I had no appetite. My husband woke up from his afternoon nap and asked, 'Why are you looking so glum?' I was going to give my usual answer – 'It's all right, there's nothing wrong' – but the time for pretence had passed, and I said clearly, 'I've been thinking of telling you something for a long time, but I couldn't think of how to say it. I don't know if I can explain to you what I am feeling, but I think you must know in your heart that we who were one when we started our life together have now become separate.'

My husband laughed and said, 'Change is the way of the world.'

'Money, beauty, youth may all be subject to change,' I said, 'but are there no eternal values?'

He then said more seriously, 'Think of women who have true cause for complaint – with husbands who earn no money, or who do not love them; you have plucked your misery out of the air!' I realized then that blindness had smeared my eyes with a salve that had set me apart from this changeable world; I was not like other women; my husband would never be able to understand me.

Meanwhile an aunt-in-law had come from her village to see how her nephew was getting on. The first thing she said after we had taken the dust of her feet was, 'Well now, *Baumā*, you have unfortunately lost the sight of your eyes. How is our Abinash supposed to run his household with a blind wife? Let him marry again!'

If my husband had jokingly said 'What a good idea, *Pisimā* – I put you in charge of the match-making', then I would have had nothing to worry about. But he said with embarrassment, '*Pisimā*, I don't know what you are saying.'

'What's the matter?' she replied. 'I'm saying nothing wrong. Well now, what do you say, *Baumā*?'

I smiled and said, 'You're not asking the right person for advice. If you want to pick someone's pocket, you don't seek their prior agreement!'

'Yes, you're right there,' said my aunt-in-law. 'I suggest we confer privately, Abinash. Agreed? And I say to you, *Baumā*, the more wives her husband takes, the prouder a Kulin girl should be of him. Our Abinash could marry instead of carrying on as a doctor, and he wouldn't have to worry about earning. When sick people fall into a doctor's hands they die, and once they're dead they don't pay him fees any more; but Kulin's wives are fated not to die, and the longer they live the more the husband profits.'

Two days later my husband asked his aunt, in my presence, '*Pisimā*, can you find me a woman of good family who could help my wife like a relative? She can't see, and if a companion was with her all the time I'd be much less anxious.' When I was newly blind such a suggestion would have made more sense, but now I couldn't think of any household task that was awkward because of my blindness. Nevertheless, I made no objection and kept silent.

'That would be no problem,' said my aunt-in-law. 'My brother-in-law has a daughter, as good as she is beautiful. She's grown up, just waiting for a suitable groom; if she could get a Kulin like you she could be married at once.'

My husband said with alarm, 'Who's talking about marriage?'

To which my aunt-in-law said, 'How can a girl of good family come and live in your house without being married to you?' That was true, certainly, and my husband could not think of anything to counter it.

I stood alone, shut in the endless darkness of my blindness, crying out to God to save my husband.

A few days later, as I came out from my morning *pūjā*, my aunt-in-law said, '*Baumā*, the niece of mine I mentioned, Hemangini, has come today from her village. Himu, this is your *Didi*, pay your respects to her.'

At that moment my husband appeared and, as if surprised at seeing an unknown woman in the room, started to leave again.

My aunt-in-law said, 'Where are you going, Abinash?'

'Who is she?' he asked.

'She is my brother-in-law's daughter – Hemangini,' she replied. My husband then proceeded to show unwarranted curiosity about when she had come, who had brought her, what her background was, and so forth. I thought to myself, 'I understand everything that's happening, so why this pretence on top of everything else? Secrecy, covering up, lies! If you have to do wrong to satisfy your lust, then do so – but why degrade yourself further because of me? Why tell lies to deceive *me*?'

I took Hemangini's hand and led her into my bedroom. I stroked her face and body, and could tell that her face was beautiful, and her age was not less than fourteen or fifteen. The girl broke out in delicious laughter.

'What are you doing?' she said. 'Are you trying to exorcize me or something?' At her simple, frank laughter, a dark cloud within me seemed to lift at once.

I put my right arm round her shoulders and said, 'I'm having a look at you, *bhāi*.' I then stroked her soft face again.

'Having a look at me?' She laughed again, and said, 'Do you have to feel me to see how big I am, like brinjal or beans in your garden?'

I then realized that Hemangini didn't know that I was blind. 'I'm blind, you know, sister,' I said. She was taken aback at this, and became more serious. I could well imagine how intently she was studying my face and my sightless eyes with her own curious, youthful, wide-open eyes.

Then she said, 'So this is why you invited Auntie here?'

'No, I didn't invite her,' I said. 'She kindly invited herself.'

'Kindly?' said the girl, with another laugh. 'Her kindness will keep her here a long time then. But why did my father send me here?'

Pisimā entered the room at that moment. She'd been having a long talk with my husband. As soon as she came in, Hemangini said, 'Auntie, when are we going home, tell me?'

'Well I never,' said my aunt-in-law. 'No sooner is she here than she wants to go. I've never known such a restless girl.'

'Auntie,' said Hemangini, 'I can see that *you* are in no hurry to leave. You're a relative here – you can stay as long as you like. But I'd like to go – that's what I'm telling you.'

She then took my arm and said, 'What do you think, *bhāi*? You're not really relatives of mine.' I embraced her instead of replying. I could see that however domineering *Pisimā* might be, she was no match for this girl. She betrayed no outward annoyance – indeed she tried to show affection; but Hemangini brushed her aside. Laughing the whole matter off as a spoilt girl's joke, she started to leave – but then had further thoughts and turned back, saying to Hemangini, 'Himu, come along, it's time for your bath.' Hemangini came up to me and said, 'Let's both of us go to the *ghāṭ* – what do you say, *bhāi*?' My aunt-in-law forbore to stop us, despite her reluctance to let us go; she knew that if it came to a tussle with Hemangini the girl would win – and besides, a quarrel wouldn't look good in front of me.

As we made our way to the *ghāṭ* behind the house, Hemangini asked, 'Why haven't you got any children?'

I smiled and said, 'How should I know why not? God hasn't given me any.'

'I dare say you had some kind of sin in you,' said Hemangini.

'That too is only known to God,' I replied.

The girl said conclusively, 'Look at Auntie, though. She has such crookedness in her, no children can possibly form in her womb.'

I had no understanding myself of the mysteries of sin and virtue, suffering and happiness, punishment and reward – so I couldn't explain them to the girl. All I could do was sigh and inwardly say to God, '*You* know!'

Hemangini hugged me and said, laughing, 'Oh dear, even *my* words made you sigh! Usually no one listens to what I say!'

I noticed that my husband was beginning to neglect his medical practice. If a call came from a long way off he did not go; if he went on a call near by he would deal with it as quickly as possible. Formerly he would stay in his surgery during gaps in his work, only coming home for his midday meal and siesta. Now my aunt-in-law summoned him at all hours, and he himself came to see her quite unnecessarily. When I heard her calling out, 'Himu, bring my *pān*-box, will you?' I knew that my husband was in his aunt's room. For the first two or three days, Hemangini fetched *pān*-box, oil-bowl, vermilion-pot or whatever else she was asked for. But after that she refused to budge, and sent the maid with the requested article. If my aunt-in-law called, 'Hemangini, Himu, Himi', the girl would embrace me with a kind of intense pity: dread and sorrow came over her. She would now never mention my husband in my presence, even by mistake.

Meanwhile my elder brother came to see me. I knew how observant he was. It would have been practically impossible to hide from him what was afoot. My brother was a harsh judge of people. He never forgave the slightest wrong-doing. My greatest fear was that he would see my husband as a criminal. I tried to cover things up with a smokescreen of excessive cheerfulness: by talking and fussing to an extreme degree, by putting on an elaborate show. But this was so unnatural to me, it increased the danger of detection. My brother, however, did not stay very long: my husband's uneasiness took the form of blatant rudeness towards him – so he left. Before he went, he placed his hand – trembling with pure love – on my head for a long time: I could feel the passionate blessing his touch conveyed; his tears fell on my own tear-soaked cheeks.

That Caitra evening, I remember, market-goers were making

their way home. A storm was approaching, bringing rain from a long way off; one could sense it in the dampness of the wind and the smell of wet earth. People were anxiously calling for their friends in the dark fields. I never sat with a lamp alight in the dark blindness of my bedroom, in case my clothes caught fire by brushing against it, or some other accident happened. I was sitting on the floor in my lonely dark room, clasping my hands and crying out to the God of my blind world. I was saying: 'Lord, when I do not feel your mercy, when I do not understand your wishes, what can I do but cling with all my might to the rudder of my helplessly broken heart? Blood pours from my heart, but how can I control the tempest? What further trials must I suffer, weak as I am?' Tears streamed down as I prayed – I buried my face in the bed and sobbed. I'd spent the whole day doing housework. Hemangini had followed me like a shadow: I'd had no chance to release the grief welling up inside me. That evening at last the tears came out; and it was then that I noticed the bed stirring a little, the swishing sound of someone moving about, and a moment later Hemangini had come and thrown her arms round my neck and was silently wiping my eyes with the end of her sari. She must have entered the bedroom earlier in the evening, but when, and with what intention, I could not tell. She did not ask a single question, and I also said nothing. She slowly passed her cool hand across my brow. I have no idea when the thunder and torrential rain of the storm passed; but at length a quietness came and soothed my fevered heart.

The next day Hemangini said, 'Auntie, *you* may not want to go home, but there's a servant who can take me back – so there!'

'There's no need for that,' said my aunt-in-law. 'I'm also going tomorrow; we can go together. Look at this, Himu, our dear Abinash has brought a pearl ring for you.' She then proudly put the ring on to Hemangini's finger.

'Now you watch, Auntie,' said Hemangini, 'what a good aim I have.' She threw the ring through the window, right into the middle of the tank behind the house.

My aunt-in-law bristled with anger and surprise and dismay. She clutched my hands and said again and again, '*Baumā*, be sure you don't tell Abinash about this childish behaviour; the poor boy will be very hurt if you do. Promise me, *Baumā*.'

'You needn't say any more, *Pisimā*,' I said. 'I shan't tell him a thing.'

The next day before they left Hemangini embraced me and said, '*Didi*, don't forget me.' I stroked her face with both hands and said, 'The blind never forget, sister. I have no world; I live only in my mind.' I then took her head and sniffed her hair and kissed her. My tears mingled with her hair.

When Hemangini left, my world dried up. She had brought perfume and beauty and music into my life, bright light and the softness of youth: now that she was gone, what was there for me when I stretched out my arms? My husband came and said with exaggerated gusto, 'They've gone! Now we can breathe again – now I can do some work.' How wretched I was! Why did he put on such an act? Did he think I was afraid of the truth? Had I ever flinched at a blow? Didn't my husband know this? When I gave up my eyes, did I not accept eternal darkness calmly?

For a long time blindness had been the only gulf between me and my husband, but now there was a further division. My husband never mentioned Hemangini's name to me, even in error; as if she had been totally removed from his world, as if she had never at any time made any mark on it. Yet I could easily tell he was, frequently, inquiring after her by letter. Just as when a pond fills up with flood-water so that lotus-flowers tug at their stalks, whenever he was affected by even the slightest elation I could feel a tugging at my heart. I was perfectly aware of when he got news of her and when he did not. But I couldn't ask him about her. My soul longed to hear about the bright and beautiful star who had briefly shone so vividly in the darkness of my heart, but I had no right to speak of her to my husband even for a moment. On this, there was a total silence between us, full of suppressed words and feelings.

About the middle of Baiśākh, the maid came to me and asked, '*Māṭhākrun*, they're loading up a boat at the *ghāṭ* – where is the master going?' I knew that preparations were afoot. In the sky of my fate there had been, for some days, a lull before the storm. Tattered clouds of doom were gathering now: Shiva was silently pointing his finger, amassing all his destructive power above my head – I knew that well. But I said to my maid, 'I've no idea. I haven't heard anything.' The maid didn't dare to ask any more questions, and left, sighing heavily.

Very late at night my husband came and said, 'I've been called to a place a long way off – I must leave at dawn tomorrow. I probably shan't be back for two or three days.'

I rose from my bed and said, 'Why are you lying?' He answered in a weak trembling voice, 'What lies have I told you?'

'You are going to get married,' I said.

He was silent. I also stood stock-still. For a long time no sound was heard in the room. In the end I said, 'Give me an answer. Say, "Yes, I'm going to get married."'

He replied like an echo, 'Yes, I'm going to get married.'

'No,' I said, 'you will not be able to go. I shall save you from this dreadful danger, this terrible sin. If I cannot do that, what kind of wife am I? For what have I offered so many *pūjā*s to Shiva?'

Once again the room fell silent for a long time. I slumped to the floor, clung to my husband's feet and said, 'What wrong have I done you? Where have I fallen short? What need have you for another wife? I beg you, speak the truth.'

My husband then said slowly, 'This is the truth: I am frightened of you. Your blindness has covered you with a perpetual shroud, which I have no means of piercing. You are like a goddess, terrifying as a goddess – I cannot go on living with you for ever. I want an ordinary woman whom I can scold, whom I can be angry with, whom I can fondle, whom I can deck with ornaments.'

'Cut open my breast and see!' I said. 'I am an ordinary woman – in my heart I am nothing but that young bride you married. *I* want to believe, *I* want to trust, *I* want to worship: do not demean yourself and bring misery to me by raising me above *you*! Please, keep me in all respects beneath you!'

I cannot remember all that I said. Does a turbulent sea hear its own roaring? All I recall is that I said, 'If I have been true to you, then God will never allow you to break your righteous vows. Either I'll be widowed or Hemangini will die before you commit such a sin!' With that I fainted.

When I regained consciousness, the dawn chorus had not quite begun, and my husband had gone. I shut myself into the prayer-room to perform a *pūjā*. I stayed in the room for the whole day

long. In the evening we were shaken by a *Kāl-baisākhī* storm. I
did not say, 'O God, my husband is on the river now, look after
him.' I said, passionately, 'God, let whatever is my fate happen,
but save my husband from his terrible sin.' The whole night
passed like this. I continued my *pūjā* through the next day too.
Who gave me strength to last for so long without sleep and food I
cannot say; but I stayed sitting like stone before the stone image
of the deity.

In the evening, someone started to push at the door from the
outside. When the door burst open, I passed out again. When I
came round I heard, *'Didi!'* – and I found I was lying in Hemangini's lap. When I moved my head, her new wedding-sari rustled.
O God, you did not heed my prayer! My husband had fallen!

Hemangini lowered her head and said slowly, 'I have come for
your blessing, *Didi.*'

For the first minute I froze; then I sat up and said, 'Why
should I not bless you, sister? What wrong have you done?'

Hemangini laughed her sweet high laugh and said, 'Wrong?
Did you do wrong when *you* married? What wrong is there in *my*
marrying?'

I hugged her and laughed too. I said to myself, 'Do my prayers
have the last word? Is God's will not supreme? Let blows fall on
my head if they must, but I shall not let them fall on the place in
my heart where I keep my faith and religion. I shall stay as I
was.' Hemangini bent down and took the dust of my feet. 'May
you be eternally blessed, eternally happy,' I said.

'I want more than your blessing,' she said, 'I want you to
welcome me and my husband together into your chaste arms.
You must not feel shy about him. If you give me permission, I
shall bring him here.'

'Bring him,' I said.

A little later I heard a new footfall in the room, and the
affectionate question, 'Are you well, Kumu?'

I hurriedly stumbled from the bed and did obeisance to him,
crying, *'Dādā!'*

'What do you mean "*Dādā*"?' said Hemangini. 'Don't be silly!
He is your new *bhagnīpati*!'[1]

1. Brother-in-law; sister's husband. Because of the sisterly relationship between

I understood all. I knew that my elder brother had vowed not to get married: our mother was no more, he had no one to push him into marriage. He had married now because of me. Tears rolled down my cheeks; I couldn't stop them. My elder brother gently ran his hands through my hair; Hemangini hugged me and went on laughing.

I couldn't sleep that night. I waited with beating heart for my husband to return. How would he contain his shame and bitterness?

Very late at night, the door opened slowly. I sat up with a start. It was my husband's step. My heart pounded. He came on to the bed and took my hand and said, 'Your brother saved me. I was in a state of madness for a while and was about to destroy myself. When I got into the boat God alone knew the weight that was pressing on my breast; when we ran into a storm on the river and I feared for my very life, I thought, "If I drown, I shall have been saved." When I arrived at Mathurganj I was told of the marriage, the previous day, of your brother and Hemangini. I cannot describe the shame but also the joy with which I returned to the boat. In these past few days I have learnt for sure that I would find no happiness in deserting you. You are my goddess.'

I smiled and said, 'No, I don't want to be a goddess. I am the keeper of your house – an ordinary woman.'

'I also have a request,' said my husband. 'Never embarrass me again by calling *me* a god.'

The next day the neighbourhood resounded with ululations and the sound of conches.[1] Hemangini began to tease my husband mercilessly, from morning to night, at meals and at rest, giving him no relief; but no one alluded to what had happened, or where he had gone.

---

the two women, Hemangini's husband will be a brother-in-law rather than a brother (*Dādā*) to Kusum.

1. Welcoming Hemangini, the new bride, into the house.

Appendix A: 'Passing Time in the Rain'

This famous poem – *barṣā-yāpan* from *sonār tarī* ('The Golden Boat', 1894) – is rightly felt by many Bengali readers to reach right to the core of Tagore's short stories. It was completed in June 1892, but was begun 'much earlier'; and in its picture of the solitary young Tagore whiling away the hours at Jorasanko, as well as in its tripping medieval metre, it has a charmingly youthful quality. But it is not quite as light and improvisatory as it first seems. There is strong cumulative energy in its evocation of the rain, the *Meghadūta*, and Vaishnava songs about Radha pining for Krishna, intermixed with the poet's own passionate aspirations. The section containing the lines that I have italicized was used by Pramathanath Bisi as an epigraph for his book on Tagore's short stories. *choṭo prāṇ, choṭo byathā, choṭo choṭo duḥkha-kathā* ('small lives, small pains, small stories of unhappiness') is what everyone quotes; but the lines about plain narrative and 'incompleteness' are just as germane, and the correlation between monsoon rain and human tears is sonorously explicit. The poem shows how deliberate the short stories were: Tagore knew exactly what he was doing in them.

> A third-floor roof in Calcutta,
> A wooden hut at one end;
> Dawn's first eastern glimmer,
> South door open to the wind.
>
> My bedding spread on the floor,
> My head close to the door,
> I cast my roving eye
> At hundreds of roofs stretching,
> Such mysteries concealing –
> Frowning at the sky.
> In a corner of the wall,
> Pressing the window-sill,
> A trembling splash of green –
> A tiny peepul-seedling,

Watching its shadow dancing,
   All day long alone.
Filling the sky all round
Āṣāṛh clouds descend,
   Rain approaches darkly:
Yoking the heavens together,
Indra's horses thunder,
   Lightning flickers sharply.
As streaming torrents pour,
I feel I am banished far,
   Beyond the universe:
Perched in my hut in the rain,
   I leave time and space.

How happy such days have been
As I sit here on my own,
   Reading the *Meghadūta*!
Outside the wind blows wildly
     In constant fruitless frenzy –
I lose myself in scenes
Of mountains, rivers and towns
   In ancient monsoon India:
Each cloud-covered village and land
So mellifluously named –
While the lovers I long have known
Yearn and grieve and pine,
   Each imagining each,
Hearts tugging them close
While a great dividing space
   Keeps them out of reach.
The Yakṣa bride paces,
Turns and listens and watches,
   Counting the days with flowers.
Or else I embrace attentively
Govinda Das's *padābalī*
   As the rain noisily pours.
I sing out again and again
That trysting-song of monsoon
   Beside the dark Yamuna:
Young, passionate Radha,
Seeking her lover's arbour,
   Nothing in the world can stop her,
 And the forest gets more lonely

As the rain falls more strongly,
  Patters and pounds and pours –
Only young Madan beside her,
No other friend to shield her,
  No houses with open doors.

As Āṣāṛh reaches its height,
I mix two *rāga*s to write [1]
  A song of the monsoon floods.
Or scanning the first stanza
Of Jayadev's *Gītāgovinda*
  I sing of sleek rain-clouds.
Or at night when the air is still
And buckets of rain fall,
  I lie deliciously sleepy
And a song about nights in Śrābaṇ,
The roar of incessant storm,
  Rolls around in my memory.
Or – 'Lying on a bed in bliss,
Melting in amorousness,
  Sunk in dreamy longing' –
I imagine that vivid scene
In ancient Vrindavan,
  Radha's lonely dreaming,
Her gently panting breath,
Her smile on her dreamy mouth –
  Her closed eyes aquiver,
Her head slumped on her arm,
Lying all on her own,
  A dim lamp in the corner.
In the mountains thunder rumbles,
Rain in the trees rattles,
  Frogs burble all night –
How joyously she dreams
Of lying in her lover's arms!
Alas, alas when she wakes
And her frenzied rapture breaks
  In mournful solitude,
She sees the lamp nearly out,
Hears the watchman's hourly shout –
  And the force of the rain is renewed,

1. Mallār and Deś *rāga*s. See Glossary.

With thunder's booming sound
And crickets buzzing all round,
    Filling the whole world.
When she wakes during such a pounding,
Caught between waking and dreaming,
    Think how her heart is swirled!

One book after another,
Dipping in out of order,
    Thus I pass the night.
I flick through some English [1] verses
But find in none of them traces
    Of the shade of this monsoon rain –
No sound of this dark pattering,
No deep, indolent yearning,
    No self-immersing pain!
The rain's relentless note,
The music, inside me and out,
    Of torrents beating the ground,
Carrying me wide and far,
Roving from shore to shore,
    Where in such poems is it found?
I throw the book on the floor,
I sit close to the door,
    Bury myself in thinking.
Nothing to do, now,
I gaze and wonder how
    I shall pass the time till evening.
But then I buckle down,
Write to a new plan,
    All day carefully –
Why should I not, if I want,
Following my own bent,
    Write story after story –
Small lives, humble distress,
    Tales of humdrum grief and pain,
Simple, clear straightforwardness;
Of the thousands of tears streaming daily
    A few saved from oblivion;
    No elaborate description,
    Plain steady narration,

---

1. *bideśī*: 'foreign', but almost certainly English.

No theory or philosophy,
No story quite resolved,
Not ending at the end,
  But leaving the heart uneasy.
All the world's unnumbered
Stories never completed:
  Buds unripely torn –
Dust of fame unsung,
The love, the terror, the wrong
  Of thousands of lives unknown.
From all the world around me
They seem to fall unceasingly
  Like floods of monsoon rain:
Momentary smiles and tears
Pouring through the years,
  The sound goes on and on.
Each lost and forgotten moment
Whirls in a dancing torrent:
  Oh may I from it gather
The clouds of life's monsoon,
And make them rain down
  What else would be gone for ever!

Appendix B: Letters

1. *chinnapatrābalī*, Letter No. 3, Shelidah, 28–30 November 1889, to Indira Devi[1]

Our boat has been moored by a sandbank opposite Shelidah. It's a huge, desolate sandbank, stretching out of sight: with slivers of river-water here and there, or expanses of wet sand that look like water. No village, no people, no trees, no grass – but monotony is broken by patches of cracked, wet black earth, alternating with dry white sand. If you turn and look to the east, an endless blueness meets an endless pale yellowness. The sky is empty and the earth too is empty: dry, harsh, barren emptiness below; ample, airy emptiness above. I have never seen such desolation. If you look round to the west again, you see a small kink in the river where the stream scarcely flows, a high bank, and beyond that huts and trees, wonderfully dreamlike in the evening sunlight. It's as though on one side you have Creation and the other Destruction. I say 'evening sunlight', because we go out for a walk in the evening and I have a mental picture of the scene as it is then. If you stay in Calcutta you forget how extraordinarily beautiful the world really is. It's only when you are here, and can see the sun setting behind the peaceful riverside trees, and thousands of stars appearing above the unending, pale, lonely, silent sandbank, that you realize how amazing these daily events are. The sun seems to open a huge book each morning, and by the evening a huge page has been turned in the sky above: what extraordinary things are written on it! And this narrow river and vast sandbank, and the picture-like bank opposite with its plain fields beyond, are a vast, silent, secluded school being taught from the book. Enough! All this would sound like 'poetry'[2] in the city, but here it doesn't seem so far-fetched.

In the evening one of the servants takes the children off over

---

1. Tagore's niece. See Introduction, p. 8, and Family Tree, p. 324.
2. The English word is used.

the sandbank in one direction and Balu, the two ladies and I also go off in separate directions.[1] Meanwhile the sun goes down completely, the last gleam of light fades from the sky, and everything is obliterated – until the faint shadow of one's body to one side shows that a slender crescent moon is weakly shining. The ample expanses of sand in the pale moonlight become even more confusing: what is sand, what is water, what is sky, becomes a matter of guesswork; so everything seems like a kind of unreal fantasy-world. Yesterday, after wandering there for a long time, I returned to the boat and found that apart from the children no one else had got back. I sat down in an armchair, and began to read an extremely obscure book called *Animal Magnetism* in the equally obscure light of an oil-lamp; but still no one returned. I put the book face down on the bed and went out on deck: nothing could be seen in the blackness all around. Everything was dim and deserted. I shouted out 'Balu' loudly: my voice rang out in all directions, but no one answered. Then my chest tightened, suddenly folded up like an umbrella. Gofur went out searching with a lamp, and Prasanna, and the crew of the boat: I sent them all off in different directions. I was shouting 'Balu, Balu', Prasanna was shouting '*Choṭo Mā*', and the boat-men's shouts of 'Babu, Babu' mingled with the rest. Together our voices made a bleak kind of music in the desert, in the silent night. No one answered us. Gofur once or twice cried from a long way off, 'I've seen them' – but then a moment later corrected himself with 'No, no'. Imagine the state I was in: picture the silent darkness, the faint moonlight, the still and deserted empty sandbank, Gofur's lantern moving around in the distance, and every now and then from one direction or another anxious calls and their melancholy echoes, with sometimes a burst of excited hope and the next moment despairing disappointment. An appalling dread took hold of my mind. Sometimes I thought they must have fallen into quicksand; sometimes I imagined that Balu had fainted or something; or else I had fantasies of various kinds of ferocious wild beasts. I recalled that 'those who do not look after

1. The party consisted of Mrinalini Devi and a maid ('the ladies'), Bela and Rathindranath ('the children', only three and one year old at the time), and Balendranath Tagore. See Family Tree, p. 324. Gofur was the cook, and Prasanna a crewman on the boat.

themselves often unwittingly cause danger to others'.[1] I turned
bitterly against any notion of freedom for women! But a little
later there were shouts that they were over on the other side of a
channel – they had crossed by using bits of sand as stepping-
stones, and now could not get back. A boat was dispatched, and
they were rescued – with Balu saying, 'I'm never going to go out
with you again.' They were all ashamed, exhausted and upset, so
I refrained from giving them a proper talking-to. The next
morning, however, I couldn't bring myself to be angry, and what
had actually been a serious alarm evaporated in laughter, as if it
had all been a joke. Ah well, at least in describing it to you three
days later I've got it off my chest.

Oh dear! Maulabi-saheb[2] is here salaaming before me with a
crowd of tenants. I want to say:

> Down with tenants! Down with the *jamidāri*!
> If only they could all get lost with Maulabi![3]

2. *cithipatra*, Vol. I, Letter No. 5, Kaligram, December 1890, to
Mrinalini Devi

Bhāi Choṭobau,

I arrived at Kaligram today. It took three days to
get here. I had to pass through lots of different places. First a big
river; then a small river, with trees on both sides, beautiful to
look at; then the river gradually became narrower, very like a
canal, with high banks on either side, very closed in. Then to a
place where the current was extremely swift: twenty or twenty-
five people were needed to pull our boat through. There is a huge
marsh which they call the 'Moving Marsh'. Water pours out of it
into the river. With a great deal of pushing and pulling, we
managed with considerable difficulty to get the boat into the
marsh. Water stretched drearily all around, with clumps of grass
or scrub on patches of land here and there: like a field flooded
after heavy rain. Sometimes the boat got stuck on the bits of land,
and it would take an hour or an hour-and-a-half of pushing and
shoving to get her afloat again. The mosquitoes were terrible. To

1. A quotation from Tagore's own play *rājā o rānī* (1889), Act II, Scene 2.
2. See Introduction, p. 8.
3. A parody of lines in Act I, Scene 2 of *rājā o rānī*.

be honest, I didn't like this marsh at all. After that we sailed along small streams, or through more marshes. At last we arrived. I don't relish the prospect of a similar journey to Birahimpur. The river here has no current at all: with its patches of floating moss, and clumps of jungly vegetation, it smells like a stagnant village pond, and at night the mosquitoes are quite something. If it becomes unbearable, I shall flee back to Calcutta.

When I got Bela's sweet letter I wanted to come straight back home. Is she missing me a lot? She's so little, I don't know what to do for her. Tell her there'll be lots of kisses and jam for her when I come. Last night I dreamt of *Khokā*:[1] I was dancing him on my knee, and he was finding it great fun. Has he started to talk yet? I think that Bela was already talking a lot at his age. Is it cold with you? I've been shivering with cold here – except that last night when we found a firm mooring for the boat and I drew all the curtains, I woke up feeling too hot! And on top of that, at one or two in the morning, right next to us, a crowd of people started singing, 'Why do you sleep so much, my love? Wake up, wake up!' If 'my love' lived near by perhaps she would have given them a beating. The boatman shut them up, but that line 'Wake up, wake up, my love!' kept on going round and round in my head: it made me feel quite ill. I slept only at the end of the night, after I had drawn back the curtains and opened the window. So today I've been feeling sleepy all the time. How is your brother getting on in Calcutta? Have you made any arrangements for his studies? How many months' allowance has he already been given? I hope to come back in about a fortnight – but I can't say exactly when.

3. *chinnapatrābalī*, Letter No. 13, Kaligram, January 1891, to Indira Devi

This great world of Nature lying silently in front of me – how I love her! I want to reach out with my arms and embrace her: her trees and rivers and fields, her sounds and quietness, her dawns and dusks. I feel that we receive the world's gifts as from a kind of heaven. I don't know what else this heaven could give, but I

1. i.e., Rathindranath Tagore. See Family Tree, p. 324.

cannot imagine it has given more of itself than in the people here – so gentle, weak, touchingly timorous and childlike. This world of Nature, our own Mother Earth, comes to us bringing, like riches in her lap, all the feelings of the humble, mortal hearts that are found here – in her golden fields, by her nurturing rivers, in dwellings filled with happy and sad tenderness. So useless are we, that we cannot protect these people, we cannot save them; various unseen powerful forces work to tear them from her breast; but Earth does all she can for them. I love this Earth so much. There is a great, outstretching grief in her face, as if she is thinking, 'I am the daughter of a god, but I do not have the power of a god. I love but I cannot save; I begin but I cannot complete; I give birth but I cannot ward off the clutches of death.' This makes me turn away from heaven and look at my Mother Earth in her humble home with even more love. She is so helpless, so powerless, so incomplete, so stirred all the time by thousands of anxious fears.

4. *chinnapatrābalī*, Letter No. 16, Sajadpur, February 1891, to Indira Devi

I see all sorts of rural sights, which I greatly enjoy watching. Just opposite my window on the bank of a canal, a group of gypsies have set up camp, stretching cloth and matting over split bamboo-poles to make tents – small awnings, I should say, too low to stand up in. They do all their domestic tasks out in the open; only at night do they sometimes pack themselves into the tents to sleep. Gypsies are like this. They have no proper home anywhere, they don't pay rent to any landlord: they wander around from place to place with a herd of pigs, a few dogs and a bunch of children. The police keep a suspicious eye on them. I often stand by my window and watch them going about their work. They are quite handsome – Hindusthani in looks. Dark-complexioned, certainly, but graceful, strong and shapely in physique. The women are attractive: tall and slender and lean, rather like English girls in the frankness and freedom with which they move – that is to say they are very confident, with an easy, swift, springiness in their gait. Yes, they are just like dark-skinned English girls. A man will put a pan on to cook, and then sit splitting bamboo to make wickerwork baskets or trays; his wife will sit with a small mirror in her lap and carefully wash her face with a wet rag two or three times, pat and pull at her sari to get it nicely arranged, squat down near to her man, and get on with some kind of task. They are real children of the soil, truly close to Nature – they are born and die wherever they find themselves, they wander around from place to place. I'm very curious to know exactly how they live and think and feel. They are out in the open all the time, in the freedom of land and air; it's an unconventional existence, yet they have their work and affections and children and domestic routines. I have never seen any of them idle; they are always busy with one kind of work or another. If a woman comes to the end of her work, she immediately goes and sits behind another woman, unties her hair and begins carefully to pick it over for lice – and maybe she gossips about whatever is going on in that small three-tent encampment: I cannot precisely tell from a distance, but it looks to me to be so. This morning this peaceful gypsy encampment was severely disrupted. It was about half past eight or nine – they had brought out the rugs and tattered quilts they sleep on at night to spread them out in the sun on top of the awnings. The pigs and piglets had all settled down in a hole, nestling up to one another so that they looked like a huge ball of mud: after the cold of the night they were obviously finding the morning sunshine very warm and comfortable. Suddenly two of the dogs came and jumped on their necks, yapping and yelping and waking them up. Squealing with annoyance they ran off in search of some breakfast.

The other day I was writing my diary,[1] now and then looking dreamily out at the road, when there was a sudden uproar. I went over to the window and saw a crowd of people round the gypsy encampment: amongst them there was a prosperous-looking type brandishing a *lāṭhi* and abusing them luridly. The gypsy-leader was standing and trying in a very meek and frightened way to explain himself. I realized he was suspected of something, so the police constable had come to make a fuss. His wife was sitting and calmly peeling bamboo-canes, as if she was sitting alone and there was nothing untoward going on. But suddenly she stood up,

---

1. Tagore did not keep a regular diary. He was working on the second volume of his *yurop-yātrir ḍāyāri* ('Diary of a Journey to Europe', 1893) at the time.

went up fearlessly to the constable, waved her arms and began to berate him at the top of her voice. At once the constable's confidence diminished by about 75 per cent: he tried feebly to say something, but she didn't give him a chance. He had to beat a retreat in a manner very different from that in which he had come. From a distance he shouted, 'I warn you, you'd better clear off from here.' I assumed that my gypsy neighbours would have to roll up their mats and stakes and shift from here with their children and pigs. But there is no sign of that; they are still here, serenely peeling bamboo, cooking and serving food, and picking head-lice.

I see many things through my open window. I'm intrigued by them all, but some of them are especially haunting. I can't bear to watch people loading up bullocks with impossible burdens and then stabbing at them with sticks to make them move. This morning I saw a woman taking her naked, skinny little boy to the canal-water to give him a wash. It's terribly cold today; when she stood the child in the water and poured it over him, he wept and wailed piteously – and he had a dreadful hacking cough. His mother then gave him such a heavy slap on the cheek that I could hear it clearly inside my room. The boy bent over with his hands on his knees and shuddered with sobs – his cough was choking his weeping. The woman then dragged the soaked, naked, shivering child back home. This incident struck me as devilishly cruel. The boy was so small – my own son's age. A scene like this strikes a heavy blow at one's ideal of man – it really makes one's faith stumble. Little children are so helpless – if they are treated unjustly their innocent distress and wails simply annoy their cruel tormentors even more. They don't know how to defend themselves. The woman had come well wrapped up against the cold, and the boy didn't have a stitch on – *and* he had a cough, *and* he had such a beating from her!

5. *cithipatra*, Vol. V, Letter No. 12, Shelidah, 19 December 1892, to Pramatha Chaudhuri [1]

1. Pramatha Chaudhuri (1868–1946) was a distinguished editor and essayist, and was married to Indira Devi. See Introduction, pp. 2, 8.

Bhāi Pramatha,

        I got your letter yesterday, but because I was busy with a poem I wasn't able to reply immediately. I find it very difficult to write good letters to order. Writing articles is easy – the pen can range unhindered over a whole subject. But in letters everything has to be expressed in hints and gestures and delicate touches of feeling – it's almost like writing poetry. But where is there the time to write letters like that? At one time I found letter-writing a joy, and maybe I was able to give joy by writing them; but the kind of adolescent indolence that is required is no more. Now everything has to be dashed off quickly. Yet so many ideas crowd my mind. Sometimes my mind feels carefree and light and fluttery, and then letters float up like coloured soap-bubbles. But when I spend all day in heavy, arduous, worldly work, then my fingers get so blunted that I can't toss off fine artistic work easily – it takes me a long time to do it. Poem-writing has been my addiction all my life: sometimes when the craving for it comes over me, then if I am *not* able to write my whole mind becomes unbalanced and life becomes unbearable; but I can't *get* the necessary time! I keep thinking I can polish off all my tasks quickly and then sit down and concentrate on my poetry in serene seclusion; but every day and every month new tasks present themselves. There's no one who can give me any help: so I just have to grit my teeth and do it all – and it's work that has to be done thoughtfully and slowly and patiently. Yet it's not *real* work: all the things that I really want to do are having to be pushed aside and postponed to some unspecified future date. There are also many duties I'm neglecting, and complaints from my family to put up with, and every day a sense of frustration and dissatisfaction with myself. But there's a kind of moral idealism in me that makes me patiently bear all the duties that pile themselves on to my shoulders. Whatever duties my circumstances dictate have to be borne and carried out. So every month I bow my head and write things for *sādhanā*, and every day I attend dutifully to all the petty responsibilities of a zamindar. Do you imagine I get any pleasure from this? Today even the letters I write are a kind of duty. I feel harassed a lot of the time, but I think that on the whole this is the best way of life for me. Flying about on a winged horse called Imagination is not very healthy exercise for a mind like mine!

6. *chinnapatrābalī*, Letter No. 98, Shelidah, 16 May 1893, to Indira Devi

At half past six yesterday afternoon, fresh and clean after a bath, I walked for an hour or so on the sandbank by the river; then I rowed out on the river in our new dinghy; then spread out my bedding in it and lay silently in the evening darkness in the cool breeze of evening. Sh—[1] sat near by and chatted on about various things. The sky above my eyes was absolutely studded with stars. Almost every day I wonder: shall I ever be born again under this starry sky? Shall I ever, in this beautiful corner of Bengal, be able to spread out my bedding in my dinghy in such a serene and absorbed frame of mind, in the still Gorai river, on an evening as calm as this? Perhaps I shall never get back such an evening again, in any future life. Who knows how the scene will be changed, or with what sort of mind I shall be born. I may experience many evenings, but will they ever, so calmly, let their hair fall on my breast with such deep love? For how can I be the same man again? It's strange that my greatest fear is of being born in Europe – because in Europe there is never any chance to bare one's soul so loftily; or if one does, people are very critical. I'd probably have to slave away in some factory or bank or parliament. Just as the city streets there are hard and paved, so that horses and vehicles can pass and trade can go on, so the mind and character have to be solidly constructed so as to be suitable for business – with not the tiniest place for soft grass or a superfluous creeper to lodge. A stiff, durable sort of mind, clipped and hammered into shape by strict laws. Truly, I don't see this impractical, self-absorbed, free-roving mind of mine, with its love of Imagination, as anything to be ashamed of. As I lie in the dinghy, I don't consider myself less important than all the more practical people in the world. On the contrary, if I rolled up my sleeves and worked like them, *then* I would consider myself inferior – inferior to all those big, stereotyped, regimented people!

1. Probably Shaileshchandra Majumdar, whose 'Majumdar Agency' published the first collected edition of Tagore's short stories. See Bibliographical Notes, p. 295. He was the younger brother of Shrishchandra Majumdar (see p. 18, n. 1).

But does this make a besotted young man like me, lying in a dinghy, greater than, say, Rammohan Roy?[1]

7. *chinnapatrābalī*, Letter No. 102, Shelidah, 3 July 1893, to Indira Devi

All last night a fierce wind was howling like a street-dog – and the rain too was incessant. Water from the fields was rushing and gurgling towards the river from all sides in little streams. As they brought the cut paddy back from the sandbank opposite, crossing over in the rain-sodden ferry-boat, some of the farmers wore large straw hats, others held *kacu*-leaves over their heads. The helmsman was soaked as he sat on the loaded boat, rudder in hand, while sopping boatmen heaved sacks on to the shore. Even in such terrible weather the world's work has to go on. Birds huddle in their nests, but men and boys have to go out. In front of my boat there were two herd-boys: the cows they were grazing made a crunching sound as they filled their mouths with fresh, rain-washed, juicy green grass; their eyes were calm and tender as they swished the flies off their backs with their tails. Rain fell on their backs continuously, and the sticks of the herd-boys too: both were completely uncalled-for and unjust and unnecessary, yet they bore both without complaint or question, and went on munching. The gaze of these cows was so loving and deep and calm and mournful. Why should human burdens be piled on the backs of these splendid animals, through no wish of their own?

The river is rising higher every day. Almost everything that could be seen only from the roof of the boat the day before yesterday can now be seen if I sit at the window. Every morning I get up and see that the shore of the river has receded further. For a long time I saw only the tops of the distant village trees, like a leafy green cloud; now I see the whole of them. Bank and water have gradually edged towards each other like two shy lovers: the line that modesty draws has become so indistinct that they have almost melted into each other. I shall enjoy sailing along this rain-swelled overflowing river – I'm eager to untie the rope and set off.

1. Tagore omitted this sentence when he printed the letter in *chinnapatra*, perhaps because he felt that the thought-connection was not clear. He may have wished to imply that the great Rammohan Roy (1772–1833) showed how it was possible to be Indian to the full, yet was as much an activist as any European.

8. *ciṭhipatra*, Vol. V, Letter No. 12A, Sajadpur, 23 July 1893, to Pramatha Chaudhuri

Bhāi Pramatha,

I'm gradually getting cut off from friends and acquaintances. I can't say why. It's certainly my own fault. My nature is perhaps getting more and more shy and self-absorbed: I'm coming to believe that instead of being swung all the time by the interest and sympathy of others, I would rather find stability – if not pleasure – in remaining alone and immersed in my own self. But when all's said and done, man is not just a work-machine; contact with others is highly desirable, and in the absence of warm companionship my enthusiasm for work has greatly diminished. One can't take on for long the task of patching the world's torn coat – especially if one has to do this on one's own, and if one's fate is to receive more abuse than praise for this unpaid work. It's best to admit as much: my skin is not like a rhino's – slander and discouragement hurt me, perhaps, more than the average man. I need smiles, kind comments, a little bit of praise and encouragement to strengthen and nourish my mind! I have for the present abandoned hope of alms from my master, and am eager to escape from his service. Your humble servant is taking a break from his efforts to improve the world! I have a longing to take the oil with which I have been anointing the feet of that ungrateful animal called the 'public', and sniff it myself to send me to sleep for a while. Then, perhaps, I shall wake again and return to massaging its feet. I tell you frankly: I set out expecting to be successful. I did not have any doubt on that score, or think myself unfit – but I've had to admit defeat. You are so far away from the battlefield that my victories and defeats, hope and disappointments must seem insignificant to you – I don't mind if you laugh at them.

I gather you are all now in the mountains. I sometimes feel like accepting your hospitality, but there are one or two obstacles: above all, after a month away from my family, I miss them, and to turn north instead of south from Kaligram would be hard for me. If I go home for a while, it will be easier to travel after that. But at the moment my financial circumstances are so bad that even the small expense of going to Darjeeling will be difficult. I hear that Loken[1] will join you in a week or so's time. So you are fixed there for some time yet. But when will you come down from the mountains?

Yes, I've noticed that *kaksa* meaning 'house' is used in several places in *Kādambarī*[2] and in a couple of other Sanskrit texts. I'm progressing slowly with *Kādambarī*. I've got through a couple of hundred pages – there are as many pages left. It's very late and I've burbled on to you for too long, so goodbye now.

9. *chinnapatrābalī*, Letter No. 149, Sajadpur, 5 September 1894, to Indira Devi

After sitting in the boat for so long it's good to arrive at the Sajadpur house. There are big windows and doors: light and air can come in unimpeded from all sides. I'm looking out at the green branches of trees and listening to the sound of bird-song. As soon as you go out on to the southern verandah the scent of *kāminī*-flowers hits you, filling every pore. I suddenly realize how hungry I was for wide open space, now that I am here and can take my fill of it. I am the sole occupant of four huge rooms – I sit with all the doors open. Here my mood for writing and desire to write are like nowhere else. A living influence from the world outside opens all doors and enters freely: light and sky and air and sounds and scents and the green ripple of the trees and my rapturous mood – all combine to create many stories. At midday, especially, there is something deeply magical about this place. The warmth of the sun, the stillness, the emptiness, the calls of the birds (especially the crows), and long and delightful leisure together make me detached yet keenly sensitive. I feel, somehow, that in this golden noon sunshine an Arab tale could be made: a Persian or Arab landscape – Damascus, Samarkand, or Bokhara; bunches of grapes, rose-gardens, nightingales singing, wine from Shiraz, desert paths, lines of camels, horsemen and travellers, clear fountains shaded by date-palms; towns, with

1. Loken Palit (1865–1915) was a close friend. Tagore met him on his first visit to England (1878–9). His father, Taraknath Palit, who qualified as a barrister in 1871, was a friend of Satyendranath Tagore. In 1879 Taraknath brought Loken to England to enter London University and study for the Indian Civil Service. In 1900 Tagore dedicated his book of poems *kṣaṇikā* to him.

2. Celebrated Sanskrit prose romance, written by Bana, poet in the court of the seventh-century Gupta emperor Harsha.

narrow streets shaded by awnings, shopkeepers in turbans and loose robes lining the roads and selling melons and pomegranates; huge palaces, with the scent of incense inside and enormous cushions and embroidered silks by the windows; ladies of the harem dressed in gold-embroidered slippers and billowy pyjamas, curling hubble-bubble pipes snaking round their feet; Negro eunuchs in gorgeous robes keeping guard at the door; and in that mysterious, unknown, distant land, in those opulent, marvellous, beautiful yet awesome palaces, thousands of probable and improbable stories made from human hopes and fears and laughter and tears!

My noons at Sajadpur are the best time for writing stories. I remember at exactly this time, sitting at this table, I thought up and then wrote 'The Postmaster'. I wrote, and the light and air all around, and the murmurings of the leaves, added their own language. There are few pleasures as great as that of composing something exactly as one wishes, submerging oneself completely in the scene all around. This morning I was writing a piece about nursery-rhymes – *charā* – I got completely absorbed in it: a great joy.[1] *charā* belong to their own separate realm in which there are no rules or laws – a misty realm. Unfortunately the material world, in which rules and laws have much greater influence, is always creeping up behind me. While I was writing, there was a sudden uproar from the office, and my misty realm was blown away – and all my time up till lunch was taken up.

There is nothing more calculated to induce inertia than a heavy meal at midday: our imaginative powers and higher aspirations are completely killed by it. Because Bengalis eat so much at midday, they cannot enjoy the intense beauty of that hour: instead they shut the door and smoke, or chew *pān* and complacently settle down for a nap – and become extremely glossy and fat as a result. But a peaceful, secluded afternoon amidst the boundless, monotonous, flat, wheat-fields of Bengal conveys a greater and deeper stillness than is found anywhere else. Even in my childhood, the afternoon moved me especially. I would sit reading on my own, on a curved settee, with the warm breeze blowing

1. Probably the essay *meyeli charā* ('Women's rhymes') published in *sādhanā* in September–November 1894, and later in *lok-sāhitya* ('Folk-literature', 1907). For an extract from an essay on *charā* see Appendix B of *Selected Poems*.

through the open door, and no one on the roof outside. I filled those long hours with so many dreams, so many unspoken yearnings!

10. *chinnapatrābalī*, Letter No. 153, 'on the boat to Dighapatiya',[1] 20 September 1894, to Indira Devi

Over the far side of the river the water-level has been going down, but on this side it's still rising.[2] I'm getting to know it better wherever I go. Huge trees, their trunks under water, stand with branches drooping into the water. Right in the midst of the shady gloom of banyan and banana trees, boats are moored and villagers bathe. Huts are dotted around in the streaming water, their yards completely submerged. No sign of the fields – just the tips of rice-plants poking out of the water. I've lost count of all the lakes, ditches, rivers and canals I've sailed through. After swishing through a paddy-field the boat suddenly entered a village pond, where there was no more paddy, but patches of lotus with white flowers blooming and black cormorants diving for fish. Next, we were in a small river: paddy-fields on one bank, and on the other a village surrounded by dense bushes, with fast streams of water snaking through them. Water enters wherever it's convenient: you've never seen land so utterly vanquished. Villagers move by sitting in large earthenware bowls, using pieces of split bamboo as oars – there are no banks or paths at all. If the water rises any more it will enter their homes – then they'll have to fix up a scaffold and live on their roofs. The cattle will die after standing knee-deep in water all the time, with no grass left for them to eat. Snakes will desert their flooded holes and seek refuge on the roofs of houses, and all the beetles and bugs and reptiles of the area, too, will look for human company. The villages here are shaded all round by jungle – its leaves and creepers and bushes go rotten in the water. Refuse from houses and cowsheds floats about; rotten, stinking jute turns the water blue; naked sickly children with swollen bellies and skinny legs jump and splash and wallow in the water and mud; clouds of mosquitoes buzz over

1. Town in north Bengal, in the Rajshahi District of present-day Bangladesh.
2. Perhaps because of the build-up of sandbanks.

fetid, stagnant water. Altogether the villages here become so unhealthy and uncomfortable during the monsoon that it makes one feel ill even to pass them. It's awful to see the womenfolk in their sopping saris rolled up to their knees, wading through water like patient beasts in the chilly monsoon air and pouring rain. I can't imagine how people can keep going at all in such difficult and wretched conditions. In every household people are plagued by rheumatism; their legs swell up; they catch colds and fevers; sick children howl and wail incessantly – nothing can save them, and one by one they die. Such neglect and unhealthiness and squalor and poverty and barbarism in human habitations are terrible to see. The villagers are victims of every kind of oppression: they have to endure the ravages of Nature *and* of landlords – and no one dares to question the age-old processes that create such unbearable misery. They ought to flee this kind of existence completely – there is no pleasure or beauty or advantage in it at all.

11. *cithipatra*, Vol. I, Letter No. 16, Shelidah, June 1898, to Mrinalini Devi

Bhāi Chuṭi,[1]

        I found your letter when I got back from Dhaka. I'll go briefly to Kaligram to tie up some business, and then come to Calcutta to make all necessary arrangements. But please, don't worry yourself needlessly. Try to bear every occurrence with a calm, peaceful, serene mind. This is what I try to do all the time in the way I lead my own life. I'm not always successful, but if *you* can keep calm, then perhaps – strengthened by our mutual efforts – I also may achieve peace and happiness of mind. Of course you are much younger than I am, and your experiences have been much more limited, and your nature is in some respects much more patient, much more easily controlled than mine. Therefore you have less need than I to keep your mind free of emotional disturbance. But in everyone's life major crises occur, in which the utmost patience and self-control are required. We then realize how silly we are to complain of trivial, daily annoy-

---

1. Affectionate abbreviation for *Choṭobau*. See Glossary.

ances, petty aches and pains. I shall love, and I shall do my best, and I shall do my duty by others cheerfully – if we follow this principle, we can cope with anything. Life does not last long, and its pleasures and travails are also constantly changing. Wounds, setbacks, deceptions – it's hard to bear them lightly; but if we don't, the burden of life gradually becomes insufferable, and it becomes impossible to fix one's mind on any goal or ideal. If we fail, if we live in dissatisfaction and tension day after day, in constant conflict with our circumstances, then our lives become completely futile. Great calm, generous detachment, selfless love, disinterested effort: these are what make for success in life. If you can find peace in yourself and can spread comfort around you, you will be happier than an empress. *Bhāi Chuṭi*, if you go on fretting over little things you will do harm to yourself. Most of our troubles are self-imposed. Do not be cross at me for lecturing you pompously like this. You do not know the intense concern with which I am saying these things. I feel such deepening of my love and respect for you, such a strengthening of the sympathy that ties me to you, that the pure calm and contentment that I wish for you means more than anything else in the world: compared to it, life's daily troubles and disappointments are nothing. These days I look at things with a new kind of longing.

A woman when young can be unsettled and deluded by love, but even from your own experience you perhaps know that at a maturer age, amidst the extraordinary ups and downs of life, a steadier, quieter, deeper, more real and controlled love develops. As her family grows, the outside world recedes. So in one respect her isolation grows – ties of intimacy seal off the married couple from the world around them. Our souls are never more beautiful than when we can draw close and look at each other face to face: real love begins then. There is no infatuation any more, there is no need to see each other as gods any more, unions and partings do not create storms of feeling any more – but near or far, in security or in danger, in poverty or wealth, the pure and joyous light of unqualified trust shines all around. I know you have suffered much because of me, but I also know that because you have suffered on my account you will one day know a greater, fuller joy. Forgiveness in love and sharing of troubles are true happiness; the satisfaction of personal ambition is *not* happiness.

These days my sole desire is that our lives should be simple and straightforward, that all around us there should be peace and cheerfulness, that our way of life should be unostentatious and full of bounty, that our needs should be small and our aims high and our efforts unselfish and our work for others more important than our work for ourselves. And even if our children gradually fall away from the example we have set them, I hope that we may, till the end, live our lives beautifully in mutual compassion and total, selfless, unambitious trust. This is why I have become so eager to take you all away from Calcutta's stony temple of materialism, and bring you to a far and secluded village. In Calcutta there is no opportunity to forget profit and loss, friend and foe: one is so constantly troubled by trifling matters that in the end all the finer purposes of life are shattered into fragments. Here one is content with little, and one does not mistake falsehood for truth. Here it is not hard to 'accept with equanimity whatever may come, happy or sad, pleasant or unpleasant'.[1]

P.S. Pramatha, Suren and a Gujarati friend of Pramatha's are here at Shelidah.[2]

12. *ciṭhipatra*, Vol. VI, Letter No. 4, Shelidah, 17 September 1900, to Jagadish Chandra Bose[3]

Dear Friend,

I was sitting quietly, flicking over the pages of a French grammar, when your letter arrived – it made me jump and twitch like an electrocuted dead frog! I was desperate to show your letter to Loken and Suren, but they are far away: I must send it to them at once. Make a declaration of war! Don't exempt

1. A quotation from the *śānti parva* of the *Mahābhārata* (12.168.30).
2. Pramatha Chaudhuri and Surendranath Tagore; the Gujarati friend has not been identified. The first Gujarati translation of Tagore did not appear till 1918, so it is hard to say if this friend had a specific interest in his writing.
3. Jagadish Chandra Bose (1859–1937) was a distinguished scientist, whose experiments on plant-reactions greatly interested Tagore. In August 1900 Bose represented India in an International Congress of Physicists in Paris. His theories about connections between organic and inorganic matter met with scepticism, and Tagore is responding here to a letter in which Bose described his determination to fight for his views. Tagore's ironic predictions of the praise that would come to Bose from his countrymen if he won acclaim abroad is prophetic of his own experience after winning the Nobel Prize.

anyone. If there are any who refuse to surrender, burn down their citadels with the fire of your arguments – as pitilessly as Lord Roberts.[1] You'll be able to combine your various armies into such a force that I firmly believe you will spend Christmas in Pretoria. And after your victory, we Bengalis will share the glory of it! There will be no need to understand what you did, no need to spend thought, money or time on it; praise from the English in *The Times* newspaper will be quite sufficient for us. Then one of our own famous newspapers will say, 'We're not such little people after all'; and other papers will say, 'We're advancing the frontiers of science'. No one will give a thought to the money you need – but when you bring in the harvest of world-wide fame we will claim you for our own. The farmer's labour is yours alone, but the profits will be ours; so when you win, we shall be even more victorious than you!

There you are, all keyed up at Point A, while I sit idly and serenely at Point B! All round me fields of sugar-cane and late rice, dewy with advancing autumn, are waving in the breeze. You'll be surprised to hear that I'm drawing in a sketch-book as I sit.[2] Needless to say, I'm not preparing pictures for a Paris salon, and I haven't the slightest fear that some foreign National Gallery will add to the tax revenue of this country by suddenly buying them. But just as a mother can feel extraordinary love for her child, however ugly, so one's heart can be attracted even to what one cannot do well. It was when I decided to give myself wholly to idleness that these pictures began to emerge in my mind. There is one major obstacle to my improving: I'm having to use the rubber much more than the pencil – so I'm getting more practice with the rubber. Raphael can sleep happily in his grave! His fame will not be threatened by me.

Loken has been trying to get me to accompany him on a trip to the Simla Hills during the *pūjā*-holiday: but I'm not budging. It

---

1. Frederick Sleigh Roberts, Earl (1832–1914). Field marshal who distinguished himself during the Indian Mutiny and the Second Afghan War; became commander-in-chief in India in 1885; and commanded the British forces during the South African War. He occupied Pretoria on 5 June 1900.

2. This is often quoted as the earliest indication of Tagore's interest in painting. But according to an article in *Desh* (5 August 1989), he experimented with portrait-sketching as early as 1880. There are also rough doodles in his earliest manuscript of all, *mālati pūthi*, parts of which may go back to 1874.

was different when the ancient sages went to the mountain-tops to practise meditation: nowadays you know how little peace there is in the mountains. I hope you haven't forgotten the friend you met on the way to Darjeeling. I'm sticking to watching the beautiful autumn assembly of squawking ducks on my beloved Padma. I think I remember that *you* were promising to take me on a trip – to Kashmir or Orissa or Trivancore – and indeed I'd like to smuggle myself into a chapter of your biography! I *hope* to meet your wishes – I'm trying to set aside some money for a future trip. My wife is sitting near by in an armchair and is pressing me to bathe and eat – it's getting late. So you must excuse me for a moment – I shan't be long.

Loken's eagerness to bring out a book of my poems has cooled somewhat since his trip to England. If he doesn't mind, I can see to this myself. You may be surprised that I'm drawing pictures, but no more surprised than you will be to hear that Loken has started writing poems! Such a state he was in – the poor fellow was finally driven to poetry! He's doing a verse translation of Omar Khayyam.[1] A brief sample will show you his condition:

> Fools you are to give up pleasure, hoping for salvation,
> Throwing yourselves in a dark gaol in search of liberation;
> No longer calling debts in, for you're sure of heavenly profit –
> I, for my part, leap at any chance to line my pocket.

But by squandering his wealth on these poems, Loken has thrown away his business prospects: he no longer cares about savings or interest – he wants to blow everything he's got, and I'm not willing to buy shares in such an enterprise.

Your brother-in-law's wife, Arya Sarala,[2] has recently begun to study Sanskrit with Bidyarnab.[3] The method of learning is my own invention. She's improving rapidly – the puṇḍit is delighted at having such an intelligent pupil. I encouraged her at the

1. Loken's translation was published in *bhāratī*, April–May 1901.

2. Sarala (her full name was Saralata) was the wife of Satishranjan Das, J. C. Bose's brother-in-law. Tagore's use of the term *āryā* ('Revered Lady') may derive from a request that Bose made to him in a letter of April 1899 that he should think of a Bengali alternative for 'Mrs'. In an article on 'Names' written in 1931, Tagore recalled this, saying that *āryā* was better than *debī* (devi), but had never caught on.

3. Shibadhan Bidyarnab, a Sanskrit pundit who also gave Tagore's son Rathindranath his first Sanskrit lessons at Shelidah.

beginning by saying that if she learnt Sanskrit by my method she would master the language within a year. I'm very pleased that she's learning. Our present-day educated women need to learn Sanskrit in order to balance the excessively English education they receive.

Dear sir, I'm not very hopeful of keeping the estate at Puri for you: the Magistrate has got his eye on it.[1] My manager there has written to say that the Puri District Board has its eye on my little plot. If the man who is claiming the land has a case, then it won't be possible to save it. If you can live there and start building a house, then maybe the fellow will not be able to get hold of it.

It's stormy today. The sky is cloudy – every now and then there are torrential showers of rain, and sharp gusts of wind which rattle the doors and windows. The storm and wind and rain throw me into a holiday mood – such as they can't understand in Western countries, where they are so addicted to work. I've done no work all week – and when it's less rainy, when the autumn sun shines or the south wind blows, I feel even less like work. I close the shutters and open the door of my room – the rain is pattering loudly as it pours down.

If you wish to get out of my expecting you to reply to this letter, then hand it over to Sarala. If she answers on your behalf, I shan't complain. Please give her my loving greetings. Don't forget that every detail of your work is fascinating to me. I'm thirsting for a *full* account of everything that's happening, everything that's being said or written.

13. *ciṭhipatra*, Vol. VI, Letter No. 5, Calcutta, 24 or 25 October 1900, to Jagadish Chandra Bose

Dear Friend,

        Is even the ship that Caesar embarks on safe from shipwreck? You've been called to so great a work – you *must* get well again soon.

I've come to Calcutta because a nephew of mine has fallen

1. The Tagore family owned some pieces of land in Orissa (see Introduction, p. 9), but the plot mentioned here was bought by Rabindranath in March 1898. He wanted to give it to Bose, but eventually had to sell it to pay off debts incurred by his Santiniketan school.

seriously ill [1] – I've had no sleep for nearly eight nights. So today I felt quite disorientated in mind and exhausted in body. Yesterday, to our great relief, he passed the danger point; now I must look to myself. I've decided to go to Bolpur-Santiniketan for a few days.

All my short stories are being published in a collected edition.[2] The first volume has appeared, but because we're still waiting for the second I can't yet send the complete edition to you. But I am, as you requested, enclosing the first volume. Most of the best stories are in the second. Of the stories in the first volume, the most suitable for translation would perhaps be: 'The Postmaster', 'Skeleton', 'In the Middle of the Night', and 'The Neighbour'.[3] But I don't have much faith in Mrs Knight's literary ability.[4]

I have passed on all your news to the Maharajah of Tripura.[5] I'm very pleased to see the esteem he has for you. He has sent me word that to help you in your work he is ready to give you much more than the amount he has already promised.

Have you made up your mind about that chance of working in England? I've given you my opinion on this before: don't have any hesitation in seizing it! If your own country is proving an impediment to your success, then you must, however reluctantly, bid her farewell.

I'm feeling terribly tired. I earnestly pray that *you* recover quickly.

14. *ciṭhipatra*, Vol. I, Letter No. 29, Shelidah, June 1901, to Mrinalini Devi

Bhāi Chuṭi,

With the palaver of the *puṇyaha* ceremony over,[6] I'm able to write again. Whenever I get the chance to write I'm

1. Nitendranath, third son of Dwijendranath Tagore.

2. The 'Majumdar Agency' edition. See Bibliographical Notes, p. 295.

3. *prabeśinī* (1900), not included in the present volume.

4. Miriam S. Knight, translator of Bankim's novels *The Poison Tree* and *Krishna Kanta's Will*. In fact Sister Nivedita was the first person to translate a Tagore story. See p. 298, n. 1.

5. Radhakishore Manikya, Maharajah of Tripura, was a close friend of the Tagore family. Tagore had approached him for help with the cost of Bose's stay and research in England. *bisarjan* ('Sacrifice') was staged in honour of the Maharajah in Calcutta on 16 December 1900.

6. See Glossary.

like a fish thrown into the water again from the bank. The isolation here now gives me complete protection, the irritations of the world can no longer touch me, and I find I can easily forgive those who are my enemies. I can well understand why the isolation got you and the children down: if I could get you to enjoy some of the feelings that I have here, I'd be very happy – but it's not something that can be *given* to anyone. If you leave Calcutta and come to this isolated place, I know you will not like it for the first few days – and later, even if you tolerate it, you will feel a suppressed impatience within. But for me life is fruitless, somehow, in Calcutta's crowds: they put me in such a bad mood that every trivial thing annoys me. I can't preserve my peace of mind there, forgiving people and avoiding conflict. Besides, I can't make proper arrangements for the children's education – they are always so restless and inattentive. That's why you will have to accept this sentence of exile. Later, when I am able, I shall choose a more suitable place than this; but I shall never be able to bury my own nature and live in Calcutta.

The whole sky is dark with clouds, and rain has started: I've shut all the downstairs windows, and am watching the rain as I write to you. From your two-storey house in Calcutta you won't get a sight like this. The dark, cool, new rain on the green fields all round is beautiful to watch. I'm writing an essay on the *Meghadūta*.[1] If I could colour it with some of the darkness of the teeming monsoon rain today, if I could make *permanent* for my readers the way in which the green fields of my Shelidah are turned a sort of bluey-green by the rain, that *would* be something. I've said lots of things in lots of different ways in my writing, but where *is* this gathering of clouds, this shaking of branches, this ceaseless stream of water, this pall of shade in which, as it were, earth and sky embrace? How easy it seems! How effortlessly the rain falls on land and air in this empty rural solitude, how casually this cloudy, relaxed, Aṣāṛh afternoon progresses towards dusk – yet I cannot retain a single trace of it in my writing. No one will be able to know *when* and

1. There are small gaps in the manuscript here. Kalidasa's *Meghadūta* ('Cloud-messenger') was a text that Tagore constantly returned to. The essay here is *nababarṣā* ('New Rain'), published in *baṅgadarśan* in July–August 1901 and included in *bicitra prabandha* (1907). Compare 'The *Meghadūta*', 'New Rain' and Appendix A in *Selected Poems*, and Appendix A in the present volume.

where I was, sitting through long leisured hours in an empty house, spinning these words out of my thoughts.

A heavy shower of rain has just finished – I must seize my chance to post this letter.

Bibliographical Notes

The following notes are restricted to giving the Bengali titles of the stories translated in this book, the Bengali periodicals and books in which they were published, and previous English translations. In order to give my selection shape and balance, I have not followed a strictly chronological order. For the stories published in *hitabādī*, exact publication dates are not known. The Bengali editions of Tagore's short stories referred to are:

choṭa galpa, published by Kalidas Chakrabarti and printed by him at the Adi Brahmo Samaj Press (Calcutta, 1894)

bicitra galpa, Vols. I and II, published by Kalidas Chakrabarti and printed by Yajneshvar Ghosh at the Sahitya Press (Calcutta, 1894)

kathā-catuṣṭay, published by Kalidas Chakrabarti and printed by Yajneshvar Ghosh at the Sahitya Press (Calcutta, 1894)

galpa-daśak, published by Kalidas Chakrabarti and printed by Yajneshvar Ghosh at the Sahitya Press (Calcutta, 1894)

galpaguccha, Vols. I and II, published by Amulyanarayan Ray at the Majumdar Agency and printed by Debendranath Bhattacharya at the Adi Brahmo Samaj Press (Calcutta, 1900 and 1901)

An edition of Tagore's stories up to 1907, *galpaguccha*, was published in five volumes by Indian Publishing House in Calcutta in 1908–9. Visva-Bharati's edition, also called *galpaguccha*, first appeared in 1926 (Vols. I and II) and 1927 (Vol. III). These volumes were expanded and rearranged in 1933–4. A new edition, adding Vol. IV, was published in 1946–7, and is the one that is currently available. All the stories I have chosen come from Vols. I and II of the current edition, or can be found in the complete *rabīndra-racanābalī* ('Collected Works of Tagore', Visva-Bharati, 1939–98).

For books of translations, the following abbreviations are used:

GBL   *Glimpses of Bengal Life*, translated and introduced by Rajani Ranjan Sen (G. A. Nateson & Co., Madras, 1913)

HS   *Hungry Stones and Other Stories* (Macmillan, London and New York, 1916)

MS   *Mashi and Other Stories* (Macmillan, London and New York, 1918)

ST   *Stories from Tagore* (Macmillan, London, Calcutta and New
        York, 1918)

BTS   *Broken Ties and Other Stories* (Macmillan, London, 1925, New
        York, 1926)

MST   *More Stories from Tagore* (Macmillan, Calcutta, 1951)

RS   *The Runaway and Other Stories*, edited by Somnath Maitra
        (Visva-Bharati, Calcutta, 1959)

HWS   *The Housewarming and Other Selected Writings*, edited by Amiya
        Chakravarty, translated by Mary Lago, Tarun Gupta and
        Amiya Chakravarty (A Signet Classic, New American Library,
        New York and Toronto, 1965)

CS   *Collected Stories* (Macmillan, New Delhi, 1974)

TR   *A Tagore Reader*, edited by Amiya Chakravarty (Macmillan,
        London and New York, 1961)

Information about Tagore in English can be found in Katherine Henn,
Rabindranath Tagore: A Bibliography (The American Theological Library Association, Metuchen, N.J. and London, 1985). Full information
about the publication of the Bengali texts of the stories is given in the
Appendix to Pramathanath Bisi's *rabīndranāther choṭa galpa* (Calcutta,
1954). I am greatly indebted to both these books. For information about
the very early translations of Tagore's stories which appeared in the
magazine *New India*, I am grateful to their discoverer, Samir Roy
Chowdhury of Santiniketan. The Macmillan editions of Tagore's stories
were published as if they were his own translations. In fact they were
generally done by friends, with or without the author's help.[1] In the notes
below, names of the Macmillan translators or co-translators are given
when known; if no name is given it should be assumed that the translator
is unknown. I have myself worked completely independently of earlier
translations, but readers may wish to look at other versions for comparison.

The Living and the Dead (p. 31)

jībita o mṛta. First published in *sādhanā*, Śrābaṇ (July–August) 1892;
included in *bicitra galpa*, Vol. II. Translations: (1) 'Alive and Dead', in
New India, 18 and 25 November 1901, possibly translated by the editor,
Bipin Chandra Pal (2) 'Living or Dead' in HS.

1. For Edward Thompson's role in the translation of Tagore's stories see E. P.
Thompson, *Alien Homage: Edward Thompson and Rabindranath Tagore* (OUP,
New Delhi, 1993), pp. 17–25.

The Postmaster (p. 42)

poṣṭmāṣṭār. First published in *hitabādī*, which ran for six weeks from 30 May 1891; included in *choṭa galpa*. Translations: (1) by Devendranath Mitter in *The Modern Review*, January 1911 (2) in MS and CS.

Profit and Loss (p. 48)

denāpāonā. First published in *hitabādī* (1891); included in *choṭa galpa*. Translation: 'Debts and Dues', by Sheila Chatterjee in *Amrita Bazar Patrika*, Puja Annual, 1960.

Housewife (p. 54)

ginni. First published in *hitabādī* (1891); included in *choṭa galpa*. Translation: 'Name', by Bhabani Bhattacharya in *The Golden Boat* (Allen & Unwin, London, 1932).

Little Master's Return (p. 58)

khokābābur pratyābartan. First published in *sādhanā*, Agrahāyaṇ (November–December) 1891; included in *bicitra galpa*, Vol. I. Translations: (1) 'My Lord, The Baby', by C. F. Andrews with the author's help in HS (2) 'The Return of Khokababu,' in HWS.

The Divide (p. 65)

byabadhān. First published in *hitabādī* (1891); included in *choṭa galpa*.

Taraprasanna's Fame (p. 70)

tārāprasanner kīrti. First published in *hitabādī* (1891); included in *choṭa galpa*. Translation: 'Taraprasanna's Masterpiece', by Sheila Chatterjee in *Amrita Bazar Patrika*, Puja Annual, 1960.

Wealth Surrendered (p. 76)

sampatti samarpaṇ. First published in *sādhanā*, Pauṣ (December–January) 1891–2; included in *bicitra galpa*, Vol. I. Translation: 'The Trust Property', by Prabhat Kumar Mukherjee in *The Modern Review*, May 1910, and MS.

Skeleton (p. 84)

kaṅkāl. First published in *sādhanā, Phālgun* (February–March) 1892; included in *bicitra galpa*, Vol. I. Translations: (1) 'The Skeleton', by Jatindramohan Bagchi in *New India*, 19 May 1902 (2) 'The Skeleton', by Prabhat Kumar Mukherjee in *The Modern Review*, March 1910 (3) 'The Skeleton' in MS (4) 'A Study in Anatomy' in GBL (5) 'The Skeleton', by Rabin Sarkar in *Amrita Bazar Patrika*, 14 May 1961.

A Single Night (p. 91)

ekrātri. First published in *sādhanā*, Jyaiṣṭha (May–June) 1892; included in *choṭa galpa*. Translation: 'The Supreme Night', by Jadunath Sarkar in *The Modern Review*, June 1912, and MS.

Fool's Gold (p. 97)

svarṇamṛg. First published in *sādhanā*, Bhādra–Āśvin (August–September–October) 1892; included in *bicitra galpa*, Vol. I. Translations: (1) 'The Golden Mirage' in GBL (2) 'The Fugitive Gold' in BTS.

Holiday (p. 107)

chuṭi. First published in *sādhanā*, Pauṣ (December–January) 1892–3; included in *choṭa galpa*. Translations: (1) 'The School Closes' in GBL (2) 'The Home-coming', by C. F. Andrews with the author's help in HS, ST and CS.

Kabuliwallah (p. 113)

kābulioyālā. First published in *sādhanā*, Agrahāyan (November–December) 1892; included in *choṭa galpa*. Translations: (1) 'Kabuli', by G. Sharma in *New India*, 31 March and 14 April 1902 (2) 'The Cabuliwallah', by Sister Nivedita in *The Modern Review*, January 1912, and HS, ST, CS and TR[1] (3) 'The Fruit-seller' in GBL.

1. This was almost certainly the first translation of a Tagore story, earlier than the version in *New India*. In a letter from Sister Nivedita (the famous Irish-born disciple of Swami Vivekananda) to Mrs Ole Bull, 29 November 1900, we read that she had already 'Englished' Kabuliwallah by then. Jagadish Chandra Bose, who had helped her with the translation, made an unsuccessful attempt to have it published in *Harper's* magazine in that same year.

The Editor (p. 121)

sampādak. First published in *sādhanā*, Baiśākh (April–May) 1893; included in *choṭa galpa*. Translations: (1) by W. W. Pearson in *The Modern Review*, August 1917, and BTS and MST (2) by Binayak Sanyal in *Amrita Bazar Patrika*, 10 May 1959 (3) by Sheila Chatterjee in *Amrita Bazar Patrika*, Puja Annual, 1962.

Punishment (p. 125)

śāsti. First published in *sādhanā*, Śrābaṇ (July–August) 1893; included in *kathā-catuṣṭay*. Translations: (1) 'The Sentence' in GBL (2) 'Punishment', by Sheila Chatterjee in *Amrita Bazar Patrika*, Puja Annual, 1958 (3) 'Punishment' in HWS.

A Problem Solved (p. 134)

samasyāpūraṇ. First published in *sādhanā*, Agrahāyaṇ (November–December) 1893; included in *choṭa galpa*. Translations: (1) 'The Riddle Solved', by Prabhat Kumar Mukherjee in *The Modern Review*, December 1909, and MS (2) 'The Solution of the Problem', by Surendranath Tagore in *The Modern Review*, August 1936.

Exercise-book (p. 140)

khātā. Probably first published in *hitabādī* (1891), or maybe written for the abortive seventh issue of the journal. The first known printing was in *choṭa galpa*. Translations: (1) 'The Copybook', by Jiten Sen in *The Statesman*, 29 November 1953 (2) 'The Notebook' in HWS.

Forbidden Entry (p. 146)

anadhikār prabés. First published in *sādhanā*, Śrābaṇ (July–August) 1894; included in *bicitra galpa*, Vol. II. Translations: (1) 'The Trespass' in GBL (2) 'Trespass', by Indira Debi Choudhurani in *Hindusthan Standard*, Puja Annual, 1947, and RS.

In the Middle of the Night (p. 151)

niśīthe. First published in *sādhanā*, Māgh (January–February) 1894; included in *galpa-daśak*. Translations: (1) 'At Midnight', by Anath Nath Mitra in *The Modern Review*, April 1910 (2) 'In the Night', by

W. W. Pearson with the author's help in *The Modern Review*, December 1917, and BTS.

Unwanted (p. 162)

āpad (lit. 'trouble', 'botheration': I am grateful to Miss Srabani Paul for suggesting 'Unwanted' as a title). First published in *sādhanā*, Phālgun (February–March) 1895; included in *galpa-daśak*. Translations: (1) 'The Castaway' in MS and CS (2) 'The Troublemaker' in HWS.

Elder Sister (p. 172)

didi. First published in *sādhanā*, Caitra (March–April) 1895; included in *galpa-daśak*. Translation: 'The Elder Sister', by Rashbehari Mukhopadhyay in *The Modern Review*, July 1910, and (revised) in MS.

Fury Appeased (p. 181)

mānbhañjan. First published in *sādhanā*, Baiśākh (April–May) 1895; included in *galpa-daśak*. Translations: (1) 'Giribala' in *The Modern Review*, May 1917, and BTS (2) 'Appeasement' in HWS.

Ṭhākurdā (p. 190)

ṭhākurdā. First published in *sādhanā*, Jyaiṣṭha (May–June) 1895; included in *galpa-daśak*. Translation: 'The Babus of Nayanjore', by C. F. Andrews with he author's help in HS and CS.

Guest (p. 198)

atithi. First published in *sādhanā*, Bhādra–Āśvin–Kārtik (August–September–October–November) 1895; included in *galpa-daśak*. Translations: (1) 'The Wandering Guest' in GBL (2) 'The Runaway', by Surendranath Tagore in *The Modern Review*, September 1919, and RS and TR (3) 'The Guest', by W. W. Pearson in *Outward Bound*, October 1921 (4) 'The Guest', by Sheila Chatterjee in *Amrita Bazar Patrika*, Puja Annual, 1953 (5) 'Guest', by Lila Mujumdar in *Hindusthan Standard*, Puja Annual, 1957.

Wishes Granted (p. 212)

icchāpūraṇ. First published in the journal *sakhā o sāthī*, Āśvin (September–October) 1895; included in *pārbaṇī*, an Annual containing writings by various authors, edited by Nagendranath Gangapadhyay, 1918–19.

False Hope (p. 217)

durāśā. First published in *bhāratī*, Baiśākh (April–May) 1898; included in *galpaguccha*, Vol. II (Majumdar Agency). Translations: (1) 'A Shattered Dream', by C. F. Andrews with the author's help in *The Modern Review*, July 1917 (2) 'False Hopes', by Surendranath Tagore in *The Modern Review*, October 1936, and RS.

Son-sacrifice (p. 229)

putrayajña. First published in *bhāratī*, Jyaiṣṭha (May–June) 1898; included in *galpaguccha*, Vol. II (Visva-Bharati).

The Hungry Stones (p. 233)

kṣudhita pāṣāṇ. First published in *sādhanā*, Śrābaṇ (July–August) 1895; included in *galpa-daśak*. Translations: (1) 'The Hungry Stones', by Panna Lal Basu in *The Modern Review*, February 1910, and HS and TR (2) 'The Spirit of the Marble Palace' in *The Comrade*, 28 January 1917, translator unnamed (3) 'The Hungry Stones' in GBL.

Thoughtlessness (p. 244)

durbuddhi. First published in *bhāratī*, Bhādra (August–September) 1900; included in *galpaguccha*, Vol. I (Majumdar Agency). Translation: 'A Lapse of Judgement' in HWS.

The Gift of Sight (p. 248)

dṛṣṭidān. First published in *bhāratī*, Pauṣ (December–January) 1898–9; included in *galpaguccha*, Vol. II (Majumdar Agency). Translation: 'Vision', by C. F. Andrews with the author's help in HS.

Addendum

New translations of 'The Living and the Dead' and 'Punishment' have appeared in Kalpana Bardhan's *Women, Outcastes, Peasants, and Rebels, A Selection of Bengali Short Stories* (University of California Press, 1990). *Selected Short Stories of Rabindranath Tagore*, tr. by Krishna Dutta and Mary Lago (Macmillan, 1991) includes translations of 'The Postmaster', 'Little Master's Return', 'Exercise-book', 'Punishment' and 'Unwanted'. *Selected Short Stories*, ed. Sukanta Chaudhuri, includes translations of 'Exercise-book', 'Wealth Surrendered', 'A Single Night', 'The Living and the Dead', 'Kabulliwallah', 'Punishment', 'Forbidden Entry', 'Ṭhakurda', 'The Hungry Stones', 'Guest' and 'Thoughtlessness'.

Glossary

Abdur Rahman Khan
1844–1901. Powerful modernizing Amir of Afghanistan from 1880 to 1901.

Āgamanī
See **Durga**.

Āgḍum Bāgḍum
āgḍum bāgḍum ghoṛāḍum sāje: Bengali nonsense/nursery rhyme accompanied by a knee-slapping game. See *Selected Poems*, Notes, p. 177.

Agrahāyan
Bengali month; mid-November to mid-December; second of the two *hemanta* or 'dewy season' months between autumn and winter.

Ālāp
Slow, meditative opening exposition of a *rāga* by a singer or instrumentalist without rhythmic accompaniment.

Ālnā
Clothes-stand, preferred throughout the subcontinent to drawers or wardrobes.

Āmṛā
Hog-plum tree; originally from Polynesia but now quite common in India. Its sour, olive-like fruit are often pickled.

Arjuna
See **Subhadra**.

Aryavarta (Āryāvarta)
Upper or Northern India where the ancient Aryans settled.

Āsan
Any seat or place for sitting, for a person or a deity.

Āṣāṛh
Bengali month; mid-June to mid-July; the first of the two monsoon months (see **Śrāban**).

Ashram (āśram)

A residential and usually secluded religious or educational community, associated with the 'forest hermitages' (*tapavana*) favoured by the sages of ancient India.

Āśvin

Bengali month; mid-September to mid-October.

Ātar (attar, otto)

Perfume applied to the face and hair, made by distilling rose or jasmine petals. Tradition has it that it was discovered by the Moghul empress Nurjahan.

Bābā

Father; also used as a term of affection or respect to a child or an old person.

Babu (bābu)

A title added to the name of a gentleman in Hindu Bengal – originally given only to aristocrats (see 'Ṭhākurdā') but later to the whole of the nineteenth-century educated class. It was used derogatively by the British ('Bengali babu'), but is not at all pejorative in current Bengali usage.

Babuji (bābuji)

'-ji' is a common honorific suffix in North India, which is why the Hindusthani Princess in 'False Hope' adds it to 'Babu' when addressing a Bengali gentleman.

Baiśākh

First month of the Bengali year; mid-April to mid-May; summer in Bengal.

Bakul

Small, white, sweet-scented spring flower.

Baṛi

Small conical ball made of pigeon-pea paste and dried in the sun before cooking.

Baṛobau

'Elder wife' – the elder of two daughters-in-law in an extended family.

Baudidi

'Wife-sister' – term applied to a wife by in-laws junior to her in an extended family; often abbreviated to *Baudi*.

Baul (bāul)

Heterodox, wandering religious sect in Bengal, famous for their songs.

In 'The Postmaster' (p. 42) the band of Bauls is 'intoxicated' with *ganjikā* (ganja), not alcohol.

Baumā
A way of addressing the wife in an extended family.

Bauṭhākrun
Term applied to the wife of a Brahmin by servants and others holding her in respect; also a synonym for *Baudidi*.

Bel
Wood-apple or marmelos, a tree from whose hard-shelled fruit a delicious 'sherbet' can be made. *Bel* or *beli* is also the name of the Arabian jasmine, a shrub with sweet-smelling white flowers that bloom from March to June.

Bhababhuti (Bhababhūti)
Famous Sanskrit poet of the seventh or eighth century, author of *malati-mādhava* and *uttarrāmcaritā*.

Bhādra
Bengali month; mid-August to mid-September.

Bhagavata (Bhāgavata)
See **Krishna**.

Bhāi
'Brother', but used as a friendly informal appellation among women as well as men.

Bhāiphōṭā
Festival corresponding to Bhaiduja in Northern India, when sisters put sandal-paste marks (*tilak*) on the foreheads of their brothers and wish them a long and prosperous life; brothers bless their sisters; and presents of clothes are exchanged. The Sanskrit name for this festival is *bhrātri-dvītiya* ('brother-second'), as it is held on the second day after the day of the new moon in autumn when Diwali (*Kālī-pūjā/Syāma-pūjā* in Bengal) is celebrated.

Bhairavī
A calm and pensive morning *rāga*, named after Shiva's consort.

Bibisaheb (Bibisāheb)
A rather archaic respectful term applied to a Muslim married lady. See **Saheb**.

Brahma (Brahmā)
Creator and first god of the classical Hindu triad, associated with

primeval fire. Brahmins are supposed to be able to curse people with 'the fire of Brahma'.

Brahmin (Brāhmaṇ)
First of the four classical Hindu caste-divisions (Brāhmaṇ, Kṣatriya, Vaiśya and Śudra); the 'priestly caste' associated with privilege, grace, purity, excellence, etc. By giving land to Brahmins ('A Problem Solved') or feeding them on festive occasions ('Son-sacrifice') or giving succour to them ('Unwanted'), one can acquire merit and improve one's next incarnation.

Caitra
The last month of the Bengali year; mid-March to mid-April.

Caṇḍimaṇḍap
Strictly, a shrine for the goddess Chandi, but it normally refers to the roofed structure used for community gatherings and festive occasions in Bengali villages.

Chadar (cādar)
A sheet of cloth carried over the shoulder or worn round the shoulders like a shawl.

Champa (cā̃pā)
The champak tree, with golden yellow flowers that bloom in summer.

Chanakya (Cāṇakya)
The *cāṇakyasloka*s are a collection of Sanskrit couplets on social morality attributed to Cāṇakya, a scholar in the court of Chandragupta Maurya (320–297 BC). Under the name Kauṭilya he is also supposed to have written the famous *arthaśāstra* (treatise on economics). The cynicism of Cāṇakya's precepts has earned him the title 'the Machiavelli of India'.

Chandimangal (caṇḍimaṅgal)
See **Kabikankan**.

Chandra (Candra)
The moon or moon-god.

Chapkan (cāpkān)
Loose, long robe; formal or official Persian-style dress favoured by the well-to-do in nineteenth-century Bengal.

Chaprassi (cāprāsi)
An office messenger or peon (*piyan*).

Choga (cogā)
Loose, Persian-style outer-garment worn over the chapkan (q.v.).

Choṭo Mā

'Young mother' – term applied, usually by servants, to the youngest wife in an extended family.

Choṭobau

'Younger wife' – the younger of two daughters-in-law in an extended family.

Dādā

'Elder brother'; also short both for *Dādāmośāy*, 'maternal grandfather', and *Ṭhākurdā,* 'paternal grandfather', and therefore often applied in a jocular or informal manner to any older man; also added to names by servants addressing the son or 'young master' in a family (e.g., 'Phatik-*dādā*' in 'Holiday').

Dadababu (Dādābābu)

Respectful and affectionate term applied to a gentleman by a less-educated person (see 'The Postmaster').

Damayanti (Damayantī)

See **Nala**.

Dashu Ray (Dāśu Rāy)

1806–57. Greatest writer of Bengali *pā̃cāli*, a genre combining music, dance and poetry, telling stories of Radha and Krishna and other traditional subjects, often in an erotic, humorous or satirical way.

Deś

A light, night *rāga*, often combined with the Mallar or 'monsoon' group of *rāga*s to create composite 'Deś-Mallar' *rāga*s.

Devanāgarī

See **Sarasvati**.

Dharma

A key word in Hindu tradition, meaning such things as duty, law, justice, righteousness, piety, scriptural rules, morality, religion etc. See *Selected Poems*, Notes, pp. 175–6.

Dhoti (dhuti)

Traditional white loincloth worn by Hindu men. See p. 190, n. 1.

Didi

'Elder Sister'; abbreviated to 'di', it is often respectfully added to Bengali women's names.

Didimā

Maternal grandmother or great-aunt.

Dom

One of the *pañcama* ('fifth') group of 'untouchable' castes outside the main Hindu castes. The *Dom*s are traditionally scavengers, corpse-removers and suppliers of wood for burning the dead.

Durbar (darbār)

A formal levee or meeting in a royal court, when the monarch listens to petitions.

Durga (Durgā)

Bengal's most popular goddess. As Shiva's consort or *śakti* she dwells on Mount Kailas and is also known as Uma and Parvati ('daughter of the mountain'). *Durgā-pūjā* in October–November is Bengal's chief religious festival ending with the ritual immersion of the images of Durga made specially for it. The song that Uma hears in 'Exercise-book' is an example of the *āgamanī* songs that are sung to commemorate Durga's arrival in her parents' home at the beginning of the festival. The reference in 'The Gift of Sight' (p. 248) is to the third eye which Durga (like Shiva) has on her forehead.

Gāmchā

A kind of scarf or napkin, sometimes worn round the waist as a *lungi* or loincloth.

Ganesh (Gaṇeśa)

Elephant-headed god, son of Shiva and Parvati, bringer of good luck and prosperity. *Gaṇeś-pūjā* in April is observed by traders and shopkeepers.

Gazal (gajal)

Popular form of love poem or song, Arabic or Persian in origin, much favoured by Urdu poets.

Ghāṭ

See Introduction, pp. 21 f.

Gītāgovinda
See **Jayadev**.

Gopī
See **Krishna**.

Govinda Das

Medieval Bengali author of Vaishnava *padābalī* (songs about Radha and Krishna).

Hanu
See **Manu**.

Haridas

Hero of *Haridāser guptakathā*, an adaption by Bhubanchandra Mukhopadhyay of W. M. Reynolds' novel *Joseph Wilmot* (1854). The book first appeared in serial form in 1871–73 and was popularly regarded as 'adult' reading for married couples, which is why Uma in 'Exercise-book' finds it under her brother's wife's pillow. There is further evidence of the popularity of Reynolds' novels in Bengal, in 'Taraprasanna's Fame', p. 73, where the reference is to *London Mystery* (8 vols, 1849–56).

Hilsa (iliś)

A fish farmed and eaten in Bengal, growing up to eighteen inches in length. It lives in the sea, but comes up the rivers to spawn.

Hookah (hŭkā)

'Hubble-bubble' or water-pipe which Persian influence introduced into Bengal; rarely seen today.

Indra

King of the gods in Vedic times; less important in classical Hinduism, but associated with thunder and rainbows (*indradhanu*, 'Indra's bow'). He drives a chariot drawn by two tawny horses, and also rides the prototypal divine elephant Airāvata.

Ishvarchandra Vidyasagar

1820–91. Famous Principal of Sanskrit College in Calcutta, a major force in nineteenth-century Bengali educational and social reform, and a pioneering writer of Bengali prose. The first part of his *barṇaparicay* (primer) includes two boys, 'Gopal' and 'Rakhal', who have become proverbially associated with good behaviour and bad behaviour respectively. *kathāmālā* – a Bengali version of Aesop as told by Revd Thomas James – was another of his many books for schoolchildren (see 'Exercise-book', p. 140).

Iṣṭadevatā

Patron god that a Hindu chooses from the pantheon as the deity to whom he offers special prayers.

Jamidār/Jamidāri

See **Zamindar**.

Jayadev (Jayadeva)

Twelfth-century Sanskrit poet, born in Bengal, famous for his *Gītāgovinda*, a dramatic poem about Radha and Krishna.

Jhāu

The tamarisk – an evergreen shrub or small tree, with feathery branches and thin leaves.

Jobbā
A long, loose, informal Persian-style robe.

Jyaiṣṭha
Bengali month; mid-May to mid-June; the second of the two summer months.

Kabikankan (Kabikaṅkaṇ)
Honorific title given to the great sixteenth-century Bengali poet Mukunduram Chakravarti. His *caṇḍimaṅgal* is regarded as the finest example of *maṅgalkābya*, a genre of Bengali narrative poem glorifying Bengal's local deities – Chandi, Manasa, Dharma, Shitala and others.

Kabirāj
Physician following the traditional Indian Ayurvedic system of medicine.

Kabuliwallah (kābulioyālā)
A native of Afghanistan or Kabul – usually, in the Indian context, an itinerant trader or hawker.

Kacu
The taro – a coarse herbacious plant cultivated for its tubers.

Kadamba
A large tree with sweet-scented, yellow-orange flowers that bloom in the rainy season.

Kailas (Kailāsa)
See **Durga**.

Kaistha (Kāystha)
Hindu caste, known as 'the writer caste', who have traditionally been writers, scholars, lawyers and judges. They overlap with the two main caste divisions, being sometimes classed as Kṣatriyas, sometimes as Śudras (see **Brahmin**, **Shudra**, **Ḍom**).

Kākimā (kākī)
Aunt; wife of one's father's younger brother.

Kāl-baiśākhī
A strong wind that blows in the afternoons in the summer month of Baiśākh, and sometimes causes sudden short storms.

Kali
The 'age of Kali' (*kali-yūga*) is the age of mankind in the sixth millennium of which we are at present living. It is the last of four *yūga*s that make up a *kalpa* or 'day of Brahma'. The age of Kali is tragically

degenerate compared to the *satya-yūga* ('age of Truth') which was the first of the four *yūga*s – hence the evils and sufferings in our present world. 'Kali' is not to be confused with the mother-goddess Kālī.

Kalidasa (Kālidāsa)

Foremost poet and dramatist of Sanskrit literature; often associated with the court of Chandra Gupta II (AD 375–414), though some scholars have placed him in the first or second century BC. His most famous works are the *Meghadūta* ('Cloud-messenger'), a poem in which a *yakṣa* (see **Kubera**), absent from his beloved, asks a cloud to carry a message of love to her; *Kumārasambhava*, a poem about the begetting of Kartik (q.v.) to destroy the demon Taraka; and the greatest of all Sanskrit plays, *Śakuntalā*.

Kalighat (Kālīghāṭ)

Hindu temple in Calcutta dedicated to the bloodthirsty mother-goddess Kali (Kālī), and associated with animal sacrifice. Tagore's famous play *bisarjan* ('Sacrifice') attacks the Kali cult.

Kāminī

A large shrub bearing bunches of sweet-smelling white flowers which bloom at night and are shed by morning. It blossoms mainly during the rain, and is often cut into shapes in ornamental gardens.

Kapāṭi

A game indigenous to India. Two teams stand on opposite sides of a line; a player crosses the line, and tries to touch an opposing player while holding his breath and uttering repetitive sounds such as *ḍu-ḍu-ḍu-ḍu*. If he touches an opponent before running out of breath, the opponent is declared 'dead'; if the opposing players physically prevent him from returning to his side of the line, *he* is declared dead.

Kartik (Kārtik, Kārtikeya)

God of war and ruler of the planet Mars, son of Shiva and Parvati, created to destroy the demon Taraka (see **Kalidasa**). Also the name of the seventh Bengali month, mid-October to mid-November.

Kashidas (Kāśirām Dās)

Seventeenth-century Bengali poet known as the author and compiler of the most popular medieval Bengali version of the *Mahābhārata*, though his nephew Nanadaram and others had a hand in it.

Kathāmālā

See **Ishvarchandra Vidyasagar**.

Kedārā

Large Persian-style armchair.

Kharia (Khariyā, Khare)

Another name for the Jalangi river that runs into the Bhagarathi (Hooghly) west of Krishnanagar. Further north, the Bhairab connects it with the Padma (see Map, p. 323).

Khokā

An affectionate term for the youngest son in a Bengali family.

Khurā

Uncle; younger brother of one's father.

Kīrtan

In Bengal a *kīrtan* is usually a simple religious song or *bhajan* (hymn), with none of the complexity of classical vocal music.

Koel (kokil)

Bird with a characteristic shrill call, rising up the scale, ending with a gentler cooing sound; very commonly heard in Bengal. Often (misleadingly) translated as 'cuckoo' because it belongs to the same order (*cuculiformes*).

Krishna (Kṛṣṇa)

Much-loved incarnation of Vishnu, famous for his childhood in Vraj, his flute-playing, his sporting with milkmaids (*gopī*s) in Vrindavan on the banks of the Yamuna, his love-affair with Radha, and his heroic role in the *Mahābhārata*. His life story is told in the tenth book of the thirteenth-century *Bhāgavata-purāṇa*. Radha's love for him is the main focus of Bengali Vaishnava devotion, and inspired numerous *padābalī* ('lyrics') in medieval Bengal. In dramatic versions of the Radha–Krishna story the *mānbhañjan* is the 'breaking' (*bhañjan,* i.e. appeasement or placation) of Radha's 'pique' (*mān*) at Krishna's neglectful behaviour. Tagore's story 'Fury Appeased' alludes to this both in its title and its content. A 'Krishna-rosary' (*jap-mālā*) is carried by pious Vaishnavas as an aid to prayer (see 'A Problem Solved', p. 138).

Krittibas (Kṛttibās)

Celebrated poet, born in the late fourteenth or early fifteenth century, compiler and author of the medieval Bengali *Rāmāyaṇa*, the most popular of all medieval Bengali poems.

Kubera

Originally a Vedic lord of evil spirits whom Brahma made one of the guardian deities of the world. He is lord of all gold, silver and gems, and is served by the *yakṣa*s – a class of elemental beings, mostly benevolent though sometimes evil. The chief *yakṣa*s guard Kubera's treasure-hoards (cf. 'Wealth Surrendered') in Alaka in the Himalayas; and it is a *yakṣa* who is the speaker in Kalidasa's celebrated *Meghadūta* (see **Kalidasa**).

Kulin (Kulīn)

Brahmin sub-caste whose practice of polygamy was notorious. Parents would marry their daughters to Kulins as an act of religious merit, and the Kulins would profit from the dowries. Kulin polygamy was never forbidden by law, but in response to changing social conditions – and campaigns against it – it died out early in the twentieth century.

Kumārasambhava

See **Kartik** and **Kalidasa**.

Kuri

Strictly speaking, a caste associated with bird-catching, but also a synonym for the Mayara or Madhukuri 'confectioner caste' of Bengal, who as suppliers of sweets to Brahmins are high or 'clean' Shudra castes (q.v.). The Rui brothers in 'Punishment' are landless labourers – showing how the identification of a caste with a particular trade has been much eroded in modern India.

Kurta (kortā)

Indian shirt with long sleeves and collarless neck, cut long to hang down below the hips.

Kush and Lab (Kuśa and Lava)

Twin sons of Rama and Sita who were brought into the ashram of Valmiki, author of the *Rāmāyaṇa*. In the last section of the epic, they are taught to sing the story of Rama, so *kuś-laber gān* are songs telling the story of Rama sung by Kush and Lab.

Lagi

A long pole, normally of bamboo, used to punt or steer a traditional Bengali river-boat.

Lakh (lākh, lakṣa)

A hundred thousand; generally used in the subcontinent when referring to large numbers.

Lāṭhi

Stick used as a baton or truncheon.

Lāṭhiyāl

Guard or bodyguard carrying a *lāṭhi*, or a person skilled in fighting with *lāṭhi*s.

Mā

'Mother'; used also to address married women with a rural or peasant background; also used as an imprecation (*'Mā! Mā!'*) because the

Mother-goddess is commonly worshipped in Bengal. See **Durga**.

Madan (Madana)
Name for Kama, the Hindu god of love; equivalent to Cupid or Eros.

Madanmohan Tarkalankar
1817–58. Bengali poet with an ornate Sanskritic style, some of whose poems became well-known anthology pieces.

Mādhabī
Creeper with pink or red or pale flowers that bloom from February to September.

Māgh
Bengali month; mid-January to mid-February.

Mahabharata (Mahābhārata)
Great classical epic of India, attributed to the poet Vyāsā, but probably created over many generations. See **Kashidas** and **Krishna**.

Mallar
See **Deś**.

Mantra
A sacred verse of scripture, or any spell or formula used in Hindu worship and ritual.

Manu
Known as the Lawgiver, mythical author of a canonical Hindu code of law and jurisprudence; identified with the first of fourteen 'Manus' or semi-divine progenitors of mankind. The 'sons of Manu' therefore means those people who are law-abiding, as opposed to those whom Tagore, in 'The Editor' (p. 123), wittily calls the 'sons of Hanu', i.e. people with the capacity for subversion and havoc associated with the monkey-chief Hanuman. (In fact Hanuman had no children: Tagore is playing with words.)

Māsī
Aunt; mother's sister or cousin-sister.

Māṣṭārmaśāy
'Master-sir' – a common name or term of address for a teacher or tutor.

Māṭhākrun
A term that might be used by a servant addressing the (Brahmin) mistress of the house where he is employed.

Meghnadūta

See **Kalidasa**.

Meghnād-badh kābya

'The poem of the slaying of Meghnād' – a brilliantly original epic based on the *Rāmāyaṇa*, but distorting its traditional values, by Michael Madusūdan Datta (1824–73), the founder of modern Bengali poetry and drama. The difficulty of Madusūdan's language and the epic's classic status had tended to make it something of a grind for Bengali students. Tagore himself disliked it when he was young.

Memsāheb

The term by which the wives of British *sāheb*s (q.v.) were generally known in British India.

Mohanbhog

A sort of porridge made by boiling cornflour in milk.

Mohar

Gold coin used in Moghul times, and also struck by the East India Company; phased out as a currency by the British in the 1840s, but preserved in treasure-hordes (see 'Wealth Surrendered', p. 81).

Moktār (mukhtar)

A legally appointed representative or attorney.

Mudrā

Any kind of coin, generally thought of as gold and/or obsolete (see 'The Hungry Stones', p. 240).

Munsiff (munseph)

A Moghul judge, but under the legal system established by the British in India an officer trying suits in the lowest civil court.

Nala and Damayanti (Damayantī)

Famous star-crossed lovers whose story is included in the *Mahābhārata*. When Nala, king of Nishadha, first heard of Damayanti's beauty, he sent a swan (whose life he had once saved) to find her (see 'Unwanted', p. 169).

Nāmābali

A scarf with the names of deities printed on it, worn by Vaishnavas and other pious Hindus.

Namaskār

Hindu greeting, accompanied by the folding of the hands in a prayer-like position; equivalent to the Muslim salaam (q.v.).

Nim tree
The margosa – a large tree with beautifully clustered narrow leaves.

Pãcāli
See **Dashu Ray**.

Padābalī
See **Govinda Das** and **Krishna**.

Paisa
Small coin/unit of currency; now (since 1957) a cent of a rupee, though formerly there were 16 annas and 64 paisa to a rupee.

Pān
Leaf of the betel-pepper plant, commonly chewed in India with betel-nut (from the betel palm, a different tree) and shell-lime, and spices added to taste.

Parvati (Pārvatī)
See **Durga**.

Peepul (aśvattha)
A large tree, related to the banyan; also known as *bodhi-taru* ('perfect-knowledge tree') or bo tree, because it was under it that Gautama became the Buddha ('enlightened one').

Peon (piyan)
See **Chaprassi**.

Pisimā
Aunt; father's sister.

Praṇām
Hindu obeisance, an expression of deep respect in which one 'takes the dust of a person's feet' – i.e., one touches a person's feet and then one's forehead with one's right hand.

Pugree (pāgṛi)
A piece of cloth worn round the head; a turban.

Pūjā
Hindu worship: anything from an offering of flowers to a deity or a ritual performed to honour a particular god or goddess on a special day, to a full-scale religious festival. See **Durga** and **Ganesh**.

Pundit (Paṇḍit)
A learned Sanskrit teacher, or a scholar of language and literature; used in English now for any kind of self-appointed expert; also a term applied

honorifically to Brahmins, who are traditionally the only people permitted to teach Sanskrit.

Punyaha
A special day on which a landlord solemnly collects rents from tenants for the ensuing year.

Radha (Rādhā)
See **Krishna**.

Rāga (rāg)
In Indian music, a *rāga* is a group of notes, usually associated with a particular mood, time, season or deity, around which a singer or instrumentalist improvises.

Rājā
King; but it can mean just a landlord or zamindar (q.v.). Tagore would have been a *rājā* to his Shelidah tenants.

Rām Rām (He Rām, etc.)
Often said by Hindus as an imprecation or prayer. Gandhi died with '*He Rām*' on his lips.

Rama (Rāma)
Hero of Valmiki's great Sanskrit epic the *Rāmāyaṇa*, and a model of human goodness and prowess, just as his wife Sita represents perfect Hindu womanhood.

Ramayana (Rāmāyaṇa)
See **Krittibas**.

Raybahadur (Rāybāhādur)
Honorific title conferred on eminent Hindu citizens in pre-British (Moghul) and British India. Muslims were given the title Khanbahadur.

Saheb (sāheb)
'Sir'; a term of respect introduced in Moghul times, and still used when referring to Muslims. Cf. 'Babu', the Hindu equivalent. The British in India also came to be known as *sāhebs* or sahibs. A *kālo sāheb* or 'brown *sāheb*' is a derogatory term for an Anglicized Indian.

Sakhī
Female friend or confidante to a woman.

Sāl
A tall tree that grows in the dry climate of West Bengal or Bihar. It is valuable for its hardwood and resin, and *sāl*-forests are now protected by law.

Salaam (selām)
Muslim greeting, accompanied by the bowing of the head and touching of the brow with the right hand.

Śāmlā
A kind of turban worn by clerks and pleaders in nineteenth-century Bengal – hence Pyarimohan's jibe in 'Exercise-book' (p. 144).

Sānāi
Reed instrument traditionally associated with wedding festivities.

Sandeś
Very popular Bengali sweetmeat made from curdled milk.

Sannyāsī
A celibate Hindu holy man, fakir or ascetic; usually itinerant and dependent on alms; sometimes disreputably dealing in blessings, amulets, quack remedies, etc.

Sannyāsinī
A female *sannyāsī*.

Sāraṅgī
Musical instrument played with a bow like a violin.

Sarasvati (Sarasvatī)
Chief wife of Brahma (q.v.); goddess of wisdom and science, of speech and music, and deviser of the *devanāgarī* script for Sanskrit.

Seer (ser)
Traditional unit of weight (about 2 lbs); used for liquids (milk, etc.) as well as dry stuffs.

Śephālī
A tree with small white flowers on orange-coloured stalks. Its flowers bloom mainly in autumn; they open out at night, falling at dawn to form a white carpet under the tree. According to the *Viṣṇu-purāṇa* it was originally a princess called Parijat, who fell in love with the sun. When she was deserted by him, she was burnt and the tree grew out of her ashes. Krishna brought it from heaven to earth as a present for his wife Satyabhama.

Shashti (Ṣaṣṭī)
A Bengali local deity who protects and promotes babies. A child is born 'through the grace of Shashti' (see 'Fool's Gold', p. 98).

Shastra (śāstra)
The Shastras are the *smṛti* ('remembered') scriptures of the Hindus in which all branches of knowledge are codified, as opposed to the *śruti*

('heard') texts normally known as the Veda (q.v.). They are humanly created works of doctrine and theology, or treatises on law, medicine, etc., rather than directly revealed Holy Writ.

Shiva (Śiva)

Major Hindu god, known as the 'Destroyer' – as opposed to Brahma the Creator and Vishnu the Preserver – but with a great range of often contradictory characteristics. In 'Taraprasanna's Fame' (p. 75) Dakshayani speaks of her 'Shiva-like' husband because in Bengali popular tradition Shiva is seen as childlike, ignorant of the world's complexities, easily pleased.

Shudra (śudra)

Fourth and 'lowest' of the four classical Hindu castes; traditionally labourers, cultivators, fishermen and servants. They have been subject to oppression, and some of them pursue trades regarded as 'unclean', such as oil-making and leather-working, but they have not been traditionally regarded as total 'outcastes'. See **Ḍom**.

Sita (Sītā)
See **Rama**.

Śiuli

Another name for the *śephālī*-flower (q.v.).

Śrābaṇ

Bengali month; mid-July to mid-August; the second of the two monsoon months (see Āṣāṛh).

Subhadra

Sister of Krishna (q.v.). Arjuna, third of the Pandava princes in the great epic of India, the *Mahābhārata*, fell in love with her when he visited Krishna in his kingdom of Dvaraka. Krishna's brother Balaram wanted her to marry Duryodhana, who was a Kaurava and thus an enemy of the Pandavas; but Krishna encouraged Arjuna to abduct her. Indraprastha was the famous capital city that the Pandavas built on the banks of the Yamuna. The reference in 'Skeleton' (p. 86) is to a moment of the battle of Kurukshetra when Subhadra appeared in a chariot to rescue Arjuna from the fray.

Śvaśur-bāṛi

'Father-in-law's house', where a bride goes to live. It is also used as a word for prison; so a pun is intended in 'Kabuliwallah' (p. 117).

Śyālikā

'Sister-in-law'. The words for brother-in-law and sister-in-law are terms of mild abuse in Bengali; there is also traditionally a bantering relationship between husband and his wife's sister. Marrying a sister-in-law is permissible for a widower, and a sister-in-law is often jokingly called an 'additional wife'. Thus when Mini in 'Kabuliwallah' (p. 113) asks her father what relation her mother is to him, 'sister-in-law' is the only one he can suggest. Other relationships (uncle/niece, nephew/aunt etc.) would be taboo.

Tatya Tope (Ramchandra Pandurang)
1813–59. Commander-in-chief of the rebel forces during the Indian Mutiny. After defeat in the battle of Gwalior (19 June 1857) he took to guerrilla warfare in central India, eluding capture for nearly two years. He was hanged by the British on 18 April 1859, and is remembered as a great patriot and military genius.

Ṭhākur
'Lord'; a term used to address a Brahmin, or a (male) deity or idol. 'Tagore' is an Anglicized form of *ṭhākur*.

Ṭhākurdā
Paternal grandfather; also used to address any old man, in a jocular or slightly patronizing way, as in the story 'Ṭhākurdā'.

Ṭhākurmā
Paternal grandmother or a respectful way of addressing an elderly Brahmin lady.

Ṭhumri
A love-song, frequently light and popular in character; often used in dance and theatrical shows. A 'Lucknow *ṭhumri*' ('Guest', p. 201) might well be subject to Perso-Arabic influences.

Ṭol
Traditional Indian grammar school, where Sanskrit would be learnt from a Brahmin pundit.

Uma (Umā)
See **Durga**

Vaishnava (Vaiṣṇava)
A follower of Vaishnavism, the religion that was the main expression in Bengal of the *bhakti* (devotional) tendency in Hinduism that developed in India in the sixteenth and seventeenth centuries. See **Krishna**.

Varuna (Varuṇa)
Vedic god who sustained the moral order of the cosmos; he was later dethroned by Indra to become the Hindu god of the sea, worshipped by fishermen.

Veda

The primary scriptures of Hinduism, regarded as divine in origin: they include the Mantras (q.v.) used in rituals, the *Brāhmana* (priestly manuals), the *Āranyaka* (treatises for hermits and saints), and the *Upanisads* (general philosophic treatises).

Vedanta (vedānta)

One of the six orthodox systems of Hindu philosophy, founded on the *Upanisads* (see **Veda**). It was first formulated by the philosopher Bādarāyana, and is also known as *uttara-mīmāmsā* (Later Mīmāmsā) to distinguish it from *pūrva-mīmāmsā* (Early Mīmāmsā) – another philosophic school.

Vidya (Vidyā)

The heroine of the *Vidyāsundara*, a narrative poem by the eighteenth-century Bengali poet Bharatchandra Ray. Her *sakhī* or confidante became a popular character in *yātrā* performances of the story.

Vraj (Vraja)

See **Krishna**.

Vrindavan (Vṛndāvana)

See **Krishna**.

Yaksa

See **Kubera** and **Kalidasa**.

Yama

Vedic and Hindu god of death, and punisher of souls after death, whose city Yamapuri is the Indian Hades.

Yamuna (Yamunā, Jumna)

North Indian tributary of the Ganges; Delhi and Krishna's Vrindavan are situated on its banks, and it joins the Ganges at the sacred *sangam* (confluence) at Allahabad.

Yātrā

Popular form of dramatic entertainment in Bengal, traditionally performed by travelling troupes of players and presenting in song, speech and dance traditional stories mixed with topical comment or satire.

Yogī

Hindu mystic; seeker of *samādhi* or communion with the godhead through the various systems of *yoga*.

Yoginī

A female *yogī*.

Zamindar (jamidār)

Under the Moghul system Bengali zamindars were landholders and revenue-collectors, but under the controversial 'Permanent Settlement' of Lord Cornwallis in 1793 they were transformed into landowners, and the Government's land-revenue demand was permanently fixed. In Muslim East Bengal most zamindars (like the Tagores) were Hindus, with houses in Calcutta, and were therefore often absent from their *jamidāri*s. This was brought to an end by Partition in 1947, and successive land reforms have removed the zamindari system from West Bengal and Bangladesh.

Zenana

A 'harem' in a Muslim palace, but in a smaller household equivalent to the *antaḥpur* or inner quarters where women lived in varying degrees of purdah (*pardā* – the word means 'curtain'). This practice was (and is) observed in Muslim households, and as a legacy of Persian influence in Moghul times was also common in nineteenth-century Hindu households. Loosely the *antaḥpur* is simply the more private part of a house, closed to strangers.

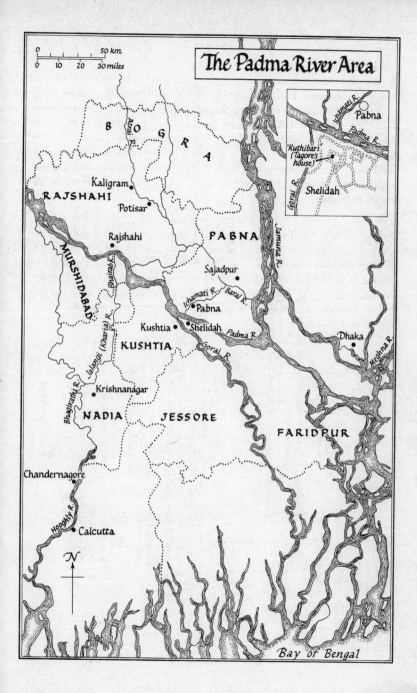

The Padma River Area

Tagore's Family Tree

3 children

DWARKANATH
(1794—1846)
m. Digambari Devi

3 children

DEBENDRANATH
(1817—1905)
m. Sarada Devi

GIRINDRANATH
(1820—54)
m. Jogmaya Devi

(2 children)

GANENDRANATH
(1841—69)

GUNENDRANATH
(1847—81)

(3 children)

GAGANENDRANATH
(1867—1938)

ABANINDRANATH
(1871—1951)

BINAYANI
(1873—1924)
m. Seshandrabhusan-Chatterjee

(3 children)

PRATIMA DEVI
(1893—1969)

10 children

DWIJENDRANATH
(1840—1926)
m. Sarvasundari Devi

SATYENDRANATH
(1842—1923)
m. Jnanadanadini Devi

BIRENDRANATH
(1845—1915)
m. Praphullamayi Devi

JYOTIRINDRANATH
(1849—1925)
m. Kadambari Devi

RABINDRANATH
(1861—1941)
m. Mrinalini Devi

SURENDRANATH
(1872—1940)

INDIRA DEVI
(1873—1960)
m. Pramatha Chaudhuri

BALENDRANATH
(1870—99)

3 children

MADHURILATA
(1886—1918)
m. Sarachchandra Chakraborty

RATHINDRANATH
(1888—1961)
m. Pratima Devi

RENUKA
(1891—1903)
m. Satyendranath Bhattacharji

MIRA
(1894—1969)
m. Nagendranath Ganguli

SAMINDRANATH
(1896—1907)

NANDINI
(adopted daughter)
(1921?—)

NITINDRANATH
(1912—32)

NANDITA
(1916—67)
m. Krishna Kripalani

READ MORE IN PENGUIN

In every corner of the world, on every subject under the sun, Penguin represents quality and variety – the very best in publishing today.

For complete information about books available from Penguin – including Puffins, Penguin Classics and Arkana – and how to order them, write to us at the appropriate address below. Please note that for copyright reasons the selection of books varies from country to country.

In the United Kingdom: Please write to *Dept. EP, Penguin Books Ltd, Bath Road, Harmondsworth, West Drayton, Middlesex UB7 0DA*

In the United States: Please write to *Consumer Services, Penguin Putnam Inc., 405 Murray Hill Parkway, East Rutherford, New Jersey 07073-2136.* VISA and MasterCard holders call 1-800-631-8571 to order Penguin titles

In Canada: Please write to *Penguin Books Canada Ltd, 10 Alcorn Avenue, Suite 300, Toronto, Ontario M4V 3B2*

In Australia: Please write to *Penguin Books Australia Ltd, 487 Maroondah Highway, Ringwood, Victoria 3134*

In New Zealand: Please write to *Penguin Books (NZ) Ltd, Private Bag 102902, North Shore Mail Centre, Auckland 10*

In India: Please write to *Penguin Books India Pvt Ltd, 11 Community Centre, Panchsheel Park, New Delhi 110017*

In the Netherlands: Please write to *Penguin Books Netherlands bv, Postbus 3507, NL-1001 AH Amsterdam*

In Germany: Please write to *Penguin Books Deutschland GmbH, Metzlerstrasse 26, 60594 Frankfurt am Main*

In Spain: Please write to *Penguin Books S. A., Bravo Murillo 19, 1°B, 28015 Madrid*

In Italy: Please write to *Penguin Italia s.r.l., Via Vittorio Emanuele 45/a, 20094 Corsico, Milano*

In France: Please write to *Penguin France, 12, Rue Prosper Ferradou, 31700 Blagnac*

In Japan: Please write to *Penguin Books Japan Ltd, Iidabashi KM-Bldg, 2-23-9 Koraku, Bunkyo-Ku, Tokyo 112-0004*

In South Africa: Please write to *Penguin Books South Africa (Pty) Ltd, P.O. Box 751093, Gardenview, 2047 Johannesburg*

Penguin Classics

A PASSAGE TO INDIA
E. M. FORSTER

'Shrines are fascinating, especially when rarely opened'

When Adela and her elderly companion Mrs Moore arrive in the Indian town of Chandrapore, they quickly feel trapped by its insular and prejudiced British community. Determined to explore the 'real India', they seek the guidance of the charming and mercurial Dr Aziz, a cultivated Indian Muslim. But a mysterious incident occurs while they are exploring the Marabar caves with Aziz, and the well-respected doctor soon finds himself at the centre of a scandal that rouses violent passions among both the British and their Indian subjects. A masterly portrait of a society in the grip of imperialism,

A Passage to India compellingly depicts the fate of individuals caught between the great political and cultural conflicts of the modern world.

The introduction, by Pankaj Mishra, outlines Forster's complex engagement with Indian society and culture. This edition reproduces the Abinger text and notes, and also includes four of Forster's essays on India, a chronology and further reading.

'His great book ... masterly in its prescience and its lucidity' Anita Desai

Edited by Oliver Stallybrass

With an introduction by Pankaj Mishra

PENGUIN CLASSICS

SELECTED POEMS
RABINDRANATH TAGORE

'It dances today, my heart, like a peacock it dances …
It soars to the sky with delight'

The poems of Rabindranath Tagore (1861–1941) are among the most haunting and tender in Indian and world literature, expressing a profound and passionate human yearning. His ceaselessly inventive works deal with such subjects as the interplay between God and the world, the eternal and transient, and the paradox of an endlessly changing universe that is in tune with unchanging harmonies. Poems such as 'Earth' and 'In the Eyes of a Peacock' present a picture of natural processes unaffected by human concerns, while others, as in 'Recovery – 14', convey the poet's bewilderment about his place in the world. And exuberant works such as 'New Rain' and 'Grandfather's Holiday' describe Tagore's sheer joy at the glories of nature or simply in watching a grandchild play.

William Radice's exquisite translations are accompanied by an introduction discussing Tagore's Bengali cultural background, his social, political and religious beliefs, and the lyric metres and verse forms he developed.

'An important book … William Radice's introduction is excellent' *Sunday Times*

Translated with an introduction by William Radice

Penguin Classics

BUDDHIST SCRIPTURES

'Whoever gives something for the good of others, with heart full of sympathy, not heeding his own good, reaps unspoiled fruit'

While Buddhism has no central text such as the Bible or the Koran, there is a powerful body of scripture from across Asia that encompasses the *dharma*, or the teachings of Buddha. This rich anthology brings together works from a broad historical and geographical range, and from languages such as Pali, Sanskrit, Tibetan, Chinese and Japanese. There are tales of the Buddha's past lives, a discussion of the qualities and qualifications of a monk, and an exploration of the many meanings of Enlightenment. Together they provide a vivid picture of the Buddha and of the vast nature of the Buddhist tradition.

This new edition contains many texts presented in English for the first time as well as new translations of some well-known works, and also includes an informative introduction and prefaces to each chapter by scholar of Buddhism Donald S. Lopez Jr, with suggestions for further reading and a glossary.

Edited with an introduction by Donald S. Lopez, Jr

PENGUIN CLASSICS

THE PENGUIN BOOK OF RUSSIAN SHORT STORIES

'Light's all very well, brothers, but it's not easy to live with'

From the early nineteenth century to the collapse of the Soviet Union and beyond, the short story has occupied a central place in Russian literature. This collection includes not only well-known classics but also modern masterpieces, many of them previously censored. There are stories by acknowledged giants – Gogol, Tolstoy, Chekhov and Solzhenitsyn – and by equally great writers such as Andrey Platonov who have only recently become known to the English-speaking world. Some stories are tragic, but the volume also includes a great deal of comedy – from Pushkin's subtle wit to Kharms's dark absurdism, from Dostoyevsky's graveyard humour to Teffi's subtle evocations of human stupidity and Zoshchenko's satirical vignettes of everyday life in the decade after the 1917 Revolution.

This new collection of translations includes works only recently rediscovered in Russia. The introduction gives a vivid insight into the history of the Russian short story, while the work of every author is preceded by an individual introduction. This edition also includes notes and a chronology.

Edited by Robert Chandler

PENGUIN CLASSICS POPULAR LIBRARY

THREE TALES
GUSTAVE FLAUBERT

'When she went to church, she would sit gazing at the picture of the Holy Spirit and it struck her that it looked rather like her parrot'

First published in 1877, the *Three Tales*, dominated by questions of doubt, love, loneliness and religious experience, form Flaubert's final great work. 'A Simple Heart' relates the story of Félicité – an uneducated serving-woman who retains her Catholic faith despite a life of desolation and loss. 'The Legend of Saint Julian Hospitator', inspired by a stained-glass window in Rouen cathedral, describes the fate of Julian, a sadistic hunter destined to murder his own parents. The blend of faith and cruelty that dominates this story may also be found in 'Herodias' – a reworking of the tale of Salome and John the Baptist. Rich with a combination of desire, sorrow and faith, these three diverse works are a triumphant conclusion to Flaubert's creative life.

Roger Whitehouse's vibrant new translation captures the exquisite style of the original prose. Geoffrey Wall's introduction considers the inspiration for the tales in the context of Flaubert's life and other work. This edition includes a further reading list and detailed notes.

Translated by Roger Whitehouse

Edited with an introduction by Geoffrey Wall